KINGS OF LUST

M.o. Absinthe

This is a work of fiction. Names, characters, places, and events are fictitious. Any resemblance to real persons, living or dead, or actual events is purely coincidental.

Sign up on www.moabsinthe.com to my newsletter to get a FREE extra-steamy bonus scene featuring Bea and her kings

Kings of Lust is not recommended for the weak of heart or for those looking for a perfect love story. This book is dark and twisted, pushing boundaries and imagination.

Kings of Lust is Book Two in The Pleasure Room Series and continues the same storyline only this time the stakes are higher and so is the cost!

TRIGGER WARNINGS

This book is written and intended for mature audiences 18+. This book is considered Reverse Harem, meaning our main female character has a relationship of sexual nature with three or more male characters. Scenes in this book contain sexually explicit acts, and graphic language which some readers may find offensive. Our male main characters are morally gray in nature and our female main character is a little too innocent for their world but is snarky and manages to hold her own.

If any of the following are triggering to you, this book may not be for you, please turn back now. Your mental health matters.

TRIGGER WARNINGS

Abuse

Alphaholes

Attempted Somnophilia

Blackmail

Beggary

Bondage

Bullying

Blood

Child Neglect

Degradation

Drugging

Dub Con (Dubious Consent)

Edging

Exhibitionism

Extremely explicit sexual content

Grief

Humiliation

Knife Play

Manipulation

Mental abuse

Mental trauma

Murder

Psychological Abuse

PTSD

Reverse Harem

Various kinks

Trauma

Slavery

Violence

Villain MMCs

Voyeurism

And the list goes on

Table of content

*For all you book babes who crave
to have your panties wet and a knot
in the pit of your stomach,*

I've got you!

THERE IS NO LOVE WHERE DARKNESS GROWS, BUT YOU COULD LEARN TO LOVE THE DARKNESS

CHAPTER 1

B ea

My eyes kept moving from one *king* to another. My emotions battling each other for which feeling would win out. My heart and mind were like a battlefield; anxiety coming out on top.

I wasn't shocked.

Shock was an understatement.

I was almost choking for air as the conspiracy against me seemed to be finally revealed.

But why?

How?

I wanted so badly to ask them, yet they seemed to be ignoring my presence completely, embracing each other as if this was some long-lost family reunion.

Strangely, even Cole appeared excited—from something different than exploiting my limits to their very edge. Nonetheless, he was still playing with my nerves, although not intentionally—this time.

I couldn't help noticing the limp in Brax's left leg, as he

took a few steps in Cole's direction to give him an almost fatherly pat on the shoulder.

I was sinking in deep shit and was acknowledging it with every single one of their friendly gestures. *Deep shit,* indeed, as I noticed even Ferris was snapping himself away from his usual melancholy and smiling back at them as if they brought a new ray of hope in his so deeply plunged into darkness world.

They knew each other. That was a certainty.

But did they also know how *I* fit into all of this? That was the thought that troubled me most. The thought that made everything a hundred times more difficult.

Continuing with the unusually warm attitude, Brax placed his hands on Ferris's shoulders, kissing both sides of his cheeks. "You were unreachable, even for a man like myself. What made you change your mind?" he asked in a sad whisper, revealing a sorrow that I knew he always hid behind his anger.

"I... I didn't change my mind," Ferris's answer floated somewhere in the air above us while it seemed to be hiding a meaning that could only be understood by the one it was meant for.

Still, I needed to know what was happening before my own assumptions would cause a heart attack. Good or bad, it was the moment of truth—or at least for part of it, because when it came to the whole truth, I wasn't so sure I could speak it out loud.

"How...how do you know each other?" Countless theories circled my mind as I asked. I was preparing for them to confess to the game they all played with me.

"Are you fucking kidding me?" Cole exclaimed with unrestrained excitement. "Brax and Ferris used to be the kings of ECU. These guys are legends!"

I drew my gaze a little to the left to fall on Brax's frowning eyebrows, then it slowly slid to Ferris's tightening jawline as he was biting back questions of his own.

How the hell did I think that it would be a good idea to open my mouth to ask questions?

Still, as strange as it may have been, while Brax and Ferris's gazes were harboring murky shadows of doubt, Cole's devious blue orbs were gleaming with fierce lust. And that puzzled me completely.

"Couldn't have made a better choice," Brax grinned, eyes gleaming at Cole as if he was his finest creation.

My curiosity couldn't be held back any longer from trying to get to the bottom of what was going on. "What choice?"

"We gave him the keys to our kingdom." Ferris reached for Cole's shoulders, wrapping a fatherly arm around them and tugging him towards his own body. "Brax and I were seniors when Cole was in his first year at the University. So, when the time came, we decided he was the most fitting person to rule in our place."

Cole was their protege. Go figure.

Some people have no luck, but I seemed to be sinking into the abyss of fucking misfortune. My three kings had finally met, and it was just a matter of time before they would start teaming up against me. If they hadn't done so already.

"Funny for us to be meeting like this." Cole's blank stare turned toward me, expecting the full explanation for their get-together.

I knew the question even before he asked it and if any doubt could have clouded my mind, the death glares coming from the other two kings convinced me that it was about time to give some answers. "I have motives for bringing you all here. This is much harder for me than it is for you."

"Is it?" Ferris arched an eyebrow as I noticed his bottom lip twitch with restrained anger. He was angry at me.

My gaze fell to the floor, embarrassment clouding my thoughts. "Yes...it is."

But I didn't find time to go on as Brax's doubtful voice pierced through me, "Why would that be?"

He, above anyone else, knew the answer to that question. It just appeared he chose to torment me instead.

"You all knew that I had other commitments," I breathed as a knot tightened in my stomach. "Well, each one of you is standing in the same room with my *other commitments.*"

"No fucking way. Talk about a small world, huh?" Brax rushed to throw a few ironic words at me, underlining the *delicate* situation I was finding myself in.

"So, what is this, Mouse? Have you called us here to choose a favorite, or what?" As usual, Cole was running on empty when it came to patience, although his guess could not be further from the truth.

"No, I called you here for a much more important reason than me trying to make sense of what's happening with my life." I rolled my eyes, irritated that Cole was seeing all of it as a joke. "I called you here because of the riots, because of the upcoming Revolution."

"What could you possibly know about the fucking Revolution?" Cole seemed somewhat amused that I spoke of such serious subjects.

"More than you." And I was certain of my words, especially after having played the involuntary spy in a battle that I unwillingly made my own.

"Let her speak." I had never heard a living soul giving an order to Cole before. Yet Brax just did, as if it was nothing.

Still, when it came to their hierarchy, the thing that shocked me most was that Brax didn't seem to hold the ruling position. It was Ferris, not by authority or force, but by the magical vibe that always floated around him. The same magic that makes every living soul drop at his feet.

Maybe the enigma of his darkness put him in charge, or

even that perfectly damaged cradle of compressed anger that I was sure lay within him. He was the ruler of their world, and implicitly of mine.

"I have information. Information that, when put together reveals the catastrophic situation we all find ourselves in. And when I say *all*, I don't mean just the four of us. I mean the whole city." I gained their complete attention, but I wasn't sure if they were listening because they were truly interested or just because they found me to be amusing. Either way, I had to go on. I had to make them listen, no matter what the price. Because knowing all three of them, I had no doubt that there was going to be one.

"The world as we know it is going to change soon. The hierarchies, social positions, everything," I continued, looking each one of them in the eyes as I spoke. "I've learned things. I'm far from being proud of how I did it, but maybe it all served a greater cause. There will be a precise division of powers soon, and if the master plan works out, all residents of the Pit will be enslaved by the Elite."

"*Enslaved* is a strong word. Maybe have their liberties restricted when it comes to entering the Hills. I don't see anyone going to such extents as to *enslave* them." Brax tried to break my theory apart, yet he didn't know the whole context. And for a man who was supposed to know everything, having *me* as the new source of information to the group couldn't have sat well with him.

"Cole..." I looked into those cobalt blue eyes, searching to see how much his father had told him on the subject, while, at the same time, exposing myself in front of him.

"Shit," he muttered through gritted teeth, "She's right."

"What the fuck do you mean *she's right*?" My king of the underworld couldn't hide his consternation, while Ferris seemed to be unbothered by what he just learned. Or maybe he was just weighing everything, so when the time came to decide on what needed to be done, he'd be ready. Either way, the darkness twinkling in his eyes was letting me know he was far more devious than any Elite plan put together.

And that should have scared me.

That should have fucking terrified me.

Still, against all rational thinking, it was exciting me.

"The plan is to turn all of the Annelids into slaves. Not figuratively, but literal slaves. Like build a fucking electric fence, give them uniforms, numbers, and fucking tracking devices." Cole was confirming every word I said as being true.

"I got information about the Elite bringing in mercenaries to stop the rebels. But slavery, that's too fucked up even for them." Brax spoke, searching his pockets for a pack of cigars.

"Bea," a voice that I'd been waiting to hear echoed from across the room. "What exactly are the three of us doing here?" Ferris arched an eyebrow, waiting for me to explain how they would fit into my plan. Although I suspected he already had a very good idea.

"I need you. I need all of you to try and stop this." Hearing myself speak, even *I* found my words amusing—asking something so important from three men who had always put themselves first.

"In case you didn't notice, I'm not in this game to *save the world*," Brax considered the message he was sending didn't get through to me clearly enough.

Though I knew better than to gullibly take everything he said as the truth. "Maybe you're not here to save the world, but I do believe you are here to change it," I intervened.

"As I told you before, I think you want to believe things about me that just aren't real."

"No, Brax. *You* want everyone to believe that you're some kind of monster, while *I* know that something good lies within you." My bottom-of-the-heart speech was quickly interrupted by Cole's hysterical laughter, unable to keep his reactions to himself. Still, I wasn't going to stop chasing the truth, bringing up a delicate subject for Brax, "Why else would you give all that food every night to the less fortunate?"

"Because it would be just a waste of good food otherwise," his words escaped in a muffled snarl, hindering the irritation at me having blown his *cover*. "I'm starting to believe that one day I will need to prove to you exactly what kind of monster I can be. You know, just so you can stop making assumptions." There was a deadly serious promise hiding between those lines. One that I feared he had every intention of keeping.

"Brax...," Ferris's voice cut through the air like the sharpest blade, drawing the line of unspoken authority. *Who would have ever guessed?*

"What I have to say is important for you too, Brax. What will happen to all your businesses when the Pit will be just that; a pit. Remodel them into what, a prison? What do you reckon they will do with your clubs, your bars and restaurants, and whatever establishment you have made in Echo City?" There had to be a way to put some sense into him since I considered him to be the main pawn in helping me convince all three of them.

"I'll survive. I always do." His specific arrogance surfaced again, revealing every mutual feature he shared with Cole.

"Yeah, it's just the whole world around you that wouldn't." And in that *world,* were my family and I.

But despite my best efforts, his shield could not be broken. "Your point is..." He was pretending he didn't care, but maybe he was right—he really didn't, and I was failing to see that. Yet, I had to try. I owed it to myself to try. I owed it to my family. I owed it to the whole city, feeling that fate had brought me the information and the means to help fix this.

"So, what's the plan, Mouse? Dress us up as fucking Vikings and lead a war against the Elite?" Cole snickered.

"No. Not *fucking Vikings*... and you won't have to lead a war, but end one. Or maybe even smother it before it begins, if we're lucky enough and time is on our side." I was asking so much of them and of me.

"And out of all people, *you* decided to orchestrate this?" Brax could not contain his irony, probably still judging me only by my nice pair of tits, or whatever his other criteria for valuing me were.

While I had every motive to show him I'm more than just a pretty face, "Someone has to do it. Don't get me wrong, I don't want to lead this. I'm not... devious enough? I'm more like the glue that holds the pieces together."

I guess my new *definition* of them didn't agree with everyone, especially Ferris, "And we are? *Devious* enough, I mean...?"

There was no point in hiding the obvious since I had a suspicion that he was the most darkly ingenious of them all. However, I didn't doubt even for a second that Brax and Cole were resourceful enough to be the masterminds behind this. But Ferris... he had something extra. Maybe it was in his nature, maybe because he successfully masked any deceitful intentions with his charming behavior. And that made him a hundred times more dangerous than Cole or Brax put together.

It was time to tell the truth and nothing but the truth. "Yes, more than enough," my breath ghosted the reply, as my eyes raised to drown in Ferris's. He was the only one in the room who still kept appearances, while my other two kings preened when called perfectly *devious.* For them, *deviousness* was their greatest quality and not by any means a flaw. And I was betting all my money on it.

"Each one of you brings a special value to the table, that when put together could give us the power to do anything we set our minds to."

"Oh, do tell, what special power do I possess?" Cole seemed

to be in the mood for jokes. Though judging by Brax's gaze, he wasn't keen on hearing about Cole's *special powers*, especially not about the ones the king of ECU considered as being *special*.

"How about you tell us? How deep do your connections in the political scene run?" I had overheard his father, but I needed to know for myself exactly how much we could rely on him.

"Ocean's-bottom-fucking-deep. My family has connections even with the president. But as all wheels in motion, every connection must be greased. And these people need a lot of grease to function."

"I guess that would be how I fit into all of this." It didn't take Ferris long to realize that his fortune would play a major part in the *greater plan.*

I loathed to tell him that I needed his money. But as Cole very well said, his bank account could set all wheels in motion. "Yes, and hopefully also with your connections. Money makes the world go round, right?" I tried to smile, intending it to be a joke, though not much humor was left in me.

"Unfortunately, not. Not connections, I mean, since public life has not interested me for the last couple of years." The sheer grief in his voice made me aware not to pursue the subject, especially since I noticed Brax's and Cole's eyes falling to the ground, sinking themselves in some kind of memory that was setting a deep sorrow on their beautiful faces.

"And I?" Brax broke the silence after a couple of minutes which seemed like a collective moment of recollection. "Let me guess. Underworld connections, access to information and how we can broker a possible alliance with the leaders of the rebels."

"Yes, all of the above, plus your men, for protection. If it comes to it." I was asking so much of them, involving them in a fight that was not entirely theirs to carry. And like all kings, each one of them would want something in return for bringing their forces to the battlefield.

"That sounds so noble in theory, even though I'm not sure any of us carry a single noble bone in our bodies. But I do have a question regarding everything you're asking of us." It was Ferris who spoke, carefully weighing all of the options. "Why would I agree to this? Why would I risk my fortune for a fight that I could so easily avoid?"

Indeed, why would he?

Maybe I was just a fool, but my mouth got to speak before my brain got to react, "I hoped **I** was a good enough reason... at least for *you*, Ferris." Ninety-nine percent spoken from the heart and a hundred percent wrong.

At least, it didn't take me long to figure that out.

Without saying another word, Ferris turned his back on me and glanced through the window, leaving me in cold stillness to reflect on my foolish innocence.

"Ferris is right, Mouse. What would we get out of this? What would we risk everything for?" Cole pressed.

"As much as I would like a noble answer would satisfy any of you, I realize that it won't be the case. So, I was thinking about a much more important prize for when the final line is drawn in the sand. I was thinking about Echo City. Or at least its leadership. I realize that there is little chance this will resolve itself just by talking. I believe that it will involve getting a few people removed from their positions. And then the vacant seats will be open for the taking..."

"And we will take them." The thought certainly sounded tempting enough in Brax's mind; whose hunger was always reaching for the top. Top power. Top authority. "I am a man of ambitions. And I do want the city."

Something was finally going my way.

"But you know what else I want, Bea?"

Or not...

"I want to be **fucking** alive when that happens, and what you're asking of us leaves little chance of that!" his roar shook the room, getting even Ferris to turn and look his way, as the wolf Brax is, was showing off his fangs.

Still, I couldn't leave things like that. I just couldn't give up. "What kind of life would we even have to live if we don't try? Did you think of the alternative? What happens if we stand by knowing what we know and do nothing? Or what if we change our minds when it's too late?"

"She's right." Out of all the people standing in the room, the approval came from the one I least expected—Cole. "How could we ever safely stay in our luxurious homes, knowing we did nothing?" *Again with that damn ironic tone.*

Shit... I should have seen that coming.

"I took you for a lot of things, but never for a coward, Cole." It was time for a dose of reverse psychology since reasoning with them had few chances of ever working.

"What the fuck did you say to me?" In an instant, he crossed the length of the room, replacing the oxygen in my lungs with his undeniable presence. The cobalt pools in his eyes flashed with anger as if preparing to tear me apart, as his hand caught me by the throat, clenching so hard I could barely breathe.

Maybe I went a little too far, bruising an ego that had already reached towering heights. I just had to try my best to somehow get through to him. To all of them.

This time, *my* courage left me hanging on a thin line between life and death.

The other two kings impassively stood their ground, just watching as I was struggling to escape Cole's wrath. They were all the same. It was making me realize that by arranging our get-together I might have just reunited the pack.

"Cole," I let out a garbled cry as I felt my feet lift off the ground, supporting my body weight only on my toes.

"Stop!" A hand laid over his, holding it in place, though not signaling him to release me. It was Ferris, sneaking behind me like a ghost in the night. He was trapping my body between his and Cole's hand, savoring every second of my torture.

"We have courage, but we're not fools." Out of the blue, Brax appeared in front of me, grunting the words as a stormy expression was rising on his face.

I was fucking terrified of what was going to happen next, trapped like a rat by a mesmerizing cage of muscles and intoxicating perfumes. My senses were running wild, on the verge of an anxiety attack, and simultaneously an instant away from having my body melt into the ground.

I hated them for spinning like hungry wolves around me, feasting on my stumbled breaths, filled with the adrenaline of my distress. They were all Alphas in their own worlds, and still, here, they maintained a hierarchy with one another.

That exact display of strength was forcing my brain to go blank, making me forget even about the hand that was locked on my neck. Though not for long as Brax's voice broke through to Cole, "Release her."

"You're taking all the fucking fun out of this," Cole hissed, loosening the grip he had on my throat and dropping my feet back on the ground.

"That's because we're not here to play games," the melody of Ferris's voice came from behind me, reminding me that my body was still glued to his.

"I was just thinking of combining work and play," the current *King* of ECU cackled, releasing me completely and tucking his hands into his pockets as if he were preparing to sit and listen to a speech. And that he was, since Ferris took a step to somewhere on my left, pinning his knuckles on the dining table's countertop until a fine cracking sound was released under his weight.

"I was certainly not expecting *this* when I came here today. But life is full of surprises, isn't it?" He took a moment to glance at us. At each one of us, weighing the events along with my proposal. "I believe I know that best," he answered his own question, allowing tiny fragments of that overwhelming sorrow to engulf him again.

No other voice was heard, even though I had a feeling that everyone in the room knew where that dark pain came from.

Everyone except me.

"I heard you, Bea. We all did, even though each one of us answered in our specific way. I know all of us have thought about the rebellions more than a few times, and how it will impact our lives. Even if some of us find it harder than others to admit it." This time, he was the one lighting himself a cigarette, crossing his feet, and leaning his back on the table to support himself against it. "I do believe that I will probably be the least affected by this Revolution, but that doesn't mean that I don't take everything into consideration. Including everyone standing here in the room today. That's why I suggest that we wait and carefully weigh everything—the current risks, the sacrifices, and the *rewards*."

When he said *rewards*, he looked directly at me, giving me the feeling that the keys to the city held little importance to him, at least compared with everything else he was expecting to *receive*.

"I'd say all of us meet here in three days," he continued. "Let us all think about what needs to be done and decide if a plan should ever see the light of day, or if everything will remain buried in this room. That is, if you both agree, of course."

"I'm in. Let's meet in three days." It didn't take Cole long to decide on how he wanted to act, though I had a feeling that our one-to-one discussion on the subject would not wait that long.

Finally, it was Brax's turn to answer. Even though, after

what he said, I suspected that it would be a no from the start on his side, his answer came as a surprise to me. "I'll make a decision when the time comes."

Ferris nodded in approval, so did Cole, agreeing on giving this a chance.

It wasn't going to be easy; I was aware of that. But it wasn't in my nature to ever give up.
And they were also aware of that.

"I have to go. I have to be somewhere with my father." Cole looked at his watch, realizing that he had stayed for too long. I guessed he was expecting a quick *fix* from his new toy rather than a discussion about saving the world.

"I'll walk with you." Brax hugged Ferris and then walked toward their *successor,* who was waiting for him by the door, but not before he made sure that his gaze stopped upon me. He still seemed slightly shocked that I could ever show such courage or insanity to ask them to be a part of my plan.

"Ferris," my voice faded, knowing that by revealing my other *deals* I had hurt him. Even if my other deals were his two friends, or perhaps it was *because* the two were his friends.

I headed toward him, maybe in a useless attempt to mend things, though before I reached his side, he moved away from the direction I was going and stepped toward the door. "I'll be back in a couple of minutes." That's all he had to say before he abandoned me in the room, leaving me prey to my own devastating thoughts.

Just as I was walking out of the dining room, Ferris returned with one of his guards, both holding numerous bags of children's clothes and toys. "I brought you these for your sister and brother."

As if called by some magic bell, Nat's bedroom doors opened and both she and Sebastian came out stumbling against one another, rushing to greet Ferris, or more likely his gifts.

I guessed eavesdropping ran in the family genes.

"Are these for us?" Seb decided to ask only after he ripped a few bags from the guard's hands and threw them on the floor, rustling through them.

"Ferris, these two little gold diggers are Natalia and Sebastian." Some introductions were in order and who better than me to make them.

My remark brought a smile to the corner of Ferris's lips, "They're just kids."

"We are not kids!" my sister had to argue. In her opinion, she was probably even more grown-up than any other person in the room. I couldn't beg to differ since I knew that feeling all too well. I had the sensation that with the first breath of real air I managed to take, I was left to carry the burden of the whole world.

Ferris also caught on to what she was thinking and used his personal charm to instantly befriend them, "I'm sorry if I have offended you, miss." He put a hand under his chin as he was thinking of something deep to say to her. "You look five or six years younger than you really are." He smiled, revealing his pearly-white teeth. "Believe me, when you're a little older you'll love anyone who says that," he whispered, giving her a subtle hint of what to expect from a perfect gentleman.

Only, I knew better, and Ferris was miles away from that distinction, maybe even further than I ever suspected.

"Would you stay a little longer?" I asked him, sensing he was searching for a way out of the apartment.

"I..." His eyes lingered on my siblings while they unwrapped their presents, then turned to look at me. "I can't. I need to think things through. Besides, I wouldn't be the greatest company. But I've made plans for us for later tonight."

"You have?" We hadn't really had a chance to talk between the time Ferris arrived and when Brax had been ringing the doorbell.

"Yes, a babysitter is on her way here. I'm expecting you at my place after nightfall." His lips curved into a murky smile because he wasn't asking me. He was *telling* me what I needed to do.

"Goodbye." Long before I could sneak in a word, he disappeared down the corridor, assuring himself that there would be no detour on my part to his plans.

CHAPTER 2

Tick tock... tick tock... tick tock.

I could hear each second passing as thoughts regarding Ferris's plans for the night ran through my mind. I had a feeling that nothing could ever prepare me for what was to come.

Even Nat sensed that something was bothering me. "What's wrong?" she asked while I changed the bandage covering the wound my father had caused her.

"Why would anything be wrong?" I asked back.

"I can feel that something is troubling you."

"It's nothing. I'm just expecting the babysitter to come," I tried deflecting.

Yet Nat suddenly decided to play parent to me. "What babysitter? And where do you think you're going?"

"A: The babysitter that man you *robbed* earlier hired. And B: It's none of your business." I wasn't ready for my siblings to interfere in my life or let them know the sacrifices I made for them.

"Of course, it's my business. I'm responsible for you," my sister said, deadly serious.

She was making me laugh to the point where I could barely control myself. "I thought it was the other way around, sis," I said between giggles.

Still, what I thought of as a joke was a cruel version of someone's reality. "After you left, I felt a responsibility for everyone, not only for Sebastian. I thought of you every single moment. I wondered how you were, if you were warm, if you had anything to eat. I used to stay awake every night wondering if you'd ever return for us."

"Oh, Nat. How could you question whether I would return for the two of you? I'm so sorry that you had to go through all of that. Just promise me that you'll keep an eye on your brother and I'll figure the rest out. You don't need to worry about me. I always land on my feet." And I planned on doing just that.

"I can see that, looking around me." This time, the giggle came from her as she laid her head on the pillow, gazing at the fine silk ivory wallpaper that decorated the room."Is he your boyfriend?"

I played dumb. "Who?"

"The rich guy with all of the presents. The one with the *dead eyes*. Who else?" Ferris was so obviously deranged that even Nat noticed. And she had only spent a few moments with him.

"What's with you and everyone's eyes?" I asked.

"They show a person for who they really are."

"When did you get so mature?" I let my arms fall all around her, pulling her body against my own, without really expecting an answer.

Our sisterly moment didn't last long since the doorbell made me tear myself away from the embrace so I could welcome my replacement for the night.

The babysitter was here.

Wow, Ferris spared no expense on this one. Just by looking at her tidy and controlled posture, I could tell she must have had a wall full of PhDs and child psychology degrees back home.

Good luck with Lucifer's offspring. And from the way my sister was looking at her, she was going to need it.

—

It was beginning to get dark outside, and that meant I had somewhere to be, without any idea of what I was walking into. A romantic dinner, an answer to *today's* question, or even maybe a cancellation of our agreement.

I guessed I would find out soon enough since, after pulling on a tight peach dress that had a deep V to show off my cleavage, and a pair of matching heels, I took the road that led straight to Ferris's bedroom.

"Can I come in?" I asked, waiting in front of his door after I had already knocked a few times without receiving an answer.

It didn't take long before the door opened to reveal Ferris's dark presence. "Now you're knocking. When did we go from almost ripping each other's clothes to knocking?"

There was something off with him, *again.* He was hiding a sadness mixed with an anger that scared me.

"I thought it was the polite thing to do," I spoke as my gaze fell to the floor.

"Yeah… polite…" The corner of his lips curved into a smile that sheltered no real amusement. "Don't just stand there, come in. It would be *impolite* of me to keep you waiting in the doorway, would it not?"

"Ferris, are you okay?" He was acting much stranger than before. This new mask he was wearing was one I hadn't seen before, something about it scared the life out of me.

"Yes, why? Don't I seem okay to you?" he chanted, although he obviously knew the answer to that question.

Something in my voice was shaking. "You seem tense."

"It's probably because of what you told me today. It got me thinking." He sounded mysterious as if he was waiting for me to get the words out of him one by one.

"About?" I quivered asking.

"Mmm," he paused, pacing to the other corner of the room. "Let's have something to drink first." The corkscrew twisted against a bottle of red wine even before he got to finish off his sentence.

I could have sworn that I heard my heart thumping in my chest as a strange sensation of restlessness ran down my body. *Something was wrong.*

"Special selection." He snuck the fine crystal glass between my fingers, tilting his own under a pale reflection of the moonlight, which was transforming him into some lost prince of darkness. Maybe he was just that, and I had just empowered him with total control of life and death over the whole city.

Maybe I was just as mad.

Maybe even madder than him.

But greatness came from ultimate madness, and I preferred to live for a minute with the satisfaction that I tried. Rather than a lifetime of regret because I did nothing.

"Just one glass. You know what happened last time," I said, letting out a smile that held no real amusement. I wasn't planning on groveling at his feet again—or who knows what else I did that night. I had some sort of recollection of that particular evening, and the memory of him impossibly hard under my touch sent a cold chill across my body from the top of my spine to the *place* that, against my will, ached for him.

"So, what are we drinking too?" I asked in a lame attempt to get an answer to what was bothering me.

"I don't know yet," his voice heavy, carrying a burden that bothered me.

I couldn't quite figure out if he was sad, angry, or even pleased in some way. The resemblance to Brax was more and more obvious as my *king of darkness* seemed unwilling to show any human emotion. He had turned to stone in the few minutes we spent together, managing somehow to petrify even my own reactions.

"You said something today that made me realize I'm involved in all of this much more than I ever planned to be." His empty glass clinked on the table as he dismissed it to fully concentrate on me.

I waited for him to go on, but his gaze was lost somewhere in a distant corner of the room, letting the burden of the unanswered question fall upon me. "Does that mean you'll help us?"

"*Us*? Did you receive any other answer?" Ferris seemed confused or perhaps, Ferris only *wanted* to seem confused.

"No." I averted my gaze, slightly embarrassed.

"So, for now, it's just you. *You* need me." And he was right. I was the only one needing him in that second. I and the entire city, though I had a feeling he didn't care about that last part.

Without much thought, I decided to let him hear what he had wanted to hear in the first place, satisfying his need for control over me, "Yes... *I* need you." The words did something to him. They lit a dangerous fire that had little chance of being put out any time soon.

"What you're asking of me... it's a lot. Getting involved in this means risking much more than a couple million, billion, whatever. I'm risking everything. My whole fortune, my companies, my social position. You're asking *everything* of me."

"I'm sorry, Ferris, I didn't realize—"

"I haven't finished yet," his now raspy voice cut me off,

continuing to divulge what he really had in mind. "You said that you thought *you* should be enough for me to make up my mind. And you're right. *You* are more than enough, Bea."

Instead of taking a step in my direction, he took one further away. He was putting himself just out of my reach as if he needed to continue what he had to say without any intrusions. "I believe that you inadvertently let a truth out. Maybe it was a momentary truth, or maybe you've felt that way for a while now. But I glimpsed the sadness in your eyes, you were hoping that you were special enough to me to get me to do this—to be a part of your plan."

My heart must have stopped for countless seconds as his words were revealing a reality I was denying.

I was falling in love with him.

"It's okay, you don't need to answer." Obviously sensing my awkwardness, he decided to spare me some extra humiliation. I'd experienced enough of that lately as it was. "Because as I said before, you are enough of a reason for me to do this. But what I need you to understand is that by doing this, I risk the impossible for you. I think it's only fair that I get everything, down to the last piece of you."

"Ferris, you know about—"

"The other deals. I know." I wasn't sure what was going on with him, but it seemed that I couldn't even finish a sentence. "I'm not talking about you being *only* mine, but I am talking about you being mine... complete control of you."

"I don't understand."

"Hmm, you're confused." He let a devilish grin set on his lips as he approached me. With a few unhurried steps, he was heading to where I was standing until his arms wrapped their warmth around me. "Like this." His lips fell to find mine as that damn spell he mastered so well was sewing itself around the dimly lit space.

Ferris was searching for something within me as his

tongue ravaged my mouth in a mesmerizing rhythm. He was searching for an answer, only I wasn't exactly sure of the question. And instead of trying to figure it out, I decided to ask a question of my own, "Does that mean *yes*?" I managed to choke the words out under the fierce effect of his touch.

"Does this mean *yes*?" He threw back the same question, waiting for the confirmation of me *being his*, while one of his hands fell on the side of my body, skimming every inch of my dress.

I wished I lived in a universe where there would be no questions and no answers, just passionate gestures to get us melting into one another. Though the reality was so different from my desires—it was just another part of the deal.

Ferris made what could have been *love,* part of a deal. He was ripping the emotions out of the night, and leaving me with the only answer I could provide him in my attempt to achieve the impossible, "**Yes**."

"Then so be it," he confirmed, catching my bottom lip between his own, biting on it so roughly that the sharp pain spread around my body like the sweetest torture.

It was happening. The wheels of the master plan were set in motion, though at that moment, I was becoming much more interested in a totally different kind of *motion.*

Yes, I hated *how* and *why* we ended up there, but my body seemed to love the end result, shivering from the sensation of his hands roaming my skin.

Maybe I was wrong.

Maybe I misunderstood his reactions because the heartless man I had found when initially entering the room was burning with the passion of a thousand suns.

Our tongues began fighting in a war of untamed lust, allowing the emotions to rule over judgment, as Ferris was doing just what he promised.

He was controlling me.

Blinding me.

Consuming me.

Destroying me.

Although his palms seemed incapable to stop from roaming over my body, my clothes miraculously managed to stay on, even after several minutes of him receiving his answer. His shirt didn't seem to be so lucky. The instant I felt him trying to dispose of it, I helped him tug it over his head, then made it fly somewhere across the room. It wouldn't have been nice of me to let him struggle all alone, would it? Especially as that intriguing map of inked skin was waiting so eagerly for me to explore it. Every inch of him was pure perfection. The way his defined muscles were shining, caressed by the orange flames, making a small squeak escape my lips. It was somewhere between excitement, happiness, and total despair, just thinking about what a man like him could do to me.

Despite my ardor, he was acting stranger than ever before, alternating fuming passion with moments of total stillness. It tested both his limits and mine, driving me to the point of insanity. It was like he was forcing himself to stop feeling —purposely trying to shut himself down while his body was screaming with desire.

But why?

Why did he want to deny himself this pleasure when I'd felt him burning with me just moments before?

"Is everything okay?" It seemed I had to ask the question too often around him, every time fooling myself that everything was fine stopped working.

"Yes... I just got an idea," he whispered with a vibe so sexual it made my skin crawl at the presumptions of what his *idea* could be.

I was spared the torment of waiting since it seemed it was something that couldn't *wait* for a second longer from being put into practice. Before I could even take a guess, I was floating toward the bed, with my legs tightly wrapped around his waist.

The *innocent* part of our evening had come to an end. It wasn't long before my body was grinding instinctively against the sheets. I was hopelessly trying to resist the fierce sensations that were coming to life in that aching zone between my thighs as Ferris occupied his rightful place, hovering above me.

At some point, between my purrs and other sounds I could no longer control, Ferris raised my hands to pin them above my head. Before I could even realize it, a fine piece of black material had wrapped around my wrists. "What are you doing?" I asked as I felt the bond tightening, fixing my hands to one of the pillars of the bed frame.

"Only what you've allowed me to," his answer came in a sarcastic tone, almost like a warning that I had committed a grave mistake. A chill ran through me, a cold warning flooding my body as the world around us seemed to stop.

My eyes instantly turned to search his, hoping in vain that I'd find even a drop of normality there. The last thing I wanted was to fear him and the first thing I should have done was just that.

This wasn't some romance being taken to the extreme, and I had a feeling that it wasn't an idea that just flashed through his mind either. It was premeditated, long before I set foot into his room.

"Ferris, what's wrong?" I asked, trying to assess the situation, when in reality, it was more like assessing the potential damage. Because when it came to damage, he was able to do the worst.

"What's wrong?" He repeated my question, lifting his body from my own, as twinkles of madness were gleaming in his onyx eyes. "What's wrong!?" He asked again, though, this time with a very familiar object flashing in my sight—the blade of his knife.

I froze as if I had been trapped in ice for ages, watching only the silvery object approaching my lips. My heart instantly began pulsing in my throat as the vibrations of the beat were reflected on my face, then on my lips, straight to the tip of his knife. I could no longer talk, but I had a distinct feeling that *he* had something to say. "What's wrong, is that you've played me. What's wrong, is that you led me to believe things that weren't fucking real." He let the blade slide millimeters away from my chin until it reached the base of my throat.

"I didn't... I didn't," I uttered in a single breath, while drops of lava-heated fear were raining down on me. All I could do was curse myself for shutting down my instincts and completely ignoring the obvious madness I noticed so often lurking within him. "I never promised you more than I could give." It was the ultimate truth. I never promised him my heart, even if for that short moment it belonged to him.

"You didn't have to say it with words. I've seen it reflected in your gestures." The blade took the path of my cleavage, mirroring its reflection on the surface of my breasts in a terrifying closeness. I could feel the cold steel resting on my skin, ready to rip it open. "But it was all a lie, wasn't it?" The calmness of a man that I felt boiling on the inside, was cascading over me.

"I never lied to you, no matter what you think. I... I care about you... I have feelings for you." That was the truth. The only truth in my life right now as I had realized that I had fallen for a monster.

"Feelings?" The knife glided through the V-shape of my cleavage, slowly tearing it apart, while the purr of the material splitting apart made me fear I was mere seconds away from his blade drawing blood from my flesh.

Was he going to kill me?

"Feelings?" He repeated as one of his hands brushed over my face, letting a lazy thumb rest on my lips. "How could you have feelings for me while you're *fucking* Brax?"

CHAPTER 3

Ferris knew. But how?

"Did he tell you?" Not that it mattered any longer. It wasn't like I could keep it a secret anyway.

"He didn't need to, I know Brax well enough to be able to figure things out by myself." I felt the anger in his voice as my bra popped open, cut by his blade.

"Ferris, please! I only slept with him because that was what he demanded out of our deal. I only did it to get Nat and Seb here." Crystal tears sprung from my eyes, soaking the pillows beneath me.

"Oh,... *only* because of that," his damn sarcasm was present again. There was nothing I could have said that would quell his anger. "As you will do with me?"

I left him without an answer, fearing his reaction to the one I would have given him. It was *exactly* the same with Ferris. Until a few moments ago, I had thought it to be something more, but it turned out I was nothing more than a deal to him. A toy.

"Did you enjoy it?" his voice clipped.

How could I answer as the metal was still pressed over the surface of my breasts and one single letter would make the difference between life and death? "Or do you hate *us*? Loath it when one of *us* touches you?" His knife, sharp like a samurai sword, skimmed one of my hard nipples. The fear instilled by the silvery blade gathered like thunderstorms inside my mind, forcing me to anchor my body into the mattress as I was preparing myself to deal with the pain.

There was no way that I could have escaped.

"Yes," I breathed. "Yes, I like it when *you* touch me. Just not right now, at the moment you're scaring me."

"What about Brax or Cole? Do you like it when they touch you?" Ferris continued.

Should I lie and risk him calling me out on it? Or should I tell the truth and risk infuriating him even more?

Whatever my decision, there didn't seem to be a right answer.

"Yes, sometimes, and sometimes I hated it. But it's not the same with you, Ferris. *Nothing is the same as it is with you.*" I couldn't stop my tears from flowing down my face out of desperation to convince him. He needed to know he was so different from the other two kings. But how could he truly understand unless he looked directly into my soul? And in the moment, I wasn't sure what he could find there any longer. "You felt it that night when I asked you to go on and I offered you the last part of me. I risked the safety of my family because of you."

"What about now? What do you feel now?" He moved his hand beneath the hem of my dress, advancing upward on my thigh while his damn knife was still resting on the goose-bumped skin of my breasts. "I asked you a question," he demanded an answer again as I could feel the edge of my panties being tugged down my legs.

How could I answer when I had no idea what was happening to me anymore?

Fear was mixing with lust while my conscience was one step away from sending me into a total breakdown.

Maybe it was time to tell him exactly the truth, "Fear!" I cried out, forcing myself to admit it while his fingers advanced to my center, yanking a second confession out of me, "And lust!"

I knew it wasn't normal. I knew it shouldn't have been normal. His fingers running through my folds, as the impetuous bulge in his pants, the spike in his breath. It was almost enough to get me to ignore the knife and focus on that tormenting movement that was sending pricking awareness throughout my entire being.

"Lust," his voice dripping the word as I felt one of his fingers probing dangerously at the edge of my entrance. "You can leave right now. I can stop if you ask me to, there doesn't have to be a new deal."

I recognized exactly what he was doing. He showed me his madness, letting the weight of the decision fall on my shoulders. *I* was the one who needed to decide if I wanted to leave or remain with his knife watching over me.

It was a matter of complete trust when in reality, *I don't think I could ever trust him again.*

Was I to part from his sweet madness?

To betray all my goals because of fear?

I couldn't think straight.

I couldn't see straight with the burden of an entire city pressing down on me, but also with the burden of my own heart.

Was it pity?

Feelings?

Fear?

Or maybe crazed magnetism.

I just felt incapable of letting him go, even if my instincts were screaming at me to do so.

All my thoughts materialized into just one answer, "I don't want you to stop. But I do want you to get rid of the knife. I told you before, I'm afraid of it."

I suppose he expected me to run. Maybe, on a subconscious level, even wanted me to. But I wasn't going to give him the satisfaction of certifying him as a monster.

Despite my request, the silvery blade remained over my nipple as his fingers were becoming impossible to bear. And that forced me to come up with a plan to quickly dispose of the sharp blade that was still filling my heart with a cold chill. "Kiss me," I called to him, my voice dripping with desire.

His lips instantly overlapped mine while he set the knife aside on the bed sheet so that it wouldn't get in our way.

I had won and lost at the same time. Something was breaking in me, realizing that no matter how hard I tried to fool myself, Ferris wasn't who I wanted him to be. Still, that part didn't even matter any longer. This was just a deal, as were the other two I had, and I would see it no differently. A means to an end. Just physical consumption of one's needs.

Everything would be so easy if I actually believed the rational thoughts that were racing through my mind. However, I was still far from doing so as my treacherous body was squirming with every flick of his tongue.

"Don't take me for a fool, Bea." Ferris said, pushing the knife farther away, knowing exactly what I was trying to do. He'd caught on to my plan and disposed of the piece of metal by choice, not because he'd fallen into my trap.

With a swift move, he raised my hips to thoroughly accommodate himself between them, rushing to ditch the burden of his pants.

I knew what was to come. My eyes closed instinctively, bracing for pain to rip through my body, and impatiently waiting for the suffering to turn into pleasure. I had no doubt that he was preparing to do just that. But to confuse me even more, he seemed to go back on his decision. "No, not like this..." It felt like he was talking to himself, convincing the beast to tone down.

Suddenly, he let his body weight fall over me, caging my chest between the strength of his arms. With unhurried kisses he reached my lips, then fell upon my round breasts, feasting on each curve with sinful longing.

It felt so good. More than good; amazing. Yet not the same as on the previous evenings. He had broken the spell and no matter what he tried, it could never be fixed. I felt it in the pain of my soul, stranded in a sea of doubt.

Trust no one.

Love no one.

Though that didn't mean I had to deny myself pleasure. I was trembling from the electric jolts of delight that were racing through my body each time his tongue circled the hard peak of my nipple. He felt rougher, maybe still angry, or maybe just more heated up. I couldn't complain. The hands clutched on my thighs and the murmur of his groans as he was discovering each new inch of me were stirring waves of ardent passion in every cell of my body. Ferris was turning me into a stormy ocean, eager to be somehow calmed by him.

After tugging my dress over my legs, his mouth drove to join my needy flesh as one of his fingers made room within me. I tensed, even if the warmth of his lips was telling me not to do so. It was an instinctive reaction, mostly caused by the emotional stress that was still altering my senses. But the discomfort I was expecting to feel was missing completely. It was like my body was waiting for him to claim me. To own me.

To make me entirely his—even if only for tonight.

With snakelike moves, another finger slid inside me, stretching me while his mouth worked in tandem to bring me to sweet ecstasy.

I understood long before that when it came to both spiritual and physical pleasure, Ferris knew exactly what needed to be done to send me into supreme bliss. And the combination of him stroking my inner walls and the piercing on his tongue, were pushing me to the brink of ecstasy at lightning speed.

My toes curled with each swirl of his tongue, the metal from his piercing swirling around my bud, teasing every nerve of my skin until my moans could not be contained. I noticed him looking up to watch me struggle with the rush he was provoking. His satisfaction of extracting whine after whine from my lips was driving him on to demolish me completely. And so he did, until the undeniable spasming of my body could no longer be avoided.

"Ferris!" I cried out to him, in desperate need of a time-out from his ravishing assault on my core as waves of ecstasy were overflowing my entire being.

With lazy moves, he seemed to answer my calling, trailing kisses upwards on my skin, to my navel, then higher and higher, between my two rock hard nipples and finally reaching my lips.

For a second, time stopped and so did his breath, as he glanced into my eyes, easing his cock into me.

He felt ready. So large that my body struggled to fit him, my core tightening as if trying to keep him out.

The deceitful kisses were still burning on my skin, as he worked every inch of himself into my throbbing center. Thrust after thrust, he was building me up to an orgasm so intense that I was beginning to ask myself how would I ever part from him. With luscious moves his muscular arms made my back glide over the sheets, guiding me to join him into the perfect delirium that he had so easily built for me.

It wasn't like my first time. I wasn't struggling to find pleasure. It was more like I was struggling to try and avoid it, prolonging the moments for as long as I could.

But it was all too intense.

Too perfect to be true.

And as life taught me, that was exactly the case.

His lips abandoned mine, only to glide along my jawline, stopping to capture my earlobe between his teeth. The sensation was devastatingly beautiful, amplified by a hand that was now tightly wrapped around one of my breasts.

I was seconds away from falling into a perfect rapture, breaking and building beneath him. But a question that was about to change everything brushed against the shell of my ear as the winter chill. "Did he feel like I do?"

My world paused as every arousing sensation seemed to run, seeking cover, draining through me and dissipating into the mattress.

It wasn't just a question.

It was a warning of the upcoming danger.

The answer was that Brax felt *different*. More desperate, more passionate, more cold, but never in control. And as funny as it may have sounded, Ferris did seem in control of everything. I was just realizing that he had followed a plan ever since I came into the room. Or maybe even before that.

"Did you enjoy sleeping with Brax more?" Another question that made his well-defined torso rise from above mine, breaking our union as the coldness of the night bathed in his reflection.

He was waiting for an answer.

Or maybe he wasn't.

He *was* just waiting for my agony.

Ferris was almost maddened by jealousy, and his bipolar nature was taking it to dangerous levels.

"I'm not going to compare you two if that's what you were after," I muttered, knowing that the answer wouldn't please him either way.

Without asking for an explanation, he pulled up his boxers, and left the bed, heading toward the table.

I didn't say a word, just watched his moves thoughtfully, as he filled a glass of wine, then downed it in only a few sips as if it was some medicine he urgently needed. He then turned to face me, with anger rising on his face while the nervous twitch of his lips was causing my heart to thump in my ears.

"I have a present for you," his voice, so devious, that I knew nothing good could come out of it.

And I was proven right mere moments later as a small black box appeared in his hands.

"What's that?" I quivered, running the possibilities through my mind, imagining all sorts of things, but not even for a second, guessing what really hid beneath the wrapping.

His eyebrow arched with molten contempt. "Something that will help you understand who's who."

What the fuck was that supposed to mean?

My sight remained fixed on his hands as he removed the paper wrapping while a knot seized control of my stomach. It didn't take him long before he took out a small pink teardrop object with a string attached and an on/off button. It was a sort of device, though I couldn't figure out its use or what was the big deal about it. But I did realize that he was going to use it on me since the moment it was free out of its wrapping, Ferris began walking towards the bed, playing with the gadget between his fingers.

Suddenly, I felt ashamed, as the nakedness of my body seemed to be too obvious, wearing only rags of the dress that was lying ripped around me.

"What are you doing?" My voice trembled at his approach, recognizing his specific madness shining so brightly all across the space.

"You ask too many questions." A crooked smile appeared in the corner of his mouth while leaning his torso above mine and searching for what I thought to be a kiss. But he stopped less than an inch from my lips as his fingers began playing between my folds, searching the last traces of dampness.

He had a message that I needed to understand. "I want you to know how it feels to be without me." Whispered words fell softly on my ears as I felt his fingers slipping inside of me, thrusting so hard it almost brought me to tears. Yet soon, I realized that it wasn't only his fingers that made room inside me. His tongue brushed a final time against my mouth, before he retreated to the couch, leaving the small pink device within me. This was his punishment for sleeping with Brax, driven by extreme jealousy, probably trying to hurt me as much as I hurt him.

Since not many *things* had ever reached that area of my body, at first, I didn't fully understand what the gadget was supposed to do, except provoke a slight discomfort.

"Can you believe that they made these things Wi-Fi-Controlled?" Ferris smiled with devilish enthusiasm as he began playing on his phone.

"What?" Maybe I was foolish, but I had no idea what his plans were regarding me.

"Give me a sec," he answered, still playing on his phone as if I could be in any way impatient regarding the object. I was scared, maybe a little curious, but not the least bit eager.

"Done," he grinned as a small vibration pierced through my walls, taking me by surprise and forcing my feet to brace into the mattress. I did expect the purpose of the gadget to be provoking pleasure. It wasn't like I thought he was going to electroshock me. Still, it was almost like I couldn't process the thought. I would have expected Cole to come up with something like this, but not Ferris.

"Why are you doing this? I told you that I didn't *want* to sleep with Brax. I had to!" My voice filled with anger. Every thought of how the night could develop was extraordinarily distant from what was really happening.

"Do you think that I'm mad or jealous because you slept with Brax?"

"You're not?" I asked, finding his answer confusing, especially since I thought I'd figured at least that part out.

As if sitting on barbed wire he quickly rose from the armchair, then paced to the table and poured himself another glass of wine. I think he stood there for minutes without providing me with an answer, just glancing straight at my body as I was nervously trying to adjust to the vibration.

Ferris knew all too well that I wasn't going to find any sort of release without him next to me. In fact, that was what he was counting on. That I would squirm, over and over again until the sensation of helplessness might break me.

I didn't even notice when he disappeared into the bathroom. I was only alerted about his presence there by the dull sound of something dropping in what seemed to be the sink. It sounded like plastic, but I couldn't tell for sure. Yet from the clinking sound as setting the object back I presumed it was some kind of tube of pills. I didn't ask—even though after a few seconds I noticed him returning to the room. It wasn't because I didn't want to know. It was because I was too afraid to know.

With hasty steps, he rushed to the table and grabbed the glass along with the wine bottle, then returned to the couch, getting comfortable to watch the free show. It couldn't be much of a spectacle since the pulse inside me wasn't doing pretty much anything except to annoy me. Either way, I wasn't going to give Ferris the satisfaction of watching me break with desire. Not this time. Not like this.

Sensing his chances of success were slim to none, his finger slid upwards on his phone, increasing the vibration. "Just to spice things up a little," he waited to receive a reaction from me.

"Why are you acting like this if not because of Brax?" I asked with sadness lingering on my lips, tinted with slight disappointment.

I was disappointed that he wasn't anything I thought he would be. He was supposed to be my support, to take my pain away, to understand me. When in reality, I felt closer to Cole or Brax than I did to *him.*

"I didn't say it's not because of Brax. I told you it's not because you slept with him. At least not entirely. You see, we weren't saints back in the days, and I never minded sharing with Brax, or with Cole from the time he came along."

"Sharing?" I asked.

"Yes, sharing. Everything and anything. Clothes, cars, and of course, the women that went through our beds."

The concept seemed impossible in my mind. Yes, I could understand clothes, cars, and whatever other things. But *women?*

How could that ever work?

How could they control their jealousy?

"You were sleeping with each other's girlfriends?" At least that was what I got out of this.

"Not exactly girlfriends. I don't recall any of us ever having a girlfriend." Ferris seemed so amused with the idea that he was making me believe they were seeing women as disposable toys. "They were in it for the fun, not for marriage and children," he continued, cackling at the thought. "And the ones I decided were worth the time, I suggested to Brax, and the other way around. Brax and I are one. We've known each other ever since I can remember, to the point we were under the impression we shared the same crib after birth." I knew from earlier that they were good buddies, but I never imagined them to be friends at *that* level. "Cole came around a little later, but we recognized him on the spot as being the chain link we were missing. That's why he took on the title. He was the only one worthy of carrying it further."

And then it hit me. I suddenly started to understand things at a whole different level—all of them shared the same stereotype. They were bullies.

If not on a physical, then on an emotional level. Manipulation or sheer force would always provide them with the result they wanted.

"So, you see. I don't mind sharing you with Brax or Cole. They both represent a part of me. But you want to know what I really fucking mind?" His temper quickly escalated to that of a volcano, making me pray that the knife was nowhere near him. "I fucking mind that you chose to sleep with Brax first!"

I recognized from the flames dancing in his eyes that he was telling the truth.

It wasn't a question of jealousy.

It was a matter of ego.

"I know you had a deal with Brax, but I thought what we had was much more than a deal. You could have told me. I would have understood!" Ferris snapped.

"How was I supposed to know that you and Brax knew each other?" I whined as my heightened pulse was bringing me into a place between life and death. I couldn't live with the torment shaking every cell of my body, and I couldn't die as nothing was destined to spare me of my misery and finish me.

"You didn't have to know. Whoever it may have been, I would have solved things somehow." Ferris was in pain. I could clearly visualize it as his beautiful face was shifting as he spoke.

"I'm sorry. I was afraid to tell you everything… but, I never lied to you. I never promised more than I could give you."

"Maybe you're right. But I *need more* than you can give me, Bea."

Luckily, I had a pretty good idea of what he was referring to.

He needed me to need him.

That was what it was all about. He needed me to depend on him. Even if he was willing to share, when it came to me, he wanted supremacy over my emotions.

"Ferris, please. I can't turn back the clock, but you know that I need you. I need you right now. This thing inside me is killing me." I muttered between the impossible pulses that were pounding within me, creating an anguish so strong that I was beginning to lose the sense of reality.

I noticed a twitch in his hand, as he was about to step up, yet something was holding him from doing it. He was fighting feelings versus retribution, wanting to loathe me and love me at the same time. And I needed to do something. Something that would make him want to choose option B. I needed to give him what he desired, and at a ridiculous point, what he desired became what I desired at that moment.

"I need you." My feet propped against the mattress, trying to hold back the pressure building down to my ovaries.

The notion of *me needing* him, almost drove him mad, fueling an existing craving with the promise of complete ecstasy. In reality, I hated him for his games. I hated him because he chose to play them with me, and at the same time, I desperately wanted him next to me.

As if listening to my thoughts, he rose from the couch and began advancing in my direction.
"Come to me," I ghosted a breath when he reached me, inviting his body to join me. "Ferris," I continued, assuring myself that

my simmering voice tied him to me tighter than the bonds on my hands were tying me to the bed.

He could no longer resist me, and that got him to take his rightful place between my thighs again, leaning, inches away from my face.

"Take it out," I begged, eager to get rid of the torture and gain some sort of relief.

Finally, he listened, and after prowling over my extremely delicate skin, he took the tear-shaped gadget out, replacing it with *him*. He didn't move, not before freeing my wrists. It was as if he was coming back to reality, changing his attitude a hundred and eighty degrees.

Not sure why, probably from the constant tremor, but he seemed bigger than before. And even though he was moving impossibly slowly, I felt myself tightening around him with only just a few thrusts. It was like he was finishing off a dying victim, move by move, letting a hand slide the length of my hip, while I managed to totally wrap myself around him.

I was holding on to him so tightly that one could say I might never let go, breaking the walls that his anger built and replacing them with the sensation of *me*. I purred and screamed, making my lips form a perfect O, as his own lips fell on mine to soothe every cry with a kiss. Honestly, I was somehow ashamed as I realized that I could barely breathe. I could only tremble and fight back waves of ecstasy, trying to prolong the moment, as I didn't seem to have any effect on him yet.

Propping against the mattress, I was arching my hips in suave rhythms, letting our bodies slide, hoping to find some element that could bring him closer to his release. But it wasn't that. It wasn't about the moment or our movements. It was about his conscience, realizing that he was wrong. "I'm sorry," he kissed the words into me, sending them to reach the deepest corner of my mind.

I knew he was sorry, but I also knew there was nothing stopping him from repeating the mistake. I had no choice anyway, just learn to live with evil. Kiss *it*. Embrace *it*. Allow *him* to bring me to ecstasy.

I could feel he was suffering and maybe I was more fucked-up even than him because I wanted to take his pain away. So, I kissed him back. Not in the same way that I'd done a hundred times before that night, but fiercely, passionately, gripping onto a small piece of his shattered heart.

"I'm sorry," he choked the words out again, running his fingers to the base of my hair as his thrusts deepened, turning the pleasure into something almost impossible to bear.

"I know you are," I whined, almost trying to get away from beneath him, heaving a long growl out of his lungs as he claimed my lips so fierce that our teeth gnashed on impact. With heaved breaths he thrusted inside me over and over again until he found his relief, holding on to me so tightly that I thought I was about to break under the grip of his hands.

I was still trembling from the thrill of the moment, when I felt his head coming to rest on my chest, stopping right against my breasts. "I don't want to lose you." Words spoken out of a damaged soul, clinging onto the same piece of sanity that he had just tried to destroy earlier.

I didn't answer, and it seemed that silence was becoming a habit for me. I just couldn't do it. Not this time, when any response would have been a lie.

I didn't know what the future had in store for us, and I didn't know if I would be able to resist another night where his madness fought the fractured parts of his goodness, that drifted away within him. Alongside Ferris, I could only live in the moment, taking one day at a time and praying his mental sanity will always manage to cling to the surface.

I wanted to hate him and I wanted to love him, but Brax's words kept spinning through my mind. *People don't love monsters. They fear them*—and I was beginning to wonder if what he said was more likely referring to him, or to Ferris?

CHAPTER 4

I wish I could say that I slept until the morning, but that was hardly the case. I tossed and turned, without actually being able to move very much as Ferris didn't shift an inch from the spot he found against my chest.

He was so peaceful, so angelic, and yet so demonic when the darkness reached out and grabbed hold of him, constantly being tortured by feelings I couldn't comprehend.

The dawn came this time, finding him sleeping, bathed in my kisses as I was trying to gradually escape from his grip. It wasn't that I didn't want to remain there any longer, but I needed to see Nat and Seb before I left for school. Besides, I had an ulterior reason for wanting to go by my place before I could leave for classes. My clothes were torn, remaining shredded on the sheets beneath Ferris.

I slipped off the bed, only to catch a glimpse in the mirror of my fully naked image. My mind refused to remember the moment my dress fell, ripped from my body, leaving it on the bed along with the pain the memories raised. I needed to do so in order to carry on, and most importantly, I needed to do so in order to maintain a small shadow of the illusion I created around him.

Biting my lower lip, I found the way to his dressing room, and without a second thought, *borrowed* a pair of jeans. They were so long that I needed to fold the legs over my ankles several times, but that did the trick. I also found a shirt that I had to tie into a knot so it wouldn't stretch to my knees. If you didn't look carefully, you could think it was just a *boyfriend* outfit. That was exactly how it seemed. Like I had just stolen my boyfriend's clothes. Though the thing was, he wasn't my boyfriend. As a matter of fact, I had no idea what he really was to me.

With my astonishing luck, I met the babysitter just as I was walking in through my apartment door. By the look on her face, she noticed immediately that I was wearing a different outfit from the one I was dressed in last night. Probably, one belonging to her employer. It wasn't like I wasn't getting used to the embarrassment anyway. Without too much fuss over the subject, I changed and went to give both Nat and Seb a kiss before I left for ECU.

New day, new life, and indeed it was just that, no matter how much I was trying to avoid it. I made my way through the University's backdoor that had been indirectly assigned to me ever since I set foot in the facility. Yet strangely, this time, it was no longer where I belonged.

The students who didn't even know who I was before were now looking at me as if I was some kind of intruder while some girls belonging to the Elite were frantically waving at me from the other end of the hallway.

Cole's end of the hallway.

My end of the hallway.

I had to go and greet them, although I would have given anything to be spared the false pleasantries. Things were as simple as day and night. I didn't want to be there, and they certainly didn't want me there either. Still, I had a title on my hands along with an invisible crown laying on my head. I was their new *Queen* and whether I liked it or not, I had to act like it.

"I love your dress," the flattery came pouring out even before I had actually reached my new end of the hallway. One by one, my *loyal subjects* came to introduce themselves, each one bearing a compliment. In less than five minutes, I was proclaimed to have the most beautiful eyes, hair, cheek structure, purse, shoes, dress, and even earrings in the entire university. If given the chance I am sure the list could go on forever.

Looking at the positive side of things, I now knew around five Kelly's, three Jennifer's, and more than a dozen other people, who guess what? *They were all my new best friends.* Kind of surprising for a person who, before coming to Echo City, didn't have any. Now, I had it all. Or at least that's what anyone who was looking from the outside would think. Because on the inside, everything was as rotten as Snow White's apple, poisoned with the price I had to pay for all of their adulations. And if you were to ask me, becoming Queen B fit perfectly into the *price category.*

"Mouse," a demanding voice sounded from somewhere behind me as the crowd of girls surrounding me began to murmur, some in ecstatic glee while others in uncontained jealousy. My *king* had arrived, a hundred percent ready to torture his *queen.*

"Leave," he growled, scattering the mob as he always did, claiming this part of the corridor for the two of us.

I didn't know exactly how I was supposed to act now. I usually didn't know how to act around Cole, but this time, I didn't have the slightest clue. I just stumbled my way a few steps away from him, between the students who were leaving, hoping that he wouldn't notice my absence.

Foolish plan.

"Were you going somewhere?"

Busted!

"Nah... I was just... just—"

"Setting a little distance so that I don't feel you up in public, or who knows what else goes through this degenerate mind of mine?" *Bingo!* Cole just read my mind.

"No... I just thought that you were also referring to me," I all but babbled.

Liar liar, pants on fire!

"Don't lie." He gestured for me to approach him by curling his index finger, which I did, forced by the *circumstances.* "If you lie, the cat will get your tongue." He pulled me onto him, shoving his tongue into my mouth to pulse against my own with delicious wrath, hungry to own me.

I was beginning to suspect he enjoyed that specific saying, and from the way he savagely explored every inch of my mouth so did I.

"Did you miss me?" He grinned as soon as his lips detached from mine, gluing one of his hands on the outer side of my thigh.

No, he wasn't having confidence issues, and he most certainly wasn't interested if my poor little heart was breaking without his presence. He was just deviously suggesting that one-on-one connection, always implying something outrageous trying to plant thoughts into my mind.

So, did I miss him?

Hmmm...

Like the plague, though that answer could have sent me straight to the pits of college hell.

Still, my reckless mouth managed to screw things up one way or the other. "I thought I was supposed to fear you, not miss you."

"Oh, Mouse, you're starting to learn." The evil gleam of satisfaction rising on his face was leading me to believe that I might have just messed up again. "There's a party tonight. On my street, three houses down the road. Be there at nine."

"How could someone resist an invitation like that?" I muttered, coming face to face with his *romantic* side.

"You can't deny any of my invitations, and you know it." Despite that he tried to make it sound like a joke, it was the truth, I wasn't allowed to deny anything that he asked.

Although it couldn't hurt trying. "Cole, I'm not in the mood for a party."

"But you are in the mood for an answer." That was indeed something that I was waiting for. "I'm not debating this. Besides, we're just retracing the circle." He shrugged.

What did *retracing* really refer to?

The party?

The date?

Or the deal?

"Bea!" A voice called out from somewhere on the other end of the building. As I turned to locate the sound, I spotted Jenna in my old section of the lobby. We shared the next class, and she was waiting for me to join her; or perhaps just trying to help me escape Cole. Either way, I needed to get over to her before he got some new idea about joining us for some extracurricular studies.

"I'm late for class," my voice ghosted the words, waiting to see the reaction.

"So?" Cole asked, unfazed.

Go figure...

"Please, I can only attend the first three classes anyway. I have to take Seb to the hospital for his treatment at noon," I tried reasoning with him.

Not that you can come to terms with a devil. "No bra at the

party, and you can go," he said, displaying a large grin.

"Are you for real?" I asked, but only got a serious nod in return. "What are you, five?"

"Then don't go. We'll spend the hour in the lobby. Either way, it's okay with me." He leaned his back against the wall behind him, getting himself comfortable for who knows how long. He wasn't backing down.

"Fine," I grumbled, knowing that I wasn't going to get out of there any time soon without agreeing to whatever twisted fantasy he had in mind. It was as if he always needed something in return for whatever little thing he did. Very much similar to Brax, and if I was to admit to it, also Ferris.

I didn't remain there to argue. My chances of winning were close to none anyway. I just hurried to get to Jenna, turning my back on *my king,* striding to my old end of the corridor.

"Aren't you going to kiss me goodbye?" Cole called after me with all the irony he possessed. "That's okay, Mouse. You'll make up for it later."

Shit. I thought *making up* for something had to come from one's own will. In his case, the tone was advising me that I'd most likely *pay* for it later.

I was out of the woods, so I only managed to greet Jenna by wiggling a few fingers. "Hey." It felt so relieving to see a friendly face in what now seemed to be the lion's den. Because whether I was the poor new girl or Queen B, I did not belong there.

"Hi!" She caught me in a long-overdue hug, yet one that hid a level of uncertainty. "I hope I'm still allowed to do this?" Her doubts came out to light, as my new position had propelled me miles away from who I used to be.

"Of course, you're allowed. Where is this coming from?"

"From you sucking faces with the devil," she answered with annoyance, then began pacing toward the classroom.

I hated to have to explain myself to anyone in general, but in her eyes, I was betraying her and fraternizing with the enemy. "He's helping me with my siblings' custody situation." That's all that I could say to her, explaining what our *relationship* was.

I guess Jenna already noticed his pattern, realizing that nothing could ever come for free when it came to Cole. "And what does he want in return?"

The question made me shut down for a second or two because, in the light of day, I didn't have the answer to it. What exactly did he want that he couldn't instantly receive from any other girl that ever set foot in this school?

"I haven't fully figured that one out yet." I just casually shrugged, trying to diminish the importance of the thought. At this stage, I was over trying to figure him out. Besides, there was something else that was worrying me at that moment. "You lost weight," I observed, knowing that the chances she was on a diet were slim; her slender silhouette was far from needing one.

As I suspected, it wasn't the case, and the unhappiness in her eyes quickly confirmed it, "Things are tough lately. I'm not sleeping well at night, not to mention my appetite. With all the riots and everything that's going on in the Pit, my parents have been left unemployed."

Goosebumps formed on my skin, I knew her situation all too well. I'd been in her shoes for too long and knew the excruciating pain of walking in them.

"You have to eat something before I'll start feeling fat around you," I giggle, pulling two muffins out of my purse and handing them to her. Ever since I started living in Ferris's apartment, I didn't lack a fresh supply of pretty much *anything*, including all sorts of baked goodies.

Jenna reached for the muffins, unsure if she should take just one or both. "Don't you want to at least share?"

"I'm not hungry," I said, making my way into the classroom.

It's not like some muffins were going to save her life, but it was the best I could do at the moment.

That unless...

Hmmm...

An idea flashed through my mind.

An idea that I had to wait until the next break to be able to put to use. I needed to focus first on the delightful hour of *Skills of Communication*. A course both Cole and Brax could have used.

"I need to talk to you before you get to the next class," I caught Jenna's arm as she was preparing to leave, guiding her through long corridors, straight to our secluded spot in the backcourt, next to the notice boards.

"What's wrong?" Her lower lip trembled with worry, assuming the worst. And why wouldn't she, since usually, the *worst* was normal back in the streets where we grew up?

"Nothing is wrong, I just wanted to give you a little something." Placing an arm around her shoulders, I tried to soothe and reassure her that I would do my best to help her.

Jenna smiled, holding on to a level of pride that had no use at that moment. "The muffins were enough, thank you."

I used to share that kind of pride as well, at least when it came to myself. That's mostly why the days begging on the streets to please my father almost destroyed me. And if that didn't successfully manage to break my personality, then my three kings were competing to crush what was left of it.

"I want you to have this." I unlocked a small bracelet from my wrists and turned it into a golden puddle of metal in her palm.

It was just a small accessory that I chose that morning out of an oversized jewelry box that I found in my dressing room.

I didn't think it was worth much, but I knew that for her it would be enough to put even just one decent meal on the table.

"I can't accept that." She rushed to return the bracelet to me, even though she had no real chance of succeeding.

I immediately pushed her fingers to close back into a fist. "I'm not sure if it's gold plated, or entirely out of gold, but you can sell it to ease things out a little."

"Won't the person who gave this to you have a say in this?" Jenna asked, still unsure if she should take it or not.

"I'll deal with him if that is the case," I nodded, knowing that Ferris would understand, if he ever found out. I wasn't going to open the subject and give him more reasons to expect something more in return, but neither was I going to deny it if he were to ask me.

My gesture caused a tear to roll down her face, "I don't know what to say—"

"Good, 'cause I don't need you to say anything. You're my friend. My *only* friend." It wasn't like I could ever consider a single one of the new acolytes as my friend anyway. Jenna was the only person close to me, except for my family. "Now go, the next class is about to start."

I was always bad at sharing emotions, mostly because I lacked receiving emotions myself. My mother was wonderful, I couldn't deny that. But she loved us in her own way, sharing a warmth that often replaced physical gestures like hugs. Words held no ground if not supported by facts. She was, in a way, a product of her society, knowing not to make us weak by over-coddling us, yet not too harsh either, denying us of her motherly love. I guess I was like her in many ways, not wanting to hear the words *I love you*, but wanting those words to be proven to me instead.

The next two classes passed, and as much as I would have liked to remain at the university, Sebastian's first visit to the new hospital forced me to leave. I had to get back home by noon, ready... or not so ready, to take my brother to the hospital. I hated going there; each time the feeling of isolation set in while walking through the gray hallways, the units looked more like an abandoned facility than a healthcare institution.

To my surprise, this place was different. I should have thought about it since I knew Ferris had set up something for us in the Hills, but what I found there exceeded all expectations. Lush gardens, just like the ones in a palace courtyard surrounded a modern glass-walled building in which everything seemed to be state of the art—design and medical technology. Totally opposite from the places we were used to and so strangely welcoming that Seb couldn't hide the large smile on his face. His treatment wasn't something that could be avoided. But at least the facility, along with the warm demeanor of the nurse who took him in, managed to dilute some of his visible discomfort away.

It was just life acting out on us. That was the part I hated most; watching him suffer. Watching anyone I cared about suffer without being able to take their pain away, to take it upon myself. Ferris's knife sounded like a much better alternative to those needles. But the way that Seb kept himself strong gave me the power I needed to go on without letting any sign of my weakness surface. I needed to be strong for him in return, and that was exactly what I let him see on the surface.

No weakness allowed—at least not externally.

We remained there until late afternoon, time during which we both dozed off—Seb dreaming of new toys and me dreaming of the day I would no longer *be* a toy.

Speaking of toys, I managed to text Ferris before I left for home, letting him know that I was meeting Cole for the night. No reply came. I could only imagine that either he was pissed off or just didn't care. Either way, the chances of me sleeping in his bed that evening were almost non-existent.

Strangely, I found the babysitter home when I arrived, sparing me the effort of having to figure out a way to convince Nat to take care of Sebastian while I was out. Besides, knowing that someone else, except for the bodyguards positioned in front of the building, was watching them made things a lot easier for me to handle. Not that anything has ever been easy since I arrived in Echo City.

I needed to find something to wear. And fast. It was almost 8 PM by the time I got my head around things, having sat down to serve dinner and eat with my siblings before I could leave. I owed them at least that much, especially since I understood I had to value each moment stolen to be together. Life wasn't going to be easy here either, knowing that they would be mostly alone due to all my other *commitments*. But them having shoes and clothes and everything else they needed, and more was encouraging. I was doing the right thing.

I finally ended up in the dressing room, searching through the shelves for something to fulfill the *no-bra* request. One step away from messing things up, I picked up a black dress that could minimize the lack of a bra, but as I was trying it on, a purple satin corset popped into my sight.

Gorgeous!

It was the only word that came to mind as I tried it on, along with a short black skirt and a leather motorcycle jacket. It brought a badass glow sparkling in my smile, and I kind of enjoyed it. Maybe it would wipe out the scared little Mouse vibe and get Cole to back off a little. Fat chance of that ever happening, but it was worth a try, especially since the outfit *fulfilled* his *no-bra* condition.

Sneaking out the door so that Nat wouldn't drown me in a river of questions regarding my clothes, the hour... and pretty much every aspect of my life, I jumped straight into the car and asked the driver to take me to the street where Cole lived.

Four and a half minutes later, I was standing in front of

another lush mansion. This one didn't seem so spectacular to me. Or maybe I'd gotten more used to their extravagances, who knows?

With a deep breath for courage, I headed inside, and even though I knew no one, everyone seemed to know me. I didn't even reach the living room and I was already waving my hand more than the Queen of England, nodding and fake smiling to everyone that I met. I was officially a celebrity and all that was missing were the paparazzi, although a few phone flashlights coming my way were suggesting that I wasn't far from the spotlight.

If the earth would just split open and swallow me whole, it would have been just fine by me. But I wasn't lucky enough for that to happen and I needed to return to reality—I was still there on a mission and had someone who I needed to meet. Although there was no sign of Cole.

Was he even here? I began wondering as I kept walking through different halls and rooms in search of him.

It wasn't like I was eager to see him. At this point, I preferred talking to anyone else except him. But I knew the longer I stalled, the bigger the chance of finding an angered king when I finally located him.

And there he was. After searching through rooms and rooms, I found him in the garden, contemplating the stars clinging to a bottle of whiskey as his sole company.

Whoever thought Cole would turn out to be a romantic?

"You're fucking late," he muttered.

So much for the romance.

I arched an eyebrow. "It's not like you were waiting for me at the entrance with wide open arms. I had to search for you through this entire place."

"Oh, you wanted to be in my arms. Why didn't you say so?" His sarcasm was getting on my nerves. "Come here, Mouse." He stretched out his hands, waiting for me to join him.

Why couldn't I just keep my mouth shut?

It seemed that I always had to ask myself this question around him. It was Cole's special gift to make me feel that way, along with giving me the sensation that I was in desperate need of someone who would read me my rights every time I was about to meet him.

You have the right to remain silent, everything you say can and will be used against you.

It was impossible to refuse him, and at the same time, I found it impossible to obey.

The terrace door just opened and a couple found their way close to his side, making camp on a decorative rock, without much thought of leaving too soon.

"I said, come," Cole snarled.

I guess he wasn't impressed with the new company, being much more focused on me respecting his demand.

Downing a few slugs of whiskey, he waited for me to approach, tilting the bottle so I could keep him company. There was no use in refusing since nothing I did around him was of my own free will.

Placing the bottle at my lips, I took a sip. And one was enough to cough the liquor out, choking from its strength.

"You need to practice." He pushed the bottle back on my lips and kept it there until I took another sip.

I cursed between my teeth as he pulled me insanely close to his chest. His grip was forcing my head to press against his shoulder while his face buried itself in the curtain of my hair and his hands began trailing on my back.

"So this was your alternative for no bra?" He playfully whispered in my ear, but his tone was the wrong kind of *playful*.

"I improvised." I shrugged, when in fact I just tried my best to take a detour from his request.

"Don't remember asking you to improvise. But if you're going to cause *trouble*, you better be prepared to attend to *them*." He took me by the hand in what was most certainly *not* a romantic gesture, guiding my palm to that hardened part of him, probably helping me to recognize the effects of my *improvisation*.

So that is what a bad clothes day really means.

"There are people watching us," my voice barely steady as I noticed another couple stepping through the glass doors.

"I'm not a prude, let them watch." He pushed himself strongly against me, allowing a long groan to surface as my fingers clenched to meet his cock. I was trying to hide this uncommon form of *greeting* with the help of our jackets but with no result.

"All you ever think about is sex," I growled as his heaving breath seemed to induce a melting effect over my own body. It was only increasing the sensation of anxiety I had every time I was near him.

"Well, me thinking about sex got you a surprise." His hand snuck into the silky interior of his jacket and emerged holding a few pieces of white paper, which he handed over to me. "Now, just to show that I don't think only of sex, I'm going to find myself another bottle of this." He tilted the whiskey bottle, which now only held only two fingers of the brownish liquid.

Did he drink a whole bottle?

I didn't get a chance to ask him, as he vanished through the glass doors, leaving me in the garden in the company of the papers I was holding in my hand.

I raised them to get a better look and the first words that I caught sight of filled my eyes with tears of undeniable happiness.

CHAPTER 5

Permanent guardianship.

That's all I could read, and all I ever needed to see as I flipped through the papers and found there were two similar titles. My siblings were mine now, and no one could take them away from me. I had legal rights over both of them, all my efforts had finally come to fruition.

Maybe it seemed weird, or maybe I had just lost my mind, but my first instinct was to run after Cole. Even if the papers came with a price, I felt that I needed to thank him somehow as the joy that was twinkling in my soul could not be contained.

I found him beside a mountain of booze, opening another bottle of whiskey, just as he said he would. He was already being assaulted by a blonde bimbo who was ostentatiously adjusting her cleavage to showcase exactly what she had to offer.

Unfortunately for her, I'd just been crowned queen bitch, and she was hitting on my *king*.

Maybe the sip of whiskey had gone to my head, or maybe

I was just tired of being undermined. Whatever the cause, it made me sneak up behind him, pressing my lips to his earlobe as I murmured, "Thank you." I let the letters slowly flow, infiltrating his bloodstream and crawling the skin of his neck.

He instantly turned, surprised, and intrigued, arching an eyebrow in my direction, "I guess that made you happy." He made his bottom lip disappear between his teeth, gleaming back at me.

"Yes," I let out a genuine answer, trying to avoid his gaze as the image of that abused lip was making me want to trace my tongue alongside it to heal its pain.

"Now, maybe when you kiss me next time, you'll really mean it." It was an open invitation to satisfy the rush of emotions that were flooding through my system.

"Okay," I whispered, sliding my hands inside his jacket all the way to the muscular sides of his torso, pressing my lips against his. Unhurried, magic, and entirely *of my own free will*. He didn't force me to do it, probably because he didn't have the time. Judging by the lack of movement coming from his side, he was more shocked by my gesture than I was.

My tongue moved slowly, teasing with gentle pulses, over and over again, until I was reminded of the unwanted eyes that were watching us. The blonde was still there, as if waiting for us to be done, so she could get another shot at him.

Over my dead body.

I pulled a hand away from the mesmerizing heat of his muscles and moved a few fingers in her direction, waving her goodbye, all while my mouth never stopped urging over his.

My gesture didn't go unnoticed, and between the rotations of our tongues I could hear a deaf whisper, "I hope now you're satisfied with my gift. Every man wants to fuck you and every girl wants to be you."

Slowly, I broke the kiss, taking a good look around me.

He was right.

All eyes were upon us, and while the men showed lust and admiration, the women gleamed with envy and jealousy.

I wish I could say that I hated it, that I wanted them all to disappear, but Cole's presence next to my body instilled a sense of authority. He was so powerful that I could see it anywhere I looked. Every one of his gestures was either envied or feared by everyone watching. Including me.

Without explanation, he caught my palm in his hand and led me to the other side of the room. We only stopped next to a large armchair that was occupied by a guy whom I'd previously seen hanging out somewhere in the middle of the University lobby. Cole didn't need words to get him to flee the spot. A simple look sufficed, getting the guy instantly to stand up as he fled out of sight.

It was that easy. What Cole wanted, Cole received, and as soon as he threw himself onto the newly vacated throne, he *wanted* me to take a seat in his lap, publicly assuming the role of *queen*.

Strangely, it didn't feel unnatural. More like I was supposed to be there, almost nestled against his chest as his subjects came once again to pay their '*What's up, bro?*' respects.

History seemed to be repeating itself to the point where I was starting to wonder how he dealt with all of the worship. Sure, at first it might be fun, having the adrenaline of leadership running through his veins. It might even give him information on everything that was going on around him since everyone was so eager to please their king. But from where I was standing it was just a waste of time and energy.

"You, go bring me a punch," Cole suddenly ordered one of the students who was an intern at his *royal servant's school*.

What puzzled me wasn't his behavior but his request. Was he going off the whiskey he seemed so fond of?

It didn't take long for me to figure out the answer. As soon as his order arrived, he put the glass between my fingers, "I know you don't like whiskey." He clinked the neck of his bottle on my cup, gesturing for me to drink up.

I first looked at it as if it was poisoned, and to be honest, that was by far more of a possibility than Cole actually being nice out of his own free will. But I left things as they were, not wanting to disturb the newfound balance of the night.

Somewhere between a few rants, a few attempts at flirting that made my blood boil, and a few brotherly pledges of eternal respect, he buried his head deep against my collarbone. "Jesus, I came here to relax, not for these idiots to do my head in," he groaned as his eyes closed and his arms snuck around my waist. The musky base of his cologne was setting in, covering my own as his eyes rose to meet mine, hiding a glimmer I never noticed before.

Or maybe it *wasn't* there before.

A determined thumb traced the edges of my lips, opening them so that his tongue could hide inside my mouth in slow circles, very similar to my earlier kiss. Lava-hot desire began flowing through my veins. Everything came so naturally, without him using his usual *methods* of constraint. It was just me and him, with shivering bodies, acknowledging a reality that seemed highly improbable—he wasn't kissing me as the result of torture, or for proving a point. It was more like a kiss between lovers as if preparing me for what was to come.

Chewing on my bottom lip, Cole grinned sensing my smile. The party started to make more sense than I could have ever believed. The music mixed with the booze was getting everyone to let their guard down, relaxing to the point where any desire prevailed day-to-day reality.

Perhaps I was a fool for only now discovering his world, but life hadn't given me many opportunities to *party* before.

It was just us, living in the moment as our crazy magnetism was settling in. Heated limbs and hearts full of desire, while our bodies screamed to be touched in the steamiest way possible.

One of his hands ran through my hair, dancing between thick locks while the other was advancing on the side of my waist, higher and higher, losing itself beneath my jacket.
"I want you to answer a question. No bullshit," he whispered between nibbles and caresses of my tongue.

"Hmmm, no bullshit. What if I'm afraid of the repercussions?" I chuckled.

"There won't be any." He glared back at me.

"Okay," I sheepishly murmured. "But you know I also have an unanswered question."

His eyebrows suddenly arched, letting me know I had his full attention. "Do you now?"

"Mhmmm," I nodded, unable to hold back my curious nature. "But I don't trust you, so I should go first." After all, who was to say I shouldn't take advantage of his moment of weakness? It was what my kings were best at anyway—one way or the other.

"I'm far from being a saint, Mouse. But I am a man of my word. Everyone else in this city might try to deceive you. But not me. One day you will find my words to be true, and learn to trust me." He seemed deadly serious about it, even though chances were that his words were just a bluff. Maybe he was just drunk. "Now for the question." He shrugged, not really concerned about what I could ask him.

"What was the bet about?" I needed to know what exactly had brought us together, even if it was just to satisfy my curiosity and not something that could benefit me. I believed everything happened for a reason, even if that reason might seem totally unimportant at the time being. It had something to do with karma and the planets lining up, even though when it came to Cole and me, I was sure the universe made a mistake.

"I remember I asked you to kiss me in exchange for an answer to that question." He leaned in to trace his mouth

73

along the side of my neck as I was struggling to hold a semi-conversation, caught between the throbbing below my waist and the thoughts that seemed to gather up just to dissipate into a million different ideas the next second.

"Which I eventually did," I whispered, my voice barely audible. I did *kiss* him where he wanted—and also a lot *lower* than that.

"Not without a large amount of struggle on your part. But I'm feeling generous, so I'll tell you anyway," he said, continuing to explore my neck, unbothered by the fact that I was demanding his attention. Although this time, I knew he wasn't doing it on purpose. He wasn't ignoring me intentionally, just letting himself be carried away by the heat of our bodies pressed together..

The secret—if I could even call it that—would be out soon, "I was drunk—"

"Kinda like you are now?" I didn't mean to interrupt him, but I needed to understand his unusually *decent* behavior.

Suddenly, he caught my chin between his index finger and his thumb, gently brushing his thumb over my lips. "I'm not drunk now."

Cole was lying. He had to be because, knowing him sober, his sensual touches and charming attitude could make me easily fall for a man like him. The ocean-deep blue eyes alongside his fit athletic physique would have guaranteed him success in case of any attempt.

"Getting back to what I was saying. I may have bragged to the guys that I'd pull some dumb stunt with my motorcycle and jump off some hill. Luckily, I sobered up in time to realize I had more chance of meeting my creator than pulling that stunt off. But Ace has had a grudge against me since... since forever."

"Maybe it has something to do with you sleeping with his girlfriend?" I let that comment slip, remembering the conversation he had with Ace on the night I accepted The Pleasure.

"Hey, it's not my fault the girl was looking for dick at every street corner. Besides, he didn't even care about her. He was just mad that I bruised his ego. And because of that, he convinced the other guys that I should pay a price for showing off and not living up to what I said I would do." Cole flared his nostrils like an enraged bull. "I may be reckless, but I'm not stupid. I wasn't going to get myself killed because I had an extra bottle of whiskey."

"How could they make you pay? Aren't you the *king*?" I asked, confused.

"I am, and I'm ready to step on their heads if they ever disobey me. But they've got an advantage in numbers. To get them off my back, I agreed to take on another bet—something more punishment than bet."

"To spend an evening without hitting on me?" I arched an eyebrow as things started to make sense.

"It was pretty hard," he laughed, tightening the hand he held on my waist and pulling me up onto his lap until I realized just how *hard* it must have been for him to hold back. "I don't hold back when it comes to beautiful women, especially if booze and parties are involved. Never needed to. Besides, it wasn't supposed to be a big deal. We used to make these kinds of bets for fun all the time. It didn't even matter if we won or lost. All that mattered was entertaining ourselves, even if in the end we would come out with thinner wallets." Cole took a deep breath. "But this time I couldn't lose the bet," he continued. "The stake was a gold Rolex I used to wear. If I lost the bet, I had to give Ace that watch so he could sell it and throw some monster party." A hint of sadness flashed in his blue eyes, "And I didn't have it anymore. My father pawned it a few months ago."

Strange for him to make a confession like that to me, but I

guess he finally felt safe enough to admit the truth.

"Ace did that on purpose, to expose you. He hoped you'd lose and wouldn't have a way to give him the watch." I put two and two together.

"Exactly. He wants my spot, and exposing my financial situation could give him just that."

"I know how you feel; I used to have nothing," I whispered, leaning my head against his, trying to comfort him.

"No, you couldn't know. Because I used to have everything." Maybe he was right, I never knew a life of luxury or the feeling of or what it was like to never want for anything. My life had always revolved around either missing clothes, food, toys, or sometimes all of them. Sure, my mother tried her best to provide for us and succeeded most of the time. But even when we had food on the table, seeing her deny herself basic necessities to provide for us always left an irreparable hole in my heart.

"Now you know my darkest secret. I always have to keep up appearances," a confession from a man who never shared the aspects of his life with anyone. Maybe he was drunk, after all.

"Now I want to know yours," Cole grinned, expecting something in return for opening up.

"My what?" I asked, unsure what he was talking about.

He let a devilish smile rise on his lips, and I felt he was pursuing a hidden goal. "Your darkest secret."

"My secrets don't get any darker than this. My darkest secrets have been exposed yesterday when you met with Brax and Ferris." What more can I hide than the fact I have two other men in my life?

"Not exactly. I want the truth, Bea." For the first time, I was Bea and not Mouse. Either I did something completely wrong or entirely right.

The warmth of his hand raised on the flank of my torso,

moving so slowly that I could barely sense it. "Higher?" The specific note of his voice let me know that was the question he wanted to ask in the first place.

It seemed that the night held many firsts because it was the first time he was really asking permission for any of his gestures. The acceptance turned out to be my *darkest secret.* He was waiting to see if I would let him go further without him asking me to.

My eyelids fell shut, aiming to push back any reactions, yet it was a moment of honesty, even if only during the minutes spent sitting on his throne. I felt my head nodding, followed by the raising of his hand, skimming the silky material and stopping somewhere beneath my breasts.
"Higher?" His question came again, hitting a nerve that exploded tingling inside my body, in pure waves of cravings.

It was anatomic.

Elementary.

Primal.

I yearned for his touch as much as I did for *the* Cole he let me see tonight. "Higher," my answer came while tugging on my jacket to keep his hand safe from all the gazes that fell upon us.

Without restraint, his hand slipped higher, cupping my breast, tracing a finger over my pebbled nipple and following its contour through the material of my corset.

"I guess now I know your darkest secret, you enjoy this." I was caught red-handed, releasing a few whimpers as his mouth bit down on mine, matching the urgency of his tongue with the circles running across my nipple.

I wanted him. I wanted to feel him—hot and slick and eager —in a swirl of many sinful thoughts, thumping straight into that needy place between my thighs.

Shaking my head, I tried to escape the thought. The unstoppable sensation of him being all around me, alluring me with his every move, and gradually enslaving me with those cobalt-blue eyes.

Cole let out a groan, "I may *fucking* get used to this." A unique admission of hidden feelings, revealing an ulterior intention.

I just laid my head back on his shoulder, letting silence be my answer.

It would never happen.

We could never truly happen since behind anything we could ever possibly become would be the truth of how it all began.

His hand never stopped moving under my jacket as his heaving breath washed over my hair, increasing the pressure until the pampering turned into an arousing pain. Through murky eyelashes, I glanced across the room, only to notice that things had gotten a lot more heated up since the last time I looked around me.

What Jenna had told me a few weeks before suddenly came to mind, *anything goes at these parties*, and these people were taking her words literally.

A guy was doing a line of coke right off a table only two feet away from us, while a little more to the left a girl's hand got lost deep down beneath the zipper of her boyfriend's pants— or whatever the guy was to her. No wonder Cole was always on the verge of outrageousness if this was *his kingdom*. Honestly, he was beginning to look like a saint compared to what was happening around us.

"I don't like it here," I whispered, leaning in to search for a kiss that would more easily convince him to fulfill my next request and leave this place.

"Why? What happened?" This room was his normality, to the point that he wasn't even aware that a normal person might find it shocking.

What happened?

I glanced in front of me to try and prove a point, though the sophomore girl who had just disposed of her t-shirt and the manly hand that had decided to cover one of her breasts made me quickly turn my gaze to Cole. "What the hell is this?"

"They're just playing. Not sure what's going to happen in the next five minutes, though," he let out a laugh since apparently, this kind of behavior was all too common at these parties.

Looking back, I noticed another guy who I recognized as one of the seniors, merging his lips with the girl's *free* breast in a lustful exploration of every inch of her skin. His gesture was so hungered and altogether erotic that I was beginning to think that I was attending one of Brax's shows.

"Do you want us to leave?" Cole was testing me to see if I was enjoying the show, and I was just about to ruin his fantasies.

"Yes," I whispered back, nudging his hand away so I could arrange my jacket.

It didn't take long before we got up, and his fingers intertwined with mine, escorting me to the grand hallway. My instinct was to walk towards the entrance door, but his tightening grip stopped me, guiding me in the opposite direction—toward the staircase.

Shit, that's what leaving really meant, I realized as he guided me upstairs.

I wasn't comfortable sitting in that room any longer, but I had a gut feeling I was falling into a trap. And judging by Cole's grip on my hand, it was too late to change my mind.

CHAPTER 6

W ith the skills of a secret agent, Cole quickly found a free bedroom, sneaking us inside and making sure to twist the key to keep any intrusive eyes outside.

"I thought we were leaving?" I snarled in a semi-annoyed tone, catching onto his plans while looking for a light switch—although luck seemed to be running out on me.

"Leaving without receiving an answer? Are you sure?" he asked.

I was sure. Sure that his docile attitude was soon going to take a turn, and at the same time, sure that I needed to hear him out, no matter how unpredictable his answer might be.

At least he didn't keep me waiting. "Okay, so let me spare you the suspense. It's a **no** from me."

"No?" I almost choked on the words.

I didn't even know why I was surprised since I suspected a refusal from him in the first place.

"Yes... NO. I'm not going to risk my future for your insane plan. But that doesn't mean the night is over. I just wanted to get that out of the way so we could continue where we left off."

Wow, just shatter my plans then let's get back to feeling each other up. Typical Cole.

Still, my instincts were telling me there was room for some bargaining, and just as a skilled trader, he was just bluffing to spike the price.

Two could play that game.

"That's it... **no**? You clearly don't understand how this separation of powers could really impact your future."

"Oh, I do understand. I'll be high up on the Hills, sleeping peacefully in my bed while the whole world can go screw itself." A simple shrug ended his sentence as he appeared to have no worries in the world—except for what was going to happen tonight between us, of course.

"Are you for real?" I refused to buy into this level of selfishness, nurturing some tiny hope that he was fooling around, or that at least I could get him to change his mind. "Your Elite origins won't be enough if not supported by wealth. How long before your parents won't be able to keep up the appearances? Think about it. Do you think they'll care about who knows who, when spots in the *life of luxury* will be limited?"

The angered distress blooming on his face convinced me that it wasn't the first time he had heard the words, and the chances were that his parents' fears were slowly becoming his own.

"And if I risk it and things turn out the wrong way, I'll lose anyhow." He tried to seem relaxed about what the future might bring.

But I wasn't giving up without a fight. "At least there is still an *if*. You know as well as I do that there will be 'no bed for you to sleep in' if we don't try to do something and stop them."

"Or I could always ask Ferris for a loan. He has more money than all the Elite put together."

That news came as a shock. I knew Ferris was rich, but I never wanted or tried to estimate his fortune. Cole was right, that could be a solution for any other person, but I knew better than to believe his words. "Somehow, I can't imagine you asking for a loan. Not even from Ferris."

The roar that broke out from Cole's throat confirmed my suspicion. I may have just called him out on his own bluff.

"Okay. Let's say I go through with this. I'm not going to do it because I'm some coward that's going to save his own ass. I want power. With my father's connections and my own, I'm heading for a political career. I might just shorten the ride by taking part in this. Or I may completely destroy it. So, that leaves me wanting more. Call it a consolation prize."

I gulped, realizing *who* was going to be that consolation prize.

"A little something to make me know it was worth trying, even if I fail," he continued, his blue orbs piercing through mine.

I arched an eyebrow. "I'm pretty sure that the keys to the city should be more than enough payment for your efforts."

"I'm pretty sure they're not," he said, almost with a grin, preparing me for what was to come. How did I think, even for a second, that the man could have even a decent bone in his body? "You see, Mouse... I've never had a girlfriend. The idea never appealed to me before."

"Are you out of your fucking mind?" I muttered.

Was he really asking me this?

"And now I will have one with a foul mouth. A mouth that I'm planning on exploiting to its limit." His hand found its way under my chin again, while his thumb was drawing the contour of my lips in a much firmer manner than he did earlier on his *throne*. "I want you as a bonus, and I'm not talking about the bits and crumbs you've been throwing me. Deal whatever you want to call it. I want what Brax received."

Was it that obvious to everyone that I'd slept with Br'

"Why would you still want me if you knew I was ⸺

with him?" I asked.

Cole's eyes fixated on me. "What's that got to do with anything? Or do you think I wanted a virgin on my hands? As I see things, he saved me the trouble."

I listened intently, waiting to sense the slightest sign of regret or distress in his voice. Yet, there was nothing except a hint of amusement.

He was telling the truth.

He actually didn't care.

"Cole, there's also something else. Someone else. Ferris... Ferris asked me for the same thing in return for his help." I tried explaining.

"A second virginity. I would pay big money to see you come up with that," he laughed.

"Cole." Maybe he considered himself amusing, but I was in no mood for jokes. "He asked me to be... *his*."

"Well, would you look at that? I'm not really surprised, we always had common tastes. But sharing... hmmm, that's a notion I've lost track of."

"What are you talking about?" I grunted, shocked at where he was going.

"Wasn't it obvious enough? I don't mind sharing when it comes to them. The list of people I respect is shorter than the number of fingers on my hand, but Ferris and Brax hold top positions. Those guys are like fucking idols to me. Mentors to say the least."

I needed some kind of explanation because the whole concept seemed so improbable that it was confusing me. "Are you serious? You're not jealous, or feeling some need to defend your manly ego?"

"How could I be jealous of family? Just because we're not blood-related doesn't mean we're not as close as it gets. We've just been separated for a while, that's all."

Maybe it made me look stupid, but my jaw fell open and I just blinked. I had just reunited the *dream team*. Or was it the *nightmare team*?

"But, Mouse, if anyone else from outside our *circle* even thinks about touching you, I will cut their dicks off. I want you to be mine. Mine to torture. Mine to enjoy. Mine to make scream."

Scandalous. Outrageous. And at the same time, my only way to prevail.

I was left with an impossible choice as the cards were now in my hands.

Could I accept and become the toy of a maniac?

Did I even have a choice?

"What am I really doing here, Cole?"

"Don't tell me that you thought I was going to play the guitar or maybe a flute for you, in an attempt to sweep you off your feet?" His hysterical laughter filled the room. "But I do want to show you my special ability. Can you guess what that is?"

I didn't want to guess.

I didn't even want to be there any longer.

"No," I answered unimpressed by his obvious excitement.

He suddenly leaned in to whisper in my ear. "I'll tell you either way. I'm going to fuck you until you can't fucking breathe."

Was this my lucky day or what? I ironically thought to myself, although my body seemed to disagree. His words were making my breasts ache with incredible discomfort while some sort of molten heat was draining down my stomach, heading somewhere between my thighs.

I arched an eyebrow while my tolerance level hit zero. "*If* I agree."

"You will agree if you want me to also *agree* to your

plan. Besides—" his body advanced dangerously close to mine, pushing the jacket off my shoulders and watching it fall to the ground, "I know you want me. You admitted it before."

"You're such a jerk," the words involuntarily slipped out as *involuntarily* seemed to be a new part of my daily routine.

"I'm starting to believe you like me as a jerk." His hand was beneath my chin again, lifting my head so I could glance straight into the icy depths of his gaze. "Bea," the depth in his words while calling my name, along with the hypnosis that seemed to be setting in, were draining me of all strength. And then there was that damn finger pressed upon my lower lip, leaving my mouth dry as if my body had been deprived of water for ages. Cole was asking a question. An unspoken one as his thumb was slowly advancing trying to obtain my permission.

That until my lips parted under his grin of satisfaction, letting myself be prey to all cruel thoughts he may ever have had.

"I'll take that as a yes." He said while the rise and fall of his chest increased with each breath, bringing with it an unstoppable lust blooming on his face as his finger moved to press against my tongue. "You've got yourself a deal." A deal sealed with a kiss similar to a storm, ravishing everything in its path, exposing me to the last bare truth.

Sneaking under my skin, crawling to my very bones, the fear I always felt around him was there again. I *feared* what he could do to me, terrified by the primordial sensations engulfing me.

Slow was a term as unfamiliar as *kind* was to him, and things were moving at the speed of light. His mouth crashed on mine until our teeth clashed, full of indescribable lust. I don't remember when it happened, but his jacket joined mine on the floor. Then grabbing the hem of his t-shirt he took it off with one hand, revealing the inked temptation I craved to see each time I was with him.

"Slow down," I managed to murmur as he reached the back of my knees, taking control of my balance and setting me on the bed.

"If I slow down, I might keep you in this bedroom until tomorrow evening." It was highly probable that his threat wouldn't hold ground. But I wasn't willing to risk it, recognizing the *various* ideas that could run through his devious mind.

With rough gestures, he dragged my corset down, pinning it right beneath the generous shape of my breasts, without removing it completely. A sound so eager and real made his throat vibrate with yearning. His lips were ignoring my own and moving on to explore the smooth skin of my nipples, lick by lick, nibble by nibble until all my power of restraint was shattered into a million pieces.

He only needed a few moments to make my skin buzz from the tip of my head, down to my toes, and he noticed. The devil stopped to look at me, raising his gaze from the place he was attending only to preen for a couple of seconds. "You're welcome." He just couldn't keep the thought to himself, serving me with a large portion of his arrogance.

An arrogance that had to be somehow kept under control. "I guess I should also thank you for the air I breathe?" I muttered with obvious annoyance.

"You will need to soon." The words came out as sharp and hard as the man who spoke them. He was just making a promise that I knew he would make good on—maybe even much earlier than I was ever expecting.

Disregarding all the laws of gravity, my skirt seemed to be slipping over my knees, being pulled off me with the speed of a falling star. Though I didn't get to make a wish, the next second, the length of his palm cupped the whole surface of my pussy with such strength that I thought I was about to break...

or cum. Yes, I was that messed up.

His touch caused tiny bolts of static energy, making them electrify the aroused zone between my thighs. A shriek burst through my gritted teeth as I could no longer control it from finding freedom.

The sound appeared to do something to him, arousing him to his very limit. Without wasting *precious* time, he pushed my panties aside and propelled a finger inside me. The move left me motionless, as if something caught my body under an invisible weight, numbing everything else and leaving just a sensation of movement alive within me. It was both good and bad, like rain and dust on a hot summer day. Not enough to cool you down, and still something that you couldn't deny yourself. Everything was utterly intense from the unearthly way his teeth bit on my nipples, to the pounding vibration of his hand, his finger stroked in and out of me as the heel of his hand ground against my clit. He quickly decided it wasn't enough—not anymore. So, he slid another finger inside of me, yet before he could properly resume, he paused, huffing in annoyance. "This fucking piece of material," he muttered, ripping my piece of lingerie and throwing it somewhere on our pile of clothes. "You're not going to wear panties any longer. At least not when you're with me."

"You're kidding, right?" The thought of walking around the university with the autumn breeze blowing between my legs was making me shudder and laugh at the same time. This man was crazy.

I didn't get to ruminate for too long as a slap hit the wetness of my core, causing such sharp pain that it made my feet brace on the mattress for support, fighting the pain and feeling it turn into a completely different thing.

"What I say, goes. Got it?" It was a punishment, and in case I didn't catch on from the slap, his irritated voice confirmed it.

Jesus, if I wasn't wet before I was dripping now, and his

two fingers took full advantage of that. Revenge or mastered skills, I wasn't sure which one of those was guiding him, but the tempo became fierce. So intense that I felt like we were setting fire to the bed itself. Cole's fingers were drilling deeper and deeper, to a spot I didn't even know I had.

As an unavoidable reaction, my body curved, raising my back from the mattress and unwillingly pushing my breasts deeper inside his mouth. He didn't just like it, he was in ecstasy. Catching my body in that exact position with his other hand, securing it behind my back.

The thrusts became violent, sadistic in a way, aiming to break me into a beautiful pain, filling me so much that I felt I was bursting into flames. It was all too impossible, too powerful, too fucking addictive, and as if that wasn't enough, the damn friction his hand was causing on my clit was making the bottom of my core contract.

Cole jabbed himself harder and harder until no matter what I did or thought about, my body decided to crash. That was it. One, two, three, and I was squirming with ecstasy, trying to break free as he kept up his torture through my orgasm. It was so intense I wanted to cry, totally unable to withstand his wicked intentions. My mouth decided to plead for mercy, "Please... Please stop," I whined as my core tightened again around his fingers, sapping me of all strength.

"Mouse, I'm just getting started." A truth I was aware of, but one which I also wanted to deny, even if only for my momentary peace of mind.

"Please," I mewled, defeated while inside my brain there was an ongoing battle between giving up or prolonging the pleasure and testing my limits.

He grunted, but finally agreed, "Okay, I'll give you a short break." Like nanosecond short, because the instant he freed his fingers from within me he reached his zipper, tugging down his pants right before I dropped on the mattress.

Deep down, I hoped he wasn't ready, and probably needed some time to warm up, but the enlarged length peeking from his boxers quickly proved me wrong. For some strange reason he seemed bigger than before, or maybe it was because I couldn't even withstand the breeze from the room's ventilation system touching my skin at the moment.

In the darkness, I noticed the liquid of his arousal as he slid his own hand over his length a couple of times. I wasn't sure if it was helping him to get ready or helping him to threaten me with unbearable ecstasy.

With agile hands, he pulled me toward him, filling me so fast that my eyes popped open to stare into his. I suddenly was motionless, powerless, and any other thing with -*less* in it. Except for *cockless*. Yeah, I certainly didn't lack that.

I didn't know how to react as my body seemed to be paralyzed somewhere between screaming and breaking the skin on my lower lip from muffling the sound. At least that surreal state of pleasure had dissipated a little, providing me with a second to recover.

Cole knew exactly what he was doing and what he needed to do, moving in short but deep thrusts, crushing me before I even got to catch my first breath. He was so focused it scared me, letting the silver piercing of his tongue show between his lips as he thrust himself further, only to exit completely in the next second.

Was he done?

Foolish question, since the next instant he pushed himself back deep into me, stretching me once again. Only to repeat *and* repeat again.

I felt the need to latch onto something but he was too far away. He was watching me from above, feeding himself on my every luscious yet panicked gesture.

My eyes fell closed, and I could no longer control the panting breath that came out in waves of moans and cries, each time louder as he thrust harder and harder.

"Don't hold yourself back. The music is so loud that no one can hear you. I want to know what I am doing to you. How badly the pleasure is ripping through this little body of yours."

The hell if I was going to let him enjoy it even more than he already was. But the thought was quickly shattered as he braced on my hips, slamming me against him as he continued jolting inside of me.

I screamed, as I couldn't hold back the spasming anymore and my body raised to find his own, burying my teeth into his chest to suppress the sound.

"Fuck, Bea." His arms wrapped around my back, pinning me against him as he threw a few more thrusts before he pulled out.

He didn't even ask me if I was okay. Which I wasn't. I was a mess of a shaking body ripped from a pleasure so intense it was making me lose control. He didn't care about that, and I didn't expect that he would. I was just happy I made it out alive, but the torture to ecstasy was far from being over as the very next second he swirled me around to face the mattress. "On your knees."

I refused to obey him. It wasn't as much of a refusal as I could no longer move even an inch. "Now!" His palm smacked my ass so strongly that I was forced to gather the last of my strength and raise it high in the air as my face got buried between some pillows. I was more like hugging the mattress than on my knees.

He didn't waste any time, propelling himself inside through the signs of me coming undone. I felt him so raw and enlarged that my head was drawn back from the shock. He took advantage of that, swiping a hand over my face to merge my hair into a tight ponytail that he caught onto, making sure it wouldn't fall apart. "You thought you could outsmart me with this corset Mouse, but all you ever did was bring me a new toy."

I felt him wrapping his other free hand around my corset, turning it into my personal leash. Then he began slamming into me, guiding me to whatever desire he may have had while arching my back to the point I began to think that his cock was hitting the pit of my stomach.

This was certainly not lovemaking. It wasn't even sex. It was fucking at an impossible velocity and if Cole wanted to prove a point, he definitely had succeeded.

The mass of muscles restlessly moved behind me as his groans picked up intensity, though not as fast as I was breaking apart. He was maneuvering my limp body while I was just a puddle of liquid desire.

How many people fainted during sex, would there even be statistics on that sort of thing? I kind of wanted to make sure I wasn't in danger of being the first one.

"Cole," I squeaked as my whole body was in ecstasy, unstoppable pleasure throbbing through me until I felt I couldn't breathe.

He was right.

The bastard was right.

I needed his approval to breathe.

"Did you have enough, Mouse?" Like it was even a question. Though he wasn't asking, he was just taking pride in his ravaging assault.

I didn't answer.

And he didn't stop.

He was thrusting stronger and wilder until a word like a moan broke through my lips, "Yesss."

Instantly I felt the hand on the corset tightening, raising me from the bed, then guiding me to meet his body in a few impossible jabs. He was finally finding his ecstasy, letting his liquid warmth flow inside me as I was still involuntarily tightening around him.

I almost fainted on the mattress as he fell on top of me, crushing me under his body weight. I was trembling when he was done. Trembling because it was just as if I'd been swiped off by a hurricane. Trembling because I liked it, when in fact, I should have been ashamed; being used because of a deal. *Shouldn't I?*

"There's a lot more from where that came from," he devilishly chuckled somewhere in my ear.

"Now?" I asked almost in desperation, starting to think of a plan on how to run out of the room—clothes or no clothes.

"Not now," he laughed so charmingly that I felt another coil running through my core. *How was that even possible?* "I'm pretty sure you'd end up in a hospital if it was *now*. But soon. Just keep that thought in mind." He bit my earlobe then placed a few kisses on the back of my neck, rolling off of me, but still remaining on the bed next to me.

At least it wasn't *now*, because *now* sounded impossible. As impossible as holding on to the thought. A thought that would certainly ravage every second of my existence.

I remember closing my eyes for just a second as he slumped against me, pressing me into the sheets while getting the tremble in my limbs to stop.

***

"Mouse, you need to wake up," Cole's husky voice purred in my ear, making me jump into a sitting position that instant.

"Did I fall asleep?" My own voice cracked and startled.

"Yes, for an hour or so. People are starting to leave. We should go too, but you can come back to my place. Continue where we left off."

Was there something left to continue?

I turned to see if he was kidding.

He wasn't, just a wide grin spread on his face—a hazard

sign flashing at me. A Nuclear hazard.

I didn't even realize when I was rushing through the pile of clothes, trying to find my own while his boxers seemed to have caught on the heel of my stilettos.

"Can I have those back? Or are you keeping them as souvenirs?" He blazed a smile while standing in the middle of the bedroom in his birthday suit.

"Y...yess," I babbled awkwardly, trying to get the boxers unstuck from my shoes. Things seemed utterly amusing to him, as I was trying to get dressed while gazing in a mirror at my electrified hair and ruined makeup. "Shit, I look like hell."

"No, you look like I've just fucked you." The devil sneaked behind me, helping me untie the straps of my corset so I could put it back together somehow.

"Can you please stop talking like that?" I asked him.

"Yeah, I'll stop. I'll stop when I'm sure that my words don't make you wet in anticipation. I'll stop when these no longer respond to them." He snuck a hand over my waist, tugging my body closer so he could devour one of my pebbled nipples with his lips.

He was right, and I loathed it. My body seemed to have a certain reaction to his rudeness. A hollow sensation bloomed in the center of my stomach and the need to hold back the tingles below my waist was growing exponentially with every stupid thing he seemed to say.
Ugh, I hated him for knowing exactly how to control me. For knowing things even I wasn't aware I wanted.

"You think you've got me all figured out? That I was dying to get in bed with you but wasn't able to find a way to directly tell you?" I let my eyes roll all the way to the back of my head, but the truth was somewhere in the middle. Maybe with a different attitude, I could have fallen for him. But not like this. At least that's what I wanted myself to believe.

My attitude seemed to have sparked his own. "I tried to

play nice. Just when I thought we were getting somewhere. I guess I'll need to reconsider the way I handle *our relationship*. A much more entertaining approach." Pulling his jeans on, Cole stormed out the door with his shirt in one hand, his jacket in the other, and a part of me tucked somewhere deep within him. A part that he'd never let go of.

What had I just done? I think I just stepped on his manly ego. But I only had a choice between bruising it or feeding it. And I couldn't allow it to get any larger than it already was, even if I was left with a 'what the fuck just happened to me' feeling.

I knew exactly what my choice meant—torture.

Cole would try his best to show me I was wrong, or worse, punish me for daring not to praise the king. But I couldn't worry about that, not in those seconds when my body was still vibrating from him being inside of me.

With the cunning ability of a cat burglar, I snuck out, clinging to any shadow I could find, hoping that no one saw me leaving the room. Sure, the chances were they noticed us entering it, as curious eyes were constantly following our every move, but at least they didn't get to watch me leave. No one had any proof—like it would even matter to anyone, except for me.

At some point between running and sneaking, I took out the phone to call for my car but remembered I also needed to text a certain someone, Ferris.

Are you sleeping?

Though no reply came, at least not by the time I arrived home.

The second I came through the door, I threw my clothes on the floor and got into the shower, as if the hot water could ever wash my shame away. Every bone in my body seemed to be hurting as I found a new meaning for sore. Pulling on a peach velvet sweatshirt and matching pants, I threw myself on the couch and picked up the phone. I was involuntary hoping that Ferris hadn't replied.

No such luck!

No. Did you finish with Cole?

Oh, I did. Though I'm not sure that he was referring to *that* type of *finishing*.

Or maybe he was. I can never tell with them any longer.

Yes. I'm at home now.

Do you want me to come over?

The babysitter is here until tomorrow.

I didn't feel like leaving again, especially since the chances were he would try and use the advantages of his *deal*. But I felt obligated to ask, so I didn't anger him further. Because I knew damn well how an angry Ferris got.

Come.

That was it, even though I waited for several moments to see the *typing...* sign.

Just great.

I picked up something to wear the next day at school because the back-and-forth drives were making me dizzy, then proceeded to Ferris's estate. To my surprise I found him in bed, half-asleep, waiting for me to join him. I couldn't say no to a few hours of rest. I quickly joined him, sneaking between the blankets while trying not to disturb him too much and risk waking up the monster—the one in his pants included.

"I was thinking... maybe I've acted poorly," he whispered, pushing a strand of hair away from my cheek while his eyes stayed tightly shut.

"You don't truly believe that, do you?" I guess I was a poisonous bitch tonight. Everything that went through my head was leaving my mouth.

With one hand, he turned me so my back was glued to his chest while one of his arms was wrapping itself around me. "I do believe it." He held me impossibly close to his heart, giving me the peace I needed and washing away a part of his sins.

Strangely, it was like he understood exactly what I needed, and was offering it to me without asking for something in return. At least not today.

My conscience was on the verge of exploding from having sex with one man and sleeping in the arms of another. And to make things worse, both were somehow my enemies, set out to destroy what was left of my soul.

CHAPTER 7

Ferris was already gone when I woke up, leaving me a note stating he had something to do today. Strange, since he usually didn't leave the house, but I figured it must have been something important for him to get up so early. Well, I wasn't sure how early it was since I hadn't set an alarm, but a few rays of sun were gleaming in the sky.

It was almost noon, I realized as I stared at my phone. Too late for University, at least for the first classes. I didn't feel like going anyway. I didn't have it in me to face Cole or whatever plans he probably had for me. Besides, I needed to prepare for something. There was one more answer I needed to receive, and the fact that Brax hadn't given me a sign by now was starting to worry me.

With uncertainty pressing down on me, I returned home so I could spend the rest of the day with my family. I felt like I was betraying them somehow—at least in terms of the time I spent with them. Constant guilt was weighing on me. Although I was giving every spare minute to them, I always felt I wasn't doing enough.

I gave the babysitter time off, at least until the evening, then asked Nat and Seb to get dressed and took both of them to the park.

The park was so different from anything any of us had ever seen. Large playground areas, so green that you might think it was some kind of artificial vegetation. The sight was a stark contrast to the gray pieces of pavement and the one square foot of sparse grass that we were used to, back in Salt City.

"Bea, are you seeing this?" Seb uttered, running toward some enormous slides. Of course, Nat wasn't falling far behind; she was running to catch up, acting half her age. They haven't been this free or happy in so long.

"Don't run!" I called out to him, knowing I'd never hear the end of it from his doctors if they saw him running. Luckily, Nat caught up with our brother, grabbing him by the hood and getting him to follow my command. Though not entirely, as she couldn't get him to stop, just slow down a little.

I chose a bench to rest as they played. Maybe on a normal day, I might have joined them, but at the moment my body felt like it was fifty, going on seventy. I just sat there, listening to the silence and watching the murky sky looking not so murky any longer. Life in the Hills was different. Even the sun seemed to try harder to break through the clouds of smog. But something was threatening to disturb everything, an unspoken panic plastered on the Elite faces. A worry that darkened their eyes and made their tongues murmur with anxiety. I could see it everywhere I looked, from the women pushing strollers through the park's pathways to the people walking along the street.

It was the beginning of the end, and they knew it. They knew better than to trust what the politicians were telling them. Possibly some of them were as scared as most of the residents of the Pit, at least as those who had nothing to do with the riots.

I was feeling on the verge of a panic attack just thinking of what exactly could happen if what I'd heard from Cole's parents became reality. A new separation of powers, so drastic that it would change everything.

A vibrating noise in my pocket brought me down to Earth, just before my chest got too heavy for me to breathe.

Brax: *Tonight. My place.*

That was all. No specific 9:55 PM timing so he could give me hell if I was five minutes late. Just *tonight*. Whatever that meant.

The message managed to calm me down a little, instilling a crazy hope that we could all try and stop this together. Sure, it seemed impossible. Mad. Maybe even suicidal, with few chances of a favorable outcome, but I needed to try.

The hours flew faster than I expected. As we were returning home, I realized it would soon be evening. Maybe the stop at the gelateria, combined with the insatiable urge of having one scoop of everything had something to do with it.

By the time we arrived, the babysitter was already back, so after an early family dinner, I rushed to the bathroom to shower and change.

No sweatshirt for the visit to Brax, or I would never hear the end of it. I went for an A-line black dress, along with a pair of short heeled stiletto boots.

Not entirely sure if I was early or already late, I passed the security guard at Brax's front door and entered the house.

"Brax?" I called with the strength of a whisper, looking around to see where he could be.

The voice of his maid answered from somewhere in the living room, "He's upstairs, Signora."

"Thank you," I replied, already making my way up the stairs. I wasn't sure why I was even in a rush, but I couldn't find peace until I heard Brax's answer.

The light in his bedroom was on, so I assumed he was there. I was right, but if finding him in the room was predictable, what I found there, wasn't. The tantalizing view of his back rippling muscles peeking through his shirt as he was supporting his weight on the dresser, blinded me for a second, numbing all my senses.

The image of him was affecting me much more than I would have liked. But as I recovered, I learned there was something else troubling me about him. He seemed to be a little out of balance, his hands too clenched to the dresser as if he was having trouble standing. At first, I thought he had one extra glass, but I quickly realized that wasn't the case. My king of the underworld was struggling to close his shirt, masking a white bandage that ran from the center of his chest to somewhere on his ribcage, where the shirt covered it.

"Brax, what happened?" I snuck in front of him to take a better look before he got a chance to cover up the wound.

A snarl broke between his lips, "Nothing, I'm fine."

"You have a bandage over what I believe to be either a gun or a knife wound. You are not *fine*," I insisted.

"I wasn't aware you were also a licensed doctor." He nudged me aside, trying to set a little distance between us so he could finish closing up his shirt—as if I hadn't already seen the wound he was trying to hide.

"Buttoning the shirt won't make it go away. *Or me.* What happened?" I asked, unwilling to back off.

"You fucking happened. This is on you if you're so curious as to how I got the wound," he muttered with anger coating his voice.

"It's from when you went to recover my family, isn't it?" I asked, although I already knew the answer.

Brax arched an eyebrow, giving me a stinging look. "What do you think?"

"Tell me what happened. Please," I pleaded, guilt gnawing at my soul.

"Holy shit, I'm not in the mood for this!" he barked,

walking toward the balcony.

"I need to know. Please," I pleaded again. I had everything to thank him for. He brought my family back safely, maybe even risking his life to do it. But I needed to know what went on there.

I could tell he wasn't in the mood for talking. He never was. Still, he wasn't in the mood to listen to my nagging either, so I guess he chose the easy way out. "Wanna know what happened? I let my dick think for my brain. That's what happened." His eyes rolled with annoyance. "I had my guards carrying out surveillance on them for a few days, but they couldn't tell clearly how many men were in the building. Things just got a little complicated when we entered. But we got them in the end. Bunch of drug addicts."

"And my father?"

Brax frowned deeply. "He got away. He was the one who put a bullet in my back. Fucking coward."

"But I saw you had the bandage over your chest?" I was confused. How was he shot in the back?

"That was the exit wound. At least the bullet got out of me. Anyway, long story short, my men are still looking for him, but there is a chance that he could turn up. Got the rest of his henchmen, though." That was it. The grand escape story, explained by Brax. Bada bing bada boom. Not writing a book any time soon—not because he lacked the ability to communicate, but because he *wanted* to lack it.

I didn't linger on the subject since the other questions I had prepared for the night would certainly drain the last drop of patience out of him.

With his story *finished*, he stepped onto the balcony and reached for a whiskey decanter from a small metal table. He filled and drained his glass in less than a minute, as if he was in a drinking competition. *Typical Brax.*

"Are you even supposed to drink?" I asked, already

knowing that he doesn't follow the laws of nature like any other mortal.

"I'm not supposed to do a lot of things and yet, I do them. I need the whiskey. It helps the pills slip down my throat," he shrugged as if mixing pills with alcohol was in any way normal.

I rolled my eyes. "Water also does that."

"I told you before, I don't drink water after six," he said, filling another glass with whiskey.

"At least he didn't shoot you in your sense of humor," I smirked.

"Probably not. Is that why you keep testing it?" Brax's words were similar to a silent warning. I was approaching a red line again. One that I wasn't going to cross tonight since I went there looking for answers, not an argument.

"Sorry for looking out for you," I mumbled, heading back to the bedroom.

"I can take care of myself. I don't need you to play Mother Teresa."

I pretended not to hear him since I didn't like where the conversation was going. He was never the kind to appreciate the people who cared for him, and he wasn't going to start now. So I realized I was running my mouth for nothing. Besides, I had more urgent problems to solve. "Can I ask you something?" I took a seat on his leather sofa, glancing at the balcony door.

"Hold on." After refilling his glass, he returned to the room with the ammunition he needed to *endure* me.

The limp in his leg was as visible as it had been two days ago. He was in pain. I could see it written all over his gorgeous face. With each step he took his jawline tightened and the green color of his eyes was disappearing under his eyelids. I wanted to put a bullet in him myself so many times, but seeing him injured left a hollow feeling in the pit of my stomach.

"You can talk now," he breathed as he took a seat on the side of the bed. He was trying to find a comfortable position, but his hand clutching the sheets and his gritted teeth betrayed his pain.

"You seem to know Ferris pretty well—" I didn't get to finish.

"Did he hurt you?" His eyes blazed straight at me, a million silent questions bubbling beneath them.

"No. But he... he has some *issues*," I stammered.

"Issues? I'm pretty sure the doctors gave him a diagnosis for his *issues*." Brax seemed to be a lot more informed than I was. That was exactly why he was the only one who could help me understand what was going on.

I took a deep breath, thinking about what could possibly be the secret everyone was hiding from me. "Doctors?" I asked.

"Yes. He was in one of those institutions for six months. The kind that tries to un-fuck your brain." Brax let out a heavy breath. "I was the one that put him there."

"Like a mental institution?" I asked, my voice shaking with shock.

He didn't answer, and by the look in his eyes, he just understood that I knew nothing about the subject.

"Brax, I'm sorry to be asking you. But you seem to care about Ferris. I need to know what I'm up against. I don't want to fix him or whatever idea you may have about me. I just don't want to do anything stupid and hurt him. It's like walking on eggshells when I'm around him. And it's not me who's in danger of breaking—it's *him*."

"I'm not sure he can break more than he already is, but have it your way. Bring me my cigs first." It felt like he was intentionally dragging this conversation, prolonging the truth I had needed for so long.

I rushed to grab the pack of cigarettes from the balcony,

along with a crystal ashtray from the outside table.

"Here." I gave him his cigs, placed the ashtray on the nightstand beside him, and returned to my spot on the upholstered sofa.

"What do you know about Ferris?" Brax asked, taking a cigarette to his mouth and lighting it.

"That he's usually isolated, a loner. I don't even know where to start. It's like he's constantly in agony."

"That's because he probably is." A deep sigh escaped him. A sign of weakness so unusual for a man like him.

I could tell from the intonation of his voice, and the pain reflected in his pupils, that he was living Ferris's pain alongside him. "I've known Ferris for as long as I've known myself. I can't pinpoint when we first met. Maybe in preschool. Maybe even before that. He wasn't always like this... like he is now. But life changed him. What happened to his family changed him."

I had a feeling the tragedy that contributed to his anguish didn't involve only Ferris. And as Brax began speaking about it, a coil of fear for what he was about to say ran down my spine.

"They say money brings misery. I guess sometimes that's true. I carry a part of the guilt for everything that happened. Call it *my family heritage*. You see, there are people who always want more. So much more that they never know when to stop. It's in their nature. Human nature in general. Except that some of them push that nature to its absolute limits.

"Someone such as my father. He was never a bad man, but his ambitions often clouded his judgment.

"I don't know if you are aware of how things work around here, but Echo City is divided into several areas. Unofficially of course. Territories divided up by streets.

"My family doesn't own all of the territories, but we do own the majority. Fuck, I'm rambling. What family? I... *I* own the majority of that turf."

"You? What happened to your father?" My curiosity pushed me to ask since he just mentioned him.

"He died. Had a stroke. I'll get to that. Anyway, my father wanted to team up with some big shot from another city. Some kind of alliance to secure us with enough manpower to take over the whole of Echo City. But he made a mistake, in choosing the worst possible person to do that with, Benjamin West.

"My father thought he could win West over by providing him with inside information. Like a who's who in Echo City and how much green they have in their bank accounts.

"Ferris's family was one of my father's slip-ups. He bragged about being friends with the Ayers', and how their international company branches will shortly raise the city's value. Therefore, helping him take full control of the Pit was a project worth investing in. Only West wasn't interested in my father. He wanted to *invest* directly in the company—or rather, take it over entirely.

"He made the Ayers' an offer to sell at a price that seemed like a joke. They refused, of course. He got to a few board members from the company, who didn't turn out to be as hard to convince as Ferris's parents. With that being settled, he only needed the Ayers' gone. West ordered a hit on them. Ferris's entire family was killed, and he—"

"He got two bullets in the chest. That's why he has the scars," I continued Brax's words. The flashback of the two silvery marks on his chest explode in my mind, freeing an overwhelming grief to flood my soul.

"You know about those?" he asked, but in the next second an indecent smile bloomed on his lips. "How could you not?" Brax just realized how I got to see Ferris's bullet marks.

I was expecting some other smart remark from him, but surprisingly his thick lips quickly turned into a thin line as he was preparing to continue the story. "It was a miracle he survived—a miracle that fucked up West's plans, as Ferris ended up inheriting the company. I also helped bring West's chances to zero after I disposed of the members of the board that had made deals with him."

Brax took a small pause as if preparing to get to the tough part. Damn, I already thought that Ferris's family getting killed was the worst that happened, but by the look on Brax's face, there was more to this story.

"You know what's worse?" he continued, "I don't think Ferris really survived—not the old Ferris, anyway.

"I went to see him every single day. At the hospital and the house. He was so changed that I couldn't recognize him any longer. It was like every single fucking time I was trying to get close he was building higher and higher walls around himself. Until one day when he asked me to kill him. He couldn't handle the nightmares anymore, constantly reliving the night his family died.

"I saw it in his eyes, he was going to do it himself if I wouldn't. There was nothing left for me to do except for get him committed into a fancy recovery institution. He was there for six fucking months. They said they fixed him, as much as he could be fixed, but when he returned, he didn't want to see me. He denied me access at the main gate and never answered any of my calls, until one day I just stopped trying to see him. I guess he had every right, given that my family was responsible for what happened to him. *I* was responsible for not seeing what my father was doing."

"It wasn't your fault." I tried to convince him because from the way he was talking about Ferris, I was certain he wouldn't have done anything to hurt him.

"If I had only stopped wasting all that time partying and trying to prove myself on the streets, maybe I would have found out what my father was doing sooner. Maybe I would have seen it coming. I could have prevented it somehow. Ferris is the way he is because of me, and nothing is going to change that. I bear the weight of his tragedy."

"No, you don't. Not even your father bears it. How could he know Benjamin was going to kill Ferris's family?"

Brax's hands clenched into fists, "We're fucking trained to know! One piece of missing information could mean death. My father was just desperate—too greedy to see things clearly.

"The rush for power accelerated his own death. He died a few weeks after Ferris's parents. We kept fighting during that whole time. Maybe that's on me too, I don't know."

"Why do you take everything on yourself? You're not responsible for everyone else." For once, I was actually feeling bad for the *almighty* Brax.

But it was as if feeling sorry for the devil himself because he was always prepared to use my empathy against me. "Look who's talking—the last person qualified to give advice on taking things personally. Not that I asked for any advice from you anyway."

"I never felt responsible for my father. I loathed the man and had nothing to do with his actions." I tried to defend myself.

But for some reason, even Brax doubted me about that, "Really?"

Okay, maybe I felt a little responsible for something, "I don't think I should be held accountable for his actions. But I do feel responsible for you getting shot. Indirectly, I sent you there."

"Do you want to kiss it and make it all better?" He was changing his approach, revealing the Brax he loved to show to the world, while masking any kind of emotion that may have slipped through his facade.

Though I wasn't going to fall for his game. "I can't kiss it all better. You'd spasm with excitement and your muscles would contract, causing you pain. I'm pretty sure I would be breaking the doctor's orders."

"I just fired my doctor," Brax said, downing the contents of his glass in one gulp.

"Well, I should rehire him then. I need you alive," I confessed. "That brings me to my next question: Have you reached a decision regarding the future?"

"I was expecting you to ask about that ever since you arrived. But I thought we agreed we'd talk about our decisions tomorrow." He took a long drag out of what must've been the third cigarette since I got there.

"I was thinking that maybe there would be a part of the conversation that you might feel uncomfortable having with the other guys present."

"Oh, so you did come back for more." A satisfied smirk appeared on his face, already considering that the alpha male had hooked another victim.

I threw him a disapproving look. "For more *answers*. I do hope that's what you're referring to."

"I thought you knew better than to insult my intelligence. You know exactly what I meant."
I guess Brax was laughing only at his own jokes, expecting everyone around him to do exactly the same.

Except I wasn't *everybody*. Never excelled at blending in. "I didn't mean to insult you. I just want to know where you'll be standing tomorrow. Will you join us?"

"Us? I get that you've already spoken with Cole and Ferris. Did they both agree?" Brax asked, unsuccessfully trying to hide his curiosity.

"Yes," I ghosted the words, knowing what was coming next.

Brax brought his left hand under his chin as he was thinking of what could have happened during my other encounters. "For what price? What did they want in return?"

I didn't answer. Not because I couldn't tell him, but because I realized I made a mistake. I let out a piece of information that automatically that—if he accepted—would lead him to ask who knows what new deal from me.

"Let me guess. They wanted to fuck you." My secret was out, though I didn't think it was much of a secret to begin with.

"They wanted to *extend* their deals," I mumbled. *Fuck me* didn't seem quite the right word choice, although that's what it really was.

"Relax, you don't need to use fancy terms with me. I already know Ferris fucked you two nights ago. Don't know about Cole yet, but I'm sure I'll catch up by tomorrow." Brax, the jerk, was there, assuring that he lived up to his words *Nobody could ever love a monster.*

I was surprised that Ferris talked to him about what happened between us. Surprised, and disappointed, but I guess being disappointed was a daily state of mind for me lately. "You... you know? He told you?"

"I've talked to Ferris. He tells me everything. He was concerned he went a little too far." Brax confessed.

"I'm not going to discuss what happens in Ferris's bedroom with you," I snapped, offended that I seemed to be the local news in their private paper.

"Then maybe you could show me." Brax was clearly inviting me to his bed.

And that infuriated me. "I made the deals because I had to. I am not a tramp to be passed around from one *man to another* out of boredom."

"Then what are you doing here?" I could feel the annoyance in his voice building up. Not because of what I said, but because of how I said it. I made him feel like a simple man—not Brax— *the king.*

Did he actually think the visit was about sleeping with

him? "I told you before. I want to talk about your help."

"And I told you before. I don't have a death wish. Besides, I'm going to land on my feet. I always do," he said, preparing to refuse me.

But something had to make him reason. "Your businesses in the Pit will be ruined. They'll be worth nothing if the Elite manage to come out on top with the plan they have."

"Not if I sell them in time. I found an investor ready to offer me a decent price for everything." That's why Brax was so calm about what was going on. He already had a plan for his empire —cash-out and probably rebuild when the time is right.

However, there was a side of the story he hadn't taken into consideration, or perhaps he didn't even know about. "They won't let you stay in the Hills. You're not Elite. You don't have their blood running through your veins."

And then it dawned on him, I could see it in his gaze. No need for words. The thought definitely crossed his mind on other occasions, but he wasn't certain of it until I confirmed it.

Maybe he hoped he had a way out. That he could buy his place among the Elite with enough money. But the thing was, up in the Hills everyone had wealth. Paying off the ones in charge just to stay afloat could prove an impossible task, no matter who he was down in the Pit.

"Then I'll relocate." Brax thought I would take this answer at face value as the truth, but I knew deep down he was bluffing. His thirst for supremacy would never allow him to give up the empire he had built in Echo City.

"You know as well as I do that you're not going to run to another city and throw everything you've accomplished here away. You're going to try and get this under control. One way or the other." I was calling out his bluff.

"You mean under *my* control." He was pointing out the obvious, as both he and I knew where this conversation was going. Maybe some self-preservation sense was telling him to stay away, but it was his other senses that prevailed. The devil sitting on his shoulder was asking him to conquer it all, asking for total supremacy.

"Do you know what's the motor that sets all things in motion? *Fear.* That's the only thing I want from the world. With fear, you can control everything. Whether it's fear of the unknown, loneliness, failure, poverty, or who knows what, fear can be a nuclear weapon if you know how to use it. But it can also backfire. So the question is: what's your greatest fear?" Brax asked so calmly that I was beginning to think that my biggest fear would have something to do with him.

Maybe he was right. However, at that point, I wasn't going to provide pro bono leverage to him. "I'm only afraid of a rebellion, a revolution. That the Elite plan will work."

"And of me?" he pressed.

"Why should I be afraid of you?" I asked, trying to seem unaffected.

"Because you gave Ferris and Cole new advantages. And I consider it's only fair that I also benefit from *those kinds of advantages.*"

\

CHAPTER 8

"You want to sleep with me again?" The thought sounded a lot more improbable in my mind than when I said it. I knew he made the exact same request before. But I believed it was a one-time thing and he wouldn't even bother with me again, especially with all the girls he had willing to bed him without a second thought.

"Sleep with you? Mmmm. You could call it that. The truth is, I'm going to fucking *break* you. You know that's what's going to happen if you agree to this. That is, if you want me to agree to the rest. To help you with your plan."

For some reason, he didn't seem regretful about it. Not even for a second. It was like he was waiting for the moment, craving to see it happen. Like he needed to break me so that he could find some twisted joy in it. Maybe even find inner peace.

It was a dose of hatred mixed with passion as if I had committed a sin I knew nothing about. There was a chance it had something to do with Ferris, but it felt so much more personal.

At least, among all the kings, Brax was the only one who had the nerve to tell the truth. Yes, he planned to break me and was the one who had the most chance of succeeding. But I was convinced the other two planned the same thing.

"So what do you say? Do I get the same benefits as they do if I agree to go through with this?" His question left me with a bitter taste. I no longer knew if he was asking me out of some newfound craving, or just because Ferris and Cole had this advantage as well.

But what I did know was that I had only one answer to give him: "*Yes.*"

This deal probably sealed my fate, but at the same time was placing the final brick in the foundation I needed to get my plan off the ground. They were now stuck playing my game, and I was stuck playing theirs. Little did I know their game would be even more twisted than that of the Elite.

"I'm starting to think that you missed me," Brax whispered, the emerald color of his eyes framed by a golden ring, glowing like eagle's eyes watching over its prey.

"You always make assumptions about me," I snarled at him.

"Most of them are accurate." He drew his upper body on the pillows until his back reached the bedpost, leaning his weight against it as his eyes closed from the short flickers of pain.

"I have a plan, but I want to talk to all of you about it tomorrow." Overly excited about getting things in motion, I let my thoughts slip past my lips.

Though Brax also had a plan, "Come here."

It was no use for me to go on about the Revolution and how I intended to stop it. His ideas were of a much more physical nature. An urgent *physical problem* that he felt needed some kind of cure right away.

Straightening my skirt, I got up from the seat and took a few steps until I reached the side of his nightstand. Although it wasn't enough to satisfy the impatience of my *king*, "I think you know what I want by now." He glanced straight at me, waiting for me to keep him *company*.

"You're not healed," I whispered, worried about the pain that even a sudden movement might cause him.

"I was shot in my ribcage, not in my dick." His irony was far from being in any way *fine.*

"Let me get this straight, you want me to sleep with you in this condition?" I couldn't contain my shock, as the thought of his wound reopening or him ending up in the ER wouldn't leave my mind.

Despite my concern, Brax seemed utterly impatient, "Are you coming, or do I have to go back on my word?"

I needed to seal the deal, so without too much time wasted lingering about it, I slid my leg on top of him, finding a spot over his knees and using it as a chair.

His index finger gestured for me to advance higher on his leg while one of his hands glided to the interior of my skirt, eagerly gripping the outer flank of my hip. With hushed moves, I listened to his command, gliding high enough that I was almost over the erect part of him. But something was stopping me from advancing as I kept fussing and turning, afraid my knee would knock against his wounded ribcage. I could have strangled him for what he was doing to me, but for some reason, I couldn't allow him to be in pain in any way, especially not because of me.

Before I could have a moment to truly figure out what was happening, he rushed to push the strap of my dress over my shoulder, freeing one of my breasts. I froze, watching him gazing at the voluptuous shape, then dragging a strong finger over my nipple and waiting for it to form goosebumps under his presence. It did just that, luring his thumb to draw more delicate circles, rotating in never-ending loops.

I was drawing out short breaths as my eyes dropped to look at his devastating invasion of my senses. Lost in the arousal of the moment, I didn't realize that he was also watching me, studying the way my lips trembled, and how my own gaze carefully followed his finger while dancing on my heated skin.

Suddenly, our eyes met in an impossible moment in which his hand decided to clench on my aching nipple, drawing jolts of pain combined with the vibration of my yearning. I gasped, trying to break free as the anguish was settling in my body, warning it of *danger.* But he didn't let go. He just remained there, watching my pupils enlarge, trying to fight the discomfort, but also mask the arousal it provoked.

Maybe he decided that I had enough, or maybe he just wanted to have a taste of me, but one of his hands slid through my dress, to my ass while the other one cupped my breast from beneath, guiding my entire body toward him until my nipple was covered by his mouth. His lips, warm and soothing over the tortured skin, were bringing me a heated relief in the most false illusion of relaxation.

Sometime between the moment I thought he was going to go easy on me, and the instant I realized I was nowhere near that, he glided his fingers between my folds, smirking at what he found there. "You like it," he stated the obvious while using the natural lube of my body to slip two fingers inside me.

The lighting pain of his intrusion took me by surprise, making me try and support my body weight on something, but at the same time, only drove me to press my breast harder against his lips. It was just what he was expecting, turning his actions to pure animalistic, one hundred percent driven out of a wicked physical need. The suckling and the nibbling became so intense that I thought he was going to rip my flesh. I wanted to ask him to stop, or at least slow down, but it felt so much like the right kind of wrong. His fingers began moving. Fast and strong, reaching each one of my walls, pounding inside so fiercely that it almost made me forget about his lips devouring my breast.

Things were developing with lightning speed, as he was thrusting his fingers into me so hard that the sound was making the red of shame fluster my cheeks. He was rocking everything around me until the room was turning only into a small image, letting velvet darkness blur my vision.

Between my heart pulsing somewhere in my brain, and the distressed sound of my panting breath, I thought I heard Brax saying something. Although I couldn't figure out if he really spoke or if I was just hearing things. I quickly forgot about it anyway as the engulfing sensations seemed to be controlling the last of my reasoning, chasing only one result. Pleasure.

"That's it, fuck my fingers." This time I **did** hear what he had to say and understood he was no longer moving against me. I was moving against him.

Initially, I wanted to stop as the realization that I was passionately playing his game dawned on me. It felt so morally wrong and yet physically right. I couldn't help myself, and the ardor that originated from his tongue circling my nipple was only making my hips move harder, trying to find a rhythm that would bring me to ecstasy.

I ground against him, increasing his own desire, while allowing my sweet moans to reach his ears like a melody played only for him to hear.

Suddenly, he curved something inside of me. I have no idea how, what, why. Anything... Everything... And with just one gesture he made my whole body squirm, seeking his torso for comfort as I was feeling the first wave of heightening release gathering to crash upon me. But it didn't get to wash over that needy part of me. His fingers withdrew, taking my tidal wave along with them.

"I can give pleasure. And I can take it away," Brax said against the nipple he was just torturing, trying to teach me a lesson in obedience—as if he would let me forget even for a single second who he really was.

I stopped, and so did his lips from the assault on my breasts, allowing me to regain my position on the upper part of his legs. No matter how confused or dickmatized I was,

I recognized exactly what he was after—he wanted me to desperately need him.

After performing a little magic trick, and balancing from one leg to the other to remove my panties from beneath my skirt, I advanced higher to reach the buttons of his shirt. My fingers moved to open them incredibly slowly. Each button I touched made me think it would somehow hurt him. Still, one by one, they were coming undone, revealing his white bandage.

The heavy anguish in his breath as he lifted his torso from the pillows so I could dispose of the shirt, followed by the angered grunt while arranging himself back in the sitting position made me jump from his lap. I was afraid that I had caused him pain, but I didn't get too far. His hand caught my wrist, bringing me straight on top of the bulge twitching in his pants.

I was in trouble.

Moving my fingers to trace the whole size of him, I skimmed his pants with lustful movements waiting for his perfect jawline to tighten, clenching his teeth, anticipating me. I wasn't as wicked as my king. Unwilling to torture a wounded man, I reached to unfasten his belt, the muffled sound in his throat was letting me know exactly how ready he was to have me. So ready, that for the first time he was admitting defeat. "You do it," he muttered so that I would be the one who would dispose of the bottom part of his clothing since he could barely lift himself to help me get rid of the fabrics that were bothering him.

Trying to mask his pain, he regained his sitting position, catching the upper side of my arm and dragging me on top of him. "I'm pretty sure that this won't work out with me sitting here and you being a foot away from me." He quickly noticed I was keeping my distance, worried that I could cause him any further damage.

His condition was still delicate. I just couldn't understand this madness, especially since I was still going to be his whenever he would ask. "Are you sure it can't wait? I don't want you to get hurt even more over this."

"Are you afraid you'll have to explain to the doctor that you fucked me to death?" Brax *the comedian* had arrived.

My eyes darted poisonous arrows his way. "I'm pretty sure that the doctor you have is trained not to ask questions," I said, crossing my arms.

"And neither should you." Before he could go on, I raised my hips, then slowly found my way back as I allowed him to slide inside me. I managed to mute him in just one second. He never said another word, just waiting for me to go on, twisting in luscious motions as I drove my body weight on the mattress, searching for support so I could move.

I was taunting him, grinding against him agonizingly slow, feeling the eagerness of every one of his veins while I was fighting to readjust to his impressive size. It was strange being on my own this time. I felt that I was doing everything wrong, yet somehow it was turning out so incredibly right. I was in total awe as his hardness was reaching exactly the anguishing spot that craved for him, over and over again, gliding to find the perfect movement.

To torture me further, Brax lifted my dress over my hips to lustfully watch the way I was moving against him in that incredible place where he ended and I began. His gaze sexual and erotic, feasting on every push, aware at the same time that his gesture was embarrassing me. Not that he would have given a fuck about that anyway.

Under the same lustful glimpse, he tugged my dress to fall over my shoulders, straight below my breasts. The view was giving him every chance to observe the tremble I could no longer control as I was moving against him. The devil was enjoying every single second of my unbelievable torment as I was struggling to remain on top of him while *knowing* that he was watching me.

In an unhurried gesture, he raised my clenched hands from the sheets and placed them over his broad shoulders, helping me find support. Yet his gesture was also giving me new reasons for worry. I could hurt him. And the crazed closeness of our bodies was leaving me one wrong move away from that.

Brax must have sensed the distress ruling over my mind and body as the shaking in my limbs was beginning to become more visible with every move. "Relax," he said in a hushed voice that for some strange reason was forcing me to do exactly the opposite. I couldn't relax because, in my mind, I must've been doing something wrong for him to notice I was tense.

Maybe I was doing everything wrong.

The thought stayed with me for a while, although slightly clouded by the tingling sensation building between my thighs. Brax's thumb soon came to move over my clit, to the point he eradicated my anxiety completely. In fact, he eradicated all other thoughts and let me be guided only by the needs of my own body.

I was moving freely, letting the odds of bringing him pain dissipate in favor of the ones of provoking him pleasure. I was preparing to explode with delirium, movements away from tightening all around him, and by the grunted moans coming from the depths of his throat, he was as close as I was.

That was until he decided to steal the pleasure away from me, "Good girl."

Those fucking words again!

"Can you please stop calling me that?" This time, I was angry, and *this time* he needed to know it. I hated him for treating me like one of his whores.

"Why, Bea? Do you think you're special? Aiming to be the queen of my heart or something?" The mocking tone of his voice left a hole somewhere in my soul. I wasn't aiming to be his queen, but I wasn't aiming to be his tramp either.

He just offended me, and yet he was acting as if nothing had happened. As if it didn't matter. As if *I* didn't matter.

But I didn't get to make a scene because, without warning, he lifted me by my waist and slammed me into him so strongly that I felt *him* somewhere in my stomach.

And then he did it again.

And again...

Until I felt I couldn't breathe, eager to escape, and at the same time, needing to find my release as the pressure building up inside seemed to reach incredible limits.

"Brax, cut it out, you're going to hurt yourself," I whimpered, sometime between my eyes rolling out of my head and his muscles forcing me to become his rag doll. He was fuming mad and was taking it all out on me, freeing his repressed feelings. Maybe those feelings weren't even meant for me, just a culmination of everything waiting to explode. I was just in the wrong place at the wrong time when it happened.

My body was there, serving him as the vessel to spill all angry thoughts as he was transforming me into just that—a passage for him to get to where he needed—thrust by thrust, until neither his words nor his attitude could keep my body from reacting to his own. I felt my core spasm so forcefully that it was close to breaking me. After crashing me one last time against him, that heaving groan I heard before filled the room, as he continued to move me a few more times, though with a lot smaller intensity.

"I can give pleasure. And I can take it away," Brax's earlier affirmation came to my mind and since I was at a point where I couldn't control my body from shivering, maybe it was a good time to take a little of that away. I could barely lift myself off him while the effects of the implosion that I just experienced,

along with the gym work session were still vivid in my mind and body.

I only remember I was lying next to him for a few minutes when I heard the sound of his lighter. No cuddling session from the man of steel. And how could I even expect that when he didn't bother to search for my lips even once?

With fading strength, I lifted my head to look at him, only to discover the sight of blood flooding his bandage.

I jumped out of the bed as if I had been burned, rushing to his side to see what had happened. "Where do you keep the medical kit?" I shuddered, rushing towards the bathroom.

"Second drawer on the left." Brax was so calm that one might have believed nothing had happened, while I was running a hundred scenarios in my head about how he was going to bleed to death.

I didn't even know what I feared most—my trembling hands, or the sight of blood. But the mixture of the two was making me one step away from fainting on the bed next to him.

"Give me the bandages. I'll do it." Brax was offering to save the incompetent me from making a fool out of myself.

"I can handle it." In reality, I couldn't. But he didn't need to know that, or at least I didn't want to admit it. I just rushed to see why he was bleeding, and only after taking a large breath, I removed the bloody wrap.

The wound was still sewn together, so he must have been bleeding from the effort—because of me.

"Just pour some disinfectant and put another bandage over it," Brax muttered, giving me instructions as if to one of his nurses.

I couldn't begin complaining since I was the main reason this had happened. Well, me and his sex drive. It seemed that not even bullets could get him to keep it in his pants.

By some miracle, I finally managed to clean his wound and replace his bandage. Still, I couldn't leave him, especially since earlier he could barely close his shirt, even though he somehow found the strength to have sex with me. "Do you want me to stay? To help you?"

My question succeeded in angering him. I was clearly overstepping a limit. One that he already had broken because of me. "It's enough that you get me to fuck you in my house. You don't get to sleep in my bed, Bea."

Funny since the last time I was here, he invited me to do just that—sleep in his bed. It was only his way of showing me how things had changed. How I had a new *place* now.

"I could have slept on the couch. I don't *aim* to sleep in your bed as you may recall. I only wanted to help you, but I guess you don't need my help—except when it involves your dick, do you?" I didn't expect an answer. Even if my little rant was going to cost me, he couldn't back out from his part of the deal after sleeping with me. That was all that mattered to me.

"Goodnight, Brax." I closed the door behind me immediately after getting dressed.

Things were clear from now on. I was no longer some centerpiece he needed to own.

I was a mere toy in the hands of a bored man.

CHAPTER 9

The extra-long hot showers, trying to wash my sins away, were becoming a routine. Just water flowing down over me, washing the scent of their lips, but never the memory.

I couldn't visit Ferris later that day, and he didn't request my presence either. No matter how hard I might have wanted to, sleeping in his bed would still feel like torture, even if he seemed to be regretful about what he had done.

I just needed some time with myself. Seconds. Hours. Maybe even days. I needed to make peace with what I was doing and work through the constant battle of my body versus mind.

The kings were weakening me. Not by the warmth of their skin, but by the coldness of their hearts. Minimizing me, degrading each moment to the point where I was to become insignificant. To disintegrate.

I guess deep down, Ferris understood. He recognized what effect the latest events had on me. That's why he didn't *summon* me to be his *slave* this evening. *Or perhaps he just had better company.*

The thoughts tormented me, consumed me throughout the night to the point I saw the dawn light rising without having shut an eye ever since I laid down on my bed.

A plan for when and whom to call out of my new kings was brewing in my mind when Ferris beat me to it. My phone lit with his name glowing on the screen.

"Did I wake you?" His voice rasped, as if he was sharing my state of mind.

"No. Not really, but what are you doing up so early?" I asked, knowing that he never woke before noon, especially when I wasn't around.

"Couldn't sleep." He seemed to have the same problem I did, only this time I knew exactly what was causing his nightmares —the trauma he'd been through.

"Since you're awake, you can come here, and we'll wait together for Brax and Cole to arrive," I invited him over. Maybe last night I wouldn't have been the best company, but the storm within me seemed to have calmed down by the morning. It had something to do with Ferris's story, and the thought that monsters weren't born that way. They were created.

"We won't be having the meeting there," his answer snapped me away from my thoughts. "You know I don't like leaving the house. I had to put in a huge effort to come by your place two days ago, but I don't feel like it today. I've already talked to Brax and Cole. They'll drop by my place in the evening. I'm also expecting you then." The tone of his voice was much more formal than before. Either he was concerned about our plan, or I'd pissed him off yet again. In any case, I knew all too well who was going to endure the consequences.

"Okay. I'll come by after I take Seb to the hospital." It was my brother's dialysis day again, no matter how much I wanted to postpone it.

"Call me if you need anything." Ferris hung up.

I guess *'Have a great day, my love'* was out of the question.

We were walking on hot coals, fully aware that both of us would get burned in the end.

Since our *meeting* was postponed, I divided my day between playing cards with Nat and Seb and going to the hospital for my brother's treatment. No sense in wasting a single moment of priceless family time, especially since it was Saturday.

After a home-cooked meal, which Nat helped me prepare, I left her and Seb with a lifetime supply of popcorn and candy. No doubt, the babysitter was looking at me as if I were some kind of misfit who broke all the nutritional rules in the book. But I couldn't really be bothered with her opinions at that point. Seb couldn't have many snacks anyway, and he knew never to overstep his limits, so I was safe.

I had a James Bond vibe, considering what my kings and I were supposed to do next, so I put on a black pair of skinny jeans and a tight black shirt that made me look like a cat burglar. I had the perfect outfit to sneak into anywhere, slipping in the shadows of dark walls to wherever I needed to be. Okay... I wasn't exactly invisible to any of Ferris's twenty-something guards, especially since I showed up in Ferris's limousine. But a girl could dream. Couldn't she?

It had just gone dark outside, so I considered I had arrived early. At least early enough to catch Ferris alone. That wasn't the case since Cole seemed to have beaten me to it. I could recognize his husky voice ever since Alfred opened the front door for me.

Both Ferris and Cole were laughing and talking so loudly that I didn't need any directions to find them. I just followed the sound of their voices down a few corridors to the left, and entered a room where I'd never been before. The place was magnificent. A massive living room, so gothic that it seemed like an old cathedral, only no angels were in the room. Just two of my devils, relaxing on an extra-large couch with glasses of vodka in their hands, reminiscing about some long-lost memories.

"And the time we trashed that party in Azur City—" Ferris was the one talking.

"Christ, I remember. They ended up drinking beer out of the bathtub, " Cole continued, then immediately started laughing.

"We were so drunk...." The joy in Ferris's voice made me realize just how well they got along, but more importantly, how similar they were to each other.

"And remember that cheerleader? The one who could open beer cans with her—"

"Mmm-hmm," I cut Cole off. I did *not* want to find out where the conversation was going. "What's with the glasses?" I was under the impression we were here to set out a plan, not to throw some reunion party.

"Relax, Mouse. You know I need a bottle of whiskey just to get tipsy. We're still here to talk business." Cole must've sensed the annoyance in my voice, although I was surprised he gave a damn about it. "Sit," he said, patting a free spot on the couch between them, which I had no intention of occupying.

At least not until Ferris made the same offer. "Come," he extended an arm, gesturing for me to join him.

I felt like I was walking into a trap, but there was no way around it. I couldn't let him wait with his arm outstretched toward me for long. Whether willing or unwilling, I joined him.

In reality, I realized it was a display of their hierarchy, and even if Ferris used a trick to get me next to him, my choice put Cole second. That was going to cost me. The evil smile tugging at the corners of his lips assured me of exactly that.

My gaze was tightly locked ahead, staring at some gothic

painting of death claiming a miserable soul on its deathbed. My eyes were pointing at the art so intensely as if I was trying to take a mental picture of every single one of its lines. In reality, I was just avoiding the two uncomfortable pairs of eyes gazing straight at me. I was being studied, becoming the main pawn in a power game.

Obviously, my kings quickly picked up my distress. "You can breathe, Bea," Ferris's warm voice seemed to be echoing from the back of my neck, but my eyes didn't turn to acknowledge his location.

"I'm fine," I answered, still gazing at the painting, imprinting the horrible view into my mind.

"You don't seem fine," Cole said, his hand reaching to play in my hair, arranging some loose locks.

The surprise of his touch made me jolt from my seat and land straight into Ferris's arms. "Bea, what's wrong? Relax." The way-too-calm order Ferris gave me was urging me to do exactly the opposite. How could I ever relax, being imprisoned between two of the most devious men I had ever met? If I were dealing with them one at a time, I might have stood a chance. But having them both in the same room, at the same time, was leading me to become a deer trapped in front of the headlights.

"I'm relaxed. I just need a glass of water." I was up, pacing the length of the room even before they could figure out what was happening. My hands were shaking on the water bottle, barely able to even fill the glass.

"I think we've scared her," Cole was mocking my timid reaction to their combined presence.

But Ferris didn't seem to be in a laughing mood anymore, "No, I've scared her." He was talking as if I wasn't even in the room. "I lost it a few nights ago. And did something I regret." He turned to look at me with a repenting gaze, though it wasn't his apology I was interested in those moments. Something else was winning my attention. Ferris was opening up to Cole, even if his confession was regarding the time spent with me.

All I could hope for was that he wouldn't go into too much detail about what happened. Not that Cole would pity me, but he would probably get ideas out of it.

Contrary to my belief, the king of ECU was showing concern, "Did you hurt her?" The tone of his voice changed as if his question was loaded with a disguised warning. *Why did everyone keep asking Ferris that question?*

"No... not physically." Ferris rose from the sofa and took a few steps in my direction, though before he could reach my side, the door opened.

For the first time in my life, I was glad to see Brax.

"You started without me," he said, his voice cracked, likely because the bullet wound was still giving him trouble.

"Now, how could I ever start something without you?" Ferris's mood improved in just a few moments as if his personal *sun* had just walked into the room. His dark eyes lit with some lost hope, watching over the man who probably still had the power to revive him.

"You never know with Bea around." Brax said, cocking a brow with a teasing smirk. I wasn't sure what he was implying or where he was going with this conversation, but I wasn't going to let things drift off to a more intimate nature. We had matters much more important to attend to than his sexual desires.

"Then, if everyone is present, I think we can begin," I cut off any other chance they might have of steering the discussion elsewhere. "I hope no one has changed their mind." And how could they, considering they'd all consummated *my* part of the agreement? "Thought so."

"We all got the same deal after all, didn't we?" Ferris was either checking to see if his assumptions were correct or teasing me about the way I chose to handle this. I couldn't decide. In any case, it was a compromise he had to accept.

Besides, he said it himself, he had no problem with sharing.

"Let's get this started." It was Brax who was helping me set things in motion. Not out of some newfound conscience, but because I suspected he didn't want to discuss his part of the deal with Ferris. They may have been besties, but apparently not close enough to keep him from asking me for a *reward* for his trouble.

"Do I go first? Or do any of you want to start?" I asked.

"You go," Ferris nodded, *authorizing* me to take the lead.

"Okay. So this is what I came up with. I was thinking that if we could try to stop the rebellion, maybe there won't be a reaction out of the Elite, or at least not one as severe as the one they're considering. Perhaps we could try and pay off the rebellion leaders to tone things down. I don't know... a nice house, maybe a car."

Brax didn't seem to agree. "These men have ideals. It won't work. They don't want nicer things just for themselves. I know their kind. They want a better life for *everyone* living in the Pit. They all stand together, forming a union."

Yet I wasn't entirely sure what he said was true. "I've lived in the Pit. I know better than anyone else that any ideal dissipates when it comes to a full pocket. People get killed there for a piece of bread and a bottle of milk. You know as well as I do, that if the price is right they would sell their own mothers. The same goes for the Elite."

Cole also decided to step in, "Even if Brax would be successful in buying off a few of the Annelids' rebel leaders, the Elite still won't reconsider their plans. It's not a decision by the Elite as a whole; it's more of a one-man show—the governor's. He's the one behind all of this. I haven't been sitting around for nothing. I did some digging. I asked my father to have an unofficial chat with him since they've been friends for ages. The man isn't going to back down on his plans. This was his idea all along—to suppress the Annelids. It's not even about the money. It's about blood superiority. He believes the Elite's superior genes cannot be tainted with free access between the Pit and the Hills. This is more of a one-man thing than the entire Elite. Unfortunately, this one man has absolute power of decision." Cole took a small pause to light himself another cigarette. "Everyone else we've spoken to in the Elite is reluctant to start a revolution or even a war. They're all scared little cowards. No one wants to get their hands dirty. The Annelids' are already their slaves, if not by force, then certainly by fiscal policies and underpaid services."

"So you suggest we rid ourselves of him, therefore eliminating the problem?" Ferris asked, also lighting himself a cig.

"He has a few acolytes, but those won't be a problem. Just leeches kissing up to the big boss to secure their places when all hell breaks loose. And it's going to happen. I don't know exactly when, but it's coming." Cole filled up his glass as soon as he stopped talking as if the speech had drained the life out of him.

"We need to find out how soon," Ferris added.

"Well, I think I have a way of making that happen. You're going to laugh now, but I can get you in," Cole said, looking in Ferris's direction. "A true royal blood supporter, with an impressive portfolio, would get a seat on his boat in no time. You could then get access to all sorts of information."

"That involves leaving the house," Ferris muttered.

"You're Ferris Ayers. People come to you, not the other way around." Cole shrugged, acknowledging his superiority. He was making Ferris look like the president or something, while to me, he was just Ferris—the slightly psychotic king.

"Okay. Set an appointment. I'll see if I can raise his interest somehow." Ferris rolled his eyes, accepting the burden of having to socialize with another living person.

"I say we kill him. I know a few skilled hitmen. Make him

disappear." Brax was the only one who could come up with that idea, or with the necessary contacts.

Ferris didn't seem to agree. He took a seat on a large armchair next to the fireplace, rubbing his hands together like he was hatching a master plan. "Murder creates martyrs. We don't need someone else filling his shoes. What we need is to discredit him. Take away any chance to present his idea to the public. At least not from the position his function provides."

"We need to ensure he is removed from his position," I continued his thought, trying to figure out a way to make that plan work.

"We need someone on the inside. Someone close to him. Someone who could give us a hint of what to look for. Embezzlement, taking bribes, playing favorites at public auctions... anything." Brax was trying out a more *docile* approach.

"I know his stepson," Cole casually said as if that *wasn't* a crucial piece of information.

And this seemed to annoy Brax. "And you're just mentioning it now?"

"I thought my father's relationship with the governor was enough. Besides, Camden is a real piece of shit."

"Kinda like you?" Brax laughed, unwillingly expressing my own thoughts.

"Yeah. Kinda like me." Cole smiled, realizing he wasn't falling behind when it came to model behavior. "He and his friends are throwing a party next weekend down in Emerald City at some fancy mountain resort. Only creme de la creme allowed."

"A party which you will be attending," Ferris assumed.

"Not exactly." A flicker of regret and anger crossed Cole's face.

"You weren't invited?" Brax asked.

"I was, but…shit… how should I put this," Cole made a short pause. "The whole thing has some costs."

The way he said it left me under the impression that Brax and Ferris weren't aware of his financial situation.

"So?" Ferris asked as if everyone else also had an unlimited bank account like his.

His ignorance made Cole take a deep breath. "Fuck. My father has made some investments lately."

"In *my* casinos," without his will, Brax unraveled Mr. Clyborne's secret.

"No. He made some investments in a congressman's elections. It will pay off shortly." For someone so smart, Cole was surprisingly blind when it came to his father.

"Brax is right," I intervened, feeling Cole needed to know the truth, "I overheard your father speaking to your mom when I was at your place."

My confession clearly shattered the image Cole had of his father. But *luckily* for him, he had someone to vent his anger on. "When, Mouse? After that time in the bathroom when you couldn't resist me even for seven minutes? Or on the night you stayed in my bed?"

I'd made him feel uncomfortable, and this was his way of turning the tables. Obviously, it worked since my face flushed a fiery red, silently praying that he wouldn't go on. In an instant, he was towering over me, consuming all the oxygen in the room, leaving me with a blank expression as I foolishly gazed up at him. I had no idea what he was about to do, but nothing good could come out of his closeness.

"You like eavesdropping," he groaned, pushing my hair aside to reveal my neckline. The gaze of a hungry vampire was upon me, as he let his lips fall next to my ear. "Just wait till I get my hands on you," he whispered in what could be an amusing threat, but coming from him, I knew it had every chance to be real.

Disregarding the other's presence, he ran his tongue over my neck, spreading a chill from the place he touched to the depths of my being. The sole purpose of his actions was to embarrass me, diminish my presence down to zero, and claim authority over his possession.

To my surprise, the other two kings didn't show any sign of jealousy, not even Ferris. More like curiosity, and a hint of amusement. I was *their* Mouse in a game of predator and prey. Now I had three Big Bad Cats to look out for.

"Leave the fun for later. Let's finish this. I need a drink." Brax was in a hurry to *numb* his senses again.

At least he made Cole stop.

Stop, but not free me. His hand quickly snuck over my waist, gluing my back against his chest just as I was about to leave.

Brax didn't seem to have a problem with our closeness, so he just went on with his idea, "Let's put a real crown on your head." He looked directly at Ferris.

"Are you fucking kidding me? I'll help you remove the governor, but I don't want to take his place," Ferris stuttered slightly.

"Do you know anyone else more appropriate to claim it than you?" Brax raised an eyebrow, looking across the room.

Ferris let out a snarl. "Even the man that mows my lawn is more appropriate than me."

"Let's get Jose on the phone then," Cole chuckled, making the sexiest sound when he laughed. Ugh... I hated him for that.

"It will only be temporary," Brax tried to explain, "You have a strong background and the purest royal blood. The Elite will eat out of the palm of your hand."

"What part of *I don't want to leave the house* didn't you get?" My king of darkness seemed determined to stick to his resolution.

"We only need this as a momentary measure until we take control and change a few laws to be more permissive for the Annelids. Better salaries, better working conditions, better life." Brax seemed to agree with my plans for them to rule the city, although I had a feeling it had something to do with more money running through the Pit, and into his pockets.

But that made Ferris also take things into consideration. "Do you think the Elite will accept this?"

Brax was weighing things. "They won't have a choice. I'll stall the rebellion until I have enough manpower to overrule them, should it be required. The Elite might have more financial options, but the Annelids are more driven to win."

"Could you stop calling us Annelids?" I asked him, finding the term demeaning, and Brax seemed to be a specialist when it came to *demeaning* people.

"I'm an Annelid too, in case you forgot. So, spare me the drama. It's just a word." Brax was stating a true fact, but it still didn't give him the right to talk and act like a jerk.

"Let's get back to the point. I'm going to cover all expenses regarding Cole's party, and everything that comes up in the meantime as well. Anything you want, just ask." Ferris was putting his assets at our disposal.

While Cole was putting me on the guest list. "You're coming with me, Mouse."

Another party, just what I had wished for...not.

"Can't wait," I muttered, trying to break free from his grip, but with no real chance of that happening.

"We're going to have so much fun together," Cole whispered the words, sounding the exact opposite of what he was saying.

"So, everything is settled. I'll go talk to a few of the leaders, Ferris is going to try and infiltrate the governor's trusted core group, and Cole... Cole is going to party his way through this."

Brax was laying out the sketch of what we just discussed, making sure all assignments were going to be finalized. "Now, give me a fucking glass of Macallan. I'm thirsty."

Ferris stood up from his armchair to pour Brax a glass of whiskey, as it was still difficult for him to walk around and serve himself.

"You shouldn't drink, Brax." I didn't know why I even bothered to warn him. I knew he wasn't going to listen to me anyway.

On the contrary, I only managed to piss him off. "Stop acting like I'm one of your fucking charity cases."

"You don't have to be a charity case for me to see you're not well," I snapped.

"Maybe you could come here and fix me," he muttered, clearly annoyed that I wouldn't drop the subject.

"Fuck you!" My foul mouth could not be contained.

Brax didn't get to react to my remark as Cole's arm tightened around me. "Watch your mouth, Mouse."

Great, now I had both of them on my back. One of them being literally on my back.

"You two are too worked up for me." Ferris took a seat back in his chair.

"That's because you didn't have enough to drink yet," Cole finally let go of me and walked over to where the guys were, grabbing his glass from the table. "What now?" He downed the contents of the glass in one sip.

"I haven't spent an evening with you two in ages." Ferris smiled, reminiscing about their past get-togethers, between many other things, I was sure.

"I'll be leaving, then." I had to try my luck and get out of there.

And to my surprise, this time it worked. "Go and rest— unless you'd rather join us for drinks?" Ferris was just giving me a way out.

A night in my own bed was a luxury I could barely afford. I wasn't going to pass on that offer, especially since the three of them and alcohol didn't seem like a great mix.

"I'm tired. I'm going straight to bed. Have fun." I forced a smile and left the room before any of them got to sneak in a word.

Although Cole's voice could be heard throughout the lobby, "See you tomorrow, Queen B."

Shit... what was that about?

CHAPTER 10

Q ueen B. The intonation of Cole's words seemed to be stuck in my mind. I was positive that he had planned something for the coming day, and I couldn't help but fear his always devious thoughts.

Sleeping an entire night in my own bed seemed surreal at that moment. It was like someone had put my torment on pause. Not a very long pause, but a well-deserved one. Everything was on fast-forward, and things were evolving so much faster than I was expecting them to. Less than a month ago, I wasn't even sure if I could save my family, and now I had the burden of a whole city on my shoulders.

The thought was giving me an anxiety attack, but in the strangest of ways, it was also soothing me. At least there was hope to put a stop to all of it. Maybe even hope for improvement.

Despite everything, I slept like a baby. Lack of sleep and tiredness didn't keep track of saving the world, so I needed to lock up my vigilante suit for the evening.

I wished the night could be longer, but I woke up feeling like only ten minutes had passed, looking at the gray sky of the morning. I must have counted to three ten times to get to the right *three* that gave me enough courage to get out of my comfy bed. And once on my feet, the only thing that I could think about was how to get back between the warm sheets.

Fighting through my morning haze, I packed up a few books, and after kissing Nat and Seb goodbye, left for the university.

Funny how for everyone else school was usually a routine. For me, it was a new challenge each day as I was beginning to learn that I should take nothing for granted.

I entered what was now my side of the hallway, bracing myself for all the unnecessary ass-kissing I was about to receive. *Nice dress, nice makeup, nice everything.* The only thing not nice anymore was me.

Strangely enough, I managed to avoid the usual crowd of fans, mostly because *no one was around.* Every single soul was gathered in the middle of the lobby, forming a huge circle, very similar to a ring. It didn't take me long to guess who was in the middle of things, since my king of bullying was nowhere in my line of sight.

"What's going on here?" I asked one of the students who was just coming out from the middle of the events.

"Someone parked in Cole's parking space," the guy explained as if it was natural to beat someone up just because he occupied the wrong square foot of asphalt.

I wasn't going to stand there and do nothing, so nudging a few students aside, I built myself a corridor directly to where the action was. "Step aside!" I had to call out to a few girls who were refusing to lose their front seats to the free show. But as soon as they acknowledged my presence, they bowed their heads as if I was fucking royalty, making me room to get in front.

By the time I got there, it was too late. The miserable guy who had confused section lot A with B or whatever it was, was supporting himself on the wall as Cole was giving him the final directions. "You fucking do that again and I'll hook your car and throw it into the river. Got it?"

The student barely nodded his head in a sign that he understood because he also needed to keep a hand on his bloody nose.

Giving a speech would have been useless at that point. Nothing could get him to change his ways, and saying anything would only bring Cole's wrath upon me.

It was too late anyway. But that didn't mean I was going to support him, so before he got himself together from the rush of the moment, I was already out of there.

My old pack had gathered at the other end of the hallway, so I decided to join them, no matter how many disdainful looks I got along the way.

"Hi guys!" I waved a few shy fingers at them, though their enthusiasm for seeing me didn't match my own. And I couldn't blame them, since I had switched camps with the enemy.

Jenna knew better than to believe it, but explaining to Darrel and Thomas why I was sucking faces with their mortal enemy was a little more complicated.

"Let's go outside. We still have fifteen before the classes start." Jenna was trying to save me from having to answer too many questions.

"Fine by me." Thomas was the first out the door, followed by the rest of us.

It was late autumn already, and the cold breeze was keeping everyone else inside, leaving our gang with the whole yard at our disposal.

"So, you abandoned us to live amongst the Elite." I couldn't tell if Thomas was joking or being serious. Either way, I didn't enjoy the tone of his voice.

"Back off, she didn't have a choice. She was *selected*." Jenna's explanation was making me sound like a pawn whose only purpose was to be chosen by the king. But the more I thought about it, the more I was beginning to think she was right. I was *selected* to be his experimental girlfriend out of a hundred other girls who would kill to be in my shoes. If it were up to me, I'd let any of them have him—shoes, and socks, and all—if I didn't need him, which unfortunately I did.

Maybe I was being selfish. I was using him the same way he used me, both aiming for a goal, impossible to reach without the other.

"We could try and take actions against him, you know. It's not fair that he gets to do anything he wants and gets away with it," Thomas was letting his feelings toward Cole out, but no matter how badly he might have treated me, I wasn't going to start to rebel against my king. We both were in the same boat now, whether I liked it or not.

"There's nothing to be gained except getting ourselves in trouble. Things are tense enough already between us and the Elite. Just drop it for now, at least until everything cools down," I tried explaining. Besides, at that point, Cole was part of the team that was trying to save his ass, although Thomas couldn't know that.

"We will soon burn the Elite and everything they stand for." Thomas seemed to be taking things to another level. One that seemed dangerously close to a rebellion.

Sensing I was onto a lead, I was trying to get information out of him. "Do you know anything about what's happening in the Pit?"

And my senses weren't failing me. "Let's just say our days at the other end of the hall are numbered." Thomas grinned. He was definitely up to something and I needed to find out exactly what.

It was time to use a little reverse psychology on him. "Just don't get in trouble, Thomas. Stay away from their rebellion and its leaders."

"A little late for that." He was confirming what I feared to be true. That only meant one thing; he was becoming an asset in our plan. The more people we knew on the inside, the more chances of stalling their actions. Now, all I had to do was ask Brax to reason with him. Another joy added to my life. I could feel a mental eye roll just by thinking about asking him to do it.

I just sent my mobster a text with Thomas's details, accompanied by a *don't hurt him!* warning in capital letters.

What do I get in return if I behave? Brax's reply lit up on my screen.

He was being flirtatious, but the improvement in his mood came a little too late. The way he acted two nights ago could only leave me with a single answer.

I already gave you everything I had.

I put the phone back in my bag while Brax's absinthe eyes were watching over me in the back of my mind.

"Thank you," Jenna whispered in my ear, snapping me out of my thoughts. "I had to sell the bracelet to pay off an eviction order, but at least it bought us 'til the end of the month." Her hand searched for mine, giving it a tight squeeze, thanking me again without letting everyone in on our secret.

"I'll figure out something to help you. I promise," I whispered back to her without letting Thomas and Darrel in on our secret.

We didn't stay out for much longer since it was about to start raining. The guys began talking about the Advanced Math class anyway, so the rain was just an excuse to get out of there.

I didn't share the first class with Jenna, but we did meet up during the break as I was still trying to ignore Cole. The little display of force he used today took him out of my graces completely, not that he was too high on my list of favorites. None of the kings were.

I didn't join Cole in his little select group, choosing to

remain in front of the door where I was about to start my next class. This one I *was* sharing with him and I could only hope he didn't feel in the mood to attend today.

I was obviously out of luck. Two minutes before the class began, he was standing right in front of me, signaling me to join him in the atrium.

He was early, and that was enough to worry me to the bone. Cole was never the most vigilant of students, so his eagerness to get to class was most odd, and could only mean he was playing another one of his games.

"Did you do what I asked you to?" Cole murmured as we were heading toward a two-seater bench.

"What?" I wasn't sure what he was talking about, but I had a feeling I didn't want to find out either.

"Regarding the panties." He grinned with devilish thoughts flickering on his lips. "Sit, Mouse." He fastened his arm around me before I got a chance to say a word. Yet, he was still expecting an answer. "So?"

"I forgot." Of course, I hadn't forgotten. I just ignored him completely, seeing it as a joke and not a real demand.

I mean, who does that? Who walks around school without lingerie on?

I guess, I should, according to him, "Give them to me." Cole stretched out a hand as if I was to take my panties off as easily as pulling a book from my bag.

"Are you fucking kidding me?" I retaliated.

"Fucking—*yes*. Kidding—*no*." He was keen on making it clear who was in control. "Now, don't keep me waiting. You wouldn't want me to get under the desk and take them off myself, would you? Because if that's the case, it's fine by me."

"I hate you from the bottom of my heart," I snarled, feeling trapped in his game.

And it seemed I was amusing Cole, "Keep your love

declarations for Valentine's Day."

"I'm surprised you even know what Valentine's Day is," I grunted, pushing him a little off me so that I at least had enough room to fulfill his request. "Can I at least go to the bathroom?"

"No, you had your chance, you're doing it here." He shrugged so casually when in fact I knew he was punishing me for my insolence at having disrespected him.

"Give me that," I mumbled, taking his jacket and throwing it over my legs as I was struggling to get the damn piece of material off of me. An impossible task without fussing and turning, involuntarily becoming the center of everyone's attention.

I was deliberately prolonging the moment, not ready to face whatever twisted game he had in mind. I dreaded finding out his plans, though I had a pretty good idea of what he was after. I was fucking terrified of his intentions, my stomach the size of a nut, and the anxiety was written all over my face.

"Hurry up before the class ends," his fine irony was destined to piss me off even more. This was payback. Maybe for what happened at the party, or because I didn't fall in line with his actions today. It didn't even matter. I was going to pay a price regardless.

"Here." I slipped the lacy fabric in his hands, noticing a certain satisfaction in receiving his trophy.

"I'll hang on to these," he said, shoving them in his pocket.

"Of course you will. Any psycho would." I was at the point where I could turn even a *Hello* into an insult.

"You really don't care how much that mouth of yours is going to cost you, do you?" He sounded almost shocked that I couldn't contain myself.

Truthfully, I was raised to keep quiet. My mother was always teaching me lessons in good manners. I respected that and honored her as best as I could. But life has taught me to be a fighter. It taught me that I needed to be cold, even distant in order to survive. It was what our society reflected. You can't deprive people of sunlight and expect them to be warm. It doesn't work that way. Society, the current lifestyle —everything put together, were creating monsters. And monsters couldn't be tamed.

"I'm not going to give you the satisfaction of me fearing you. That wasn't part of the deal," I snarled at him.

"You're right, it wasn't." He let a few tense seconds hang between us before speaking again. "It's a bonus," he quipped, fixing his hand beneath my jaw and pulling me into a kiss.

I could feel his anger in every swirl of his tongue, kissing me like he was intent on stealing the air from my lungs. He just didn't give a fuck about anyone else in the room, or about the professor who had just walked in. It was just *lust, and the need that it would be satisfied.* The only thought that ruled his mind in those moments. That, and the sadistic thrill of watching me melt into a mix of fury and shame.

For a guy who didn't enjoy kissing, he was certainly doing it a lot. Not that I could complain. Sure, I was angry about the timing and the place. But that sensation. That unbelievable sensation of him owning me in a fleeting moment of raw dominance could not be denied.

His lips finally withdrew their warmth, leaving me alone under the scrutinizing gazes of our classmates. I was the main attraction again, and he was my twisted protector for one more time since with a single warning glance from him, everyone's eyes quickly darted away.

I hoped he was done. That he was just trying to scare me a little, get my blood pumping. But deep down I knew he had something more in store for me.

Halfway through the lecture, his hand slid onto my knee, and I froze, my breath catching as a hot surge of adrenaline coursed through me, igniting every nerve in a mix of fear and something dangerously close to thrill.

What the hell was he trying to do? It was the only thought that governed my mind.

He casually draped his jacket over my lap, the same damned jacket that had shielded our last indiscretion. Its presence felt heavier now, like a silent accomplice to his every move. I was beginning to hate that fucking jacket, even thinking of getting my hands on it and burning it. Although I didn't doubt he had an entire wardrobe of replacements ready to cover for the loss.

With snail-like moves, his hand advanced further up on my inner thigh, as my feet tightened so close together that I thought my knees would break.

"Mouse, do you want me to put on a show? Open your legs." He didn't even look at me as he spoke. So detached that his calmness was provoking a reaction between my thighs. Maybe it was the feeling of being controlled. Or maybe knowing that absolute way he controlled everyone.

Cole was a man of power and whatever I was trying to do to avoid it, it seemed to be backfiring on me.

"What did I say?" He gently smacked that needy place that had already dampened at his touch. The click echoed through the room, and I was under the impression that every single one of his actions was being broadcast live on national TV. But no one turned. I couldn't tell if they were oblivious to the noise or too intimidated to investigate its source.

At least I was partially out of the woods—*partially* being the keyword in the sentence.

With the unavoidable sensation that the end of the world was coming, I opened my legs, making room for his hand to move directly over my pussy, working up and down at a growing pace.

It was torture. A torture so perfect that I wanted to scream my pain looking into those cobalt blue eyes that were sipping every single reaction that my face could no longer contain. It was the fear of getting caught that was driving me insane, spicing up every natural reaction my body was having.

"You're mine," he groaned, visibly turned on from the way my heels were anchored into the floor, as I was trying to keep myself together.

I hated to admit it, but he was right. He owned me.

I was his, I could feel it in my bones. Despite the fact that we were in a full room, he was becoming the only person there as he and his magic fingers were captivating all of my attention.

I could have asked him not to do it in the classroom. Maybe even promise him something in return for using a more private location to put his plans to use. But I knew there was no point. He wanted it—the adrenaline brought by the risk of public exposure, the heart beating, the eagle eyes pointed at the rest of the class, dreading the moment someone would catch on. He wanted the complete experience like it was some package deal at a luxury resort.

I gasped feeling the sudden intrusion of two of his fingers within me. I even snuck my hand beneath the jacket to catch onto his own and try and have it still. My instincts did me no good. Sensing my desperation, his teeth clenched with excitement, waiting for tiny beads of sweat to form on my forehead. Waiting to ruin me. And he was doing just that. With every one of his movements, he was building something so strong that it was giving me no chance but to shiver in ecstasy.

The fingers increased in their depth, going each time further to a place that was making me curl on top of the bench. Guilt, fear and pleasure were conjoined into a tidal wave crashing; a reaction that was making it almost impossible to hold back a throated moan.

Driven by the adrenaline, I was extremely close to a delirium drift-off. I was barely holding on and he knew it. He was living for the moment.

"I want you to look at me," he ordered, eager to witness the full results of his actions.

He wanted to completely dominate me, and I had no choice but to obey.

I was looking at him. Well, as much as I could since my eyes could barely stay open through the excruciating thrill. And then he decided to end the game. With a single pinch of my clit, the strongest orgasm ripped through my body. This time, my heels scratched loudly into the floor in an impossible trail to still my sweet anguish. The unavoidable was here and all eyes were upon me, as Cole's hand was refusing to leave the warmth of my core.

"Please!" I whimpered in his ear, feeling him trying to bring me into another moment of frenzy while we were surrounded by our very own live audience.

He didn't listen. How could he? His hand kept moving inside my soaking pussy as I was trying to keep a poker face, pretending to be writing down what the teacher was saying.

One by one, the students' heads turned back to their desks, afraid of getting under the radar of His Royal Highness.

"I'm not someone you can ignore without consequences, Mouse," Cole growled right before sending another wave of pleasure coursing through me. It *was* a punishment after all. A consuming punishment, though one that didn't fully satisfy his wrath. My flushed cheeks and trembling hands weren't enough. He aimed straight for my heart. "You purposely ignored me to be with your so-called friends."

That was true, but it was still his fault. "I ignored you because you were beating a guy up over a parking space."

"I could kill someone and you'd still need to support me," he rasped with annoyance. The king's actions could never be condemned. "But you'll know how to behave next time. I'll make sure of that. Meanwhile, you're not allowed to talk to

Jenna anymore."

"You can't do that!" I protested.

"Watch me."

"Our deal didn't involve my friends or freedom." He was stepping out of bounds.

"No, it didn't, but it involved you being my girlfriend. So let's just say it's not fitting for a queen to waste her time with someone from the other end of the hallway."

I couldn't lose my only friend just because of one of Cole's mood swings. "Please reconsider," I all but pleaded.

"I will. When you learn to behave. You made a fool of me today by leaving." He sounded offended.

"I didn't know..." *Of course, I knew.* "I didn't realize this would affect you."

"Now you know. And Mouse, if you disobey me, you won't be the one paying the price. Jenna will."

Shit, he was stepping up his game, taking all the necessary measures to ensure I was left with no option.

"Jenna has nothing to do with us," I gasped.

"My mind is made up. If you have something else to add to the matter, I'm expecting you to unfasten my zipper as you speak."

He might have had a way to get me to shut up. But never a way to make me give up.

CHAPTER 11

I managed to stay by Cole's side for the rest of the hour. Then, abiding by his request, I played the girlfriend role for a few extra breaks.

I wasn't sure he even liked the role he'd cast me in, but he sure loved how I was reacting to it. I guess he found it exciting, helping him detach from his daily routine. *Sick bastard.*

In any case, I wasn't going to stand by, waiting for another one of his fantasies to become my command. The second my last class ended, I snuck out of the university like a burglar into the night, hoping that Cole wouldn't catch a glimpse of me. I was out of the woods, but entering an entirely *different* kind of woods, since there was a certain someone who I owed a visit to. A proper one this time. *Ferris.*

With only five minutes to spend at my apartment before I had to rush out, I left the babysitter instructions for the night, changed, and kissed my family goodnight.

Alfred was surprised by my arrival at the mansion before nightfall, and even though he didn't tell me this in words, I could see it in his eyes.

"Is he in his room?" I asked, thinking that Ferris was probably still sleeping.

"No, he's in the day room, watching the news. Follow me. I'll lead you to him," Alfred guided me toward the day room since the place was still a labyrinth to me.

The news? I dreaded the news, to the point that I wasn't even turning on the TV. I knew where things were going, and how they were going to end if we didn't intervene.

Ferris was so focused that I don't think he even heard me step into the room. I didn't want to make him aware of my presence either, since the news that was on captured my attention completely.

It's been a quiet day in the Pit. The number of protesters has slightly diminished since yesterday, as a few of the rebellion leaders seem to have taken a different approach and are now asking for patience. There are rumors that the protests and acts of violence will decrease in intensity during the next couple of days, as people have been summoned to go back to their normal activities for a while. What we do not know is if this small setback could mean an attempt to return to normal, or the calm before the storm.

The rebellion leaders haven't made their intentions public, but the word on the street is that they're setting up a plan of attack.

On the other side, in the Hills, the governor declared, during a press conference he attended earlier today, that the Elite is ready to hold its ground, and I quote, **"No one can threaten our security without repercussions. We are ready for whatever action they could manifest against us. I just hope they are also ready to face the consequences."**

We return with the global news, but tune in at seven for the entire press conference and the after-interviews from the governor.

"Do you think Brax got to the commanders?" I asked as soon as the news report ended, causing Ferris to turn toward me, slightly shocked.

I guess I forgot to let him know I was in the room.

"I just transferred 4.5 million dollars to him. I think it's safe to say that he already convinced a number of them."

"Yeah, I have no doubt that Brax can be convincing," I muttered, remembering exactly *how convincing* he could get at times.

And it seemed Ferris also knew about Brax's ability, "Like convincing you to sleep with him again? That kind of *convincing*?"

Fuck, he knew about my visit to Brax. Though, despite what my crime lord probably told him, Ferris didn't seem so pissed about us sleeping together. I just hoped it wasn't a fake calm like last time and that I wouldn't end up under his blade again. It sure didn't feel that way. More like he was content with the situation—as strange as that might seem.

"Do you guys talk about everything you *do*?" I was concerned about my nights spent with them being their main subject of conversation.

"More or less. It just came up last night when I talked to him." Ferris shrugged like it was the most casual thing—them talking about me.

The *three* of them were talking about me, since Cole was there too.

I could literally beg the ground to open up and swallow me whole, just thinking of what their discussions could have been about and how exactly Ferris found out that I had slept with Brax. Did he give out the details? My motives?

In a strange way, I was bursting with curiosity. But it wasn't something I could ask very easily.

I just decided to play it cool. "I don't even want to know what you've talked about. Unless it involves the rebellion, and from the look on your face, it doesn't seem that was your main topic of discussion."

"We settled that subject while you were still here. There was nothing left to talk about regarding it. Besides, I have to meet with that piece-of-shit of a governor tomorrow at some politician's brunch. And that *does* involve me leaving the house!" Ferris seemed really pissed off about going out, especially since the plan for the governor to come and see him personally didn't seem to have worked out.

"I'm sorry, I thought Cole could convince him to come and see you here," I tried to apologize.

"His schedule is too tight. He could only come to me next Friday, but that would throw our plans off track. So I agreed to meet him tomorrow." A hint of anger mixed with frustration as he spoke, made me realize that this was anything but easy for him. "Fucking brunch," he continued cursing, taking a deep breath to try to calm his nerves.

I had to do something to improve his mood, and I knew just what. "I'm sorry you have to go through that. But I do have an idea on how to make things a little easier for you."

My *having another plan* didn't sound too good to him. And who could blame him? "What idea?"

"You'll see. But I need to borrow something from you first." I was winging it along the way.

"I was going to talk to you about having your own card." Mr. Billionaire thought I was after his fortune tonight.

"Jesus, not money." I laughed. "Just come with me." I headed toward his bedroom, going straight into his walk-in dressing room.

"What do you need? Maybe I could help," Ferris offered his assistance watching me as I was actively going through his shirts.

"Here, put this on." I threw him a simple black T-shirt, then carried on searching for one for myself.

"What's wrong with the one I'm wearing?" Nothing was wrong. He looked devilishly delicious with or without a shirt, but the designer brand logo imprinted on his chest pocket was interfering with my plans.

"I need you to look less... royal." I smiled, trying not to give too much of my plan away.

Not that it was an easy task when it came to Ferris. "Why?" he asked, cocking an eyebrow at me as if he was losing his patience.

"You asked me to trust you. Now I'm asking you to trust me. Put this on and turn around." I threw him a black cap, and as soon as he turned around, I tugged one of his shirts over my head.

"Did you just make me turn so I couldn't watch you change?" He instantly burst into laughter, realizing what I was up to. Defying my request, he whirled back to look at me. "I think I've seen you naked enough times to be able to look at you while you change." With two swift steps, he was by my side, sliding a wandering hand across the small of my back.

"This is exactly why I told you to turn. I want to get dressed, not *un*dressed." I smiled, reaching for a pair of his jeans and pulling them on, "Do you have a belt?" I asked.

His mind went straight into the gutter, "Kinky. I like it."

"For the pants, Ferris." I chuckled.

"You can take mine off," he offered.

"Okay.," I smiled again, reaching for his buckle and unfastening it under his already-lust filled gaze.

I guess he didn't get the dressing-versus-undressing message, as he was still waiting for me to continue, right to the moment he noticed I was really putting his belt on. "Do you have a pair of joggers?" I couldn't see what was what through so many clothes.

"What do you think?" he asked as if he owned a whole store of joggers—which he probably did.

"I think you should put them on." I shrugged.

Ferris was becoming suspicious of my plan, "Okay, but first, tell me what's going on here."

"We're going out." I tried not to make a big deal out of it.

"The fuck we are." That was a decisive *no* on his part.

But when did I ever let a negative answer stop me? "Please. It will do you some good. I promise."

My request put Ferris into a defensive mode. "Since when do you know what's good or not for me?"

"Listen, I know I'm probably just some new toy for you. And maybe you don't even believe me, but I care about you," I explained.

"You're not a toy," he murmured, allowing that same consuming darkness to invade his eyes. "I fucked up, big time, I know."

"Well, unfuck it, then. Trust me. Give me an hour of your life." I was playing with his emotions—if he had any to begin with.

"An hour outside these gates." He made it sound like I was asking the impossible of him.

I was raising the stakes. I wasn't going to let him crawl back into his darkness. "An hour with me."

"Step aside," he muttered, walking past me to search a shelf for a pair of joggers. "Do I look baggy enough?"

"Not really, but it will do." His clothes could be torn to pieces, and he would still look like royalty. I just pulled his cap lower over his eyes and hoped no one would recognize him. It was the best I could do on such short notice.

"Let's call for a cab." I took my phone out to give the order to the dispatch.

"A cab?" His Highness was used to traveling in style.

"Yeah, we can't take the limo where we're going. Alfred taught me that." And I never forget a lesson.

"I'm not going into the Pit if that's what you're thinking." Ferris was backing out of our *date*.

But I had an exact plan for where we were going, and it didn't involve entering any of the dangerous zones, "I promise you'll be safe."

"I'm not afraid if that's what you're implying," Ferris tried to justify himself. Men will be men. He was afraid, and I knew it. But it wasn't the normal kind of fear people get when walking into the unknown. Ferris was afraid of triggering his memories. He was afraid of his nightmares.

"I know you're not afraid. I didn't mean it that way." I snuck my hand into his, hoping his temper wouldn't resurface. "I hope you're hungry."

"I was going to call you to invite you to dinner, but you beat me to it," Ferris said, and I was sure he already had some chef ready to make us dinner. But I needed to get him out of his comfort zone somehow, and a trip to the Pit was the shortest way there.

"My treat this time," I laughed, pretty much determined to show him what a good day in the Pit really meant.

The cab arrived, but unfortunately, we couldn't leave without a car full of bodyguards somewhere on our trail. At least they kept a decent distance—enough so we could have our privacy but also be safe. I was getting used to their presence anyway, to the point I even forgot they existed.

I paid the cab driver right after he stopped in front of a local fast-food joint. "We're here," I let Ferris know.

"Here?" Ferris almost shuddered, convinced that a hospital bed and a food poisoning diagnosis were waiting for him.

"You've put way worse things in your mouth than this food." I chuckled, almost dragging him inside. "Let me order. I know exactly what to get.'

"Not doubting you on that one." Ferris stayed with me, just quietly observing my every move and pretty much everything else around him. He was like a curious child, stepping out into the real world for the first time.

"A small chicken strips menu to go," I ordered while Ferris was looking back at me slightly confused.

"That will be $6.50." The cashier took out the receipt as I slipped her a $10.

"Keep the change." I smiled.

She just nodded, turning her back on us to prepare our order.

"I have some cash on me," Ferris offered, probably noticing that I'd ordered a single small menu.

"I told you it's my treat." I didn't get to explain since the waiter was already handing me a paper bag over the counter, "There you go. Have a nice evening, and don't forget to come again."

"Thanks." I winked at the girl, then turned my head to Ferris. "Come on, let's go."

"Go where?" He was confused, since he probably thought we were going to share a chicken strip over dinner.

"To get drinks. Come." Taking his hand, I led him to a supermarket across the street. "Beer or soda?" I asked, approaching the drinks aisle.

"Soda. Not really a beer guy."

Go figure.

"Okay." I reached for two cans of soda and dropped them on the ground, not hard enough to break them, but enough to make the tin cans bend.

"Are you out of your mind? What are you doing?" Ferris was almost in shock, probably waiting for some local authority dude to charge us with vandalism.

It was kind of funny watching my psycho look at me as if I was the one missing a few screws. But it wasn't about that. It was about survival. About what I've been doing all my life.

"Relax. I'll pay for them." Taking the sodas from the floor, I went straight to the cash register. "These ones are a little bent."

"Let me see." The cashier picked up the sodas for a closer look. "50% discount. That'll be 65 cents for both."

"Thank you!" I handed him the money, and walked out, followed by Ferris's laughter. He found it amusing. And it couldn't be any other way for a man like him. But for me, it was something else. It was survival. Doing whatever you needed to stay alive.

"Can you also do that with cars?" Ferris went for a joke.

"We can't really afford cars down here, so no." I was letting him in on a truth he never could conceive existed. And who could blame him? He knew luxury all his life, so missing a pair of shoes or a piece of bread that could still your roaring stomach seemed impossible to him.

"Let's get out of here." Reaching for his hand, I guided him through dark lanes until we ended up in an abandoned building. "We'll have to go up about seventeen floors."

The shock on his face was priceless. "What? Are you fucking kidding me?"

"Come on, you look like you live in a gym." I pulled his hand to join me.

"I work out. But what you're asking me is Rocky Balboa's level," Ferris began laughing as he started up the stairs.

"It'll be worth it. I promise."

We were out of breath when we finally managed to reach the top, and even if it was almost below zero outside, neither of us could move even an inch.

Our heads simultaneously raised to look up at the purple sky, watching death and beauty put on a supreme fight on the same dark canvas.

The pollution rate was incredibly high. We could feel it in the thick air we inhaled, our lungs almost fighting for each breath. I'd gotten used to the better oxygen levels in the Hills. But even though my body was barely getting accustomed to such stress, my brain wasn't going to let me forget where I came from.

"This is as amazing as it is deadly." Ferris took a seat on an old pipe, lighting himself a cigarette.

Great, he was adding to the pollution. "That thing you just put in your mouth is as deadly as that cloud."

"Then I'm just racing toward my death." He shrugged, taking a drag from the cigarette.

"Don't talk like that, Ferris." I knew why he said it. I recognized his pain, though that didn't mean I could ever agree with the way he was acting. "You have so many things to look forward to."

"Name one," he asked me so suddenly, making me think he truly believed he had nothing to look forward to—not even our time spent together.

"Helping someone, and not the giving them a glass of water, kind of help. Like really helping a person. Change someone's life." I was trying to show him how good it could feel to make a difference in someone's life, especially since for a man such as him it wouldn't have come with great effort.

"I thought I already did that with you," he said, referring to how he already changed my life.

"I didn't mean me. A random person. Like all the people we're going to help if we manage to pull this off." After all, our plan was to save an entire city.

"Like you did with your friend Jenna?" Ferris asked, to my surprise. I didn't know he had any idea who Jenna was.

"What did I do with Jenna?" I answered his question with a question, as I was still trying to figure out what he meant.

And Ferris was wasting no time to clear things out for me. "You gave her one of my presents. A diamond bracelet. Unless she stole that from you."

"No, she didn't steal it." I turned to look at him, trying to gauge how pissed off he really was about the gift I'd given. "But diamonds?" I was slightly shocked since I had chosen the bracelet out of a jewelry box filled with at least fifteen similar pieces.

"It had a serial number. The pawnshop where she sold it called me to ask if I wanted it back since it was registered under my client account," Ferris explained.

"I had no idea. I only wanted to help her. I didn't even know if it was real gold or not." I took a moment of silence, thinking about how to mend things, not that I could really fix anything. "I'm sorry. She's going through a rough time. I didn't think for a second that the bracelet could have real diamonds. Damn, I'm sure they paid her scraps for it."

Ferris flared his nostrils. "That's probably why they called me. To cash in the big bucks."

"I didn't realize. I thought I was doing the right thing," I apologized again since now *I* was the one who had messed things up.

"I'll give you a card with a monthly sum for expenses. You can decide what to do with that. I don't care, as long as you stop giving your personal things away. I bought that for you," Ferris said, a stinging tone in his voice.

"I didn't think of the consequences, but I'll make it up to you." I wiggled the takeout bag. Like that could ever compensate for anything.

"I guess that will do," he smiled, waiting for me to take our picnic dinner out. He was just trying to make things easy for me. But I did manage to surprise him—instead of the lousy menu, I got a bag full of French fries and more than enough chicken strips for both of us.

"Where did that come from?" He looked at the food like Jesus had multiplied our food.

"The extra $3.50 did the trick." I smiled, setting out our paper bag dinner cloth over the ventilation pipe, then took a seat next to him.

"I'm starting to think you're an expert at this," he

murmured while helping me set the *table.*

"At romantic dinners? Not by a long shot." I chuckled, pulling his leg.

"Getting by with basically nothing. That's what I was referring to."

"Oh...story of my life," I raised my shoulders, opening *the fine bottle of wine*—the soda cans in our case.

Ferris was literally licking his fingers after the first bite. The fast-food carbs worked their magic faster than a Michelin starred chef menu could.

But no matter how stress-free our dinner was, the thought that I had wronged him didn't give me peace. "You know, I don't want you to think I don't appreciate what you do for me." I wanted to clarify things between us because the more I thought about it, the more I realized that the subject was going to eat me alive if I didn't talk things through.

"I know you had good intentions. I would have just liked it if you would have told me. I guess the truth is, I didn't give you too many reasons to trust me," he took a small pause to gather his thoughts. "You know, I'm also thinking of the harm I've caused you." He seemed truly repentant. But one thing I'd learned since I'd met Ferris was never to put my full trust in him.

He was 99% psychopath and 110% perfect madness, though this time his madness had manifested into something unbelievable. "I hope you'll be able to forgive me. And to ease my way, I did something."

"What?" I asked, unsure if I should be happy or terrified.

"Do you remember my business trip right before Brax got your family back?"

I forced a smile, recalling the exact moment when he decided to give me that phone as a gift. "How could I forget?"

"Not very nice of me." He smiled back with the certainty

that he knew exactly the effect his sinful gaze had on me.

He was doing it again—casting his spell into the air so subtly that untrained senses could hardly detect it. But I knew it. I knew it all too well, and despite that, there was nothing I could do to stop it from enveloping me.

"No, it wasn't," I arched an eyebrow, climbing down from the windpipe and walking in front of him, waiting to hear what he had to say.

Though with Ferris, every step I took meant walking into another trap. The second I got next to him, he stretched his legs, then curved them back, catching my thighs between his calves and the pipe. I was his prisoner, entrapped by his body to gaze right into his onyx eyes. So devious and so undeniably seductive that he could easily be mistaken for a demon. And maybe that's exactly what he was—my personal demon, escaped from the depths of Hell to slowly torch my soul to extinction.

"You were saying something about your business trip," I had to remind him about where we left our discussion since it seemed things were alternating between me acting indifferent, to being one step away from jumping him and kissing him. I wouldn't allow myself to be that weak. Not when it came to Ferris or anyone else, although what he had to say had the power to change my heart.

"Yeah, it wasn't exactly a business trip. At least not company business." His confession suddenly saddened me, as I realized he had lied. My mind instantly made room for a thousand thoughts of how, when, and where he was spending the night in someone else's bed. I shouldn't have been jealous. I had no right to be. And if I had a single sane neuron in my brain, I should be thankful at the thought that one day someone else might take my place.

But I wasn't.

I hated all the ways he did me wrong, and altogether I

didn't want to let him go. I didn't want him to let *me* go.

"Hey, what happened?" He interrupted his *confession*, sensing my visible distress.

"Nothing. I'm peachy," I muttered, amazed at how ineffectively clumsy I was in hiding my emotions.

"Peachy?" The word amused him as he slid both palms to mold on the round curves of my ass. "Hmmm... peachy," he chuckled deliciously in my ear, brushing his lips along the nape of my neck. A second longer and our discussion would have been history, but I couldn't give in to him so easily.

"We're getting nowhere like this," I whispered as his tongue piercing slid against my skin, making every single inch of me shiver. And I did mean *every* inch.

"What are you talking about? We're getting to dessert." He was playing smart-ass on me.

"For someone who hated being out of the house, you're certainly thriving in the city." I caught his face between my palms and forced him to look at me. "Are you going to tell me?"

"Okay, I guess it's the right time for me to tell you this. Nothing can jinx it now." He took a short pause, just to get on my nerves again, but quickly continued. "During my trip, I visited someone who holds an important function in the healthcare department. Names are irrelevant. But let's just say, I pushed someone up on the transplant list."

"Sebastian?"

"Yes. He's the first choice on the list when a donor arrives," Ferris was giving me the best possible news.

"Oh my God, Ferris. I can't believe it." I closed the distance between us, throwing my arms around his neck, burying my head against his chest.

I wanted to kiss him, but it didn't seem right—not because he didn't deserve it, but because he did. For what he had accomplished, he deserved an honest kiss, while my heart was still in doubt regarding him.

"There's more—" he continued.

"More?" I asked, unsure of what *more* could be.

"Yes, I asked Alfred to talk to the board of Echo City's School of Elite. They need an education, and I will make sure they get the best one. If you agree, Nat can start next week and Seb when the doctors give their okay." Ferris was leaving me speechless. Like selecting the mute button on a remote control, I was randomly moving my lips, but without any words coming out.

I must have stayed still for a good while, trying to process all that information.

"Say something." He grinned. "Yes, no... anything."

"I have no idea what I could say. This wasn't part of our deal." Was he doing all of this without asking anything in return?

"It's not. Consider it more of a bonus for putting up with me. I know I can be more than *difficult* at times." I knew exactly what he was referring to. The moments when he crossed all the limits, racing for madness. The knife, the ledge, the toy but most of all, the moments when he was pushing my boundaries to somewhere between craving and hating him.

"I've already talked to the babysitter. She'll drive them to and from school every day. Of course, under the watchful eyes of one of my guards." Ferris cared to add that to his *miracles list*.

And I couldn't hide my shock. "You thought of everything."

"I always think about a lot of things," his tone thickened with subtexts, opening a hundred invitations to all sorts of devious possibilities.

"Such as?" I was playing the fool, only for the sake of it.

The night seemed different. He seemed different, yet somehow the same. I was seeing him in a new light. What Brax told me had something to do with it, and even though I promised myself I wouldn't mistake compassion for feelings, I was doing just that. My body was listening to my soul—or the other way around. All I knew was that my demons were hungry to play with his.

"Such as dessert." His smile spread into a full grin, casting an undeniable proposal.

A proposal I gladly accepted. "Then dessert it is."

CHAPTER 12

Searching for Ferris's hand, I let our fingers intertwine as he cupped the side of my jaw. His free hand wove through long strands of my hair, securing his grip while claiming my lips. Sorrow, regret, and uncontrollable passion were brewing to reach the surface, so strongly that the mixture was destroying me completely. I felt naked in front of his emotions, stripped of any resentment over his actions, and prepared to believe him again.

That was his spell and my curse. Every time he opened up, he was erasing all of our past and capturing me in the ephemeral moment he was painting only for us.

I knew I couldn't believe him. And despite that, I was blindingly following his lead, craving for the warmth of his lips as if it were the only thing that could keep me alive.

I couldn't believe him. I could never trust him. Still, I was doing it once again.

Through muffled groans, his hand lost itself beneath my jacket, searching for the voluptuous shape of my breasts. Things were heating up at a blinding speed, and I was losing ground with each trail of his tongue. I had to do something, anything to slow down the dynamic of the evening. I owed it to my conscience not to be swept off my feet again by the man who had guaranteed suffering written all over him.

"Dessert," I whispered, trying to stop the thoughts flooding my mind.

He quickly slid a hand inside my jeans to cup my ass, thinking I was trying to rush things. "That's what I'm getting to."

"No, Ferris. Dessert," I couldn't hold back a chuckle as I retreated so that my pussy would prevent a visit from his eager fingers.

Ferris arched an eyebrow, looking so confused it was as if he didn't actually know the true definition of the word *dessert*. "I thought you were dessert?"

"Well, I'm not. Come on." I escaped the cage of his legs and stepped back to get him to move.

"Don't tell me you were only teasing me." The disappointment in his words, combined with his unsatisfied lust, warned me I had no chance of our night not ending this way.

Just like an eager child, I stretched out my hand to grab his and pulled him from the pipe. "Then, I *won't tell you*."

"Okay... okay. Where are we going?" he asked.

"There's a donut shop nearby. I want you to have the complete experience of living in the Pit on a good day." I rushed him because the rooftop view seemed to be putting ideas into his mind.

As we walked back through the narrow lanes, Ferris didn't miss the opportunity to sneak in some feverish kisses, especially since the night's blanket was covering us in its dormant secrecy.

I admit, what he did for me and my family was pretty amazing, but it couldn't wipe the slate clean of what happened between us a few nights ago when he freaked out on me. He was bipolar and I couldn't help but fear the silent danger lurking within him.

"We're here." I squeezed his hand to stop as we reached a tiny donut shop, hidden between the outdoor grocery shelves of the other stores around.

"How could you even spot this place? I would have passed by without even noticing it existed." Ferris looked at me in surprise.

"I can smell it. The sweets these people make are amazing. Come on." I crammed him between the display shelves to get in front of the shop. "Two house specialties," I told the woman behind the counter.

"What's the house specialty?" Ferris leaned to look over the window and glanced inside at what the cashier was putting in our bag.

"The most delicious cake they have. It's made from scraps." I was about to introduce him to the best part of living in the Pit.

"Scraps?" he asked, the notion bruising his noble senses.

"Trust me on this one."

"$0.90 it's 50% off. Closing time," the woman behind the counter pointed at the clock, though I already knew that. You needed to learn all the tricks in order to survive in the streets. It was pretty much the same everywhere else. Survival of the fittest. And by now, I was capable of doing *anything* to survive.

"Thanks!" I paid the cashier, then picked up our bag.

"Do you get everything at sale prices?" Ferris laughed, probably because the word *sale* made no difference to him, something being on sale meant there was something wrong with it.

"Ferris, there were times when I couldn't even afford what was *on sale*. And I'm not talking about clothes or who knows what luxury. I'm talking about food. Everyone in the Pit lives like this, and even if, from time to time, they could afford a normal meal or something nicer, they still choose the discounted one because you never know what tomorrow brings. We don't have government allowances to live off of. Hell, we don't even have bank accounts. Most of the revenue goes undeclared anyway, so the employers won't pay taxes. No premium healthcare. In fact, no healthcare at all." It was time for me to get him down to earth.

He quickly understood how detached he was from what was really going on down in the Pit. "Sometimes I'm.... let's just say I'm spending too much time in the house."

"That's why I wanted you to come out with me today. To see the reality. Most of the people here share your pain. It may not have resulted from the same events, but their struggle is real. *This is* who I want to help. *This* is what I want to change."

"And we will. *Together.* Now, give me that bag. I'm like the fucking Cookie Monster. I need to see what's in it." Ferris didn't wait for me to take the cake out; he just snatched it straight out of the bag, "This is delicious!" The Elite's manners were replaced by the ones of a three-year-old stuffing his face.

"It's made from all the dough that is left over from when they make other cakes. They fill the dough with different flavored cream." I was letting him in on the secret recipe which wasn't so secret since the ingredients were on the price board.

"I never had a reason to get out of the house, but now... now I'm an addict." He finished eating the rest of his cake at the speed of a tornado.

"I thought I was your reason. Maybe take me out on a walk." I was teasing him.

"On a walk to get cakes, you mean?"

"You just broke my heart." I faked a pout, taking my cake out of the bag. "Here you go, Cookie Monster. Have mine since you're ditching me for a piece of dough."

"A *delicious* piece of dough. You're seriously not going to eat that?" he asked, already eating the topping.

"No. I'm not going to eat that." I caught on to his hand and rested my head against his free arm.

"That's the best thing I've heard today." He literally stuffed his face again, instantly wiping my cake from the face of the earth. "My sugar rush got the best of me." He snuck his other arm around me the instant that he was done, then signaled for a cab. "We really need to get back."

"Why? Is it curfew?" I was playing dumb.

"Something like that." He flashed a vicious grin, and as soon we got into the car, he pulled me on top of him.

Oh, it wasn't curfew by far, and the nervous twitching in his pants was letting me know it wouldn't be *curfew* for a while now.

"Hey, get a room. Don't get freaky in my cab." The driver also seemed to notice Ferris's excitement.

"This isn't your luxury limo." I chuckled, since Ferris was forgetting how things worked around here. Or possibly didn't know in the first place.

"Really?" He raised an eyebrow searching for something in his pocket. "For your trouble," he handed the driver a $100 bill.

"Hey, for an extra hundred, I'll let you rent the car for a couple of hours." The driver suddenly became extra-generous.

"No, thank you. We're good," Ferris answered him right before losing his tongue inside my mouth.

"You're so sweet," I murmured, tasting the sugar on his lips.

"And you only found out now?'" He drew his hands to cup my ass, as I was still exploring his lips.

"Do I taste strawberries?" All those cakes had left their flavor on him.

"You taste of lust and very, very dirty thoughts... and probably some strawberries."

"Dirty thoughts?" I feared his *dirty* thoughts.

"Oh, you're going to love my dirty thoughts, this time." His hand snuck inside my jeans, getting skin-on-skin with my ass.

He wasn't just warmed up. He was already boiling by the time we reached his mansion. The whole ride there he focused on exploring my lips along with every single line of my panties.

I had no idea when the cab left or even when we entered the house. I couldn't see basically anything, being completely fused with his lips. Not that I was regretting it in any way. It was like he was relighting that fire between us, and the foolish me was allowing it to burn through all our other memories. It felt so far from a task or a deal or whatever it was between us.

It felt real.

So real that my heart desperately wanted to believe it was true.

"I have to stop myself for a minute," he ghosted the words, placing me on the living room couch.

"Is everything okay?" The monsters of his past concerned me and, for an instant, I thought they had returned to haunt him.

"Everything is perfect. Trust me. I just need a minute to do something." He gave me a quick kiss goodbye, then disappeared down the hall.

I had no idea what he was planning or doing, but I couldn't deny that I felt slightly anxious about his intentions. And somehow that was bringing my feet back on the ground, alerting me to what really lurked beneath the Prince Charming attitude. It was like I was constantly fighting against being brainwashed by him, and never really succeeding in not letting that happen.

Tonight was no exception, and the seductive tone of his voice was erasing all reason once again. He could say *chair,* and the word would still sound sensual falling off his lips. *Get on that **chair**.* Just thinking of the sentence was making my skin crawl. I needed a quick reality check because I was already reeling and he wasn't even around.

"Were you daydreaming about me?" The carnal vibe of his voice almost made me fall off the couch.

How did he know exactly what I was doing? I was so busted, but I couldn't figure out what exactly sold me out. Was it my face? The tremble in my legs acknowledging his presence? Or the beat of my heart?

"You were." He threw me a smile, walking toward the couch. "Come, we're not spending the night here. Well not in this room." Taking my hand, he led me out of the living room and straight into his bedroom. "Let's change the rhythm to my own," he whispered, pushing the door open and revealing what seemed to be a scene from a movie.

The fireplace was lit, and around a hundred candles were glowing, turning the room into a beautiful ring of fire while a blues tune played in the background.

"This is for putting up with me." He whirled me around so I could fully observe the results of his effort, then pressed his lips on the top of my head.

He might have known how to break dreams, but Jesus, when it came to building them, he seemed to be unmatched. The candlelight, the champagne cooling in the icebox, and the fluttering curtains fusing the warmth of the fireplace from the cold of the night were creating pure magic. The lost paradise we both so desperately needed to hold on to.

"You do know how to impress," I barely got the words out; it felt like my voice was fading.

He let out the most charming laughter, abandoning the spot he had behind me and coming into my range of vision to take pride in his surprise. "Oh, this. I wasn't even trying."

"All of this, and I look like a bum." I ostentatiously shook my hands so he could look at my outfit—his clothes, in fact.

"I think you look amazing dressed in my clothes, but if

you have a problem with them, I suggest we get rid of your burden." His hands caught the hem of my jacket, "Let's start off with this." The coat flew onto a chair somewhere on our left while he grabbed my waist to slowly follow his lead.

"Are we dancing?" I asked, surprised that we seemed to be moving with the rhythm of the music.

"We're floating." He tugged me against him until I raised on my toes to reach his lips.

"I wasn't aware that you could go from the Cookie Monster to Don Juan."

"¿Por qué no, señora? As you can see, I can be anyone you'd like me to be. So who's next?"

Although I knew he was making fun of me, I had only one answer to give, "I want you to be yourself. To be Ferris."

Sadness replaced the sparks in his eyes. "That I can't do. I guarantee that you wouldn't like me that way."

"What if I would?" I asked, trying to let him know that I could accept him even if he was broken.

"You've seen glimpses of me and I nearly lost you over it. I don't want it to happen again. I'm doing my best to avoid it," he was confessing his deepest fears.

And I couldn't watch him suffer. "You're not the monster you describe yourself to be."

"I didn't say I am a monster. But a monster does lie inside me—and unfortunately, I'm not talking about the Cookie Monster this time. I can be both a glacier and an active volcano at the same time, Prince Charming and The Big Bad Wolf in the blink of an eye. I'm not like Brax, always determined to be made of stone, or Cole, who needs obedience and adrenaline for his world to keep functioning. I can't provide stability, except for the material one. Because, when it comes to my emotions, I don't even know what's going to happen next. I have no idea if I'll wake up wanting to rule the world or burn it to the ground. But I do know one thing. *I don't want to lose you*. I meant what I said. I want you here with me, in both my darkest and my brightest hours." He took a short pause, giving me a little space to hear the difficult part, "But I also know that I'll end up hurting you along the way."

I feared he was going to try to back down, and I wasn't going to let him go back into his shell. "What if I think it's worth it?" I asked.

"It's not. There's nothing more about me left to unveil. I'm exactly how you see me. I'm everything and nothing, emperor and slave. There isn't anything perfect hiding inside, just something perfectly broken."

"I understand. I won't try to fix you," I murmured, wrapping my arms around his broad shoulders. "But I do want my Don Juan back. I was getting into the spirit." I let out a chuckle, capturing his bottom lip to hold him hostage until he would obey my command.

It was a diversion to get him back on track, but also a diversion for me to stop the knot in my stomach from twisting and turning. I knew he was telling the truth; I just refused to believe that he was irreversibly broken. It felt like I was losing him before I even found him. But for the night I could settle with the illusion of the man he could be.

"Mmmm. I kinda hoped you would say that," he murmured against my lips while hauling my shirt over my head. "Can I have this dance, Miss?"

"And you couldn't ask me while I still had the shirt on?" I chuckled.

"It was getting in my way. These too." He unbuckled my belt—which was technically his belt—pushing the already loose pants down.

"I feel I'm at a disadvantage since you still have your clothes on." I pointed out.

"That's because you are." In a swift motion, he scooped his hands beneath my knees, lifting me in the air and high on his waist until my legs wrapped around him.

We never broke the kiss. Mostly, because I was afraid I would ask more questions again or say one of my little foolish things and shatter our spell. No, I definitely didn't want that. I needed to feel—even if it was just an illusion—anything beyond the constraint, to feel warmth, maybe even love. No matter if it was real or not.

We danced across the room—if you could call our beautiful entanglement of limbs dancing. But we had rhythm. One from the music and one within us, guiding our bodies to move one to another between candles and champagne glasses.

With a tactical dance move, he leaned his body to lay me on the bed. "Don't go anywhere." Like I ever had a chance of leaving, or a different place to go to, without him owning a piece of me.

The clink of a bottle cap captured my attention as a whiskey bottle was being opened. But that wasn't the only bottle that was coming undone. Ferris also popped a champagne bottle, filling two crystal glasses.

"Whiskey and champagne? That's an odd mix," I teased.

"I like a glass of whiskey once in a while. Champagne not so much. I just wanted to toast with you, to tonight." He clinked his glass on mine. "To the first evening in a long time that I feel free."

His words both saddened and brought me joy. I was the one who managed to free him of his burden, even if for only a couple of hours.

I never responded, just laid the glass aside, trailing my finger to search for the place where his shirt met his joggers, snaking my hands around him to glide over the length of his back.

I tried to prolong the unavoidable, but his shirt was becoming an unwanted accessory. Without too much thought, I lifted it over his head. It was like pouring gasoline on a flame, instantly raising a firestorm within the man standing in front of me. His lips were no longer joining with mine but quickly left to explore the rest of my body. A long line of warmth and metal was hovering against my skin from the base of my collarbone to the edge of my navel.

Surprisingly, my bra was still on, but the lost tongue against my belly button was making me forget about that. It was making me forget about everything, glide by glide, driven by my hushed moans. Until I thought I sensed him moving.

I wished the gesture didn't bother me, but when it came to Ferris, every second could foresee a danger. I pulled my mind away from the delirium created to see what he was doing, yet before I could figure out what was happening, he brought a lit candle on top of me.

"Ferris?" I let a startled sound out, convinced that he was going to do something that would hurt me.

"Relax. This one doesn't burn. It's a massage candle."

I had no idea what the fuck a *massage candle* was but the fire moving in Ferris's hands was alerting every one of my cells to oncoming danger. I guess he sensed that since he breathed a few words as he drove his hand to play with my aching breast. "Trust me."

He let the drops fall on my skin like hot lava tumbling off a volcano. Only the wax wasn't so lavalike. In fact, it was warming my skin, but in no way close to the point of burning. It just felt hot. A strange yet arousing sensation like my body was about to boil with a new craving.

But he was far from being done awakening my senses. He stopped for a second to take a sip out of his glass of whiskey, though that's not all he took out of the glass. I was about to discover the pleasure of fire meeting ice as his cold tongue descended to trail the path of the melted wax.

My toes instantly curved as every touch seemed to be imprinting itself within me, deeper and deeper until *he* seemed to be imprinting himself on my skin, setting each cell on fire.

I was never so conscious, and so lost at the same time. I was living only to feel the heated drops, knowing that they would be soothed by his tongue.

With patience I didn't know he possessed, he unclasped my bra, moving the candle to melt over my breasts. The power of the fluid hit differently on my silky skin, but so did the arrogance of his tongue. The moves were so precise that they were drawing moan after moan from my mouth as the cold chill overcame the burning sensation.

And then that hand. That hand that fell down my panties, roaming each nerve of my core, electrifying it with the need of him. I no longer knew how or what he was doing. Not that it mattered anymore. I just needed him to go on, over and over again until I would disintegrate into tiny pieces, and he would own them all.

I was so hot and so cold at the same time, feeling I had drunk an entire cradle of champagne all at once. Though it wasn't the alcohol that was getting me high. It was him. The king of my senses, ruling over all thoughts and flesh, lifting me higher than any mountain peak. So high that one pulse could fully break me.

I could have gone on like that for hours, with this utter intoxication of senses, but I realized that I needed something more than his touch. I needed his presence.

As if he knew that, he put the candle aside, and came towering above me. Feeling his mouth crashing on mine, my own breath ceased, my body freezing as if trying to stop time while the subtle groan from his throat was vibrating throughout me. I never was *so* ready to belong to someone, never so willing to be swept off my feet. And he did just that, slowly easing himself into that part of me that was waiting for him.

I kissed him with everything I had. Maybe the way Cole kept asking me to kiss him, but I wasn't able to because the emotion belonged to someone else. It belonged to Ferris, the way I belonged to him. Or probably only to the dream he was creating.

He was moving slowly, yet rocking my world so fiercely, burying himself deep within me with every steady thrust, and every melting kiss.

I couldn't help myself from wrapping my arms around his neck, drawing one of my legs high over his waist, clinging to him with all my strength. It was so out of my element to ever do this, but it was as if my heart refused to respond to my mind's commands.

I felt as if I was about to cry, though it wasn't only from the undeniable pleasure. I felt like crying because I was helpless in stopping time around us. I was helpless in holding him there with me. *This best version of Ferris.* The version I'd fallen in love with. Though as he said, he was made of many pieces, and when put together, he was far away from anyone I could ever love.

Undoubtedly, he was whisking me off my feet, turning me into a puddle of liquid lust, and making me melt under the shattering orgasm he was building within me.

It seemed unfair to be so powerless, to purr like a playful cat from the way one of his hands was dancing over my hardened peaks whilst his length was grinding on my inner walls. Our bodies flowed through the sheets, turning the silky linen into a stormy sea, our limbs sliding in futile attempts to keep stability. And for a short second, the world belonged to us.

This was so far from being only sex. It was giving. We were each giving ourselves to one another, finding the heaven of our own existence.

No doubt I wanted to prolong it for a lifetime, but my body was betraying all my requests. I was shaking with the chills of the upcoming ecstasy, unable to hide the panting of my breath. The tremor in my core could no longer be avoided, crashing under the power of his palms clutching somewhere on my hips.

Ferris was groaning through his elation, while I was ripping the sheet off the bed to withstand the typhoon of my release.

Maybe it was time for round two or three or four, but the night was asking something different of us. It was no longer time to spoil our bodies. It was time to try and heal as little as we could of our souls.

Without wasting a second longer, he pulled me onto his chest, wrapping an arm around my back to hold me as close as possible against him.

"It will be okay in the end." A whispered promise was evading his lips. I didn't know what end he was referring to, but I felt *the end* was much further away than either of us could ever imagine.

My eyes closed, but not really for sleeping. It was as if I was trying to take in whatever piece of him I could find, sinking against his muscled chest and bathing in his spicy cologne— anything to get *him* to stay with me for a second longer.

Anything to get him to be mine.

CHAPTER 13

I woke up with Ferris's hand playing in my hair, twisting a wandering lock between his long fingers. If it had been any normal day, I would have stayed in, losing myself between his sheets and hiding from the whole wide world for another stolen moment in this paradise. But today was 'Brunch with the Governor day', and no matter how much Ferris was trying to avoid it, I wasn't going to let him use me as an excuse to stay in bed.

"I need to get dressed and get to ECU." I turned to search for the safety of his chest, allowing myself to rest there for a few more minutes.

"Fucking brunch," he muttered from time to time, cursing the moment he agreed to be a part of my plan.

Ferris was as reluctant as I was to leave our secluded piece of heaven and face the outside world. But sweet dreams never lasted long, and ours was just about to come to an end.

"At least you can stay in bed for a little longer. I have to run before I'll be late for class." I quickly shrugged on my clothes and rushed out the door, giving him a knee-melting kiss on my way out.

Things were quieter than usual at the university. *Things* but not Cole, who seemed to be in a bad mood ever since I arrived in the hallway. "You better get your bags packed for the weekend. That fucking party is already doing my head in."

"What do you mean?" I asked, not entirely sure of what he was referring to.

Cole became increasingly agitated. "Camden has like an entire fucking list of rules to follow. And I don't follow fucking rules!"

"What kind of rules?" I questioned.

"They want to assign things to everyone so that they don't have to do anything. He thinks I'll be in charge of hiring a chef and a team to cook for us. Do I look like fucking Ratatouille?"

The comparison made me laugh, but something else amused me much more. "The insolence of these people. I don't understand what they were thinking, giving a task to someone of your caliber. Tasks are for staff, not for kings." I had to admit it was pretty funny that a living breathing soul could consider itself more important than Cole.

Though I was beginning to think that Cole didn't find it funny at all. "You dare patronize me because of a bunch of idiots?"

"*Dare?*" I retorted. *Did he really consider me his puppet?* I wanted to give him a piece of my mind, but Jenna's presence at the other end of the hallway made me reconsider my reactions. I could pay the price for my mutiny, but I wasn't going to let my friend pay for my actions.

"Do you have a problem regarding my authority, Mouse?" His words were so crisp I knew they could bring nothing but trouble. And trouble it was since he jerked me to stand by his side and claim the role of his loving girlfriend again.

"Do you get a kick out of forcing me to be your girlfriend, or whatever you consider me to be?" I snapped.

"I get a kick out of torturing you." He slid his hand up to cup one of my breasts through the material of my shirt.

"Are you insane? Everyone is watching us." I tried pushing him away, without any sort of result.

"That's exactly what I want." He only squeezed his hand tighter. "Those shivers of embarrassment and fear. The way your body stiffens against me."

I tried to shake him off, but the harder I struggled, the harder his grip became. I was trapped in front of a live audience that was witnessing the complete display of my misery as all my anxieties were transforming into a full-on panic attack.

Maybe out of madness or desperation, I did the only thing that came to mind. I raised my lips to claim his, hoping my sudden obedience would help him calm down.

That was hardly the case. He caught on to my game before it even began. "You're that desperate, huh?" His tone fueled by my agony, while I felt I was drowning under every gaze pointing at me.

He didn't let go. How could he? Just captured my bottom lip against his own, keeping me glued to his face as his fingers were spreading to cup the whole of my breast. "They all want to be you, my Queen B."

"Then choose one and leave me the fuck alone," I snapped back, finally managing to detach myself from his grip.

I didn't look back. I didn't even care who or why anyone was watching anymore. Just walked straight into the courtyard, trying somehow to calm down.

The gym's brick wall served as my support and cover, as I pressed my body weight against it. My nerves seemed

185

to be stretched to the limit. Not that I cared about public humiliation anymore. I was so much more concerned about Cole's deviant behavior, about the need to constantly prove himself. The Herd and everyone else saw him as a god. And, in some way, I knew he was right—they also saw me as his queen. Their gazes were full of lust or jealousy, not one repulsed or shocked that he was publicly claiming control of my breasts.

Maybe I was the one messed-up, hanging on to some moral values that didn't even exist. And if I had any doubt that morality was becoming extinct, the man who appeared in front of my eyes convinced me of it. Thomas just passed me on the left, probably rushing to classes. Nothing out of the ordinary about that, but judging by the new set of clothes and modern sneakers he had on, Brax had probably paid him a visit at my request.

So much for ideals.

Then it only meant I was the one seeing things wrong. Morality wasn't a must anymore, and I was learning it the hard way.

***

It was Seb's treatment day, so until Ferris's promise could come through, I still needed to take him to the hospital. That was cutting my school day short, and also the time spent with Cole. Not that I was complaining about that.

The day followed its usual routine from there on. Hospital, dinner, then back to Ferris's place. I needed to know how the governor's brunch went, and it wasn't something we could talk about over the phone.

Strangely, I heard music as soon as my limo was passing through the Ayers' estate front gates. Loud music, as if someone was having a party. It couldn't be Ferris, that was for sure.

Following the sound, I discovered it didn't come from the

main house. It was coming from somewhere in the garden. As I approached, I realized something was going on at the guesthouse. All the lights were on and twenty-something cars parked outside confirmed it was indeed a party.

Cole and Brax couldn't have been too far away; neither of them would miss such an event, especially since I reunited their *dream* team. Lucky me.

My first instinct was to turn and leave the estate. But the chances of getting a call or a text from one of the kings, even before I reached my place, were too high to even bother with an escape plan.

Pushing the door open, I entered the main room, to find the current king of ECU lazily lying on a couch with a bottle of whiskey in his hand and three bimbos almost throwing themselves at him.

The scene had Cole written all over it—the welcoming image and the party.

"What's going on here?" I asked, still finding it hard to believe that Ferris had agreed to throw a party.

"What does it look like?" Cole asked, casually taking a sip from the bottle of whiskey while one of his bimbos was laughing at the way he was defying me.

"It looks like you're entertaining yourself a little too much," I muttered with an annoyance I didn't want. Yet there it was. Some stupid jealousy of him belonging to me when things couldn't be further from the truth.

"You told me earlier to choose one. I just couldn't decide," he shrugged, looking at the three girls who were sitting next to him. I knew he was doing it on purpose, to hurt me, and against my every attempt to prevent it, he was succeeding.

"Where's Ferris?" I continued with unhindered discomfort. I was determined to find out what Ferris did today, then make up some excuse, and leave.

"Were you looking for me?" Before Cole got a chance to

answer, Ferris's arms wrapped around my waist from behind while his lips melted against my neck.

I immediately froze, knowing Cole was looking straight at us, although he seemed much more excited than jealous. Then I realized I was the jealous one, watching his hand rest ostentatiously on one of the girl's thighs, as if placed there specifically for me to see.

I just couldn't be here any longer, so I turned to find Ferris's lips into a kiss. "Yes, I was looking for you. Let's get out of here."

He didn't wait for any more requests. Taking my hand, he guided me through a black wooden door into a secondary living room. The place was similar to the rooms at the main house. The same gothic elements. The same mesmerizing fireplace, bringing the space to life with its flames.

With his hands running up and down my dress, Ferris didn't get the memo that I was looking more for a debriefing than a hookup. I had no idea what got him so turned on so quickly, but I was beginning to think the vodka taste on his lips had something to do with it.

"What did you do with the governor today?" I asked as he lifted me onto his waist and placed me back on the edge of the couch's backrest.

"Who cares right now?" The rest of the world held no importance when it came to his needs.

There was something utterly wrong with the evening, and I was just about to find out how *incredibly wrong* it was. "I want you." He bit my lower lip so passionately that I immediately recognized there was no escape from his desires.

On a normal day, his words might have sounded flattering, even arousing, but the pitch-black darkness in his eyes, for some reason, made me fear it.

"I want to have you on my balcony." I was right. I had every reason to fear him as his monsters came out to play.

The balcony, the railing, the knife—flashbacks flooded my

mind, making me jump from the couch and take a few steps away from him.

"Ferris, are you okay?" I stuttered, glancing at the irritation growing in his gaze. I was saying no to him without actually saying it, leaving my actions to replace any words.

"Do I not look ok?" He took a step in my direction with that specific madness scribbled on each one of his facial expressions. And that was terrifying.

"Am I interrupting something?" Brax's familiar voice was bringing me my salvation as he just entered the room somewhere from another door behind me.

"No. We're good," Ferris grumbled, looking at me as if I had an unpaid policy with him.

"Since I'm not *interrupting* anything, I came here to learn what you did today. I didn't really get a chance to ask you earlier with Cole doing my head in with his party and everyone coming in." Indeed, Brax probably wanted to know how Ferris handled things today, but there was something more going on. He caught a glimpse of the madness trying to surface and I'm not sure if he was trying to prevent it or control it.

Ferris took a seat on the couch, preparing for Brax's questioning, "I didn't get much. But he asked me for funding. For a special project, he said. Not too much info though."

"When are you meeting him again?" Brax took his role seriously.

"Next Wednesday. He said it's an urgent matter. I think he wants to convince me to fund some of his actions. Give him enough money to hire mercenaries," Ferris answered.

"Perfect. Stall the payment, and see if you can get more info out of him. Dates, contractors, affiliates. Whatever you can find out." We were in desperate need of information and Brax was perfectly aware of that. We needed to start somewhere, we just didn't know where yet.

"What if we don't get anything on the governor? Any info

to bring him down," I ask Brax, trying to see where we could go from here.

"Then we'll have to set him a trap. Invent something. If it was up to me, I'd show up to your meeting spot and kill him myself. But you'd only go on and on with that making him a martyr shit," Brax muttered.

"I think you've done enough killing." The sentence involuntarily slipped my mouth.

"What is she talking about?" Ferris's interest piqued.

I had just fucked up big time. So big that I didn't even dare to think of the consequences.

"Will you tell him how we met? Or will I?" Brax shot me the most pissed-off look I'd ever seen.

"I....I—," I stammered, lost for words, so lost that I had no idea what I was doing or saying anymore. My temper got the best of me again, though this time it managed to bring the *criminal* to light.

"Come," Brax gestured for me to join him, but my feet could hardly move to obey his command. With agonizing steps, I found a place next to him, my body shaking so fiercely that I thought something in me was about to break.

"I did it, Ferris. I paid my debt. I killed Benjamin West, the man who murdered your parents." Brax's confession seemed to petrify Ferris on the sofa. Not a single word came from his lips or any kind of other gesture that could betray a reaction.

It was as if the news left him cold; dead-cold.

"I avenged them." Brax was looking directly into Ferris's eyes as he pulled me against his chest with one hand. "And this fox was my cover that night. Although I see she's unable to keep her little mouth shut."

To my surprise, Brax shifted his focus away from Ferris, probably giving him time to adjust. But that was no longer my main problem. My problem was that all of Brax's attention was now dedicated to *me.*

"You really need to learn who is in charge here. You never know when to keep quiet and when to speak." Brax's hand stopped somewhere on my throat and despite the visible discomfort he was in, caused by his wound, he was choking the breath out of me.

"What the fuck did she do to you two?" Cole's voice filled the room. He must've just walked in.

Great. I had all three of them pissed off at me now. Maybe I was the one who was screwing things up after all.

"This mouth of hers is going to put her in an early grave someday," Brax growled, his grip tightening so strongly that even he had trouble sustaining the effort.

Luckily, his savior was on the way.

Cole came from behind me, replacing Brax's hand around my neck with his, snaking his other arm around my waist, gluing me to his crotch. "I can feel your heart beating so loudly that it turns me on," Cole's mouth descended to trail a warm line along my neck, in his sadistic ritual to claim supremacy over my body.

"What the fuck did she do to you?" Brax asked with curiosity.

I could hear Cole take a deep breath as if answering this question took a considerable amount of effort out of him. "She told me I could choose whoever I want to replace her, and then she comes in here and almost throws a fucking tantrum."

I don't say a word to defend myself, mostly because Cole is telling the truth.

"But don't worry, Mouse. We only want you." His tongue slid upwards claiming my earlobe as he spoke.

We?

What the fuck was *we* supposed to mean?

I didn't ask out loud. Nor did I have to, because the answer I dreaded came much faster than I was expecting.

"Let's give her a little lesson in obedience," Brax growled as Cole's hand tightened around my waist.

"You need to know who owns you and absolutely everything else related to you, including the stupid shit that comes out of that mouth of yours," Brax was giving me a direct threat, though not entirely one made out of words. Between the pounding in my head and the trembling in my stomach, I felt a hand playing with the hem of my dress—Brax's hand, judging by the determined fingers that were quickly ascending on my inner thigh.

"Stop it," I whined, feeling Cole's heavy breathing crushing on the column of my neck while the beautiful emerald color in Brax's eyes was turning so dark that I could barely distinguish the green.

Oh God, I almost forgot about Ferris being in the room. My breath hitched at the thought, and as I turned my head to look at him, my worst fears came true. He was in the exact same position, maybe even calmer than before, closely observing the revenge the other two kings were plotting against me. And doing nothing to stop them.

"It's not funny, Brax," I ground out the words, feeling his fingers already reaching the line of my panties. Though by the look on their faces, they didn't find it in any way amusing either. They found it arousing.

"I can do whatever I want with you, remember? We have a deal," my king of the underworld reminded me, as if any of them would let me forget about it, even for a second.

I knew both Cole and Brax weren't shy about a little public exposure, but this crossed the line. "In your house or a bedroom. Not *here!*"

"Here," Brax answered just as *here* was beginning to have a double meaning. His fingers just shifted to beneath my panties, searching for the dampness of my core.

"Brax, please," I murmured with a last hope that I'd get him to back down. But I knew he wasn't going to stop. He wanted my cries. He needed my cries of ecstasy to assert complete validation of his dominating power.

"You need to learn that every action has a consequence. That whenever you do or say something that goes against us, you will be taught a lesson," Cole was whispering in my ear as his hand kept tightening over my neck, his grip bringing my head a little upwards, forcing me to glance straight at Brax's satisfied gaze.

"But you know what, Mouse?" Cole continued his *speech* into my ear, "I hope it takes you a long time to learn this." He was living for every hitched whimper, for every second in which my embarrassment was becoming a reality. I could see it in his every gesture.

I was so angry at them for playing with me as if I were only a toy to keep them distracted. But most of all, I was angry with myself, of the way Brax's hand was slipping against my skin, gliding through on the signs of my own excitement. I had no power of control over my body once again, and I didn't escape without a remark from King Brax. "I'm starting to think you were waiting for us."

I snapped. "Like I wait for my death."

"Now don't get dramatic on us. Better do yourself a favor and spread them." Without waiting for a reaction from me, he pressed a hand between my thighs, forcing them to open and sliding two of his fingers inside my core. The sensation took me by surprise, drawing my posterior to arch from the thrust, crushing against the shape of Cole's hardened member that was threatening to break through his jeans. The encounter made me shift forward again, only to meet the velocity of Brax's fingers, driving inside me over and over again. I hated all of them to the point I wanted to be the one locking them in the Pit and throwing away the key. But there was something more than hate teasing me—the adrenaline, the lust, the testosterone floating in the room, breaking through my skin and infiltrating my veins. Their excitement was somehow transferring to me, awakening some fucked-up sense; a devious illusion that I could own them all, and not the other way around. A little surreal considering my position, imprisoned by Cole's cage of muscles, tortured by Brax's wicked desires, and overlooked by Ferris's demonic gaze.

They all wanted the same thing from me—to see me suffer, yet at the same time to see me addicted to each one of them, to crave for their presence and their touch. *To become a junkie as they would become my drug.*

I tried once again to get away from Cole's grip, uniting my knees to stop Brax from going forward with his game.

"Stop fussing, Bea. Or are you too afraid of what my touch is doing to you?" Brax was just speaking out my thoughts, expressing my deepest fears, and multiplying the humiliation they were subjecting me to. It was a game of uncontained lust and sinful needs where rules didn't apply as long as the goal was achieved.

"You're close," Brax whispered, getting a rush out of the way I was trying to reject any sign of elation. Yet it was almost impossible for me to keep composed. His masterfully trained fingers knew all my weaknesses, attacking each one of my weak spots to get me to crash against him.

"Ferris!" Cole called for him. I wasn't sure if it was to request his presence or to make sure he was okay.

"Go on, I'm fine here. It kind of reminds me of the old days," Ferris let out a soft chuckle, keeping his place on the couch.

I was expecting to sense at least a hint of jealousy in his voice, but he seemed to enjoy the show his friends were putting on. The feeling must have transported him into the past, finding a part of the old Ferris. A part that I didn't want to meet.

"This is better than the old days," Brax snarled through gritted teeth as he was grinding so possessively into me that my body was curving into a ball, unable to withstand the rippling surge of ecstasy flowing throughout me.

"It *is* better." Ferris curved the corner of his lips into a dangerous smile as I understood exactly what he was referring to. I wasn't a bimbo or one of their whores. I was the good girl who was breaking all morality to become a willing prisoner in their devious game.

"I can't wait for your punishment the next time you disobey one of us." Cole slowly bit on my neck to mark his presence on my body, probably giving me the biggest hickey of my life.

I could barely stand as Brax was stroking his fingers over the last flickers of my orgasm, bringing everything I ever thought of them to a whole new level. I genuinely feared them now, and Cole's threat seemed more real than ever. He obviously had a plan for my next slip-up, and that was exactly what was forcing me to assure myself there wouldn't be a *next time.*

I really needed to hold back the *fuck you* and *drop-dead* greetings.

"I think she will *want* to defy us. Won't you, Bea?" Brax grinned, pulling his hand from beneath my dress, then rearranging the fabric, as if nothing had happened.

I couldn't answer. Not in a civilized manner anyway. Just flared my nostrils, and the second Cole loosened his grip, I stormed out the door.

"Don't go off too far. The party isn't over yet!" Cole called after me as I was determined to walk straight back to the limo.

The party wasn't over for me and that only meant one thing—my torment wasn't over either.

Just fucking great!

CHAPTER 14

I stormed out of the room, while my kings' precise instructions still resounded in my mind—I couldn't leave the party. Not without further consequences. That meant I had at least five or six hours in which I needed to mingle between the wolves while my kings played alpha male.

Deep down, I loathed my body for craving more, for crying after their touch, dreaming of the consuming flames that only they can create.

And that feeling. That cursed feeling that everyone knew what I had done.

What they had done.

That feeling almost made me throw up, not because I attracted their wrath. But because I allowed myself to enjoy it.

With shaking hands, I poured a glass of whatever alcohol I could find, forcing myself to down its contents in just a few sips. I didn't even know what it was. Gin, vodka, anything to numb my senses. Just needed something to clear my mind and switch off even for a nanosecond. Something that would help me part with reality.

Cole, Brax, and Ferris left the room one by one, losing themselves amongst the crowd while I was trying to stay as far from them as possible. There was no party mood left in me anymore. Not sure there was much of a party mood to begin with, but being forced to attend the gathering of stuck-up students was making the music sound like scratching on my eardrums. And if I found that annoying, the company that kept stumbling to me was horrific. The unending praise of every piece of clothing I was wearing and every lock of hair styled to perfection were doing my head in. Then there were the countless drama queens going on and on gossiping about people I didn't even know and I didn't want to hear about.

At least no male presence was around to hit on me or try to buy me a drink from the free bar. I guessed my three protectors had something to do with that. Strangely enough, they weren't with any female company either. Not even Cole or Brax, who I expected to have two or three tramps hanging around their necks halfway through the night. It was like the rule applied both ways. No one could touch me, and no one was allowed to touch them either. At least not from now on.

I think I was on my second glass—not that I could even count to two after the first one anyway—when the air in the room got nearly suffocating. The smoke from cigars or the heavy perfume had nothing to do with it. Just my three demons, always watching over me.

I needed some air and the cold atmosphere outside could bring me back to my senses in no time. The trouble was how the hell was I supposed to even walk outside when everything around me was slowly spinning?

After a few calculations on how to get from point A to point B, avoiding point C, I found my courage, and the moment I spotted a straight corridor I began pacing toward the front door. I was a soldier on a mission, finding the only free path to pass while dodging the bullets. Or in my case, the people, because I wasn't sure that if someone were to walk in front of me, I would still have the time to avoid them and not to walk straight through them.

Mission accomplished. My stiffened legs managed somehow to carry me to the garden, making the freezing temperature wake me back to my senses. I had sobered up in just a few minutes, but despite the shivering in my legs and the thin dress I had on, I didn't want to go back. At least not straight away. I needed a little time by myself before returning to be their slave.

With unsteady steps, I walked around the guesthouse, and into the back garden, where nobody seemed to be around. One of the sunbeds seemed to be calling my name. Weird to see sunbeds outside when we couldn't really see the sun, but I could never underestimate Ferris. It seemed even the yellow orb was empowered from time to time to shine for him.

I watched the party inside through a large glass window. The laughter, the clinking glasses, the phoniness of it all— those people were all a part of my kings' world.

And so was I.

Maybe it was time to admit it, or at least accept it somehow. But I had to do it on my terms, not be forced or constricted by the will of my *gods.*

I kept delaying the moment I would return. Kept telling myself *after this song,* though I would find myself halfway through the next melody just repeating the *after this song* again. However, it was getting late, and I didn't want to pay the price for defying a direct order again.

I was finally just about to stand up and leave when a set of footsteps caught my attention.

"It wouldn't be fair of you to freeze to death. How would you keep your part of the deal if you were six feet under?" It was Brax who spoke. He, out of all the kings, was the one who came looking for me in the garden.

"It's not that cold." I—the-purple-lipped-girl—answered through chattering teeth.

"I brought an extra jacket. But I'm just going to hold on to it if you don't need to keep warm." As always, Brax knew how to prey on my weaknesses But I would have rather frozen to death than ask him for the coat.

Luckily, that was not the case, since just after a few seconds of blankly staring at each other, he walked right next to my sunbed. "Not entirely sure if you're trying to catch a tan from the outside lamp or pneumonia, but you should put this on." He wrapped the jacket around my shoulders while I was trying to understand why exactly he was doing it.

It didn't take me long before I got a clue as to his newfound kindness. Once he had set aside the jacket he had been holding, a whiskey bottle came into view. By the looks of it, this had been his companion throughout the night.

I wasn't going for the *stop drinking* lecture since I knew it would have no impact on him. On the contrary, it would probably just awaken his temper again. And I couldn't handle an annoyed Brax for the second time tonight.

"What are you doing outside? I thought Cole told you to stay at the party?" he asked.

"I haven't left. Have I? I just needed a breath of fresh air." I was lousy at hiding my anger.

"You've been outside for more than an hour. That's a little bit more than a breath," Brax cared to observe.

While I caught on to his plan. "Well, you brought a jacket. So, you weren't really planning on taking me back inside were you?"

"You have a point." He admitted I had caught him at his own game.

But I needed more than just some dry confession, "So, why's that? Why don't you want me to go back?"

"Maybe I'm not ready to share you tonight," he said, his absinthe eyes pointing at me.

"I think it's already too late for that, Brax," I muttered, turning my back on him. I wished my words would have done the trick, and gotten him to leave me alone. But his heavy steps as he walked around the sunbed to be in my line of sight again convinced me of the opposite. I was about to get hell for disrespecting him again. I needed an imaginary slap on the face for giving in to my impulses and talking back to him.

"Do you regret it?" His tone, much more casual than I expected. Was he really asking *that* question? Did he think I wanted to be their toy of the night?

"Regret? I don't think I'm the one who has something to regret. I didn't enjoy it either—if that's what you were really asking," I snapped.

"That's not what I saw from where I was standing." His arrogance was blazing straight at me while I continued to curse the betrayal of my own body.

I needed to diminish the importance of what happened, in his eyes and also in mine. "What you saw was a physical reaction to an external stimulus. Bodily anatomy, no feelings whatsoever."

"No *feelings*. Right. People don't have feelings for

murderers. Do they?" I couldn't tell if there was a hint of self-pity or disappointment lurking in his voice, but after what I'd learned tonight, he wasn't a killer in my eyes.

He was the one who avenged an injustice.

The one closing a circle.

And it was time to let him know that. "I'm not sure how many others you've killed, but if you're referring to the night of the party, you're not a murderer. You were just a loyal man seeking justice for his friend. I do hope you also found the power to forgive yourself for your father's mistakes. Not that you were the one to be blamed for them in the first place."

"What the fuck do you see in me, Bea?" He asked, taking a large sip from the bottle as if trying to drown everything that I said into the brownish liqueur.

"I see a great man. A loyal friend to both Ferris and Cole. But I also see a man incapable of managing his feelings." I was giving him my honest opinion.

"The feelings I have for you?" His question came like a bullet to the heart.

"You don't have feelings for me." My eyes became as cold as my voice while I spoke the words. Maybe it was an obsession, an ambition to make me his, but definitely no feelings. Although the look in his eyes that replaced any verbal answer was making me doubt my words.

A few more sips of whiskey went down his throat, as if gathering courage for what he had to say. Even though Brax was a man who definitely didn't lack courage.

I was looking. No, not looking, *staring* at the green in his eyes as it was slowly disappearing, letting his sight narrow to watch over me from the depths of his soul. The image frightened me, giving everything such a real note that I was beginning to wonder just who the man standing in front of me was. "You think your pussy is so special that I would've risked my life for it?"

His question made something shudder within me. It made everything insanely real. Like he was admitting to one of my deepest desires. Desires that in our world had no chance of ever becoming true.

The whiskey bottle clutched in his hand led me to believe that it was the drink freeing his tongue. A hallucination of exaggerated emotions, and not by any chance a moment of bravery to disclose what could secretly rest in his heart.

"I think your need to own *things*, to collect them is so special to you that you would risk your life for them. The need for no one saying *no* to you."

"Is that what you *need* to believe in order so that you can carry through with your end of the deal?" Such truth in his question.

Yes. That was what I needed so I could go on.

I thought if I could get him to care even a little, it would make things easier for me. But now, the hint of a confession was making everything a thousand times more complicated.

"Yes, that's what I believe." I couldn't let him see the uncertainty in my soul. "You wouldn't have touched me with Ferris and Cole being present if I wasn't more than just a piece of *pussy* to you."

"You really don't get it, do you? I didn't do that to embarrass you. Sure, that torment in your eyes turned me on, but I did it so that you would realize I *don't mind sharing when it comes to Cole or Ferris!* It wasn't a bluff. The punishment was just an excuse. I did it so that you'd understand that you like it, even if you won't admit it."

"Are you done?" I suddenly stood up, preparing to leave.

I wasn't going to listen to him putting words in my head. My body probably liked it, but my conscience didn't.

"No. I'm not fucking done with you, Bea. I don't know when the fuck I'll be able to be done with you." The anger in his words made me stop and glare straight at his feral expression, which was uselessly trying to mask his fear. He was afraid of what he was letting come to light. Afraid, yet unable to stop it.

"I don't want anyone else," he ghosted the words, sending them to slip somewhere so deep in my heart that nothing could ever take them away.

"You're drunk," my own words came out, almost choked.

"Maybe I am, but that doesn't mean I'm not telling the truth." Keeping the bottle in his hand, he snuck his arm behind my waist, crushing me against him.

"What... what are you doing?" I stuttered, worried about what the impact could have on his wound.

"I don't know what the fuck I'm doing anymore." Suddenly sealing his lips to mine in a tortuous kiss, letting himself fall back, and taking me along with him into the heated water of the swimming pool.

We sank to the bottom, then slowly found our way to the surface, never detaching our lips. It was like we needed each other more than the air from above the water, pulsing our tongues to suffice a need that could never be fully fulfilled. It felt as though we just found each other, and I was struggling to fight off the pain of knowing we were about to lose ourselves again, living in the moment, with the looming certainty of saying goodbye.

And I couldn't. I couldn't handle such pain, of having him,

then being forced to let go. Because I knew *he would never let me stay.* Not the way I would want to, anyway. Not close to his heart.

Yes, we could probably own each other's bodies, but never what I craved—his love.

I had to go. At least for the night. I had to go before it would be too late. Before I would let him break me.

"Brax...," I whispered almost in a moan, trying to separate myself from his grip.

"Don't... don't go." He covered my mouth again with his, guiding us to the edge of the swimming pool. But not to get out. Just to catch me prisoner between the mosaic tiles and his chest.

His lips never stopped, urging through groans of despair mixed with lust. He was setting all fears free, living just for the moment of *us together.*

"You can't do this to me, Brax," I begged.

"I can't stop it either." His lips moved harder, more passionately, with the intensity of a wild storm. It wasn't about sex. I didn't even care about that anymore. It was about the need to stop him from claiming the last part of me he didn't already own. It was about me trying to survive, and him drowning me in frenzied kisses until his scent was infiltrating my lungs.

In all the storms of passion plunging upon us, Brax stopped for a second to place the bottle that never left his hand on the edge of the swimming pool. A reminder that he was drunk.

"Brax?"

"Yes, baby."

"You're drunk."

"Maybe I am, but nothing about this moment is any less real." He caught my bottom lip between his own, "I want you. I want you so fucking bad, I can't even control myself."

I couldn't stop a gasp, acknowledging that what he said was true. I'd seen it in his gaze before. The viciously cruel mask he puts on every single time he knew I was looking. And the anguished torment reflected in his eyes when he knew I wasn't.

We kissed until our lips began to feel sore, and all lights seemed to be fading, letting our moment of ardent passion lose itself beneath the steam rising from the pool.

Unable to hold on to any sense of morality or self-preservation, my legs wrapped around his waist, asking for him to own me again. He was so right. He wasn't fucking done with me. Far from it. And I was accepting that with each one of my stumbling sips of air.

He slowly pushed the cups of my dress down, but stopped as if asking for permission. So strange yet almost heartwarming for him to do that.

I didn't say either no or yes, just let my head fall back, eagerly awaiting his lips to merge with my breasts. And he didn't waste any time listening to my desire. With uncontained hunger, he claimed my nipples, rolling his tongue over the hardened nubs as.

"I want you... I *want* you," he groaned. His request was making me wetter than the water in the pool, driving his hands to replace his lips as he lowered me slowly to welcome him inside of me.

"Oh, God!" I mewled, stretching to accommodate his arousal, feeling him so large that I feared he would make something tear.

"God is so far away from here now," he growled, driving himself gently, yet incredibly deep inside my core.

I arched, ready to renounce myself in whatever game he was playing, but a simple request changed everything, "Stay with me." I was to remain here, not wasting a single second drifting away to paradise. Just living there with him, in the heaven he was creating.

He never let me lose myself, making sure I knew exactly what was happening to me—so real that his touch seemed to be intensified a thousand times.

His thrusts found a rhythm that was awakening each one of my senses, building them up with a master craftsman's skill to a rapturous feeling and getting my legs to fully wrap around his, drawing him even deeper within me. I couldn't get enough of Brax, no matter how hard I tried. His kisses weren't enough, his hands holding me to him, weren't enough, his thrusts aiming for the pit of my stomach weren't enough to still my undying need for him.

I needed every breath of air he had to give. Every second of raw truth, because I feared the moment he would claim back his mask, and sink into the lie he was mastering so well.

I tried avoiding the unavoidable for as long as I could, but tension bundled his shoulders as he focused to turn the storm against me, firm and steady, building it with each new thrust within me.

I couldn't control the rising pressure in the pit of my stomach anymore. With a long gasp, I almost fell upon him as he kept going over and over again. My back was slowly banging against the mosaic tiles in a fluid reaction of our bodies intertwining as his name was rolling on repeat from my lips. "Brax....Brax..."

I didn't know any longer if I was asking him to go on or stop. I wanted more, but I couldn't handle another single thrust. The claustrophobic panic was setting in, assuring me that I might break from within if he went on.

With beautiful rapture pulsing off my lips, I pleaded for his release. And for the first time, he understood.

Steadying himself against the rim, he jolted a couple of times more until another uncontrollable squeak was freed from my throat. It was the sign he needed. Fighting the urge to go on, he drove his lips to claim my shoulder, and found the electrifying jolts of his own relief.

I was expecting him to leave immediately, find some shit excuse, and bolt right away the next second. But he didn't. Brax remained there with me, tugging my body against his own and without words, promising me the impossible.

It was so beautiful that I almost believed it. I almost believed I could be happy. Until I saw it—the reflection that made my stomach churn, and my mind teeter to the edge of normality. The lights in the house were out by now, the party must have died down. But through the dark windows peering right into our part of the garden, a pair of eyes was watching us.

"Ferris?" I uttered, breaking our embrace, setting distance as if Brax was about to burn me with his heat.

Brax still seemed relaxed, but much more down-to-earth than a few seconds before. It wasn't a question whether Ferris saw us or not. It was only a question of how much he saw.

"I can't," I almost choked on my words as I climbed out of the pool, looking back at all I was leaving behind.

No mean remark from Brax this time, like he usually let out. He just remained, supporting his body on the edge of the pool, and drawing the whiskey bottle to his lips to keep him company.

I ran straight to the car, my wet clothes almost frozen by the time I got there. That wasn't even important anymore. "Home, please," I asked the driver as my head fell on the backrest. Brax was there again, living in my memories. Focusing only on me. As if only *I* could ever get him into a state of total freedom. And that look in his eyes. Nothing could ever erase that look from my mind. He etched it there for me to remember what to be loved by a man like him felt like.

CHAPTER 15

I felt as if I was in heaven only to be immediately sent to my personal hell. Ferris's gaze kept haunting me, and at the same time, Brax's lips still felt vivid on my skin. That was how I spent my night, continually fighting between nightmares and sweet dreams. Not that I didn't deserve it. I did. I had wronged them both and the time to pay the price was approaching quickly.

The next day brought nothing special. Cole missed classes, probably too wasted from last night's party. I couldn't be more overjoyed about the lack of his presence. I even snuck a few words in with Jenna, trying to explain the delicate situation we both found ourselves in. But I couldn't spend too much time in her company because I was convinced Cole had Nick or Jason watching over me.

It was a day I would have rather spent at home, but the urgent matters of the world were pressing me to return to Ferris's place, as much as I would have liked to avoid it. Cole and I were supposed to go to that out-of-town party the next day. And honestly, between being constantly caged up and haunted by them, I didn't have time to find out anything about the event. Luckily, Cole stepped in, and even before I managed to get home, had sent me a text.

Meetup at Ferris's tonight.

I was going to wear pants this time for sure.

Dinner with family followed by another dose of daily torture. You would think I would've gotten used to it by now, and just accepted my fate. But that's what quitters do. And I couldn't be a quitter at a time like this.

I had a spirit within me. One that, though often defeated, was never broken. A strength that made me find success in every challenge.

I have no fears. I repeated in my mind over and over again as I walked into Ferris's mansion, to the point that I was sure I had succeeded in imprinting the words on my brain. The words maybe, but not their meaning. Fear began creeping in as I approached the room the guys were in.

Brax was running late, again. Strange for the man who puts such value on time, but I was starting to think he just enjoyed torturing me about being late myself.

"Hi," I wiggled a few shy fingers for them to acknowledge my presence, but then quickly retreated to the furthest corner of the room.

"Anything new at school?" Cole asked from the couch, while he and Ferris were busy saving the world on the PlayStation.

"Your parking spot was free, if that's what you're asking." I shrugged, knowing that I would annoy him again, but still, unable to stop myself from doing it. "You still have your crown, don't worry."

"The university could burn down and I would still have my crown. I wasn't worried about that. You're the one who should be worried—about the weekend." It sounded like a warning coming from Cole.

"Why's that?" I asked, waiting to get more info out of him.

"We're walking into unknown territory. Or maybe a too

familiar one." He let out loud laughter, although I wasn't exactly sure what he was implying. But I had a bad feeling I was going to find out soon enough.

"Do you want me to call Alfred to fetch you a drink?" Ferris asked out of his typical practiced politeness, too caught up in his ammunition quest in the game.

I didn't need Alfred to come up from twenty rooms away just to pour me a drink from one of the bottles next to me. I may not have been royal, but at least, I was acting decently. "No, thanks. I have hands of my own."

"Suit yourself," Ferris said without catching the irony in my voice. He was far too focused on saving the world from zombies.

So much for *the planning* to save the real world for the night. Not that I minded. I just sank into a seat and waited for Brax to arrive. My heart was pounding in my ears at the thought of seeing him. I was excited, and at the same time worried about what the new day might bring.

And as if all fears had come true, the man who stepped into the room was the old Brax. *We* never existed. He ignored me completely, striding over to the couch to break the guys' game. "Bang. You're out." He turned off their screens right when they were about to free a city from the walking dead.

I hoped that wouldn't happen in the real world, too.

"Fuck off," Cole muttered, throwing his controller across the room. "You're fucking evil, man!"

"And your brain is the size of a walnut. Leave the fucking games for later. I'm here to talk business. Something regarding your best interest," Brax snapped as he walked toward an armchair.

"We had like two fucking minutes left in the game. Couldn't it wait?" Ferris didn't seem pleased with the interruption either. Still, he rose from the sofa to get Brax a drink. "Here. Just because you're crippled." He extended him a whiskey glass.

"I'm not fucking crippled," Brax snarled with a hint of amusement in his tone, "Just momentarily restricted in my actions."

"You didn't look *restricted* last night," Cole began laughing.

Shit. Did he also see us in the swimming pool?

I think I must've turned fiery red under Brax's cutting gaze.

"Do you want to hear what I fucking have to say, or not?" My king of the underworld was almost losing his patience with Cole. The other night was definitely becoming a taboo subject for him.

"Why you so tense, man? Chill." Cole shrugged, making Brax realize he was overreacting about something that, to them, shouldn't have a special meaning.

"Just don't test my patience, okay?" Brax was softening up, unwilling to let his secret out.

And Cole quickly understood not to insist. "I didn't know you were stressed out. I'm paying attention. What's this all about?"

"About me doing the math and erasing some debts." Brax pulled out his phone to check something.

"Debts?" Cole asked.

"Yeah. From a certain gambler. I know your father didn't lose money only in my casinos, but the ones that ended up in my bank accounts were just transferred back to you. I don't trust your father not to gamble again. It's enough to get back to your old lifestyle. My accountant just texted me that it's done." Brax was being extra generous.

But Cole didn't seem to agree, "I don't want your pity."

"Who said anything about pity? I expect the money back, with interest, when the time is right. You're smart. You'll multiply it and fill my pockets, I see it as a win-win deal."

Cole paused for a second as if assessing the offer, before

pulling Brax into a man hug as they'd found common ground."That, I can do. Thanks."

Although Brax's wound didn't seem to agree, "Fuck, ease up on me. It's not healed yet," Brax winced but couldn't hide his smile.

"And it's not going to heal if you don't take a break," Ferris intervened from the couch. I couldn't tell if he was as worried for Brax as he was for the reason *why* his wound wasn't healing.

"I don't do breaks." Brax laughed, slipping his phone back in his pocket. "So, what are you two doing tomorrow, after all?" he asked Cole, referring to our little getaway.

"We leave in the afternoon to get to the resort. I had to get a fucking chef, staff, and all," Cole barked, irritated once more that he wasn't getting the royal treatment.

But Ferris decided to bring him back to Earth. "Chill, you're not carrying them there on your back. You only placed a few phone calls."

"They only did this to undermine my authority. Camden wants to make sure of who is who, and what is what between us," Cole muttered again, annoyed that he had to leave his territory and go to a place where he wouldn't be seen as royalty.

"I thought you said you were friends?" I asked, remembering Cole mentioned Camden was a friend of his.

"We are, but they're also jackals," Cole grumbled under his breath, clearly annoyed.

"Nick and Jason are also jackals. You don't seem to mind them." I raised my shoulders, speaking a painful truth to him.

Cole only seemed amused by my observation, knowing precisely their value. "They're *my* jackals."

I guess he made a good point there, especially since he's the one leading the pack.

"Are you packed?" Cole asked, taking charge of the

operation *Party in the Mountains*.

"More or less. I put *a few* things in my luggage." *A few*, meaning two full shelves of clothes since I couldn't decide what to pack.

And it seemed Cole was coming to my help regarding what I should take along. "I want you looking bomb."

I began laughing, remembering the job at the Pleasure Room when Ace asked for a bomb. "The *bomb* thing again?"

"I want you to be so bomb that they'll charge us for terrorism." Cole devilishly smiled.

"He wants to show you off. He's always competing with Camden," Ferris said, coming by my side. "Come, I'll pour you a drink." Draping an arm around my waist, he guided me toward a small bar cabinet.

"So what's been decided, if we can get dirt on the governor?" Cole asked, probably thinking of the larger plan.

"We'll get everyone to support Ferris as the new governor. Besides being wealthy as fuck, he's also royalty, so he'll have every chance of pulling it off." Brax explained the decision he probably made by himself. Not that anyone had the power to go against him.

Not even Ferris, who muttered while prepping me a drink. "Fuck you and your ideas, Brax. This will only be temporary—an emergency measure until we find someone we can trust."

"You'll need to get rid of your piercings," I said, knowing his rebellious look wouldn't suit the political arena.

"I thought you liked my piercings," Ferris flashed me his tongue, seductively playing with the metal between his teeth.

I didn't answer, just took a sip out of my drink. A looooong sip, keeping the glass to my lips until their gazes moved away, giving me some time off.

"Hmmm. Ferris as the governor. It's like replacing one psychopath with another," Cole commented as a joke. Though there was truth in his words.

"Better say your prayers then. I may pass a law to put you, and your jackals in the zoo." Ferris also seemed to be in a really good mood. A stinging good mood.

"You'll need to put him into the pussycats' cage." Brax stepped in, making both of them burst into laughter.

I rolled my eyes. Men and their jokes.

"Don't worry, Mouse. I'll still keep the piercing," Cole's attention turned toward me in the worst way possible. Not that anyone asked him in the first place.

"I'm fine, thank you." I downed my drink between their laughter.

I wasn't sure if it was from the atmosphere or from the glass of alcohol I'd downed in under five minutes, but it was getting hot in the room. "I need to step outside," I breathed, sliding the balcony doors open and stepping out to catch a breath of fresh air.

After a few minutes in the cold of the night, I was feeling a little better. Still, going back inside right away didn't seem like a good idea at the moment. Not that I got the chance to return to the room before Ferris made his way to the balcony to ensure I was all right.

"You're cold." He placed his jacket on my shoulders.

"I'm okay, just needed to get out of there for a second." I couldn't be the lost zebra among the lions… and jackals.

"Here, I refilled your glass. You really need a drink."

"I'm starting to believe I do," I said with a smile, taking the glass from his hand and bringing it to my lips.

"You don't have to worry about the party. I know Cole. He has things under control, even if it doesn't always look like it."

"Oh, I'm not worried about Cole not having things under control. More like the opposite." I took another sip, realizing that an entire weekend with a still pissed-off Cole lay ahead.

"You're the one who wanted to save the world." Ferris pointed out, as if saving the world was a bad thing.

"Not the entire world, but at least the city."

"The city isn't worth saving, but have it your way." Ferris tilted his glass to clink against mine: "To saving the city!"

The extra sip didn't sit well with me, causing a light dizziness that made me put my glass down.

"Is everything okay?" Ferris wrapped an arm around me for support as I threw my own arms around his neck.

Was it the magic of the night, or the alcohol vapors that drew me to his lips?

Not entirely sure, but that feral magnetism between us was leaving no room for regrets. Our tongues pulsed with the beat of desire, for minutes, maybe hours as the notion of time was becoming blurred, overshadowing everything around us.

It felt surreal as if I were living in another dimension, watching everything from outside my body.

"I want you," that statement escaped his lips. "This night is so beautiful that I can't even feel the cold. Let's go to my room. I want to have you on the balcony."

That should've sounded so dangerously wrong, but in that moment, being with him was all that I could think about. Probably the alcohol to blame, but my head nodded in agreement, eagerly waiting for his lips to return to mine. Nothing seemed to matter anymore as long as I got to feel the sensual warmth of his skin.

Not entirely sure when we left the balcony for his room, but somewhere between the lobby and the staircase, Brax stopped us.

He was far from happy with our escapade. I didn't understand exactly why. He just asked Ferris to join him in an empty room, leaving me to wait in the lobby.

Though waiting was almost impossible. My feet didn't

seem to stay put. At least not without getting the impression I would fall straight on my face. Luckily, I found a comforter to lean on in my time of need. But just as I settled, Brax's arms formed an anchor for my body. "Bea... Bea, look at me."

Easier said than done since I was looking, but not really seeing anything.

"Fucking look at me," he roared like a lion, though without much success.

At least not the one he was expecting, because his voice *did* have a result on me. "You're so fucking hot when you groan like that." Yup, that was me speaking, as I felt his tone tingling a very aroused part of me.

"Let's go." He started walking.

"Where are we going?" I asked, trying to get a few neurons to work.

"To my room."

I had to admit, at that point, it didn't sound bad at all, but wasn't I with Ferris just a few moments before? "I don't understand."

"There's nothing to understand. You're going to bed." Brax... bed... all the information I needed to get my panties wet.

My head was spinning like a carousel. But I couldn't let a bit of dizziness stand in the way of my cravings. The slight storm in my mind couldn't compare with the hurricane raging through my body. And when it came to satisfying urges, Brax had a wall of degrees.

Despite my limbs being tangled on his shirt, he seemed incredibly calm—maybe even a little annoyed by my insistence, while all I could think about was taking things to a more sensual interaction.

"Get on the bed. I'll be right out." He left me alone in the room as he closed the bathroom door behind him.

"Okay," I nodded, though without any real intention of

getting on the bed. I was too agitated. I felt more like climbing the ceiling than getting on the bed.

Brax's order to wait for him lasted around three nanoseconds before I pushed the handle to open the bathroom door. I found him standing in front of the mirror in a mouth-watering image of some kind of modern gladiator. Petrified muscles scarred with the signs of street wars adorned with black ink intricate art pieces.

"What are you doing?" I asked, noticing him search the bathroom cabinet.

"What does it look like I'm doing?" he groaned, pulling away the bandage from his back to check his wound.

Luckily for him, his private nurse was there. "Let me help you. You can't clean the wound on your back."

"I have a doctor for that. Besides, in your condition, you might end up killing me." Brax muttered, visibly displeased by my presence there.

"What's my condition?" I asked, sneaking up in front of him, molding myself between his body and the sink.

"You're drunk," he muttered as if alcohol was invented only for him.

"So?" I raised my shoulders, unfazed.

"So, go back to bed," he snapped, clearly frustrated.

But I wasn't going to let myself be intimidated by him, "Not before you let me help you."

"Fuck. Okay, but just on the entry wound. I already patched up the other one." He took a step backward to create enough space so I could see his new bandage.

I imagined it would be a lot easier to clean the wound. But by the time I put disinfectant on the cloth, I was seeing two wounds instead of one. And to make things worse, they seemed to be spinning in circles.

Fuck. He was going to shoot me over this.

I had no idea with what heavenly strength I managed to clean his wound and apply a new bandage. But by the time I was done, the contact of my fingers with his tense muscles had left me in agony.

"Brax," I whimpered, calling him to do something to me. Anything to satisfy that desire to have my body squirming between the sheets.

"Bea, get in bed before I tie you to the bedpost." *Was that supposed to be a threat?* Because it sounded more like an invitation to me. Besides, it felt impossible to get between the sheets without him by my side. My breasts were crying to break free, to have the aching in my tips soothed by the warmth of his tongue.

"Let's stay in the bathroom for a little while," I seductively whispered, pushing my dress along with my bra down to my waist. If that didn't do the trick, I don't know what would.

"Are you trying to torture me?" Brax smiled, looking down at my naked body that was ardently waiting for him.

"Not at all," I breathed with the last of my strength, melting my lips against his shoulder tattoo, then letting them descend on a decisive path to reach his V-line. I needed to hear him groan. I needed to know I could make him groan so loud the walls would shake with his ecstasy.

I let my teeth run over the heavy shape of his length, reaching for his belt while a groan escaped his throat, then lost itself between curses.

"This is some kind of punishment for growing a conscience," he grumbled, kneeling down to help me stand up.

But standing was the least of my concerns as he was taking away my only chance to still the vicious tremble between my thighs. "Brax, is there something wrong that you don't want me?" I didn't understand what I did to him to refuse me, especially since he always seemed to be in *the mood*. He compelled me to sleep with him a few days after he got shot.

Turning me down now made no sense at all.

"You're fucking drunk. That's what's wrong." Before he could finish the sentence he pushed my dress down, leaving me only in my silk panties. "Bed, now!" Wrapping an arm around my waist, he took me to the bed, then tried to get me between the sheets.

I couldn't listen to his demand, since it seemed impossible to sleep alone. And for some reason, I had to make him perfectly aware of that. I arched my hips, grinding against the mattress, fighting the urges that were devouring me. But despite my best efforts, Brax was still playing the ignorance card.

"Come and tuck me in?" I gave him my most seductive smile I could manage, given the circumstances, running my palms against my aching breasts, hoping he'd come to replace my hands with his own.

I didn't even get to see his reaction. My vision was blurring and the room's image was fading into a tiny colored dot. I just felt him getting into bed, next to me, molding the shape of his taut chest against my back. One of his arms fastened around my waist, securing me to stay still, no matter how hard I struggled to break free and turn to face him.

"Don't you want me?" I whined, feeling totally abandoned at the moment. I needed to be loved, in every possible way.

"On the contrary." His lips molding to the back of my neck, opening his palm to cup one of my breasts.

"Then?" I demanded an answer for denying me of *his* presence. I just needed some quality sex. *Was that so much to ask?*

"Then... I told you. We'll talk when you sober up. And stop grinding your ass over my cock. I don't know how long I can stop it from breaking free," he muttered, in futile attempts to get his body to relax so he could go to sleep.

Huffing, I finally admitted defeat. I've come to know Brax

and once he made up his mind, there was no way around it. So, after a little more tossing and turning, I glued myself onto him and found a comfy sleeping position of my own. My back snuggled to his chest as my hips arched against his cock to make sure he'll have *sweet* dreams. I wasn't going to be the only one aroused and unattended.

"You're going to give me blue balls by the morning, and I swear I'll make you pay for it as soon as possible." His threat was the last thing I heard as the blur spread inside my mind and took me into a different world.

Morning arrived, and so did a pair of lips to fuse with my own moving gently, though not gently enough to not interfere with my headache. I couldn't hold back a soft moan as *a* hand snuck beneath the sheets searching for the roundness of my breast while a strong *set* of arms were drawing my back closer to Brax's chest, alerting me of his morning *mood*.

I purred like a lazy cat, struggling to open my eyes and shake off the booze still living inside my head. Though something wasn't adding up. The kiss seemed different from Brax's. Not different bad, but just different. "Cole?" I snapped my eyes open, thinking I wasn't seeing straight.

Fuck! The lips and the hand over my breast weren't Brax's. But the annoyed voice behind me certainly was. "Cole, get the fuck out of here before I shoot you."

"I was just having some morning fun!" Cole laughed, giving me another peck on the lips before withdrawing his hand.

"Go have *morning fun* in your fucking room. You're interrupting my sleep." Brax was definitely not a morning person, and judging by my headache neither was I.

"Just make sure Bea wakes up. We leave in an hour," Cole cackled more than spoke, leaving the room.

Not before Brax called after him. "Bring back an orange juice if you don't want her throwing up in your car on the way there."

I could certainly see his point, though the volume of his voice was piercing into my head like a sharp hot pin.

"Shit, how much did I have to drink?" I asked, trying to prop myself up into a sitting position while keeping a sheet wrapped around me.

"Not that much. What do you remember from last night?" Brax asked.

Was that a trick question? Because the parts I did remember were too embarrassing to admit.

"I had a drink, then went outside to cool down. I think Ferris came after me and—" It was pretty much a blur from there on.

"And?" Brax insisted.

"I remember Ferris and I kissed, then... then I was in your bathroom—" As I was retelling the events, I became more and more confused about what really happened.

"I think Ferris drugged you," Brax said all too casually while pulling up his pants.

Wait... What!? "What do you mean *drugged me*? Why would he do that?"

"For fun. How should I know why?" Brax raised his shoulders while zipping up.

"It doesn't make sense. He already has the same deal as you do. It's not like I could refuse any of his *requests*." But the truth was, I could never tell what really went on in Ferris's mind.

"Maybe it's not about refusing, but willingly agreeing to it. Or maybe I'm just fucking hallucinating. Just drop it and get dressed. Cole will be back any minute." But I couldn't drop it, and he wasn't hallucinating. He was giving me a warning, and it was about time I listened. Brax was right. Vanya was right too. And as terrible as I may have felt admitting it, Ferris did have a request that I would never willingly agree to. He wanted to have sex on the balcony—at the edge between life and death.

He would need to force it out of me, and that would break everything we'd built.

But drugging me? That seemed so wickedly extreme even for him. That would tear apart any connection we had.

Still, Brax was the one in the room with me, and I also had some unanswered questions when it came to him. "Brax, why didn't you... you know...?"

"Fuck you?"

"Can't you talk like a normal person?" I muttered.

"I *am* talking like a normal person." He arched an eyebrow, taking out a pack of cigarettes from his pocket. "I don't need to get a woman drunk or drugged to fuck her. You included. If I wanted to do that, I could have done it when you first slept at my place." He did have a point. After we finished The Pleasure he initially hired me for, I was unconscious in his bed for half a day.

"Thank you. I kind of remember giving you a hard time about it." Okay, maybe *hard* wasn't the best choice of words.

"Don't worry, I won't let you owe me for long." Brax winked, reminding me that no good deed went unrepaid when it came to him.

Still, there was something else bothering me. I felt like this before: the same headache, the same getting drunk from two glasses, the same uncontrollable lust, the same place where it happened—Ferris's house.

But why would he have drugged me back then, since Ferris rejected my advances the same way Brax did a night ago?

The question tormented me for a while, and there was a single reasonable explanation for it. He wanted to gain my trust, or maybe even get me to fall for him. And the bastard succeeded.

"Are you ready, Mouse, or do you need help getting dressed?" Cole just stepped into the room, disrupting my thoughts and making me an offer I didn't even need to think about.

"No. I'm fine," I said, looking in the mirror while adjusting one of my dress straps.

"Keep an eye on her!" Brax warned Cole as he was leaving the room.

"Oh, that I'll do," Cole smiled sinfully. "Come, Mouse. The *fun* is about to start."

*Why was I under the impression that **fun** wouldn't have much in common with **fun** after all?*

CHAPTER 16

A bitter taste invaded my soul as the thought of Ferris's deceit settled into my mind. Nothing would ever be the same again. Not that anything was any different with him, just with my perception of the man I thought he was.

I could have loved him. Maybe even loved the splinters of the monster he let out. But I was starting to believe that, in reality, that's all he ever was. A monster.

I sank into my silence, muting the outside world into just background noise. The trees blurred into a thick line as Cole's car was racing along dusty roads, taking us to the next city. I think it was the first time I wanted to give up. Not just the plan. All of it. The strength I used to have was abandoning me, fleeing to mingle with the memories of Ferris.

Even Cole sensed my restlessness and decided to ask, "Is there something wrong?"

"No. Everything is okay." What could I have said? That Ferris had got inside my head and totally fucked up my life?

"I don't really believe you. But *I'll make it* okay." He bit the thickness of his bottom lip, filling his mind with vicious thoughts. "Just try to sleep for an hour or so. It's a long drive. You seem tired, and I have plans for you tonight."

More plans. A thought that made me dream of jumping out of the moving car.

My instincts normally rejected any advice from Cole, but the one about getting a little rest was perfectly welcome, especially since I knew there was a hidden truth in his playful warning.

I wasn't sure where the hour went. In fact, I think that more than a couple of hours had passed because, by the time I got up, it was dark outside.

Cole must've kept an eye on me, and was already aware I was waking up. "That's your coffee," the second my eyes opened, he pointed towards a large cup of to-go coffee sitting in the car's cup holder.

"Did we stop?" I asked, taking a moment to figure things out while stretching out my feet from beneath the blanket I had snuggled into.

Wait... did he cover me?

"Thank you for—" I didn't get to finish my sentence.

"You were shivering, and I hate the heat blowing in my face as I drive. It's not a big deal." He was trying to minimize even the slightest chance of him ever being nice, since being *nice* was probably the most horrible thing that could happen to him.

"I was talking about the coffee." I would have loved to see him come up with an explanation for that too. But he didn't bother to say a word, just pretended he didn't hear anything, and totally ignored me.

I wasn't planning on saying anything back, or even speaking to him, but a large roar coming from somewhere in front of us gave me a panic attack. "Where is that coming from? What's happening?" I asked, my knuckles white while I gripped my seat. By the sound of it, we could be swallowed— car and all.

Though Cole didn't seem to be even slightly bothered by the noise. "Don't get your panties in a twist. It's coming from the air vents."

"Air vents?" I asked.

"This city is even more polluted than our own. You can barely breathe in the streets, so the Elite ordered some massive air purifiers to be built. They're the size of apartment buildings, surrounding the wealthy part of the city." As Cole was explaining about the machines, we were getting closer to the deafening sound, the sky-high ventilators were the only thing around for miles.

"I... I've never seen anything like this." I was shuddering, looking with a certain level of anxiety at the monstrous machines. I wasn't raised in the woods. I'd seen strange tech before, but there was something utterly wrong with these purifying devices.

"Nothing you will ever see again. This place is unique." Cole tried to explain.

"By the looks of it, these machines pollute more than they purify the air." It felt like such a tremendous waste of energy. Maybe on one side, the air purifiers were giving life, but on the other, it looked like they were taking it away.

"They don't pollute the Elite. The rest is irrelevant in their world." Cole was simply stating the sad truth that ruled in every city.

"But doesn't that mean the poorer residents are even more polluted from the machines spitting out the heat and toxic residues into their part of the city?" I was having trouble believing that something like this could happen.

"What did I just say? No one cares. The poor people could move if it bothers them." Cole wasn't letting me forget that he was also a part of the Elite.

"They probably don't have the finances to get out of here."

"Listen, Mouse, the guys you're about to meet are right at the top of this food chain, so I suggest keeping your mouth shut. We're here to deal with our problems, not theirs." As much as I hated to admit it, Cole was right. This wasn't our fight, and it wasn't as if we had even started solving our own problems. We were here to get info on what we needed, not to stir trouble. And for the first time in my life, I was putting all my effort into doing it while keeping myself off the radar.

"We'll be there in an hour. The location is somewhere in the mountains. The chef and his staff just texted me. They've already arrived at the cottage."

"I still don't understand why they need a chef and staff at the cottage." Haven't these people heard of pizza?

"Have you ever seen anyone from the Elite cook?" He did make a point. "I didn't think so," Cole shrugged, lighting himself a cig. "Everyone was in charge of something: DJs, drinks, decorations, and who knows what else."

I could never understand aristocracy. "This sounds like a lot of trouble for a simple party."

"They don't really care as long as someone else is doing the work. It's an honor to even be invited." Cole made air quotes with his fingers, getting angry again for not benefiting from the royal treatment.

"Just suck it up for the weekend."

"I'm not the one *who's* going to do the sucking this weekend," Cole arched an eyebrow, looking straight at me as my head instinctively turned to look out through the window. I bit back my tongue, trying not to snap back at him. It would have been the worst timing possible, as we were going into unknown territory.

I never turned back to look at him. Not before we arrived at the cottage anyway.

Cottage—a laughable description of a two-floor house with ceiling-high glass walls to show off every single piece of exquisitely furnished wood and rustic chandeliers.

"Come on, Mouse." Cole opened the door for me to get out of the car, then picked up our luggage from the trunk.

Was he growing manners? Because I was mentally prepared to drag my bag out through the snow.

"You, dumbass, get his bag." A man in his early twenties pushed the entrance door open, gesturing to another guy to relieve my king of the weight of his luggage.

"Camden!" Cole faked the largest smile he could. With open arms, he walked over to the man and caught him in a brotherly hug.

"So glad you could join us," Camden exclaimed, making sure to oversee that his friend was taken care of, then directed his attention my way. "If I'd known you have pieces of ass like that in Echo City, I would have come to visit sooner." He smiled, opening the door so I could get inside, "Ladies first."

That was the first moment I had a chance to take a look at him. Okay... more like stare at the twinkling madness dancing in his eyes—so similar to Ferris, yet different in so many ways. His icy blue eyes like pools from the pits of hell, his full lips crawling with wicked temptation, and his raven hair arranged in a perfectly styled messy look. He was a danger to any woman around, armed with a rare kind of undeniable attraction and altogether something pure evil enrooted deep within him. A lump formed in my throat, racing to the pit of my stomach. The thought of spending the next couple of days in this place scared me to death.

"Come on, Mouse. Let's get you unpacked." Cole snapped me out of my momentary shock and escorted me to follow the guy carrying our bags. "Take your clothes off," he instructed as soon as our assigned bellboy left the room.

"I have to open my bag first and find something to change into." I was searching for any excuse to avoid him.

"Who said you were changing into *something*?" The evil grin he perfectly owned was stirring all thoughts running through my mind—fear, contempt, and unwanted desire.

"It's up to you if you want to trade making an impression for half an hour between the sheets." I raised my shoulders, took my jacket off, and threw it on the bed.

"Only half an hour? You must've gotten your *kings* mixed up," he muttered since I unwillingly offended his manhood. "And don't try to use reverse psychology on me. It won't work." My cover was blown, and my plan backfiring.

"It isn't reverse psychology." It was, but he didn't need to know that. "It's just that I felt the competition the second I walked in, and I figured that you wanted to be on top of that. It's a jungle out there and you shouldn't be walking in with a *mouse* on your arm. You should be holding a feline." I tipped him a seductive wink, assuring myself that we weren't going to wrinkle the sheets less than ten minutes after walking into the room.

"Oh, so tonight you're the feline." Cole let out a loud laugh, taking a step toward me. "But the problem is, I don't want to hold a feline. I want to fuck it." His words reverberated through me, awakening the exact instinct reflected in his gaze. Feral. Raw. Consuming.

"Get dressed." Opposite to what he said earlier, he *was* preparing to put on a show. One that will consolidate his position in the winners league. "Give me the best you've got, *Mouse*."

"You can't handle my best." I smiled, as I was already going through my luggage.

"Unless you're wearing something that shows off your full Brazilian wax, I don't think you have anything to surprise me with." Cole took off his shirt to search for a new one in his bag while I had just found an outfit of my own.

Holding my clothes in one hand, and my make-up kit in the other, I ran straight to the bathroom, before Cole got a chance to come up with some new idea and ask me to change in front of him. "I'll be right out."

A pair of skin tight leather pants and a black corset were my choice for the night, and by the look on Cole's face when I stepped out of the bathroom, I had played my cards right. Plus, I was having a good hair day. I was preening on that, letting my locks cascade in silky waves over my breasts.

Still, my look wasn't entirely ready. Something was missing. A detail that would tie everything together. "I'll be wearing that tonight." I snatched his university jacket from his bag and put it on. It was a sign of ownership, a mark of belonging, drawing very precise lines on what's what and who's who.

Cole might have thought I did it to swear some unworded allegiance to him. But I was doing it out of a dreaded sensation of anxiety. I needed protection. I felt there was something completely wrong with everything that was going on here, no matter how perfect things may have seemed in the daylight.

"Would you look at that? Turns out you are a little feline after all." I could see the hidden admiration in his eyes. I was going to solidify his position amongst the Elite of this city, and he was perfectly aware of that. "Let's get downstairs. You took for-fucking-ever to get ready."

"Oh, so you would have had time for sex, but I don't get five minutes for makeup?" I muttered.

"More like fifty minutes for some doodling I'm going to ruin as soon as the party ends."

I got the hint. Even if I preferred I hadn't. But that didn't mean I couldn't still ignore him. "Well, ready if you are," I headed toward the door, trying to avoid any further hints of how we would spend the night.

"You like to play games with me." Racing through the door, Cole caught up with me. The softness of his lips melted on the crook of my neck while one of his hands molded onto my ass. "Don't leave my side," he whispered into my ear as soon as we got into the extra-large living room.

Despite my initial gut feeling, the party was very similar to those we had attended in the past. With one exception— here, Cole wasn't the center of the universe and no one came to bother him with false oaths of allegiance. Pretty nice, if you asked me.

Even though refinement was the keyword of the evening —the food, drinks, and even the decorations were polished to an extreme shine—the same refinement didn't extend to the people attending. Sure, they were all rich, but there was something utterly wrong with each and every one of them. Their souls seemed so rotten that they made the Elite residents of Echo City look like angels compared to what I found here.

Gossiping and envy were the main themes of the evening, as that was all I could ever hear in the murmurs around us. Who has what and how could someone else benefit from that? These people were even faker than my own supporters back at

ECU.

"You know, you do look really fucking pretty tonight, Mouse." Cole brought his thumb to wander on my lips, asking them to part and welcome his tongue.

As much as I usually told myself I hate him, and everything he represents, his mouth was something I was beginning to be fond of. Luckily, I didn't have to part from it too soon, taking our union of lips so far that uncontained soft moans began escaping from my throat. I liked it, and he knew it, wrapping his fingers around strands of my hair to support the back of my head as he adventured to tease the depths of my mouth.

"I could ask to cut in, but Camden told me your girl is off-limits. Wouldn't want to start a war or something like that," a six-foot-three mass of muscles and piercings spoke from less than ten inches away from us.

"Treyton," Cole broke off the kiss but didn't let go of me, keeping his hand tightly clutched over my waist. "I haven't seen you in a while. Did you get even fucking taller?"

"Yeah, a few inches short of getting a blowjob while the girl's standing." Treyton considered himself to be funny.

I for one wasn't laughing.

Wish I could say the same about Cole. "Just buy a stool, man, or get a really short girl." He cackled, giving Treyton some knuckle-on-knuckle greeting. Judging by his expensive clothes and the arrogant look in his deep green eyes, I was convinced Treyton was part of Camden's close circle of friends, especially since he knew Cole.

"Not NBA material, though. I needed a few extra inches. At least they went to my dick." Treyton shrugged, satisfied with nature's plans for him. And come to think about it, he wasn't the only one satisfied.

"No sneak peeks, man. I'm good." Cole laughed again in a rehearsed amusement. Being sociable didn't suit him well. Actually, he lacked any real skill in it. But desperate times called for desperate measures, and trying to act friendly once in a while never hurt anyone—even if *friendly* meant talking about his friends' dick. Go figure.

Men would be men, acting like little boys all the time.

"Yeah, man, listen... catch you later. Zale is pissed off about a guy muttering something about him for fucking his girlfriend last night. And the motherfucker has just shown up. I need to deal with him." Treyton took a few steps toward the opposite corner of the room.

While my date offered to help. "Want some backup?"

"He's only five feet tall. But you're welcome to watch... and learn," Treyton said with amusement.

"Learn? Are you on crack? I could be the coach when it comes to fighting." My king was eager to show off, especially after all that practice in ECU's lobby.

"Be my guest, then. This shirt cost me a fortune. I just got it custom-tailored. I don't want to splatter his blood all over it. And I have no idea where Camden or Zale are."

"Oh, this party is about to get electrifying. Which one is it?" Cole asked, scanning the room.

"The curly-haired one. The one with the green shirt."

Cole seemed to be locked in on the target, as I kept hoping he wouldn't be the one to play justice. Although I had a feeling it was all part of his plan.

"Stay here, Mouse." He didn't wait for an answer before he stormed off on his new mission.

The poor guy with a target on his back didn't stand a

chance against the onslaught of Cole's fists, which sent him reeling straight outside.

A choking sensation was almost making me gag as an unsettling thought was vivid to mind; I had to be next to my king. I had to play the loving girlfriend and support him for the sake of our plan. I may have dodged that bullet in the past, but it was time to put my best acting mask on.

With hesitant steps, I followed the crowd of people to the front of the house, making room between all the curious gazes, to go and applaud my king.

The second I reached a spot from where I could see, my stomach began churning, noticing the velocity Cole was hitting the guy. Deep down I was hoping he was doing it out of the need to stand out and gain even more of Camden's trust. But I knew he was also doing it out of fun. That wicked idea of fun that always made him detach from reality as his arrogance put an imaginary crown on his head.

I was one step away from fainting when a guy got in my way, obscuring my sight. From there on, it wasn't my fault I couldn't see the whole fight. Not that I had any plan on doing that.

The murmured voices in the crowd stopped for a second, just to be followed by a large wave of sadistic joy. My king was victorious, and I needed to suck it up and congratulate him.

Trying not to hyperventilate, I snuck between a few people, aiming to reach the improvised ring. I didn't get too far. Not before I accidentally hit a rock-hard body blocking the way to my winner. I had to look up, because all I could see in front of my eyes was ink—black, mesmerizing ink. Like the gods came down to earth, and scribbled their magic into the guy's skin. The tattoos ran up to his sculpted jawline, though not a single black line touched his face. And it would be a pity if any had done so. He looked like a sculpture you see in a museum.

Exquisite, perfectly shaped, and deadly. It was like venom was spilling from his eyes. A darkness so twisted that one may believe he was a direct descendant of the devil himself. *What was wrong with the men in this city?*

"Zale," Treyton appeared from somewhere behind him, "Cole fixed him."

Both Treyton and Zale stepped aside to look at the improvised ring, where the poor guy's blood had stained the ground red while Cole nonchalantly wiped his hands clean.

"Go kiss your winner." Treyton winked back at me, nudging me to congratulate *my fighter*. Which I did. False smiles and all, loathing him for beating up the guy, and at the same time enjoying Treyton's large, approving grin. Cole had just taken a step closer to Camden's crew, and one step further into sustaining our cause.

My arms wrapped around *my boyfriend's* neck, crashing my lips on his to congratulate him for the *smashing* success. No doubt he seemed pleased with the gesture, responding with his pulsing tongue.

"Mouse, go get me a towel from the house," he asked, as soon as we broke the kiss to breathe. His knuckles were smeared with blood. I just couldn't figure out if it was his or the other guy's. I don't think he knew either since the adrenaline still crackled through him. That's what he needed the towel for. ASAP.

I ran into the house to find a towel, but the bathroom door closed right in front of me, and any attempt to knock didn't come with a result.

Kitchen—that was another place where I could find one. I stormed straight into the secondary kitchen to search for a cloth. Any kind of cloth. But to my surprise, I found something unexpected..

There was a reason why Camden wasn't around. It had something to do with a certain brunette kneeling in front of him, offering her mouth services by giving him a blowjob.

I couldn't look. Just needed to take the towel and get the fuck out of there. Maybe they wouldn't even notice my presence.

But *he* noticed.

Camden noticed, staring back at me with icy blue eyes.

It was like a fucking trainwreck. I wanted to look away, but couldn't, to the point that I think I was staring at the woman bobbing her head to please him.

"I can send her away if you'd like to take her place," he casually said, tilting his head to look at me as he was thrusting into her mouth.

"Hey," a muffled sound came from the kneeling girl.

"Weren't you doing something else with your mouth?" His angered tone came with a few more thrusts, reminding her to respect who knows what rules.

I didn't really understand what was going on. Or why did he offer to ditch his date so quickly? All I knew was that I needed to get out of there, and once I had the towel in my possession, I ran back to the garden.

I was surprised that Cole didn't get a crown of flowers by the time I got back. The crowd seemed to still be ecstatic, praising him as a king while my stomach was still twisting and turning from the bitter taste the fight had left.

Nonetheless, I rushed to clean the blood off his hands. He may have been a bully, but he was *my* bully. Him being wounded was unsettling to me, even if I wouldn't mind throwing a few fists at him myself.

After wiping all the excess blood off, I found just two cuts on his knuckles. Not too nice, but not severe either.

"I like it when you act like this," Cole was making a confession that I really didn't care for. We weren't here for his likes or dislikes. We were here for information.

"That's because I give you the attention needed to feed your ego." I smile, finishing cleaning the blood away.

"What's wrong with that?" he asked so casually that he was making me question my judgment.

"Nothing. It's just that attention might come in many ways. I'm not sure you want the *right* kind now."

"Oh, I want the *right* kind." He snaked his arms around my waist, lifting me to reach his lips. "I want to go upstairs," he groaned in anguish because it wasn't going to happen any time soon.

"You know we can't." I let myself be lost in his arms. For the first time, I wanted to be locked away in a room with him. Anything to escape the party.

But Camden cut in. "I heard you had fun."

"Yeah, well, I was getting bored." Cole unglued himself from my lips and squeezed my hand into his fist, guiding my body impossibly closer to his.

"Do you want extra company? Just tell me who you like and I'll get her for you." Cam looked across the room for anyone who could catch his attention. "Do you like the blonde that's with the guy in the plaid jacket? She's got nice tits."

But Cole protectively wrapped an arm around my waist. "I'm good with what I've got."

"I can see your point," Cam tilted his head to study me from head to toe. "When you get bored of her, let me know. I can lend you *ours*, she's good with pretty much everything."

Ours? What the hell was that supposed to mean?

"Irina," Cam gestured toward somewhere in the crowd.

A beautiful girl with ebony hair and a body to die for made her way across the room. A very different person from the one giving him head earlier in the kitchen. "If you decide you're bored, she can assist you two in any way you want."

I was pretty sure the thought agreed with Cole. As far

as I was concerned, if he even came close to considering the suggestion, I was making a run for it.

"My pleasure." The woman smiled, with a hundred underlinings hiding between the curves of her lips. Her caramel skin, a perfect contrast to the ivory cutout dress she was wearing, and the more I looked at her, the more I was getting worried Cole might take Camden on his offer.

"We're good." I nodded, taking Cole's arm and wrapping it around me. I was doing it again, letting my damn possessive anger control my actions. I wanted to stop. I just couldn't. I couldn't stop acting like he was my property.

"Then if you don't mind, I have a little unsolved business with this one," Treyton's tall figure appeared from somewhere behind Irina, wrapping his arms around her, and clutching his hands over her voluptuous breasts. He was turned on as fuck. Maybe from the rush of the fight, who knew? But his large palms squeezed her tits so tightly that tears were spilling from the corner of her eyes.

I tried to look away and not stare at the show he was putting on, but as my gaze went up, it met his own, staring straight at me.

I had no idea what he was trying to prove, but it felt like a statement. He was trying to establish some kind of dominance over me. And I was far from being impressed. "Let's go," I whirled to snuggle in Cole's arms.

Turns out my kings weren't so bad after all. Not after what I'd just seen. And I was certain it wasn't even close to the end of it.

Strangely enough, Cole didn't put up a fight when it came to fulfilling my request. We left Treyton and went to mingle with the crowd. But we couldn't leave the party just yet. We needed things to calm down so that Cole could find a chance to properly sneak himself into a conversation with Camden. I was starting to believe that meant waiting for their appetites to settle down. I observed them one by one picking different women from the party—unattended or *not*, and disappearing with them into different rooms of the house. Maybe this was a regular party for all the other people attending, but it was a sexual feast for Camden and his crew. They got whoever they wanted, and it seemed to be an honor to all the women selected. They were fucking gods in Emerald City, and they took that literally.

I just hoped Cole wouldn't get any ideas out of this visit. He seemed calmer than before—except for the fight, of course. It was like he finally understood the importance of what we were doing, and he was trying to hold back his urges. And that, for some fucked-up reason was making me crave him.

Despite the endless sexual hints that were turning out to be part of his personal charm, Cole was acting decently—almost docile, just sneaking a kiss or two while keeping his hands no lower than my waist.

"Are you okay?" I had to ask since things were getting ridiculously weird between us.

"Yeah. Why?"

"You're... I don't know... behaving." The words seemed weird as they escaped my lips—Cole behaving.

He cocked an eyebrow. "You don't like it when I behave? That's interesting."

"You scare me when you behave, Cole. Makes me wonder what's really going on."

"They won't dare lay a finger on you, if that's what concerns you. I just need to keep my focus for a while. But Mouse, I do promise I won't behave for long." And the truth was that I wasn't sure I wanted him to behave any longer. It felt as if something was missing from our game, or maybe I was beginning to fancy the role of his queen just a little. Even if being the queen in his life meant giving in to every dark desire. He certainly had that going for him—that undeniable force to keep a wave of heat between my thighs burning. I hated him and yearned for him to make me his at the same time.

"Let's have a drink," Cam appeared from nowhere, ordering more rather than asking Cole. "I'm sick of all these bitches going the extra mile so I would fucking look at them."

Cole sighed, as the feeling was all too familiar to him. "Tell me about it…"

"Irina will keep her company. Come, the guys are making a fire outside." Camden left without waiting for an answer. Not that anyone could ever refuse him.

"Fucking shit," my king muttered, overly annoyed by Cam's air of authority. "Spend ten minutes with the girl, then excuse yourself and get back to our room." He leaned to whisper directly in my ear. "And Mouse, be prepared for when I return." His tongue left a hot trail against my earlobe, making his promise more vivid in my mind.

"Let's have a drink," Irina gestured for me to join her a few feet away while Cole put on his jacket and left to go outside. "What are you having?" she asked.

"Sex on the beach." I laughed, naming the last cocktail I'd had throughout the night.

"We don't have beaches around, but I'm sure I can find someone to help with the sex part." She smiled, showing off her perfect white teeth. "Just kidding," Irina extended a hand to bring me by her side. "Hey, you. A Sex on the Beach and a Hugo," she ordered from a guy who didn't seem to be part of the staff.

"Is he a waiter?" I couldn't stop my curiosity.

"They *all* are my waiters," she answered so casually, as if the whole world belonged to her.

"What do you mean?"

"It's pretty simple. I do what Cam and the guys want, and the whole world does what I want in return," Irina replied with such pride that it got me to realize she was queen around here.

In my opinion, selling your body to get respect really doesn't get you any respect at all.

"That must be nice." I had no idea what else to say to her.

Yes, what we both did might be similar, but the reasons were worlds apart.

"Are these babies fake?" she asked, grabbing one of my breasts to test its authenticity.

"No. All mine," I shrugged as she arched an eyebrow as if she was having trouble believing me.

"I just got mine done." She guided my hand to verify the quality of her new implants. "Best doctor in the world. Cam's money bought that."

"They do feel natural." I took back my hand, again with no idea of what I should actually say.

She was scanning me in search of any signs of Botox or filler. "So, what have you had done? Let me guess, your lips?"

"Nothing." I was a little surprised she assumed I had to have something done to my body. But I guessed this was the main topic of conversation around the place.

"A natural beauty, huh? Good for you." I could feel a hint of jealousy in her voice.

"Drinks," the guy assigned to be our waiter returned with our cocktails. Irina just took her drink while I took mine. No *thank you* wasted on him from her, while I had to follow her lead. I didn't want to risk embarrassing her and ruining our plan.

"You should have seen me a year ago. Unrecognizable. Now I'm a fucking beauty star," Irina continued.

More like a porn star, if anyone had asked me, but I couldn't really say that to her.

No surprise that she went on and on about shoes, clothes, cosmetics, and more plastic surgeries to the point where I was bored to death. Maybe this was what girls talked about. Perhaps I was the one fucked up. But I couldn't give a damn about her plastic surgery or implants, or whatever her position brought her. The humiliation wasn't worth any of that, and I knew that firsthand.

"I'm a little tired, and besides, I have to get ready for Cole. He'll get cranky if I'm not perfect by the time he returns. You know how these things go," I tried excusing myself.

"Oh, I know, believe me." Irina smiled with a hint of worry resting on her lips as if she's been there, done that. "Wear something red. I bet it will look great on you."

"Oh, that's exactly what I had in mind. Nice meeting you." I drifted off, making a quick escape to get to my room without further intervention.

My plan worked. I arrived safely, and after a hot shower, I changed into something red, just as Irina suggested. Although, I wasn't sure if she was referring to the red flannel pajama I put on. Maybe I was getting my messages mixed up that night. I got between the sheets to wait for Cole and prepare myself for when he would return.

I just hoped he'd find me in *dreamland.*

CHAPTER 17

I heard him walk into the room, but there wasn't a chance in hell I was going to wake up, and welcome him. Not when I knew what welcoming him would really mean. I just pretended to be asleep, biting the tip of my tongue to contain my curiosity.

Did he get something out of Camden, anything that could help us?

I didn't ask. Just kept my eyes shut as I heard him turn on the water in the shower, then slip out of his clothes. Next thing I knew he was getting into bed.

I was patiently waiting to see if he would remain on his side of the mattress. My curiosity didn't take long to be satisfied. Before I knew it, his arm wrapped around my waist, snaking one of his hands beneath my fluffy blouse and reaching for my breasts. His fingers locked tightly over my throbbing nipple, hardening it on touch. Still, I held my ground, trying the impossible to withstand Cole's delicious assault while still pretending to be asleep.

A few cusses left his tongue, keeping his thumb and forefinger playing with my aching tip. The sensation tormented me, raising a fervor I knew couldn't be stilled—at least for that night. I wasn't going to trade the last drops of dignity for soothing the flesh, even if I was vibrating with the agony of being deprived of him.

By some miracle, I managed to fall asleep. I just wished the miracle would last throughout the next day since the morning found me with *a surprise* wrapped around my core. Cole's hand was deep down in my panties, rubbing with a light touch against my clit while the other was playing with my hardened nipple again.

How was I supposed to pretend to be asleep when my body seemed so fiercely awake? His hand kept moving like slow torture on my skin, gliding against my pussy to awaken my need for him. Each time a little stronger, each time, driving me further out of my mind. I could feel him tense behind me, grinding his teeth while pleasuring me. He was turning my arousal into his own, and I just couldn't hold back a moan as my irrefutable ecstasy was closing in.

"I know you're awake, Mouse." He ground harder against me, getting my body to arch into the sheets. "Does it feel good?"

I nodded. There was no point in denying the obvious.

"Of course, it does." He began moving his hand harder and faster. "The only problem is that you haven't been a really good girl, have you now? You pretended to be asleep last night. Like you did earlier." He pinched my clit, making my face bury itself into the pillow, purring with incoming ecstasy. "And this outfit. I always wanted to fuck Little Red Riding Hood. But I know you didn't choose it to fulfill one of my fantasies. You wanted to discourage me from touching you," he muttered, insisting on an impossible spot that was making even my ovaries ache from the pressure. "I guess that doesn't apply now. You want me to touch you now, don't you?"

"Yes," I whimpered into the pillow, allowing my body to speak instead of my brain. I was one second away from convulsing with shattering pleasure, when—

"Too bad you didn't stay up and wait for me." His movement stopped, leaving me with an anguish so impossible to handle that I was even thinking of stealing his hand and making it my prisoner. But I couldn't let him see my desperation, although it was becoming quite obvious as a few cries lost themselves between the sheets. "Now, get your ass up. We're invited to a small afterparty."

"Did you get anything out of Camden?" I asked, still unable to turn and look him in the eyes.

Cole smirked, deciding to keep my curiosity on the edge. "I'll tell you later. We have to get dressed now."

"You can't let me boil like that," I pouted.

But this was about payback. "You let me boil last night."

"And you just got your revenge a few minutes ago," I all but whined.

"I turned down twins last night to come and be with you." *Was he for real?*

He was seriously pissing me off. "Oh, and should I feel honored for winning in front of two tramps that would've slept with you after two words, and a drink from the free bar?"

"Ah, you're jealous again."

"I am not." I was lying.

The '*I can see through you*' smile bloomed on his face, "You don't have to hide it, Mouse. I love it when you're jealous. Turns me on."

"I repeat. I AM NOT jealous." I insisted, hoping I would convince him, although I wasn't that convinced myself.

"Have it your way. I guess I'm going to take them up on that offer a little later. I think they said 13B... or was it C? Who cares? I'll just search around."

Okay, I was jealous. "Just close the door behind you when you leave. I need to call Brax."

Cole instantly arched an eyebrow. "What for?"

249

"For...a thing." Besides being as jealous as it got, I was also a lousy liar.

"You think you can use some reverse psychology shit again to make me jealous with Brax? Nice try. I do appreciate the attempt. Makes me want to fuck the coils of anger rushing through your veins." I felt he was one step away from going back on his plan. "But not here."

"What's that supposed to mean?" I retaliated.

"You'll see. Get dressed before we're late. Everyone was invited to the party last night. It's *this* one that you need a special invitation for."

I didn't really feel like dressing up again. "What should I change into?"

"Think casual sexy and toss on a dress." Music to my ears.

"Your wish is my command. I'll be ready by the time you finish with the twins." I could never keep my mouth shut and that brought his lips one inch away from mine the very next second.

"I just told you that it turns me on when you're jealous." Taking my hand, he guided it straight to the bulge in his pants. That part of him was definitely awake. "Now, if you don't want to continue from where we left off, I suggest you get fucking dressed, and we get going." Tough decision on my part, especially since the ache between my thighs hadn't yet found a chance to settle down.

Strangely enough, things with Cole were turning more into a game than a task I needed to fulfill in order to keep my end of the bargain. And that was going to be a problem no matter how hard I was trying to deny it.

"Ready." I returned from the bathroom dressed in a tight wool-blend black dress, and a short pair of matching boots. "Do you want me to change?"

"Nah, you're perfect like this. Besides, we match." He was

right. The black shirt he had on, dark jeans, and matching black stylish boots would lead one to think we planned our outfits to match. Pretty cool coincidence, if you asked me.

The afterparty, because I believe that is what it was—an afterparty, seemed much more tempered than the one from last night. Fewer people were attending. So few that I actually got to see the room we were in. Turns out, our location was an immense living room that stretched throughout the whole first floor, being separated into several sitting areas. In the center was a gigantic U-shaped set of couches, orientated toward the biggest TV I'd ever seen. It was kind of giving me *Gulliver's Island* vibes. No money was spared for supreme luxury.

"Let's get something to eat. I think we skipped dinner yesterday." Cole escorted me to the food stand.

"And breakfast and lunch." I was famished. Oversleeping in Brax's bed had made me skip a few meals.

"I guess I should take better care of you then." Cole wrapped an arm around my waist as I tried to decide if he was kidding or not.

His efforts to snare a Michelin chef along with his staff were paying off. The food was sublime, and that wasn't just because I hadn't eaten in almost two days.

The atmosphere was much cozier than the one the night before. There was still a weight floating in the air, but the danger seemed to have dissipated—a little. Maybe because everyone still had a hangover, or was still drunk.

Camden and Treyton came to greet Cole at some point, each with a new conquest buzzing around them. Though I wasn't sure *conquest* was the right word. Anyway, I was willing to bet I saw the girls coming here with different dates. The *gods* must have spoken to them.

Not too many interactions after that. Just a few hours spent with Cole among people who were either carrying out last night's party or sobering up. My king's attitude was a lot different from the one last night. If the night before, he could keep his hands to himself, today was a whole different deal. Our lips were sealed while his hands seemed to have been glued to my ass, squeezing it so tightly it was beginning to hurt. A nice pain. An all-consuming pain. The kind that pulsed below my waist, drawing my body to his in an undeniable need to feel him close.

"What did you find out last night?" I whispered, letting my tongue trace the curve of his ear, savoring the way his breath hitched in response.

"Just don't move, and I'll tell you," he groaned against my neckline, his fingers twisting in my hair to keep my head perfectly still. He liked knowing that I was acting out of my own will. And I, in return, loved knowing that, for once, he didn't want to control me. "I did good, and I'm going to need a reward soon," he groaned again as my lips brushed against his jawline.

"Mhmmm," I delicately murmured. Judging by the dampness of my panties, I would also be in need of a reward soon.

"It looks like Camden hates his stepdad. That's why he never moved to Echo City and decided to remain here—the city his real dad used to run." Cole stopped for a second, exhaling a breath so heavy that it seemed it was a burden on his soul. I had to slow down somewhat before he'd decide the party was over.

"Go on." I changed the beat into just gentle kisses.

"Okay, so his dad died when he was twelve, and his mother remarried the governor five years later. But turns out the man is a real piece of shit. They're getting a divorce. And guess what's the reason?"

"The Elite enslaving the Annelids?" I gave him my best shot.

"None of these people give a fuck about the Annelids. What the governor did, affected her on a more personal level. She found sex tapes of him and a range of different girls and *boys*. Some of them, she even thought were underage. Hundreds of recordings. He destroyed the data before she got to download it onto her personal drive. But you know what they say. *The wolf changes his coat, not his nature.* He's definitely doing it again, maybe just at a more discreet level. Cam said that if he's right and the governor's still fucking around, the tapes are either on his home computer, password-protected, or in his safe."

"Damn. How the hell are we supposed to get access to that? Even if we get in there, who's going to crack the safe or the password?" I felt like we just made a huge breakthrough and turned out it was impossible to accomplish.

"If we *could* manage to somehow sneak in—which is highly unlikely because his house is guarded—maybe Ferris could figure out a way to work through the surveillance cameras. He's like a fucking genius when it comes to technology."

It seemed there were a lot of things I didn't know about Ferris. "I didn't know that about him."

"I'm not sure if he'll agree to help us though. He hasn't exactly been working on his skills since what happened with his parents," Cole said with sadness in his voice.

"Oh, he will agree. It's part of our deal." I hadn't slept with him in vain. Not that the last time I slept with him had anything to do with any deal. "I'll talk to him when we return."

"In the meantime," Cole whispered, "let's find a spot on that couch. I'm tired of standing."
It was already late afternoon. Time had flown by pretty fast considering the company. The couch idea wasn't bad at all, and as I took a seat, Cole decided to get more comfortable. He stretched himself along the length of the couch, and placed his head on my lap.

"Are you sleepy?" I asked, running a gentle hand through

his coal-dark hair, and looking at the two cobalt orbs closing with each one of my touches.

"Maybe just a little. But don't stop." I didn't. Not necessarily because he asked, but because I liked it. It felt like a normal thing to do, or maybe it was completely wrong—considering this was just a deal. Either way, I just couldn't stop myself.

Contrary to what I thought would happen, he didn't fall asleep, and neither did I. We were just sprawled on the couch, living our short moment of relaxation while being in a public place, with no one coming to talk to us. It must've felt strange for him. But it was a good kind of strange.

People came and people left while my fingers still played with the ebony locks of his hair, only moving from time to time to graze the short stubble of his beard.

"Okay, motherfuckers. I'm tired, and I want to watch a movie," Treyton decided to cut the party short. "Whoever wants to stay, pick a seat, whoever doesn't... well, you know your way out the door."

I immediately looked down at Cole. In response, he just raised an arm above his head, wrapped it around my thigh and signaled me that we were staying.

Everything seemed to have organized itself at Treyton's command. In just a few minutes, the music became a murmur in the background. The guests were either getting comfortable on the sofas and couches or grabbing their coats to walk out the door.

What a party pooper I thought to myself, since I was sure that if Cam, or any of them, were still in the mood for partying, the music wouldn't stop until the morning.

"You're such a dipshit," Cam laughed. "Learn to fucking share, and don't fucking ruin everyone's mood."

Treyton didn't answer, just turned toward the girl by his side "leave," he didn't have to tell her twice. The girl just evaporated into thin air as he walked toward the door, stopping a brunette who was on her way out. "Are you going somewhere?" His question, more similar to a warning. I guess not, since two minutes later, she was searching for his tonsils with her tongue while straddling him on a sofa.

What the Kings of Emerald City wanted, the Kings got. This seemed to be the main rule in this place.

"What was that about?" I asked Cole, because I couldn't really make any sense of what had happened.

"Treyton is lashing out over that Irina chick. She likes Zale's dick better than his." He laughed, gently moving his head against my lap.

He was right. Irina was sitting on the couch next to Zale, running her hand up and down over his tattoos, while he barely acknowledged her existence—except for a satisfied smirk beaming on his face. Not because of the overzealous company, but because he had managed to get to Treyton. Clearly, they had something to share—other than the girl. And I couldn't care less what that was, as long as it didn't interfere with our plans.

"If we already found out what we came here for, why aren't we leaving with the rest?" I asked since Cole seemed one step away from dozing off.

"How would leaving with the other guests look to Camden? We're spending the night. Besides, I have some unfinished business with you."

"Go back to sleep," I chuckled, without having any idea of his real *intentions*.

"Come here and lie with me," he murmured with sleepy eyes. *Devious* sleepy eyes.

"I'm not going to lie there. Besides, I was thinking of going upstairs to change into something else. The entrance door keeps opening, and my feet are beginning to get cold."

"Come here then, I'll keep you warm." His invitation seemed tempting enough, and as I looked across the room, more than half of the couples were getting as comfortable as they could. Some watching the movie that had just started while others were dozing off.

Still, I hadn't answered Cole. I could feel there was something off about his offer. And my delay made him turn his head to rest on my abdomen, "I could raise your dress right now, and get you more acquainted with my tongue." He smiled in a hidden threat.

"You wouldn't," I retorted, calling his bluff.

"Wouldn't I?" he purred the question which made me realize he *would*.

"Okay... okay. Get up so I can get next to you."

He raised his head from my lap, and I slid onto the couch next to him, facing the TV with his body somewhere behind me. Not that I wanted to see the apocalyptic movie that was on. We had an apocalypse of our own, thank you.

Cole was thoughtful enough to pull a fur blanket over us, to cover my freezing feet as I kept rubbing them against his own to warm them up.

"Get closer, Mouse." He tugged me impossibly close to his body, sneaking a hand beneath the blanket to cup one of my breasts, and fusing his warm lips with the back of my neck. I just wished it didn't feel so damn good.

To my surprise, for the first part of the movie, he remained still. So still that I even thought he had fallen asleep. I was shortly about to join him; the movie was boring anyway. I was one second away from dozing off when the wet heat of his tongue traced my neck, so sensual that he was waking up pretty much everything in me.

My eyes snapped open, waiting for him to go on. But nothing else followed. Not for long minutes during which my body finally managed to calm down. I couldn't go back to sleep though. Just let my eyes wander across the room until they met Zale's figure. He was lazily lying on a double sofa with Irina snuggled next to him while both shared the same blanket.

A blanket that was fucking *moving*.

I wanted to look away, but I couldn't. It was impossible to make my eyes drift anywhere else but there. Maybe I was a freak like Brax, but for some reason, I needed to know what she was doing.

Was she giving him a handjob?

It didn't take long for me to find out as I soon noticed how his squared jaw clenched, and the dark tattoos on his neck came to life. Fuck, did she just make him cum?

I had to look away. My gaze trailed throughout the room where everyone else seemed to be enjoying the movie. That's until I noticed Camden with a girl on his lap, and his hand deep beneath her skirt. Not sure if she was having a panic attack or something similar to that. But she was sure having trouble breathing.

My eyes drifted again, finding Treyton, with the same new acquisition straddling him while his face got lost somewhere between the borders of her open jacket.

The guys wanted sex. *Public sex.* This was what the whole thing was about, maybe even the party itself. I recognized their hungry looks from Cole's. The same kind of twisted adrenaline rushed through their veins.

I drew my head a little more to the right, trying to somehow look away, but suddenly that same warm trail reappeared on my neck while Cole's hand began massaging my breast.

"Cole?" I asked with a hint of worry lingering in my voice.

"Turn, Bea." *Bea?* What happened to Mouse!?

Fuck.

Double fuck.

Triple fuck.

Cole's voice didn't sound right. Yet, I turned, knowing there wasn't any way to avoid his command.

"You didn't fight me on this. I'm surprised."

"What exactly is *this*?" I feared asking.

"Raise your leg over my hip," he whispered, brushing his mouth on mine, so unhurriedly that the gesture seemed incredibly intimate.

"Noooo," I whispered back.

"Yesssss." That devilish smile appeared on his lips again, and I was starting to believe it had even more power over me than our deal. Slipping a hand beneath my thighs, he spread them apart so I could get my leg on top of his. "Just stay still and no one will know."

I thought it wasn't about standing still. Besides, "I don't want you to be like them." I buried my head against his chest, hoping I could get him to empathize and hold back. Not that he had a heart to empathize with.

"It's not about me being in any way. It's about the adrenaline." I could feel him unzipping his pants, freeing his cock—so eager that I could feel its shape against my stomach. "You won't find this kind of thrill anywhere else." He drove his fingers to grind on my silky pussy which seemed to be in the exact same stage he'd left it that morning—aroused, sensitive, and fucking drenched.

Cole immediately let a muffled groan out, discovering what devastating effect he had on me. And it seemed it worked both ways. "What the fuck did you do to me?" He sounded annoyed but resigned, almost defeated by what fate threw at him. This wasn't something any of us planned for but it was something we couldn't control anymore.

I raised my eyes to drown into his own while his hand slid between my thighs again, pushing them further apart so he could get me to fit his length. I froze, feeling that all eyes were on me. My lips stopped working, and my body suddenly became rigid.

"It's okay. It's okay, Bea. Just relax. No one is going to know," he whispered, chewing on my bottom lip. Maybe he was right, because he was barely moving, but hot beads of sweat were making room on my forehead and standing still was becoming an impossible task. My body needed to consume his, and to be consumed by him. Grinding my teeth as I was fighting my primal instincts, I nestled my head into his chest, pretending to be asleep. That was the best I could do, since continuing kissing him would draw even more attention upon us.

For some reason, he felt enlarged. Maybe it was just because of the almost nonexistent motion, allowing me to feel every vein probing at my walls. I was all too aware of everything surrounding us, and at the same time careless about everything else. Cole succeeded to entrap me in his moment, melting his lips on top of my head while moving as gently as he was breathing.

"You're fucking beautiful Mouse, did you know that?" His words made a long moan escape my lips and crash upon his chest. Cole was freeing his deepest feelings. He didn't need any lies to get me to submit to him, or to make me remain next to him on the couch. He was just stating the truth as he saw it. And knowing that he could be so gentle, yet so ruthless when it came to what he wanted, was making me understand he was never going to change.

I wanted to stop my hushed moans muffled only by his chest, as I felt him twitch within me. At first, I thought it would be impossible to find ecstasy at that rhythm, but the first flicker of an incoming orgasm crept up on me. It was his presence combined with the adrenaline. And those damn fingers. Fingers that began moving against my clit in slow circles, as if lightning bolts were dancing on my sensitive nub.

"No." I arched against his hand to catch it between our pelvises, and keep him from making me scream right there with our live audience. The action did more harm than good. His fingers began moving faster as he rearranged himself to plunge deeper within. My temples were literally pulsing from holding back, but if I could still somehow control my moans, the tightening sensation in my core was making an orgasm inevitable.

"Shush." Cole kissed the top of my head again, driving his fingers into a vicious assault—stronger and stronger, faster and faster until that twitching sensation ripped through me. Suddenly, my pussy contracted so fiercely that I could hear his throat vibrating with a moan. He needed just a couple of deep thrusts to cum. Thrusts that had me biting into his shirt, trying to keep quiet.

At that moment, I perfectly understood why he was seeking the thrill. The adrenaline awakening your senses, multiplying every sensation, and bringing it to a boundary where it almost becomes impossible to handle.

"Christ, that felt so fucking amazing," he groaned, continuing to kiss the top of my head. "You okay?" His hand snuck under my chin, trying to get me to look at him.

But I wasn't okay.

I was disappointed with him but mostly, with myself—of who I'd become, enjoying something so fundamentally wrong.

"Why do you even care?" I broke all eye contact, turning my back on him. "Zip up, I have to use the bathroom."

I left as soon as I felt him rearrange himself, rushing to the ladies' room. I couldn't breathe. I felt like the whole world was choking me, refusing to accept that I could somehow integrate or even enjoy their madness.

"Hey, where are you going? You look like you're about to faint." Irina snuck up on me just when I finished cleaning myself up, and I was leaving the bathroom.

"How do you do this? All of this?" I asked, my voice shivering. I needed to know what made things work for her.

"Simple. I never say *no*. Makes everything a hell of a lot easier." She arched her plump lips into a smile.

"Leave," a harsh tone made her evaporate as her presence was replaced by Camden's. The guy owned all the good looks in the book, gorgeous by everyone's opinion, yet hiding something so diabolical that it made my body churn. "Next time, I might join you on that couch," he grinned, gazing straight at me.

Fuck, he knew!

My cheeks were about to explode with shame, and I was certain I had trouble hiding it.

"If you ever want to hang out with the big boys, you know where to find me." Camden winked, implying exactly what I thought he did, as I almost ran away from the bathroom.

I went straight outside to catch my breath and cool down. I needed the air, but more than that, I needed the world around me to make sense again. Yet, Cole managed to track me down before I even got a chance to realize how freezing cold it really was on the porch. "What about those cold legs?" he asked while walking toward me and removing his jacket to place it over my shoulders.

"He knows. Maybe everybody knows." I was so angry that I let a tear fall onto the white carpet of snow.

"*Everybody* doesn't know. Stop being so dramatic. Who knows?" Cole had no idea what I was talking about.

I could barely breathe. "Camden."

"Oh…" I didn't like his tone.

"Oh?"

"He might suspect something because of the blanket. But trust me, he *doesn't* know. Unless you led him to believe it was true."

My gaze was blank.

Did I?

"Okay, so maybe you did. Why does it even matter? He fingerfucked that girl he was with. It's not like you got seen by

Holy Mary."

"You're right, Cole. You're always right." I couldn't argue with him. I felt I didn't have the strength in me to do anything anymore.

I knew he sensed the tone of my voice, but for the first time, decided against punishing me for my insolence. Instead, he just ignored my remark, almost pretending he didn't hear it. "Let's get you inside before you catch a cold."

"Can I go to the room?" I asked, more than fed up with this party, or maybe just with him.

"Yeah. Go. I won't be long either. Just need to have a word with Camden."

I closed the door the instant I got inside the room, racing to the bathroom to fully wash him off of me. I wanted to cry, but even tears were refusing to accompany me as the torment of the person I'd become was ruling my very existence. The touches. The kisses. The fucking feelings I nurtured for each one of them. All leading me to be someone else. Someone that I needed to fight from surfacing.

Despite my internal struggle, I decided to take Irina's advice *'never say no'*. It was some kind of self-punishment for allowing myself to be their toy. Maybe consciously being their toy would get me through the day. At least through *this* day, because I definitely couldn't fight Cole any longer. Deep down, I hoped that by making myself no different from every other living, breathing girl around him, I wouldn't pose such an attraction to him.

I decided to wait for him on the bed, dressed in a sexy multi-string bra and a tiny pair of panties.

My king returned to the room less than half an hour later to find me waiting for him between the pillows. "Either you can't get enough of my dick, or you have mixed personalities," he said in an angered tone, walking next to the bed. "So? Which one is it?"

"I'm just giving you what you want." I tried to make things sound simple, but we both knew it was far more complicated than that.

"You don't have the slightest idea of what I want, even if I keep telling you." He got into the bed, next to me—shoes and clothes on. "Move over, Mouse."

I moved to make room for him, but instead of lying on the mattress, he caught me in a hug, burying his head against my stomach. "What's wrong?" he asked, his warm breath caressing my skin.

"Nothing." *Lies.*

Lies that Cole wasn't buying into. "You see, I can't take you seriously when you give me bullshit answers like that. I asked *what's wrong*?"

"You keep saying I should play girlfriend, but you treat me like a tramp." The thought had been weighing on me for a while.

"I haven't even touched you. Are you on drugs?" he retaliated.

"Not now. Earlier." He made me feel as cheap as the girls who got chosen by their *gods*.

"Why? Because we had sex on the couch? If you remember, you came in like five nanoseconds. But okay... you didn't like it..."

"Me liking it doesn't excuse the fact that you forced me into it. For you, I'm no different from the girl who got fingered by Cam." This was what really troubled me.

"First of all, I didn't force you into it. And second, you're miles away from any of those girls. You are my *girlfriend*. You're the only one I kiss, the only one I fuck, and the only one I protect. So you tell me, where does that leave us?"

Cole didn't wait for an answer. Not that I had one. He just stormed out the door and never returned, abandoning me with the question: *Where does that leave us?*

CHAPTER 18

Cole didn't return until the morning, and I hadn't slept until the morning. Judging by the dark circles under his eyes by the time he decided to come back to the room, neither had he.

"Did you pack?" he asked, looking around the room.

"Not everything, but most things."

"Good. I'll get my stuff, and we'll be leaving." He was beyond pissed off. He was calmly pissed off, and that was worrying me. Especially the part where he didn't deviate from his plan for even a second. Just packed his things, took both of our bags, and we were off.

"Did you get any sleep?" I asked him, knowing that he needed to drive for a few hours.

"I'll stop for coffee." It wasn't like Cole was the most communicative person on earth, but his answers came as short as they got. We did stop for coffee, but no other words were wasted between us. He just bought me a cup, and we continued on our journey. Not for long, though; I just had to say something because the silence was getting ridiculous.

"I was thinking I would be the one who goes into the governor's house." At least I didn't keep my eyes open all night for nothing. I was going to be the one who'd try and get something on the governor. It was my idea, after all.

"Okay." He answered like he didn't even give a fuck.

I guess things were settled then. "We'll just need to talk to Ferris when we return, and see if he can help." I tried starting the smallest conversation.

But only received another dry answer in return, "Okay."

He was getting on my nerves, "Is *okay* all you have to say?"

"Pretty much. I did my part." He raised his shoulders, still watching the road.

What was his problem? "What exactly does that mean? You're not going to help us further?"

"I'll help you, don't worry. It's just that I want to end the deal." *Excuse me?*

"End it?" It felt as if my mind couldn't process the words.

"Yes. *Us* or whatever. Let's just say I've grown out of it. *It's not you. It's me* kinda crap." He seemed dead-serious.

"And what about school?" I feared his answer, but I needed to ask that question.

"You can still keep your *title.* I don't fucking care. So, take out your glass and celebrate. You finally got rid of me," he muttered.

"Cole—"

"Drop it."

I wasn't sure what I was going to say anyway. He was right. I should take my glass out and celebrate. The only problem was, I didn't feel like celebrating at all.

Cole kept his eyes on the road the whole drive. Every single feature of his face was telling me it was over.

It was really over. I'd finally gotten rid of one of my kings, and could still keep him to assist us when needed.

That was a good thing.

Wasn't it?

I called Brax and Ferris on the way to Echo so we could meet. I had a plan that needed to be urgently put into practice, but the moment Cole parked his car in front of Ferris's mansion, I realized he wasn't coming in.

"You." He signaled a bodyguard. "Get her bags inside."

"Are you leaving?" I asked. I thought he said he would still help us.

"Yeah. I called Ferris last night on a secure line, and explained everything I got from Cam. He knows what to do."

"I guess this is—"

"Take care, Mouse." And he drove off, leaving a trail of dust behind him to fall upon all the memories we shared.

If only things were that easy.

"Ferris, Brax," I nodded as I entered the room. It was my game from there on.

The two seemed surprised by my new boost of confidence, especially since I was returning without an important link in our chain.

"Cole filled us in on what you got. Good job," Ferris was the first to congratulate me. First *and* last, because no one else followed.

"Let's hear it. I have a meeting with one of the Annelid leaders in less than an hour. Apparently, some of their funds ran out. I'm growing fucking sick of their crap." Brax seemed unsatisfied with the Annelids spending even more funds than the Elite.

"Okay. So we need someone on the inside to search the place, and see if any of those videos actually exist," I said, preparing myself for the plan. "And since he has a passion for young women I was thinking about entering the house through the main door. I'm going to pose as his escort for the night."

Both of the guys blazed back at me with undecided gazes, then turned to look at one another, just to burst into laughter.

"You don't think I can do it?" I asked, convinced that my physique would help me out a little. I mean, it got me *them.*

"I *know you* won't do it." Brax barked, in a cutting reply.

I felt a surge of anger. He didn't get to dictate what I could and could not do—except in his bedroom. "Why?" I asked, crossing my arms.

"Because it's not safe," he snarled. "We'll get someone else to go in."

"And risk having another person involved? Think about it. It's the perfect solution. All we need to find is an agency that supplies girls for him. Well, that and one more thing. We need Ferris's help. Cole said that maybe you could handle the safe or the computer."

"Maybe," Ferris brought a hand under his chin as if he was still weighing the options. "But I don't like the idea of you going in there."

"We have to act quickly. There's no telling how long we can hold back the rebellion, or the governor from putting his plan into action. We don't have time to convince someone new to join us. Especially someone who could seduce him, and at the same time who we can trust not to betray us."

"It's a no," Brax decided, speaking so determinedly that he didn't leave too much room for anyone else to argue.

"Why? What is it to you?" Maybe the aftershock of Cole's departure was still raging in my veins, making my blood boil, and my mouth say stupid things.

"You know what. You're right," Brax angrily replied. But in reality, I was the one who indirectly put the words into his mouth.

At least I got him to agree, even if the cost was higher than I expected. I was hoping for either a daylight confession out of him or an agreement. I guess it paid off in one way. Just not the one that I'd hoped for. "I'll make a few calls, and see where he gets his girls. He has to have a source. It's not like he can put an ad in the paper. Someone on the streets must know." Brax was already formulating a plan to cover up the fact that something inside him wanted to try and stop me.

"That means I should also get to work," Ferris let out a sigh.

"Are you okay going in there? I know it's been a while," Brax asked him, while I had no idea what they were talking about.

"Yeah. I think I'll be okay," Ferris said, his voice distant.

"Do you want me to come with you?" Brax insisted, sensing that Ferris didn't seem comfortable with the new task.

"No. I should be good. Now, if you'll excuse me. I'm going to try and talk to some people I know, and upgrade some of the software I have."

"Do you think we can pull this off?" I asked Ferris, unsure what to believe anymore. He seemed unstable.

"It's not the fucking Pentagon. Yeah, we can pull it off. If *you* can," Ferris said, leaving the room, almost slamming the door behind him.

"Why did you offer to go with him? What happened?" I was trying to put some light on things and who better than Brax to tell me what was happening?

"His father used to be an engineer. Software and artificial intelligence. That, and some good business skills made him rich. Ferris used to work from time to time with him in the garage but I don't think he's been in there ever since his father died. And *we* just sent him into his past."

Fuck! "Maybe we should check and see if he's alright." Despite everything he did, I still cared for him. And I couldn't have one of his breakdowns be on my conscience.

"Even if he isn't, there's not much you or I can do. He needs to fix this from the inside. We did everything we could do from here." Brax seemed tired of trying to fix Ferris. So he just stopped.

Maybe that's what I should have done too. Try to live with who Ferris was now, and accept that the Ferris I want maybe didn't even exist in the first place.

"I have to go. Do you want me to drop you somewhere?" Brax asked, picking up his phone and cigs from the table, and heading toward the exit.

"I'm fine. I still have the limo." I watched him leave, then found my way to my apartment. Nat and Seb were waiting for me there, eager to spend whatever time we could together. I just needed to put my happy mask on, and ignore last night.

Much easier said than done.

Seb was a little under the weather. Nothing that I hadn't seen before, but knowing that he was having even the slightest discomfort got to me like nothing else.

We were just preparing to have dinner when my phone lit up with Brax's name on the screen.

"The Pleasure Room," he said as soon as I picked up, sending a cold chill down my spine. *"The governor sometimes takes contracts from there. The ones willing to put in the **extra work**, of course."*

Just hearing of the place was transposing me right back to the time that key-shaped door first opened for me. A door to a new life.

"Did you fucking hear me, Bea?" Brax was getting annoyed, making me realize I hadn't said anything in return.

"Yes... Yes, I can hear you." My voice barely above a whisper, drowned out by the cacophony of thoughts racing through my mind.

"Do you want me to go with you and speak to Vanya?" He asked, noticing my stuttering.

"No. It's fine. I'll deal with it." I was already rehearsing a speech about what I'd tell her.

"Okay, because she's expecting you now."

"She's what? *Now?*"

"Didn't you say we're in a rush? Well, I called her, and sped things up."

I guess my speech had to be ready a lot sooner than I thought.

"I'll go get changed," I said, hearing him hang up immediately after. Suddenly I wasn't sleepy anymore. I was so wide awake I could feel the acid raindrops falling on the fields across the city.

Things were falling into place so easily that I felt it was too good to be true. And I feared that part. *The too-good-to-be-true* always bit me on my ass. I'd learned that the hard way, like a lesson repeating itself over and over again.

The ride to The Pleasure Room was as if in a daze. I just drifted away, suffocated by my thoughts, and dreading the burden that was to follow.

I couldn't even recall how I ended up in her chair, looking straight into her inquisitive eyes while casually trying to sip from a coffee mug. Like *casually* could still be a word in my vocabulary at a time like that.

"It must be important for Brax to call me personally, and set up an appointment for you. You've come a long way. I'm impressed," Vanya said while twisting a pen between her fingers.

I just wasn't sure what impressed her. The fact that I was sleeping with Brax or Ferris. Or both? I bet she didn't even know about Cole. Not that I was so sure there was something to be known about Cole anymore.

Still, there should have been something other than Brax's call to get her impressed. And I realized Ferris had something to do with it. A message from him appeared on my phone's screen.

Tell Vanya I'll pay <u>whatever</u> it takes to get you in.

"So, what can I help you with?" Vanya lit a long cigarette, rising from her desk to walk toward the window. She was stressed, probably bracing for something serious.

I had to begin somewhere. "I need a favor. Maybe an impossible task, but nonetheless, deadly important."

"Let's hear it." She curved an eyebrow trying to figure out what I could have to say before I actually said it.

I decided not to beat around the bush. "I need to get a contract with the governor. The kind he *specifically* asks for."

"I have no idea what you're talking about." She was playing dumb, but unfortunately, picked the wrong person to take part in her game.

"Brax seems to have an idea. And I don't remember him ever being wrong." My gaze pointed straight at her, assuring her there was no room for her bluffs.

"He is this time." Still no recognition from her.

"You don't understand. This is critical. It involves all of us. Yourself included." I was giving her a hint of the danger we were all in.

"Then start with the beginning. First, tell me what's happening, and then, let me decide." Vanya wasn't the kind to ever be left on the outside.

But I couldn't let her in our plan, not as long as I couldn't tell for sure if she was an enemy or a friend in our game. "I can't. And believe me, it's better you don't know. I just need that piece of paper that grants me access to his house. That's all."

"You've worked here. You know the rules. I never sell out my customers or my employees. Not to the press, not to judges or cops, and I certainly won't do it for you." She was sticking to her principles.

"I know the rules. But do they *also* apply to the governor? I thought it was an employee's decision to stop or go further with the pleasure—if asked."

"It is. I just make sure to send the ones who say *yes*. That's our agreement."

"Then send me. I'll say yes." I uttered.

"Exactly, the very fact that you're considering saying *yes* makes me hesitant to send you. What's really going on?" Vanya's impatience was beginning to show.

"Ferris. He needs some information, and he's willing to pay big to get it." I felt bad lying to her, but it wasn't a total lie if you came to think about it.

"Ferris knows better than to ask something like this of me."

"But I don't." I raised from my seat, resting my knuckles on the table to support my weight. "Vanya, he's willing to pay whatever it takes. I promise that no one will hear a word from me, if you're worried this will blow up in any way."

"If this comes out, it will destroy everything I've built. Customer confidence is the most important part of this business."

"I promise, nothing will be heard. Besides, I'm a former employee. Just make me a new contract, and send me in there the next time he asks. If I work with legal forms, I can take everything on me in case anything goes wrong. *Which it won't.*" I reassured her, although I was perfectly aware I couldn't offer a foolproof guarantee.

"Shit," she grumbled, taking such a strong drag of her cigarette like she wanted to finish it in one go. "What's Brax got to do with all of this?"

"He and Ferris are friends, and he's also directly interested in the matter." I was telling a fractured truth, throwing details here and there so that she could determine the severity of things.

"I can't believe I'm doing this. It's only because I know Brax. And the consequences of not complying with his demands." I could hear a masked fear in her voice every time she mentioned Brax's name. Vanya was working on a fine line between the Pit and the Elite, meeting supply and demand. And since Brax controlled everything that went down in the Pit, by default, he also controlled her.

"If you fuck things up for me, I'm going to come find you and bury you alive. Got that?" She was threatening me, although direct threats weren't exactly in her nature. That was unless she was scared.

"Got it." I nodded in acceptance. It was my ass on the line from now on.

"Two nights from today. I'll slip the letter under the door at 7:25 pm. Your job, how you handle things from there. I want nothing to do with this deal besides what we discussed here."

"Don't worry. No one will suspect a thing. I'll just come to work like you gave me my old job back. That's all they'll ever know. I'll tell the others I was out of town for a while."

"Okay. Better not disappoint me," Vanya said, taking another long drag out of her cigarette.

"I won't." At least, I didn't plan to. Because disappointing her meant disappointing everyone I know.

"And tell Ferris I just ordered a new limo. He's paying the bill." Vanya was playing in the big league. But Ferris was also a big boy. He could handle it.

"Got it," I smiled, understanding that Vanya was more compelled by necessity than profit. She was doing it because she had no other choice, and I felt bad forcing her. "I wish we had a different solution. I promise to tell you what this was all about when it's all over."

"What use would I have for it then?" She asked, lighting herself another cigarette seconds after she put the other one out.

"You would know that our intentions were good, but the limited time left us with no other choice."

"I know you're a good kid, Bea. What the hell have you gotten yourself into?"

"Something I can't back out of." I reached for my bag, "I'll be here in two days."

"Bea, wait." It was bad. I could sense it. I felt she had something to tell me ever since I stepped foot into her office. I was just too afraid to ask what that look in her eyes was really about. "I've been questioning whether I should say something or let you go without knowing. But what the hell? I'm breaking every rule in the book anyway," she gasped, preparing to take a burden off her chest. "How are things with Ferris?"

I dreaded that our conversation would be about him. I feared it to the point that I was considering leaving without hearing her out. But I couldn't ever be at peace with myself if I did that.

Still, I couldn't answer her question either. What could I have said? *Great. He just drugged me a couple of days ago, but everything else is peachy.*

I just looked at her, probably confirming something that she already suspected.

"The reason I'm bringing this up is that a few former employees of mine have taken Pleasures with him in the past." Vanya was breaking her guidelines again for me.

"I know." And for some reason that hurt.

"How should I put this more delicately? One of the girls that worked with him became particularly fond of him."

"He has a specific charm." I completed, still trying to defend him for some unknown reason.

"Bea, he tried to kill her." Vanya's confession instantly made a loud humming noise vibrate inside my head.

I couldn't really put that past him, but the news still came as a shock. "He what?"

"He had a breakdown. Not sure exactly what happened. She didn't tell me everything. But it made her leave town and never return." Vanya continued, slight worry spread across her face.

"Thank you, Vanya. I'll watch out." I just couldn't let her go on without being in danger of fainting right there on the floor.

Closing my eyes, I was trying to take in the information, and slowly smother it. That's what I did with every troubling suspicion or unsettling thought about Ferris anyway. *That's what I did* not because I loved him, but because it was the only way I could keep the plan on course, no matter the personal cost.

CHAPTER 19

I stormed out of Vanya's, locking myself in the limo as if someone was chasing me. Maybe my own soul was after me, at least that part that belonged to Ferris, and I was making one last attempt to leave it behind.

Out of breath. That's all I could ever think about lately. I was always out of breath while the confusion in my mind grew exponentially with every new gesture of my kings', and every new piece of information I was fitting into the grand puzzle.

My phone was ringing—six, seven times. I lost count of the missed calls and messages before I managed to pick it up.

"Yes, Brax?" I answered annoyed, with the exhaustion of a woman who had been through hell and back, and just bought the ticket for journey number two.

The arrogance in his voice was set out to match my tone. *"Am I disturbing you?"*

"I just got out of Vanya's," I answered.

"And where are you now?" he asked.

"I haven't left yet. I'm recollecting my thoughts." I didn't feel like going anywhere at that moment. In fact, I had no idea where to go.

"Stay there." And he hung up only to instruct his driver to

stop his car next to mine two minutes later. "Get in." He rolled down his windows, then opened his Jeep's door.

I couldn't do much but follow his order, even if this was the worst time for the two of us to interact.

"What did Vanya say?" Brax asked with the coldest tone he possessed. I noticed from the instant I got into the car that he was trying to keep his distance, practicing wearing a mask so thick that nothing could break through it.

"You scared her well enough to accept, if that's what you were asking." My tone bitter.

"No, that's not what I was asking," he snarled with the same annoyance in his voice. I thought being the Big Bad Wolf would be an honor for a man in his position, not an offense.

My eyes rolled instinctively. Maybe I just couldn't put up with his bullshit anymore knowing what laid behind it. "She said we have a window in two days."

"Two days?" Brax was surprised by how quickly things were coming into place. But also definitely worried.

We shared that same worry since only *two* days separated us from our goal.

But as usual, he quickly recovered from the news. "How do you plan on doing this?"

"I'll pretend to return to my old job, and just take the letter she indicated. Direct access into the governor's house."

"Bea, I could ask one of the girls from my strip joints to do it." Brax was giving me a way out.

But I was too tired, or maybe even too stubborn to see things for what they were. "I bet you could." I felt betrayed by all of my kings, in one way or the other, and imagining Brax surrounded by all his strippers left a bitter line down my soul, splitting it in half.

"What's that supposed to mean?" His gaze so raw that it felt like he was darting fiery arrows my way, bringing the backseats of the Jeep to incendiary temperatures.

"What do you really want, Brax?" I was tired, completely drained, sick of all the games, fights, and whatever new obstacle life threw at me every single day.

"For you to show some fucking respect. That's what I want." He was growling so loudly that the driver felt the need to push the brake. "Fucking drive!" Brax snapped at him too, making the man speed up to the point he was barely able to stop at a red light. "You know what your problem is, Bea? You need to stop confusing sex with feelings. You're too fucking naive for your own good."

Brax was calling out the source of all my misery. He was right. I was letting myself seek affection where there was never a trace of such a thing from any of them.

"Then maybe you should stop lying to me." Every time I pulled myself apart from his influence, he managed to bring me back in. And that night at the pool changed everything in my heart, even if my mind knew the truth—it was the effect of the whiskey and he was just about to admit the same thing to me.

"I was fucking drunk that night at the pool. That's why I said you're naive. You need to stop believing in fantasies and take a good fucking look around. Survival, wealth, and sex. The existential impulses that make people change their entire nature to obtain them." Brax was teaching me a lesson. One that he had no intention of stopping too soon.

"I understand, Brax." I really did understand, and definitely didn't need him to spell it out for me in a hundred different ways. "Can I call for my car now?" I wanted to go home to try and sleep my misery away.

But Brax had entirely different plans. "No," he barked, picking up his phone and sending out what I believed to be a text.

Suddenly, the car took a turn, heading in the opposite

direction from Ferris's mansion. "Where are we going?" I questioned, recognizing the evil sparks gleaming in Brax's eyes. He had every intention of hurting me this time.

"You'll know when we get there." Opening the minibar, he poured himself a glass of his favorite drink while his lips formed a thin line revealing his level of tension.

Just a few streets later, the car stopped in front of an all-too-familiar place—his nightclub.

He wouldn't. I hoped. I prayed.

"Get out of the car," he groaned, opening the door on my side, waiting for my petrified body to move somehow. "I don't want to drag you out. But you know I will do it." He extended a hand which I didn't take. "It's either your hand or the back of your neck. You decide." His words were so menacing that I truly believed him capable of dragging me out. That finally got me to slip my trembling hand into his own.

"Much better," he hissed, helping me get out of the Jeep, then showed me toward the club's entrance.

I recognized the path we were following, and knew exactly where it would end. I was just praying we would stop before it would be too late. "Brax, I don't want to go in there."

"I do. I'm tense. And I need something to help me relax," he snarled, pushing open a door.

The room with the glass wall. Only this time, the room we were in was identical to the one behind the glass wall. A large armchair and a black cushioned table, one of each on both sides, perfectly arranged to mirror the ones in the opposite room.

"We're going to play a game tonight," Brax came from behind me, wrapping his arms around my waist while whispering in my ear. "Kind of a mirror action." He turned me to face the glass wall, keeping the same position while brushing his stubble on the silky skin of my collarbone.

Suddenly the lights in our room went off, and the same

projector fully illuminated the second chamber. A perfectly shaped brunette was letting herself in. It was not the girl from last time, which made me wonder how many employees like her Brax had.

"I want you to do exactly what she does," he purred against the column of my neck, giving me an impossible task.

"Are you out of your fucking mind?" I retorted, although I knew he wasn't kidding. He was just being the self-entitled bastard that I was already accustomed to.

"Now I'm going to have to make you pay for that sharp tongue of yours. Do what she fucking does. We have a deal," he ordered as the woman on the other side was standing in a confident position, placing both hands on her breasts to cup them, then letting her open palms sensually fall to her hips. Only my palms weren't moving. I was refusing to let Brax break the last of my pride.

This wasn't about teaching me a lesson; I'd never learn. I don't think it was even about his sexual satisfaction. It was about him trying once again to diminish my existence, turning me into one of his puppets. Turning me into something that he could never really care for.

"If you don't do what she does, I'll take you over there. Maybe you'll like things better if she can see us, too." His lips were restlessly brushing the side of my neck while his arousal at the thought was beginning to press onto my thigh.

He wasn't kidding.

He was just laying out new rules, waiting for me to refuse him so he could go further with his plan.

I had no choice but to rest my palms on my hips in the same position as the woman who seemed to be staring back at me.

"She can see us," I protested, noticing a smile blooming at the corner of her mouth.

"She can't see us. The window has a mirror on the other side, just like the ones in interrogation rooms." That calmed my mind a little, but what I was supposed to do next, didn't.

A tall man made his entrance into the room behind the glass wall, heading toward the brunette. She was looking at him through the window's mirror, and even if she had probably done this a hundred times before, she seemed excited. Maybe she lived for the pleasure, or maybe she shared something outside the club with the man, because as soon as he came behind her, she let her back melt on his chest in a closeness that she eagerly displayed.

I couldn't really repeat the gesture since Brax's body was already like a solid rock behind me, reinforcing his dominant position in front of his subdued slave. Or maybe not so subdued after all because, despite my best efforts, I wasn't melting against him. On the contrary, my flesh stiffened, rejecting his touch. It was an effect of his lies, sending me to a place where I was fighting to figure out what was true or not.

The man's arms began moving, gliding on her waist and gripping her hips while Brax's fingers were digging deep into my own hips, letting his feral thoughts come to play.

She suddenly turned. Her lips joined with his in a kiss that expressed all captive emotions.

Without too many options I repeated the gesture, although my lips moving on Brax's had lost all passion. It was mechanical, rehearsed. *All* that he ever wanted.

Maybe he should have taken more consideration to the saying *Be careful what you wish for* because the colder my lips got, the more heated up his became. He was going through an avalanche of feelings, trying to ignite something that he just fought to extinguish.

Everything was surreal. I was looking in a mirror that was showing the same gestures, but not the same reflection. The concept itself was intriguing, to say the least, though maybe better at another time, with another state of mind, and with a different version of Brax.

The woman began unbuttoning the man's shirt, and so did I, tracing the defined muscles with the tip of my tongue while following her lead. Only this time, the beautiful tattoos carved on the rocks of Brax's body were lifeless. Just dull scribblings on a canvas that didn't speak to me anymore.

Everything was getting much easier. Maybe Irina was right. *Never say no.* And I wasn't. I wasn't opposing anymore, just going with the flow. That way I could never get swept away by my feelings again.

I knew Brax was enjoying it, but I also knew he felt something was fundamentally wrong. The warmth of my tongue might have managed to push his unease away, though the doubt remained, slowly infiltrating his system.

The brunette ended up kneeling in front of her partner's belt. So did I. And if the metal buckle coming loose didn't have an effect on me, the hardened shape revealed by his boxers did. I felt a warm coil running down me, flashing through the place between my thighs that he so badly craved. A coil that I decided to ignore completely.

Continuing the game of seduction, the woman raised her eyes to look with satisfaction at the man standing in front of her. I followed her gesture, only *satisfaction* was miles away to describe what my gaze was letting on. For the first time, I was just like Brax, shutting down emotions to put a hollow mask on. Sure, I was hiding disappointment, contempt, and a dangerous type of smothered passion, but all he could see was a rock. The petrified gaze of his puppet, as dead as the ragged material he wanted me to be made of.

I slowly pushed his boxers down to set him free, peeking through the glass at what the brunette was doing. She was already ahead of me, making her partner's arousal lose itself down her mouth. I gasped, knowing I couldn't fall far behind, so without wasting any more time, I took him between my lips, sliding them down the whole length of him.

Brax was beyond aroused, reaching a hand to catch the holstered table for support as his body was gently thrusting inside my mouth. It was all about seeking pleasure, making everything fade in front of the primal urges that ruled us.

Against my will, I was beginning to react to his pleasure. My body was involuntarily heated by the groans leaving his lungs as I was bobbing my head in his direction. I wanted to stop feeling anything, to numb myself back to the puppet Brax wanted. But the faster I moved, the more motionless he remained, letting me decide how I should bring him to ecstasy. He was eagerly waiting, and even if I was determined to disappoint him, the heat of the moment didn't let me. It was like I was on a mission to get him to shudder.

My tongue began moving alongside my lips following a straight line to his tip, making sure he knew exactly when I reached it. With each glide, stronger, draining him of any strength to oppose the oncoming release.

Without warning, his hand caught the back of my head to steady my movements. He couldn't take my assault for long. Right after a few of his determined fingers got caught pulling on the roots of my hair, he drove his hips to move a couple of times, then finally found his yearned ecstasy. I could feel the taste of his orgasm disappearing inside my mouth. I just didn't want to give him the satisfaction of watching me suffer while doing it. My head turned to look toward the glass wall where the woman was still working to raise the ripping waves of elation within her partner. It just seemed he wasn't there yet. Who ever thought that I could beat a pro at bringing a man to ecstasy with my mouth? Not that it would ever be a record to take pride in, considering it's part of a deal.

I hoped I had a break since the couple seemed far away from getting to a *liquid* result. Contrary to my beliefs, after only a few more seconds of moving her head against him, the man lifted her directly onto the table.

It didn't take long before I was on the same piece of furniture in our room, and Brax's lips were searching for the taste of him inside my mouth. He was fired up. I could feel it with every pulse of his tongue, oscillating between keeping a practiced mask of control and breaking all his barriers again. Although the mask seemed to be winning this time around.

His hands slipped to my back, and after a few minutes of one-on-one combat with the zipper of my dress, Brax won. The metal bond had been defeated, although the victory didn't bring any cheering sounds. I just clenched my teeth as hard as I could, hiding any unwanted signs of excitement my body could betray. I imagined I was slipping off my dress to change into something else. The same natural gesture I did a few times a day, ignoring the feverish fingers that urged against my skin along with the fabric.

My attempts to withstand him did not go by unobserved, but this time, there was nothing he could blame me for. It was just a matter of physical attraction, and I just put a fire hose on any flame that aimed to sparkle between us—externally, because on the inside... let's just say things were on a whole different level. A wicked turmoil was building around my waist, rushing toward my core, fueling it with small jolts of smothered signs of excitement. It was as if the harder I tried to oppose it, the more violent the sensation became.

And I needed to take all measures so that it wouldn't surface. No matter what.

A large grin set to rise over Brax's face, as he was trailing a finger from over my lips to down between my legs to skim the center of my panties. He wasn't exactly mirroring the motions of the man from over the glass wall since the guy was already on his knees, exploring the depths of the brunette's core with his tongue.

Brax didn't kneel. It was probably tough for him because of his gunshot wound, yet also at a mental level because of his *rank*. But he did have a plan. He always had a fucking plan. With a swift move, he lifted me higher on the table, pushing my thighs to fully part so I could welcome his stubble against my panty line.

Maybe the gesture gave him pain since his nostrils flared in a smothered annoyance. I just couldn't think about him at that moment—at least, not any longer. He was the one responsible for inflicting on himself every second of this pain, but mostly, the psychological torture he was uselessly subjecting himself to.

The devastating force of his tongue coursed through me. With every rise and fall, he was drawing pressure lines that sent electrifying jolts to the depths of my being. I could feel he had only one thought in mind—to hear his name leaving my lips. His hands digging into my hips, his thick lips alternating kisses with nibbles on my clit. Fucking torture. But I couldn't allow myself to be fooled by Brax once again. I couldn't allow myself to give into him although I wanted to scream and whine and curl and twist, surrendering as the humblest prisoner to his subjugation. Yet no matter how much he worked to get me there, I didn't fall into ecstasy. I might have done it a hundred times in my mind, but I was forcing my body not to respond to him. It wasn't because I didn't have feelings for him, or because his touch couldn't send me jolting straight into the depths of the sky. It was because I wanted to deny him that kind of power over me.

My face was removed of any facial expression, defying his every attempt to make me come, and trying my best to demolish every sensation that he could raise within him. And it felt almost impossible to survive it.

My cold-as-stone attitude didn't go unnoticed. It only drove him further. Two of his fingers slipped to grind in an impossible arousal of senses. He was giving his best, curving them so skillfully that I was certain I would start crying the moment he would stop.

I could barely hold on to my ignorance mask. My muscles were contracting, and my brain was nanoseconds away from popping a vein from all the unreleased pressure. I don't know how, but my head fell somewhere on my right, catching a glimpse of my *mirrored reflection*. She was in ecstasy. Her eyelashes batted between open and closed while her lips cried out, forming a perfect circle.

Brax noticed her too, and I could read the slight annoyance tugging at the corner of his absinthe eyes. Despite his best efforts, he was failing to bring me there.

If only he'd known the truth.

But I was never going to tell him. Instead, I had something much more stinging to say to him. If he was going to break me, then I was going to break his pride. "Do you want me to fake a moan? I'm not sure where our *deal* stands regarding that."

"She didn't fake it two weeks ago when I fucked her," he hisses a confession that just made my manufactured indifference kick in even harder. I knew he said it because I attempted bruising his manly ego. But I also knew he *wasn't* bluffing. "Face down," he ordered, whirling my body to face the cushioned material while he guided my hands to raise above my head, and catch onto the edge of the table. "You're going to need to hold on." The underlining of his voice so dangerously vindictive it was instilling a silent fear deep down to my bones. But I didn't let it show. I just turned my gaze toward the window where the brunette was eagerly waiting for her partner. I was far from doing so. The thought that she could have shown the same eagerness waiting for Brax a few weeks ago made my stomach churn with painful repulsion.

I had serious issues—jealous of her for sleeping with a man I hated, equally infuriated with myself, and yet at the same time, curious to evaluate the competition. Yes, I was *that* mentally fucked-up. She probably had the same leverage as Irina, the *'never say no'* one. That made her perfect for the job, and at the same time so terribly wrong for hopes of any kind of moral backbone. Not that I still had one, but I kept tiny slithers of hope that, maybe one day, I could stand straight again.

The incursion into my soul didn't take long. Brax's palms dug into my hips, and I felt him stretching me to my limit in just one painful move. So different from the last time. Like my mind was asking my body to refuse him. He felt rough. Possessive and ruthless. Moving as if he was trying to break me, and punish me to the deepest extent. He was trying to bring me pleasure through pain, to prove I didn't stand a chance in front of him. But this time, I wasn't willing to fall into his trap.

"What are you doing?" I asked through clenched teeth, feeling him studying his every gesture, deliberately aiming to make me feel the whole size of him. Though I knew the answer well before he said it. I could feel it in my clenched fingers buried in the table's plush.

"Making you regret what you said earlier," Brax rasped, quickening his velocity as my anguish seemed to gradually bring him pleasure again. He was feeding off his monsters to the point where *they* would become one step away from feeding off him. I could hear his breath pacing, making his chest rise and fall with a hindered agony, fighting against the pain his wound was still causing.

He was trying to dominate me, but no one was there anymore. It was like he was knocking at the front door of an abandoned house. And that infuriated him to his very last limit.

I was doing my best to hate his intrusion within my body. Numb myself in all possible senses. Numb him out of my mind. And as a twist of fate, I had every chance of succeeding, at least succeeding in covering up all traces of pleasure.

I watched in satisfaction as the brunette in the next room was stumbling on her breaths, instants away from giving into ecstasy. That was exactly what I wanted—to make Brax boil with the impossibility of getting me to that point. I didn't even need to know him to see it was a competition for him. And his mirror reflection was winning. His muscle mass had just slightly fallen over the brunette in the last flickers of ecstasy.

"You're fighting it, aren't you?" Brax recognized my tricks as I had just made him lose at his own game. He wasn't going to give up. Far from it, especially since I knew his incoming ecstasy was impossible to set back.

Deciding to go in for the kill, he stretched his hand into a fist full of my hair. My clenched fingers immediately lost all grip as I was arching my back with an unbearable curve. He was rushing for something only he knew—a spot that was dragging me to dance on the line between pain and unbearable ecstasy, and with each thrust he was setting it more and more alive.

The last drop of the strength of self-suggestion was draining through my cells, scattering under the sensual stamina of his moves. All of a sudden, he raised my body higher, leaning further to whisper something so undeniably true in my ear. "You can't help yourself with me. No matter how hard you try."

He never retreated, just remained there, fighting against me with a few more thrusts as he was sensually biting on the back of my neck. Without being able to hold back, I felt my core contract with the unstoppable thrill of orgasmic pleasure. I muffled all sounds and shrieks. Maybe I even muffled the beat of my heart, but no matter how hard I tried, I couldn't stop the jolts wrecking my inner walls and entrapping him in a vise.

"Good girl," he groaned through that tightening feeling, finding his release for the second time that night.

The words didn't matter any longer. He could do no further damage to me because there was literally no room left for anything more.

We weren't going to hold hands and cuddle. That part was clear from the start on both sides. It made no further sense to stay at his club any longer. Besides, that was the normal moment when his tramps usually left.

"Are you done with me?" I asked, gathering my clothes from the floor, and putting them back on.

He didn't seem to be in any hurry, just pulled up his pants and took a seat on the sofa to enjoy one of his well-deserved cigarettes.

"Don't play victim with me, Bea. You knew what you were getting yourself into from the start. This is a sex deal. One, no one forced you to enter. No room for love and emotions." He really still thought I didn't get it.

Oh, but I *did*, "It's okay, Brax. I don't need your love. I never knew love except for my family. It's okay not to have feelings for me. I would be much more concerned if you did. For you, I'm an object meant to bring pleasure. And that is what you should seek in me. Only pleasure. That's why I asked the question earlier. Are you done with me? Am I done *pleasuring* you?"

"Get out!" He snarled from his seat, letting the full weight of my words sink in.

How could I refuse such a command since it seemed impossible to be in the same room as him even for a second? I just walked through the door, abandoning shattered pieces of another illusion. Unfortunately, lately, I had been developing a bad habit of collecting pieces, and drops of broken dreams.

CHAPTER 20

I couldn't even remember what day it was, or how many days had passed since I took on the deals. But what I did know was that we had only one day left on the clock to set up our plan.

After another troubled night's sleep, I stayed in bed, rolling between the sheets until noon. It was like I was trying to avoid the inevitable, dreading a new encounter with the kings even more than the plans I had with the governor.

But as usual, my fears usually came true. Before I knew it, I was climbing the entrance steps of Ferris's mansion.

"They're waiting for you in the living room," Alfred let me know as soon as he opened the door, escorting me to where the guys were.

Cole was there too, even though I hadn't expected him to return to help us with this part of the plan. I couldn't say anything about it without feeding his already large ego, but his gesture impressed me more than I was letting it show.

"I see everyone is here." I put on a smile—a bitter one, as I walked into the room. Still, no matter how bitter it was, it couldn't match the one on Ferris's lips. There was something off about him. The same way there was something wrong with me. I was acting on autopilot, tossing all feelings aside and focusing only on the plan. It wasn't like too many feelings were involved in the first place, at least not on their side.

"Do you want a drink?" Brax walked to the bar, probably to get his signature whiskey. I couldn't tell why he even bothered to ask. *Polite* wasn't even a word in his vocabulary. Maybe it was because his conscience was telling him to, aware he took things a little too far last night—not necessarily by his actions, but by his words. It was too late for regrets anyway, maybe even too late for forgiveness.

"I'm fine, thank you," I answered, taking a seat in an armchair next to the fireplace. "So, how are we going to do this?" I looked toward Ferris since he was the one responsible for the tech part.

He didn't answer, lost somewhere in a parallel world, as if he was thinking about something else.

"Ferris?" Cole got his attention, and how couldn't he when he almost yelled at him to snap him out of his thoughts? "Bea was asking about the plan. How are we doing this?"

Still no real answer from Ferris. He just ran his hand through his hair, his eyes narrowing like he was just making sense of things. "Right... the plan," he finally murmured. Then, as if nothing had happened, he asked for my phone. "I'm going to install some basic decoding programs, and a little something to help me operate the phone remotely."

"So, you said his office and the safe. All we have to do is learn where the safe is," I was still trying to figure out how I was going to find out where the safe was, or if the governor even had any compromising videos hidden in there.

"I've been to his house a few times with my father. I don't think the safe is on the ground floor. He always has people over;

parties, brunches, lunches, and whatever else kind of excuse for any kind of event to get to mingle with the Elite. No one would keep a safe in a place with so much traffic. It must be on the second level." Cole tried to explain the Elite's lifestyle to me.

"Communication," Ferris cut us in, acting strangely again. "A wireless micro earpiece that no one could detect, and a camera with a microphone hidden in the earrings."

"Which earrings?" I asked since he didn't tell me to bring a specific set of earrings along.

"These ones." He pulled out a small velvet black box from his pocket.

The last time I saw a box from Ferris, things didn't turn out that great. I just hoped this time would be different. And it was. A pair of diamond earrings that looked exactly like a majestically crafted set of jewelry, and not at all like a device of any kind.

"Perfect," I murmured, putting them on to see how they looked while Ferris turned his laptop toward me so I could view the screen. Live footage of me looking into the monitor was reflected through the earrings at an astonishing quality. "It's like seeing through someone's eyes."

"It's something that my father and I used to work on. Nanotechnology with the highest clarity level available. We'll see everything you see, and hear everything you say as if we were there with you." Ferris stood up right after he finished speaking and walked to the opposite corner of the room to get something from a table.

"What's that?" I asked, noticing another small box in his hands.

"Air pods. At least that's how they look to the untrained eye. They have a USB cable to connect to the computer and a cable for your phone," he said, pulling a cable from the small box.

Brax cared to continue, "They'll probably have you go through a security check. I don't want you to have anything suspicious on you."

I didn't say anything back. Maybe I should have, but Brax wasn't *the keen-on-words* kind, and I wasn't in the mood to waste any on him.

"You'll have a tracker in the earrings, in addition to the one in your phone," Ferris explained while taking a drag from his cigarette.

"I have a tracker in my phone?" That was new to me.

"Relax, every phone can be tracked these days," Cole jumped in to explain before I went for Ferris's throat because of the intrusions in my personal space. Not that I had any personal space lately.

How was I supposed to know? My old phone looked like it came straight out of a wall—a brick wall. It didn't even have a touchscreen. Pretty sure a tracker was out of the question for that one.

"Cole and I will wait outside, along with a couple of my men. Just for backup in case anything goes wrong," Brax shared an aspect we hadn't discussed before. Sure, extra security measures should have given me some peace of mind. But if Brax by any chance would break into the governor's house, what would it lead to? Everything would be out in the open. Everything we were trying to achieve would be ruined.

"I don't want backup. It could jeopardize everything." I said, having considered the alternatives.

Though Cole didn't seem to agree. "Did you notice the part where we didn't ask?"

"I'm not letting you risk everything. I'll be fine." I wasn't going to let it drop.

But then again, I didn't have a choice. "It's not negotiable, Bea," Brax placed his glass on the table, "Cole and I will handle this part. You two handle the rest."

"The *rest* isn't entirely finished. I need a few extra hours to install some programs on Bea's phone and sync a few things before we're good to go. I guess I'll be ready later this evening." Ferris stood up, heading for the door. "Bea, drop by in a few hours to get your phone," he said in the same unusual tone, then disappeared somewhere into the lobby.

"That's that. I should get going." Cole also decided to leave. "We'll meet tomorrow, Brax."

"Hold on," I called out to him, not before I walked to Brax, and asked him for a *favor* to help me make our plan work. "Walk me to the car," I almost ran after Cole the second I was done. Being alone with Brax in the same room didn't seem like a good option at the time.

"Now I'm the good guy?" Cole asked with a hint of sarcasm lingering in his words as we walked back through the hallway.

Come to think about it, if I had to choose out of the three of them, Cole was the *good guy.* But I wasn't going to ever admit that. "You've just chosen to play a different type of game with your *toy*," I answered, getting back into the car that was waiting for me, without waiting to see if Cole had something to add.

I spent the next few hours playing Monopoly with Nat and Seb. Strange how it seemed more like some kind of training for life, and not really a game this time around. Maybe I'd been spending too much time with Ferris and Brax because the road to Boardwalk didn't seem to be paved with gold anymore.

It was around midnight when I tucked Seb in. Strangely, I hadn't received any word from Ferris yet. I decided to call him, but no one answered. Something was off again, and I was getting tired of things being *off* with Ferris, but this time I needed him more than ever. It wasn't even a choice, he was an essential piece of the puzzle. I needed my phone by tomorrow, and I had to make sure everything was going to plan.

I decided to go and pay him a second visit, even though every sign advised me against it. And if the signs weren't enough, then a verbal warning from Alfred should have made me come to my senses. "Ferris is... not up to receiving visitors," he said, opening the door.

If only I had ears to listen, "I need to talk to him. Sorry Alfred, but I can't take *no* for an answer this time."

"Miss Bea, he's not well." A second warning that flew straight by my ears.

"When was he ever *well*?" I smiled, passing by Alfred and heading to the stairs.

Turns out, this time he wasn't *well* at all. I recognized it the instant I entered his bedroom. Smashed furniture and shattered glass were scattered everywhere I looked. Like a typhoon swept through the whole place, utter destruction down to the last piece of what that room stood for. All warnings of the disaster that lay within him.

Despite the devastation, my phone seemed to be lying on the couch. It was still in one piece. That came both as a surprise, and also a relief since we needed it tomorrow—if it was ready.

"Take it. I've finished," Ferris's voice echoed from a dark corner of the room. All the lamps were broken, and all the candles spilled on the floor so I couldn't really notice him there, to begin with.

"Did you install everything?" I asked, trying to get a better look at his face.

"Yes. Everything should be good now," he answered without moving from the spot he seemed to be hiding in.

"You have your own meeting with the governor in the morning to talk about funding. Are you okay, to go through with that?" I asked, trying to start a conversation with him. I couldn't leave him, not before I could understand what was wrong with him, and knew he had fully calmed down. His meeting with the governor became irrelevant in the meantime anyway since I was going in to search for any dirt we could get on him. Still, we did need a backup plan in case something went wrong on my end.

"Do I not seem okay?" he asked with a touch of irony.

I took a step toward him, walking straight into the lion's den. "No, you don't. What's going on?" I was afraid he might have done something stupid and hurt himself.

"Redecorating." He tilted his head backward to support it on the wall behind him as I was getting close enough to distinguish the shape of his body.

"Just don't register for architecture school any time soon."

"What is it that you really want, Bea?" I could see the red sparkles of his cigarette lighting a cloud of smoke as he took a drag.

"To help you." I reached out a hand to touch him, and like a vampire in the night, his darkness pulled me in, crushing my body against his own, and merging our lips into the most sinful kiss.

"There is no helping me," he growled between the flickers

of his tongue on mine, wrapping his arms around me so tightly that the flesh he was hugging was about to bruise.

Maybe I was insane myself, but I didn't want him to stop. I couldn't even think about him stopping as the rush of him was drugging me on the spot. It was like falling into a dark abyss, plunging into danger and somehow craving to do it.

I wished I knew better, but I couldn't fight the taste of his lips—toxic, like the most venomous snake, sending out his poison to the very last piece of me.

He was chaotic, and at the same time incredibly determined, raising my body on his hips, entrapping me between him and the wall. He was supporting me there so he could find my lips in decadent pleasure, roaring sweet lies to glide within me through the cracked pieces of my soul. "I need you. I need you like never before."

I was stupid enough to believe him, helping him break an innocence that could never be put back together again. I still loved him at an unconscious level, and against his own warning, was hopelessly trying to heal his soul. Little did I know, he needed to still have a soul in the first place so I could try and heal it.

"Ferris, tell me what's wrong, please," I insisted, hoping that maybe there was a way to get through to him. I guess some fools never learn, and I was the fool this time.

"Nothing is wrong now that you're here," he whispered between ghosted breaths, running his thumb over my cheekbone, then securing a hand to the back of my head.

I couldn't trust what he said. Everything seemed incredibly wrong, falling into an abyss of fabricated illusions, so magically charged with every single emotion brewing between us. And that made it seem so dangerously right.

The constant on and off between me and my kings must've caused it, altering perception, changing my perspective of reality so much I couldn't tell what was what anymore. The games, hidden feelings, the ambiguous confessions— everything culminating in a fog engulfing my world, making me get lost in the moment while missing out on the picture as a whole.

As if trying to bring me back to earth, his fist fell on the wall right next to me. The vibration of the impact was so strong that it reverberated throughout my entire body. "Ferris? Ferris, what's happening?" I asked again, wrapping my arms around his broad neck, and fusing my lips to trace the line of his jaw.

Surprisingly, this time, I did receive an answer, "I need to take my mind off everything. I need to stop the memories." His forehead pressed against mine as if he was trying to be rid even of a little part of his pain.

I would have taken it all upon myself, if only it could have been that easy.

"Just come back to me. Be here with me, in this moment," I whispered, pressing my mouth on his, in the hope of giving him the distraction he so desperately needed.

Only it wasn't a distraction that he craved. It was total chaos, a madness taken to the extreme.

He never wanted to join me. He wanted *me* to join him. Ferris needed to break something, other than objects, so he could finally feel safe.

So, he chose to **break me.**

With a rushed gesture, he caught the back of my head in a tight grip, forcing me to look straight into the pitch-black color of his eyes. His monsters were all there again, surfacing one by one with one single goal—to destroy me.

I didn't have time to react as he drove his hands beneath my knees, securing me on his waist, and began walking towards the double glass balcony door.

"What are you doing?" I asked with a trembling voice, even though I knew exactly what he was doing.

"I need this," he said with a hint of madness lingering on the tip of his tongue, striding toward the ledge with me straddled on his hips. "I've got you. All you have to do is trust me."

The most impossible request. I could do anything he asked of me—except trust him. That I couldn't do ever again.

My body turned to stone against his own the second I felt the cold rim nudging on my calves. Then the coldness spread toward the back of my upper legs and higher to my ass as he gently placed me on the edge of the railing. "Ferris, stop it," I begged, hoping that my plea would tear through the veil clouding his mind.

It didn't.

He was so much more lost than I could ever realize. "I can't. I need this," he answered in a dying murmur, with such agony that I was one step away from believing this could be his only salvation.

His salvation—*my destruction.*

With the hunger of the predator, he ripped the top of my dress apart so he could discover the round shapes of my breasts. A snarl escaped his throat at the encounter, biting his bottom lip with uncontained lust right before he could unclasp my bra, and reveal my pebbled nipples. His gaze raw, visceral, waiting an extra second to visually feast on his meal before going in for the kill.

I felt his grip on my back loosening just a little the second he drove his lips to search for the sweetness of my nipples. The movement startled me, waking me from my petrified trance and bringing me to wrap my arms around his neck while his mouth began moving over my aching tips.

I think it was freezing outside, but somehow the atmosphere seemed one step away from catching on fire. Every cell within me was brewing either with monstrous fear or with the anguishing throbbing produced by the adrenaline rushing through my veins. His lips were dancing with the intensity of a storm as his teeth were grazing painfully into my skin, testing that thin line again between agony and ecstasy.

A desperate craving to have me. I could see it in his every single gesture, rushing his palm to discover new areas of my skin while his other hand was forced to remain tightly wrapped around my back to keep me from falling into the abyss.

If I were to base my judgment on the clasped muscular arm that was keeping me secure, I was completely safe. But that wasn't what worried me. It was the madness. The irrational moment in which Ferris could decide to let go of everything. He wasn't thinking straight and that made him dangerous.

"I never felt something like this," his lips murmured a confession while raising to join mine. A confession I couldn't take for granted; just add it to the list of possible lies and deceit.

Maybe I could have believed him. It made no difference anyway. On the contrary, it meant he was trying to destroy all feelings with that speed he rushed to destroy me.

The bulge in his pants threatening to break free was becoming more than obvious, propelling itself against my leg. That's what brought his hand to push the hem of my dress so high that in just one move, he reached my panties. I prayed he would stop since every new move seemed to unbalance me a little further, pushing my body deeper into the abyss beneath us.

But he didn't.

He just pulled on the material, ripping it apart to find the place he was anxious to reach. I couldn't even think of that. I could only focus on the gap below us, as the darkness beneath was spreading its wings, hungry to grab us.

His eager fingers were already probing my pussy, searching for ways to give me pleasure. But fear continued to replace any different thought while daggers of cold chills were piercing through my sensitive flesh.

"Don't be like this." He curved the corner of his lips into a decadent smile, feeling me completely frozen against the warmth of his own body.

"If you want to ruin me, then take out that knife and do it already," I snapped back, urging him to finish off his plans. If he wanted my blood, then it was time for him to claim it.

"I'm not ruining you, Bea. I'm setting you free," he groaned, releasing himself from his clothes imprisonment, and easing the tip of his length inside me.

The sensation I knew so well by now made me close my eyes, steadying my feet against the bottom of the railing, expecting the sensual assault that was to come. I had never seen such fire burning through him before. Lava-heated waves of his passion seemed to be spilling directly onto my skin. His feverish lips were still melted over my own, but his free hand ran with primal desire from the inside of my thighs to cupping my breasts from beneath.

He began to gradually move, gliding further and further in a delicious intrusion that I wanted so badly to despise. But the adrenaline was kicking in, mellowing all defense mechanisms and raising tiny jolts of unwelcome pleasure within me. It was all too intense, too taken to the extreme; and along with the increase in his pace, Ferris was pushing the line between life and death. My arms were still tightly gripping his neck. But he was moving so firmly that I felt I could slip off at any time and maybe even pull him into the gap.

"Slow down!" I cried out between the rush of ecstasy, and my world falling apart.

"No. Just trust me," he answered, his jaw clenched to the max, seeking to drain the very last drop of our luck while thrusting deeper, and more sensually within me. "Relax. Put your hands here," he unclenched my hands from over his neck and shifted them to hang onto his forearms, setting a small distance between us so he could move more freely. A distance that was sending me even closer to the abyss, only to be pushed even further by the rhythm of his movements.

He was growling loudly with excitement as my eyes filled up with tears, in a combination of fear and thick waves of rapture. It was as if he was bringing all my fears to life, crushing me with the uncertainty of his next action. And the moment I dreaded most could hold no postponement. In just one gesture, he lifted me higher until I felt that only the back of my knees was touching the ledge. He was raising me somewhere in the air, pushing my body away just to bring it back to crash against his own the very next moment.

It could have been sublime, an erotic demonstration of powers, making every cell in our bodies vibrate with the tempo he was creating. Except I was four hundred feet away from touching the ground.

And still, that didn't stop me from exploding with the pleasure he was forcing within me. I was moments away, and he felt it, setting a distance between us. He was keeping his hand on the small of my back but brought the other to pinch my clit, instantly turning the signs of my release into fucking euphoria.

He didn't let go, just parted my body from his to bring me back again, uniting us so deeply that I could feel him shuddering through his release in the pit of my stomach.

My body probably loved him for the undeniable thrill, but I hated him for risking our lives over an ephemeral sensation. I loathed him as much as I truly feared his madness, just thinking about the moment when even a risk like this wouldn't be enough anymore for him.

He had broken me. So irremediably that a future for us couldn't exist. Not that he ever wanted anything else besides a cheap thrill anyway.

Strange how the moment he set me down, I felt like I was attending a funeral, saying goodbye to someone I had loved, but was never really mine.

His lips uselessly searched for movement against my own, as the experience seemed to have brought him a strange mental relief. He was entirely different, almost overflowing with happiness to the point I thought he had become blind to what his satisfaction really did to me.

I rushed inside the instant I was back on my feet, searching through the piles of scattered clothes to find a jacket and cover my ripped dress.

"Bea... Bea, what are you doing?" I could hear him ask while he followed me back to the room. But I couldn't answer. I couldn't even speak.

I felt him somewhere behind me just as I picked up one of his hoodies and pulled it over my head. And as soon as I finished, his arms wrapped around me, trying, as he had every single time before, to erase the madness with a kiss. "Bea. It's okay. I'm okay now."

He... *he* was okay.

"It made me feel alive," he breathed with relief.

"I'm happy *you're* alive because you just killed *us*."

CHAPTER 21

I guess it was irrelevant to say that the night with Ferris ended with the last of my words. I couldn't be there anymore, and he didn't have the nerve to ask me to stay. I just grabbed my phone and headed straight to the safety of my own bed. Not that anything would ever feel safe anymore after what happened in my life lately.

University was the last thing on my mind. I simply refused to take the quilt off my head until noon. I wasn't really sleeping. Maybe just hiding from the rest of the world beneath a shallow illusion of protection. But it was time for me to get ready to go to the Pleasure Room. It wasn't like I could show up at 7:15 p.m. and take the 7:30 p.m. Pleasure. I had to wait a while so that nothing could connect things to it being a setup.

Nat and Seb weren't home from school yet which made me think about how far we'd come—the two being in an Elite school now, when a few months ago they weren't allowed to attend classes. I didn't even have time to kiss them goodbye. It's not like we were really saying goodbye. I was only going to be away for a few hours. Though this time I felt I needed to do it—just in case. I guess I missed that shot too because of my evening spent with Ferris.

Comforting myself with the thought, I got dressed in whatever I found first and left for the Pleasure Room. It was a walk down memory lane as every minute closer built up the same state of anxiety. Only this time, I wasn't traveling from the Pit. I was traveling from the Hills. Things had changed, and so had the sheepish girl who first entered through Vanya's door to discover a whole new universe—a rotten one, yet the only option to salvation.

I couldn't even remember how exactly I had arrived there, but I found myself standing in front of the wooden-carved door, looking at the sculpting grinning back at me. It took every drop of courage in me to push it open, knowing that once I walked into the room there was no way back.

All eyes were staring at me the instant I passed through the door. I knew most of the people present there, but there were two girls that I'd never seen before. Poor souls.

A friendly face I hadn't seen in a while came to greet me. Laura, the person who made the experience so much easier to handle, especially since I was a newbie at socializing—amongst other things.

"I haven't seen you around, stranger." Laura spread her arms widely to hug me, as I responded to her gesture.

"I needed a vacation." I smiled, trying to avoid the subject.

"After only two weeks?" Laura giggled, knowing I was lying. "This had something to do with the Pleasure you took at the mansion up in the Hills. Didn't it?"

"Maybe just a little." I still didn't want to get into too many details with her. "Do you still have coffee around here?" I asked, looking toward the beverages area.

"I wouldn't come to work otherwise." Laura caught me by the arm and guided me to the table while a red envelope sneaked through the door. "You're kinda new today, so you can take the Pleasure if you want," she let me know while the girl who grabbed the letter was signaling me to go and read it.

308

"I need to reacquaint myself with the place. You take it. I'll open the next." I signaled to the girl who picked it up as I poured myself a cup of coffee.

"They probably won't be as kind to you as you are with them," Laura cared to advise me, even though in reality I didn't plan on staying. But she wasn't aware of that yet.

"That's okay. I wasn't expecting to take the first Pleasure anyway." The truth was, I didn't expect to walk through the door and be served an envelope, especially since I wasn't exactly a newbie anymore.

The next few envelopes came requesting specific employees, so I didn't need to find an excuse not to pick them up. I only opened one.

Making an impression at company dinner

Woman early to mid-twenties

$1000

8 PM

That could have actually been fun. Still, I refused, claiming I had food poisoning two days ago, and my stomach was still too sensitive to eat who knows what they would serve. I was becoming an ace at improvising, especially with the role of my life coming up in just a few hours. And the letter that was bringing it finally arrived under the door.

Deluxe entertainment

Attractive woman

Starting at $1500

9 PM

"Don't take this Pleasure." Laura snuck up on me, asking me to decline, probably knowing that I never went beyond the agreed limits of a Pleasure.

She was right to warn me, but this time the hidden warning was exactly what had brought me back to the Pleasure

Room. "Sorry, but I can't pass up on this one," I answered, nodding that I accept the Pleasure.

"No, you don't understand. He will ask more of you," Laura tried to clarify things.

"I can't refuse. I need the money," I whispered, walking toward the changing room to get ready as her disappointed gaze followed me to the door. I couldn't tell her the truth. What *was* the truth, after all? I was still selling my body, exactly as she assumed, just not to the person she was thinking of.

I was a girl on a mission, and that meant I had several parts to my plan. After picking up a black lace bodycon dress and a sexy coat to go with it, I refreshed my makeup and fixed my hair a little. Well, not really a little; more like somewhere around 45 minutes, but finally, I was done. All I had to do was put on my new earrings and earpiece.

"Can you hear me?" I checked with Ferris who was listening on the other end.

"*We can all hear and see you. You're good to go,*" Brax was the one who replied, assuring me we were all set.

Unwilling to drag things out or to have to talk to any of *my kings*, I was on my way out, as soon as I knew everything was working.

I remembered the terrifying feeling I had when walking toward my first Pleasure. This was ten times worse. And this time around, no one was holding my hand to cheer me up.

I entered the limousine destined to take me there, knowing exactly where I was going. Such a huge difference from the other Pleasures. Fear and determination were the only elements vivid in my world as I was looking out the window, hoping to prolong the moment for as long as I could. This was my idea after all. I was responsible for what would go on.

One of Brax's glasses of whiskey could have come in handy to help calm my nerves—especially since I was getting new ones only when thinking about him.

After less than twenty minutes—that actually felt more like a lifetime—we'd reached the governor's residence. The same grotesque luxury, taken to the extreme to prove the extent of his wealth, and of course, his membership in the Elite.

While going inside, I glanced at all the bodyguards scattered around the property. No way would this many guards ever be needed to guard an *untainted* man—no matter what his importance. And no way could Brax or Cole interfere if anything would go wrong. But I needed to be optimistic. Nothing would go wrong.

"I'm here for this." I extended the letter to the guard who was watching the main door of the house.

"Can you show me your handbag?" The man asked to check my things just as Brax suspected he would. I don't even know why I was nervous about that part. Ferris made sure nothing could draw suspicion. Well, nothing except a very sexy piece of lingerie that I was carrying. But that brought more like a smile to the guard's lips. "This way, miss. I'll walk you." The man immediately offered to escort me to the place I needed to be. "In here." He opened a large door which seemed to lead to an open spaced living room and gestured for me to go inside.

"You're new," a surprised voice welcomed me the second I set foot inside the room. It was the governor. I recognized him from TV. A libidinous man in his late fifties with more hair growing out of his ears than on his scalp, and a grin so sick that it made me wonder if all residents of Echo City were blind when they voted for him.

"New *here*." I smiled, rearranging my posture, showing all

my weapons of feminine seduction.

"Vanya didn't tell me she had someone new when I paid for this." He seemed slightly reticent when it came to new interactions. And I couldn't allow that for long.

Catching the collar of my coat between my fingers, I traced it down in a sensual line over my breasts. I only stopped at my waist to unfasten the cord and reveal the extremely tight dress. "Don't tell me you're disappointed?" I asked, slightly pouting my lips. Not enough to seem phony, but enough for him to notice.

"No. Definitely not disappointed. But I do have some doubts that you have what it takes to play my games." He showed the same resistance as earlier.

And I had every intention to break it.

With feline steps, I approached the place where he was standing, letting my coat slip to the floor

"Oh, but maybe I want you to play *my* games," I whispered, lifting the hem of my dress to adjust my garter belt.

In that second, I had hooked him. Not completely, but I could feel the bad-girl attitude was working for him. And if I had any doubt, his hand racing to glide onto my hip just confirmed it. "No," I pushed his hand back. "Rule number one: don't touch unless I say so," I whispered, raising a finger to bring it millimeters away from his lips, but without really touching them.

"Maybe I could use a change once in a while," he grinned in the most despicable way, eagerly waiting for me to go on.

Which I did. "Rule number two: when I say everything goes. That means *everything* goes." I could see the excitement in his gaze, chewing the corner of his lips with uncontained eagerness. "And three: well, three is usually very pricey, but it's not every day I get a man like yourself. Three: you will get a taste of each setting, and I'll let you decide on the one you want before we begin. How does that sound?"

"Amazing." He was mesmerized, driven only by the sexual vibe I had activated within him.

"I'm very excited that you agree. Now, Mr. Governor... for the first scenario, I would need an office. You do have a home office, right?" In reality, I needed to explore the place and the little game I had in mind was giving me that opportunity.

"Yes, it's upstairs," he answered, eager to get things going.

"Show me," I exclaimed, rearranging my dress so we could leave the room.

One of his hands moved onto the small of my back, showing me the way. "This way, Sexy."

"What did I say rule number one was?" I asked, planning to use that rule to keep his hands off me.

"Don't touch unless I say so." He repeated my rule.

"Then don't." I peeled off his hand. "It ruins the wait," I turned to throw him a wink, then slowly walked in front of him, waiting for him to guide me toward his office.

*"Thought you didn't like **scenarios**,"* I could hear Brax mutter from somewhere in my earpiece, but it wasn't like I could answer—or even wanted to.

"Here," the governor announced as soon as we reached the second floor, pushing a door open, and revealing his office. Impressive woodwork and decorations, along with diplomas to match it. Most of them bought with a few checks, I was sure. But the surroundings weren't of my interest, my eyes were drawn to a certain object in the room. The laptop was on a massive wooden desk right in the middle of the room. I was in the right place, just as I suspected. That's all I ever cared about.

"Now be a good boy, and wait for me in here."

He nodded, getting comfortable in his presidential chair.

"Tell me where the bathroom is so I can get ready," I asked.

"Second door on the left."

I delicately walked out, taking my bag with me. There were four men only on this floor. There wasn't any chance in hell I could pull this off with them present, and I only had a few minutes to figure out how to get rid of them. The second I stepped into the bathroom, I took off the lace dress, revealing an extremely sexy red teddy—garter belt and all.

"Did I buy that?" I could hear Ferris's voice echoing in my ear, reminding me they could also see everything I did.

"It's going straight to the trash after tonight," I muttered so he could hear me, pulling out an office-tight buttoned dress that closed up to my neck. I looked like the innocent hiding *a sin*. Maybe that's what I was until tonight. But not any longer. Now I was *the sinner*.

I returned to the office, not before scanning the guards one more time.

"Did you miss me?" I trailed my teeth on my bottom lip, casting the governor a smile that seemed to hide anticipation. In reality, it only hid disgust, but I was doing my best to mask it.

"I was getting impatient," he confessed.

"Tsk... tsk... First, you see what I have to offer, and only after you choose," I moved my finger as a no, to signal him to stay still. "Now, I don't want to play secretary. That would be too trivial. Who do you fantasize about from work?"

He instantly let out a sleazy laugh. "You're right. I've already fucked my secretary."

"Then tell me. Who do you crave? Who gets you hard just by walking in front of you?" I was trying to unveil his secrets.

"Jesus, you're good. Mrs. Finley from accounting. She's not too pretty, but she's got that innocent–evil attitude."

"Oh, I see," I let out a sigh while my mouth slightly began to shiver, and my thighs firmly pressed together, repulsed by the thought that he could ever get access to the place between them. "How does she wear her hair?" I asked, trying to get in character.

"In a bun." He looked at me with real interest while I drove my hands through my hair and lifted it to catch it in a bun.

Mission accomplished.

"Like this?" I asked, approaching his desk, careful enough to sway my hips on my way there.

"Exactly like that," he grinned, eager to see my next move.

"Then Mr. Governor, it's time to discuss our monthly budget." I gently leaned over his desk, continuing the same sheepish gestures.

"Did you do the revenue graphics? Or do I have to punish you?" he asked, falling straight into my trap.

"Mr. Governor... I... I didn't get to finish them." I unclasped the first two buttons of my dress, "Is it hot in here? Or is it just me being nervous?" I asked, playing around, and opening an additional button.

"Let me help you with that." He rushed to assist me with my buttons, but stopped just in time. "Only if you say so. I haven't forgotten about the rule this time."

"Only two buttons for this presentation, Mr. Governor," I answered seductively, waiting for his approach.

It took him a second to get next to me and start unbuttoning my shirt, trying to run his sleazy hands over my breasts. I froze, barely holding back from throwing up. "Just two." I brought it to his attention that he was wandering off a little too far. "You wouldn't want to miss out on the second setting," I said, releasing my hair to fall back on my shoulders.

"But I want Mrs. Finley," he whined, just like a toddler about to lose his toys.

"I have more. *So* much more to show you. Just tell me who you *really* want. Who do you really want to fuck? It can be out of lust, regret, maybe even revenge. Who gets to you?" I asked, trying to move on with my plan.

"My ex-wife. She does all of the above to me," he said, with a trace of regret blooming in his voice.

"Then let me be *her* for you." I moved my finger along the line where his shirt fit together. "But first. I just have one request," I whispered, one word at a time.

"What is it?" he asked, willing to comply, willing to do anything it would take just for me to go on.

"You see, I only do Elite. Top Elite. This body—" I pulled at my cleavage to give him a more thorough look. "This body is reserved only for royal eyes."

I could see the satisfaction growing on his face as I had just touched his weak spot—the disdain he felt for *all* Annelids. Little did he know it was all a part of my plan.

"That's why I don't want your guards to look at me, especially since I'm sure we won't be needing these clothes soon, and especially since we're trying a few scenarios to see what *really* turns you on. I want to be *free* in my actions."

"I fucking hate Annelids," he whispered, opening the door and walking into the hallway. "Clear this level."

"Boss?" One of the guards seemed almost shocked by the request.

"Clear this level, and close all cameras. I don't want you to look at her," he roared as if defending some newfound piece of property.

"Yes, sir." The men immediately scattered, complying with his command.

"That was hot. You deserve a reward. I'll throw in a bonus for you," I came from behind him, whispering in his ear, trying to give him the security of my trust.

"I sure do, Sexy. So where to next?" he asked, waiting for me to lead him.

My plan was to search the other rooms. "Give me something your ex-wife used to wear. And some accessories. Jewelry or something she liked."

"The bitch took all the jewelry, but I still have a few of her clothes in a spare room." *Bingo!*

"Take me there." He didn't wait for me to ask him twice. Taking a left turn, he opened a room that seemed to be full of random stuff piled there.

"Take whatever you want," he gestured toward two racks full of gowns, furs, and other clothing items.

"Please wait outside. I don't want to spoil the surprise," I rushed him out, closing the door behind him.

"Oh, and there's a small detail I missed out on. My ex didn't wear lingerie," he called out from the hallway. That *little* detail made my stomach churn with a rotten, disgusting sensation.

The second the door closed, I started taking my clothes off to change, keeping an eye out for the safe at the same time. I still couldn't find it, but I couldn't let an opportunity go to waste.

"Check the room for paintings, and look behind them for a safe," Brax instructed, as if I hadn't seen any heist movies myself. But despite my best efforts, I couldn't find anything.

"Don't forget about the lingerie," Cole *cared* to remind me. *"I* **have** *to meet Camden's mom."*

"Shut the fuck up. We need the line clear," Ferris cut in, breaking Cole's enthusiasm.

I would have liked to sneak in a word or two, but I couldn't talk and risk the governor hearing me. I just pulled on a red silk dress I found on one of the racks, and an oversized fur collar that made me look like I had just come from the Oscars.

"You can come in!" I called out to the governor, although I wasn't really prepared to see him. I didn't think I could ever really be prepared to see him, knowing that his sleazy eyes would lustfully travel every inch of my body. I was just praying I could keep things only at a visual level. "Like what you see?" I asked while letting the fur fall just a little over one of my shoulders, revealing the shape of my silhouette that was so visible through the satin that I felt almost naked.

I needed to keep his interest, no matter what.

"You look so much like Louise." I could see the shock on his face as he closed in on me, this time all too eager to touch. "Game over," he snarled, bringing his arms to wrap around me in a human cage.

"Mr. Governor, you're not playing by the rules. And do you know what that means in *my* game?"

"What?" he asked with a trembling voice.

"That you're going to lose out on an important part of the night." I needed a way out. Fast!

"What would that be?" He pushed the fur collar to fall off completely, staring directly at the way the silk arranged itself over the V-shape of my cleavage. "I can't wait. Besides, I want you... I want you to be Louise tonight."

I needed plan B.

"That's a shame. I pegged you as a fan of straps. And I'm not usually wrong," I moaned in his ear as his lips were already trying to make room on my collarbone.

"Straps?" he stopped, intrigued even by the way the word sounded.

"It's okay if you don't like straps, I guess I was wrong." I was pushing his buttons.

And it was working. "Tell me more."

"I have one other scenario in mind for you that I think you would love. *The eccentric mistress of a billionaire.*"

He arched an eyebrow. My plan was working.

"I have a very, and I mean very tiny boudoir teddy made out of straps," I said, running my hands over the fullness of my breasts.

"Okay, let me see that one too," he nodded, doubting his decision a little, yet unable to refuse my proposal.

My arms wrapped around his neck, searching the depths of his gaze. "Let's use the bedroom for this one. Shall we? I don't usually like beds, but I have some ideas I'm very eager to share with you."

"I have a feeling this is going to be the last stop," he bit his lips in excitement, waiting for me to go on.

"We'll see, Mr. Governor... We'll see. Just take me to where I can get changed."

He walked me to another door that once opened revealed his Victorian bedroom. "The bathroom is in there." He pointed toward a second door.

I rushed to get inside and change. I had a feeling I was playing with his patience, so I needed to make the plan work at that moment.

Letting the dress slip to the floor, I pulled on the strap teddy, which only covered the area between my thighs with a line of material. Same for the breasts. Only my nipples were fully hidden, leaving most of the cups in sight.

"*What the fuck is that?*" I heard Brax growl from the other side.

"It's called lingerie," I murmured, still trying to arrange the impossible straps.

"*That should be a weapon, not lingerie,*" Cole laughed from somewhere in the background.

I couldn't risk another answer, so after figuring out what went where, I pulled a thin robe from my bag, and pushed the door open.

"You can come, and see this one for yourself," I seductively called out to him, placing one foot in front of the other so that my robe opened slightly, to reveal the shape of my leg.

"Oh, I will." He paced my way, stopping right in front of the cord that held the robe together.

"Not from there," I purred between my lips. "I don't want you to fully open it until you're sure we're sticking to this scenario. I don't want you to ruin the surprise." I smiled with devious intent. "From here." I guided his palm over my knee, pushing it a little upwards, encouraging him to drag it higher on my thigh.

No wonder he was more than eager to follow my command. His lustful gaze combined with the touch on my leg, made my skin crawl—and not in a good way.

"I've turned you on." He noticed my body's reaction, making me almost let out a raucous laugh.

Still, I needed to play my part in the game, "How could you not?" I said as he was already reaching the upper side of my thigh, revealing the straps.

"We're sticking with this. Definitely." He groaned, preparing to further *investigate* my outfit.

"Okay. But I want to make things more exciting. I need some props. Do you like props?" I lusciously brought my lips to his ear, making sure I brushed it as I spoke.

"I love props." A foolish grin spread all over his face. "What do you want? Handcuffs? Plugs?"

Cole laughed in the background hearing the last one.

"No. Something much more exciting. Something that shows off your power, and everything that you stand for," I was putting pathos into my every word, rubbing my hand against the base of my neck and down my breasts. "I want money. A room full of money."

"Money?"

"Yes. I want you to fuck me while we're sitting on money —bond certificates, titles, whatever. I want you to feel exactly as powerful as you are. To feel the adrenaline running through your veins." My request seemed to have muted him, leaving his eyes just to stare back at me for a few moments.

"That wouldn't be too wise of me now, would it?" The tone of his voice so much colder than earlier.

Shit. I was blowing it.

I needed to regroup. That instant.

"You don't trust me. Okay...," I let my gaze fall to the ground, pretending to be offended by his mistrust. "I think you should know something about me. I don't take the Pleasures just for the money. I take them for the *fun*." I said purring the last part, as I extended my arm to play in his hair. "It's okay if you don't want to do this. We can go back to a different scenario. I could always go change," I said letting a visible trail of disappointment show as I let a small part of the straps covering my breasts fall.

And that made him quickly come around to my idea. "No. I think we could do this."

"Mr. Governor, I promise you that everything will remain here. You can *thoroughly* check my body before I leave to convince yourself of that."

"Oh, I will definitely do that." He snickered, driving his head to brush on the crook of my neck. "What's your name?" he asked.

"It's Carla." Obviously, I was lying, but he didn't need to know that.

"Carla, I have the feeling I'm going to put you on my all-time favorite list. Let's do this!" The governor shouted in excitement like a kid who just got a new toy. "Come, Sexy. Tell me what you need." He walked out of the room, into the lobby, then stopped in front of another door. "Follow me," he called, entering what seemed to be the game room judging by the large pool table by the window and the poker table in the middle of the room. "The safe is in here." He walked toward a wooden sculpture that nearly covered an entire wall, then, moving his hand behind it, pushed it open.

I would have never found it there.

I was expecting a safe similar to the ones they have in the banks. That was just my imagination running wild from watching too many movies. It was much more like a regular home-safe. Except for one thing; it opened with his handprint. He needed to put his palm on the door to access the content.

"*Shit*," I could hear Ferris cursing in the earpiece, but I couldn't tell how bad things were.
Was our plan compromised?

"Let's only take the money, I don't want to get any titles ruined," he said, taking out five stacks of dollars while I tried to peek into the safe without him noticing that I was staring.

Anyone else would have probably left me in the bedroom to keep the safe's location hidden. But I recognized his type. Although cautious, he was infatuated enough to show off, proving to me that no matter what, he was untouchable.

"That's perfect!" I flashed a satisfied smile when in fact, there were no real signs of satisfaction. Besides a few stacks of foreign currency, I didn't get to see too much, so I still had no idea if any recordings or anything else we could use against him were in the safe.

"Back to the bedroom." He shook the money in front of me, expecting another fake *yayyyy* on my part.

"Can you call someone to get us something to drink? Alcohol has this effect on me..." I purred as if that would be the fuel to set the night on fire.

"No need," he walked toward a bar on the other end of the room, and pulled out a chilled bottle of champagne, along with two glasses from a rack. "You take these." He extended the bottle to me since he was busy carrying the money packs.

At least something was falling into place. We needed to get back to the bedroom. This was it!

The most difficult part of the mission was coming up next.

"On the bed." I jumped a few times with enthusiasm as he threw the money on the bed, preparing *the scene* for our foreplay—the murder scene in my opinion.

"Now, for the robe." He said, literally drooling all over me.

It was time.

The fucking robe needed to go.

With shaking hands, I pulled the cord and opened the robe, letting him see the exquisite lines of my teddy.

"Jesus," I heard him murmur with a faded breath. "Vanya was so right to send you here."

"Let me pour us both a drink," I whispered seductively, heading toward a small table where I had left the bottle and the glasses.

"No, let me do it," he cut in front of me.

"How chivalrous." —and how wrong for my plan.

"To new people in our lives," he toasted, but before I could clink my glass on his, my fingers *slipped,* spilling champagne on the carpet.

"Oh My God, I'm sorry. I don't know what happened. I'm never this clumsy."

"I *bet* you're not. Don't worry, I'll refill it." He rushed toward the table to replace my drink, giving me just enough time to slip a sedative into his glass. That was the favor I asked Brax for the day before. I needed drugs for the governor.

"Again, to new people in our lives." He returned with the glass, waiting for me to toast.

"To intriguing new people," I murmured as if there was a chance in hell I could be seduced by a man like him. "Bottoms up." I downed the full contents of the glass, expecting he would follow—he didn't. However, he did drink half of the champagne in the glass.

I just hoped that would be enough.

"I want you to stay right there." I kept him at the edge of the bed as I lazily rolled between the bills, making sure my body remained in the sexiest pose I could think of. "Look at me," I whined, drawing all of his attention while my hips arched into the mattress, and my eyes were calling out to him. "I want you to get hard for me, Mr. Governor," I continued purring, slowly grinding my hips over the money.

"*Why don't you talk to me like that?*" Brax was the one trying to be funny this time, but *fun* wasn't exactly his main quality. Besides, nothing he could say or do could ever mend things between us.

"I am." The governor began unbuckling his belt as my pulse began pounding strongly.

It wasn't working! The sedative wasn't having the effect, probably because he didn't drink the whole dose.

What now? What now? The dreadful question kept spinning in my mind as the other alternative—sleeping with him—seemed impossible.

"Are you ready?" he asked, prepared to release himself from his underwear.

"Not so fast. Come and have me like a real king. Take my teddy off," I launched the invitation, trying to buy some more time.

He didn't reply, just got to his knees on the bed and crawled on top of me, preparing for the mission that was just assigned to him.

"*Bea, what's going on? Why isn't he passing out?*" Brax asked, his voice tinged with panic, knowing that the effects of the sedative should have kicked in by now. *"Get out of there!"* he roared, although I couldn't respond; or get out of there.

"So sexy." The governor made room between my hips, leaning in to kiss me. A kiss I couldn't deny him. I just needed to force myself, and pretend I enjoyed it.

My eyes closed, expecting the stench of his lips on mine, as each second just dragged out the unavoidable. But as his lips approached, I felt him collapsing over me.

It worked.

It worked!

He passed out, thankfully before I needed to welcome him all over my body.

"It worked," I uttered so that the guys could hear me.

"Good job," Ferris congratulated me. *"Now you have to go to the safe."*

"Can we open it?" I asked since the task seemed impossible without chopping the governor's hand off, and I wasn't ready to do something like that.

"An app like a scanner will appear on your phone in the next minute. I'm just uploading it. You need to put his hand on the screen."

As soon as the scan thing appeared, I followed Ferris's instructions, dragging the governor's inert hand over the screen.

"Now go to the safe, and place the scanned picture over the access pad. This model only reads the pattern of your palm. It doesn't have a pressure or heat sensor. I'll configure it to work by the time you get there."

He didn't need to tell me twice. I just walked straight to the game room and pushed the sculpted wall apart to access the safe.

"Great job. Now put your phone over the access pad and keep it there. I need to run an extra program to trick the system that it's a human hand and not a device," Ferris continued instructing me. But it wasn't only instructions I was about to receive. *"Bea, there's something you need to know."*

"Not fucking now, Ferris," Brax's angered voice echoed in my ears.

"It worked," I murmured, hearing the clink made of the opening door. "What is it?" I asked Ferris as I was already rushing to search through the safe.

"Nothing important, just check the safe," Brax was trying to cut me off.

He should have known better than that.

"Brax, tell me what's this all about," I asked him again since there was no backing out now.

"Finish this and I will."

My hands sped through the safe, but there was nothing there except money, bonds, some watches, and property titles.

"There's nothing we can use in here," I said with disappointment.

"The computer. Close the safe, and go to the office," Brax instructed me as if I didn't already know what to do.

After putting everything back in its place, I followed my previous path, and walked straight to the office.

"I'm in the office. Just opened the computer."

"See if it's password-protected or not." It was Ferris who was speaking to me this time.

"It is." I confirmed, as the locked sign appeared on the screen.

"Okay. No big deal. Just connect the cable to your phone, and then to the computer."

"On which port?" I wasn't too good with technology, mostly because I didn't have that much access to it.

Still, I seemed to have pissed Ferris off. *"It doesn't matter 'on which port'. They're all the same. Jesus, I have to break into some high-level security encoding, and you don't even know what a USB slot is."*

He was getting on my nerves, "Then maybe you should put on a garter belt, and come rub up against the governor next time."

"You fucking rubbed on him?" Ferris seemed repulsed by the thought.

"It was a figure of speech. We didn't need to get to that part."

I could hear Ferris muttering something on the other end.

"Now tell me what you were going to say earlier," I insisted.

"Ferris is a moron," Brax answered on Ferris's behalf, still unwilling to let me in on the secret.

"Cole?" Maybe he could give me an answer.

Except Cole didn't seem to be there anymore.

"Cole?" I asked again.

"He's not here." It was Brax who replied.

"Did he leave?" I was a little disappointed that he decided he'd ditch us in the middle of everything, but I couldn't say I was surprised.

Brax seemed to know something. *"Promise me you're not going to freak out. I asked Ferris not to tell you before you got the job done. But apparently, he can't keep his fucking mouth shut."*

"I promise." My words didn't truly reflect the truth, as I was already freaking out.

"Shit... Okay, I'll tell you. Cole had to go to the hospital."

"Why? What happened?" I asked, surprised since I had just talked to him a couple of minutes before.

"Nothing bad. They found a donor for your brother. So, one of us needed to go and make sure everything went okay." Brax continued.

"A donor? Now?" *Out of all possible moments, it had to be this one.* Another irony of fate, as life seemed to be mocking me again.

"I got a call from the hospital just now, while you were changing into that strappy thing. Just hold on there until I finish, and Brax will be waiting outside to get you to the hospital. The password should be cracked in a few seconds." As Ferris spoke, I saw the desktop background lighting up. He was in. *"I'm a fucking genius."* Obviously, modesty wasn't one of his qualities.

I kept watching the screen, seeing folders closing, and opening up again as he kept searching through the files. None of it made any sense, and in those seconds there was little chance it would. Sebastian was receiving a new kidney, and all I could possibly think about was how badly I needed to be there for him to hold his hand.

"Did you find anything we can use?" I asked while watching the second tick on the clock. I needed to get out of here so badly that I felt I could hardly breathe anymore.

"I can't tell yet. I'm just copying everything I find, and uploading it through a secure connection on my laptop. But from

what I can see I didn't get any picture files."

There had to be something, anything.

"I'm scanning for hidden folders," Ferris continued as I thought I heard movement outside.
My eyes went straight to the door, but after a few moments of carefully listening, I managed to convince myself that paranoia had kicked in.

"Bea, is everything okay?" Brax noticed from the camera that I was fussing and turning in the seat.

"I thought I heard something," I whispered, still keeping my eyes on the door.

"How fucking long, Ferris?" Brax groaned into the mic, growing even more impatient than I was.

*"I... just... need... to... **Bingo!** Got you, motherfucker. Hidden desktop files JPG and AVI images. Anyone want to take a guess what it is?"*

We just struck gold.

"One minute to the full download."

One minute and I could go to Sebastian. My heart was thumping so loudly that I thought it might escape my chest. I watched the countdown drop, counting the seconds until I could see him.

25

20

15

10

5

And then it happened. Five seconds on the screen, and the office door burst open, letting in the governor along with an army of his men.

It was game over.

"You bitch!" He jumped straight to the desk where I was, grabbing me by the arm and smashing my body on the wooden counter.

"*Bea? Bea, are you okay? Beaaa!!!*" Brax's desperate shouts crackled through the earpiece, but his screams seemed so far away—almost unreachable.

"Who hired you?" The governor's palm fell to slap my face with such force that it knocked me to the ground. "Who are you working for?" He shouted again as I noticed him picking up a little something from the carpet. My earpiece had fallen out from the impact. "Shoot to kill anyone that gets inside, and call to double the guards," he roared frantically, glancing at his men. "As for you, bitch—" His hands clenched in my hair, dragging me toward the computer to disconnect the phone, "You thought I didn't read straight through your game? You're dead, bitch."

His words became an echo in my ears as a sharp pain pierced through my head, straight into my brain, breaking all visual contact on the spot, and plunging me into total darkness.

It all ended there. The struggle. The plan.

Nothing mattered any longer.

I was just floating above it all, surrounded by voices that seemed to be slowly fading away.

I was dying!

End of Book 2

"Kings of Lust" is book 2 of The Pleasure Room series.

The Pleasure Room reading order:

1.Kings of Desire

2.Kings of Lust

3.Kings of Seduction

4.The Book of Kings- optional -the kings' POVs

5.Kings of Destiny

ABOUT THE AUTHOR

M.O. Absinthe

Ascending author with a sweet tooth for alpha males, and a guilty pleasure of making your darkest fantasies come to life.

Follow me on:

-Instagram :@m.o.absinthe -for sneak peeks and events

-TikTok: @m.o.absinthe

-Facebook Page : M.O. Absinthe
-Facebook Group: M.O. Absinthe's Dark Sinners

-Email : absinthe.is.writing@gmail.com

Sign up HERE www.moabsinthe.com to my newsletter to get a FREE extra-steamy bonus scene featuring Bea and her kings

BOOKS BY M.O. ABSINTHE

The Sin of You

A vampire dark romance that will make you shiver in unknown temptation

The book is suitable for a mature audience.

I invite you to take a dangerous path where nothing is forbidden. Desire, lust, deceit, and betrayal revolve around an ancient prophecy that can build or break destinies. You're soon to find out if passion and love are enough to stand in the way of antique forces, or it will all be dust with the first ray of light.

"The room darkened with his presence as every step he made towards me took me closer to my downfall. He was death, and life merged in a predator's body. Strength and dominance oozed from his every pore. But it was something else too... Something more that made a cold chill flash through my body. His beautiful absinthe eyes captured the depths of time, making him irresistible, undeniable, but also fatal. All of my instincts were telling me to leave as fast as I could, but there was something stronger that kept me frozen to the spot. An unspoken link from the dawn of time brought me here, in this place, meant to fulfill my destiny. He is the living dead that people whispered about while looking, with fear, out the window... He is a vampire."

Il Capo's Seduction

An enemies-to-lovers passionate mafia romance.

The book is suitable for a mature audience.

One dreadful night changes Angelo's and Elise's lives forever, sharing a dark secret that can never be revealed.

After her mother's tragic death, Elise finds herself trapped in the dangerous Italians' penthouse caught up in a wicked game of smothering lust and wild passion - mind versus feeling.

To escape, she has to win his trust -yet she ends up losing her heart in the process.

"The water drops path while rolling over his inked body was becoming mystical. A sparkling road her famished hands craved to thoroughly follow, to feel his ripped muscle tense beneath them while sliding her fingers towards the wet towel. It felt like a sin, just to be looking at him. "

Blackjack- A game of cards and destiny

Adam Delmont Rocher, Monte Carlo's famous billionaire with a shaky reputation that needs immediate mending offers his teenage crush, Lynette, a deal with a modern devil. A Blackjack game of cards and destiny which finalizes with the fake marriage he desperately needs to keep his company, though sometimes, the word fake can get really blurred when true feelings are involved...

Contrary to what M.O. Absinthe usually writes, this book is NOT a dark romance!
"A feral sound escaped him, bringing down his carved lips on her with an unstilled yearning. The kiss was almost brutal, releasing something chained for too long as his tongue searched hers in crazed swirls, hoping to make the very last drop of her his own."

Printed in Great Britain
by Amazon

61602658R00191